LOVE
IN
writing

DANA LeCHEMINANT

First Printing: September 2022

ISBN: 978-1-951753-14-6

ONE

ALL THINGS CONSIDERED, MAYBE BEING mauled by a dozen twelve-year-olds in laser gear wasn't the worst way to go. It could have been death by a weeks-old diaper in the ball pit, and likely no one would have found him for months. At least this way he had an audience, and Ben Nakamura knew too well the irony of being so noticed.

He had never been noticed in his life. Not the way he wanted to be.

"For the love of all that is good, just leave." He knew he was begging, and he knew it wasn't helping anything, but at this point he was seriously considering letting the group of preteens accomplish their goal of playing the world's longest game of laser tag. It wasn't like the fun center had closed an hour ago. Or the kids' parents were growing more impatient by the minute. Or Ben could almost feel his phone about to start ringing with a call from his manager, wondering why the neon sign at the front of the building hadn't been turned off.

Oh wait, it was all of those things.

The general manager had an uncanny ability to know when that O'Reilly's Fun Center sign was still on after closing time. Ben suspected he had access to the street cameras and never went to bed until the sign was off.

"We haven't conquered Team Voldemort yet," one of the boys said. He was a particularly nasty-looking kid, with the kind of pinched expression that came from trying too hard to look intimidating. And he had somehow managed to wedge himself between the ceiling and one of the many walls that created the laser tag arena, which meant he was a good three feet over Ben's head and firmly planted in his spot.

Ben knew for a fact the other team would not yield, which was the reason he was standing in the middle of the arena despite the very real threat of being tackled by someone not paying proper attention in the misty, black-lighted space.

His attempt to turn on the lights and end the game over an hour ago had resulted in a particularly feisty thirteen-year-old girl from Team Voldemort screaming at him until he turned them back off. It wasn't that he was terrified of kids, but after working a double shift to cover someone who got sick, he didn't have the energy to deal with this tonight.

And maybe he was a little terrified.

"Look, kid," Ben said, doing his best to sound like he wasn't completely unnerved by the unseen movement all around him. All he heard were laser gunshots and shouts of preteen death threats. "I know it's your birthday, but I gotta close up the building. Your mom is waiting outside, and —"

"Team Godzilla Dragon will never surrender!" the boy shouted, and a resonating cry of agreement rose up around Ben, reminding him how completely surrounded he was.

Oh, how he hated working laser tag.

"And Team Voldemort will prevail!" another shout responded, followed by a chorus of demonic shrieks from the other end of the arena that made Ben wonder if the new generation of girls would be the one to finally take over the world. They were certainly fierce enough.

Ben just wanted to go to bed. Was that so much to ask? "Come on, kid. There's honor in admitting you're outmatched. They beat you in the last three rounds."

The boy shook his head wildly. "I will not be defeated by a bunch of girls!"

"You just were," the leader of Team Voldemort said from right behind Ben, and her very presence seemed to turn the air around them to ice.

The demonic shrieks returned, only now they were everywhere, and boys were falling left and right as the girls shot them with terrifying precision, until one by one each remaining Godzilla Dragon carried nothing but a useless gun and oversized equipment that flashed to tell them they had been thoroughly demolished.

Everyone except the king, whose laser sensors were protected by the wall and ceiling he had wedged himself between.

"You can't beat me!" he screamed while eight girls aimed their guns at him.

Ben knew he was standing right in the middle of a massacre, but at this point he pretty much hoped he would be a casualty of the battle.

They didn't pay him enough for this.

"Surrender!" ordered Team Voldemort's leader.

"Never!" squeaked the dragon king.

A door opened just to Ben's left, bringing with it blinding light from the outside lobby. All of the kids hissed like vampires hiding from the sun.

Recognizing the silhouette of the person who had just come in, Ben had never been so glad to see anyone in his life. "Kit," he breathed. It was about time.

His best friend in the whole world came to stand by his side, squinting up at the lone survivor. "Ah, the top of the wall trick," he muttered knowingly. "I remember that one."

"I don't remember you refusing to come down," Ben replied. Surely Kit would know how to convince the kids to give up. He spent his whole work week with kids—granted, his students were a little younger—but if anyone knew how to force someone to get in line, it was Kit Morgan.

Taking in the situation, Kit gestured to the nearest girl and took hold of her gun. "The trick," he said as he took aim in the opposite direction from the boy, "is to know the field and play it to your advantage." He fired the weapon, and King Godzilla's vest lit up with a techy explosion sound.

The girls burst into cheers and began hugging each other, and Kit—who was a good deal taller than Ben—reached up and plucked the kid off the wall, catching him before he hit the ground.

"Never underestimate a woman," he said before the kid hurried off after his friends, sniffling as he went.

Ben felt like crying himself. "How did you do that?"

Kit chuckled. "Mirror. Oliver found it when we were ten, and it's positioned just right to get whoever tries the wall trick."

Ben had known Kit since they were eleven, so that must have been just before they met. Kit had been friends with Oliver practically their whole lives, and the two of them were thick as thieves. It was strange, thinking about how Kit might have been Ben's best friend, but Ben wasn't Kit's. That spot would always be claimed by Oliver Hamilton.

Not that Ben was jealous. Usually. He had never been one to demand attention—or even get it—and he wasn't nearly as cool as his friends. But sometimes Ben really wished he could stop being the one they always pitied.

Kit had only come tonight because Ben texted an S.O.S. Otherwise, they probably wouldn't have seen each other for another week at least. When it came to Ben's friends making time for him, they were doing it less and less.

It wasn't their fault. Maybe if Ben wasn't stuck working every night, he might have actually had more free time.

Once all the kids had been hauled off by their irritated parents, Ben worked as quickly as he could to close up the fun center. Kit tried to help, but he mostly played one of the arcade games while Ben scrubbed the bathrooms. Ben was just glad to have some company. He knew Kit wasn't great with late nights during the school year, so he worked as quickly as he could until he was finally able to lock the doors—after he had to run back in and turn the sign off when his boss gave him an irate call.

The man definitely had access to the street cameras.

Though Kit was silent as they walked to the only two cars left in the parking lot, Ben could feel his comment lurking just beneath the surface, and he gritted his teeth. He knew it was coming—he always did—but that didn't mean he wanted to hear it. It was the same thing every time. The same conversation for the last decade.

Finally, when they reached Ben's crappy car that probably should have died years ago, Kit opened his mouth. "When are you going to quit?"

Ben forced himself not to show any frustration in his face, knowing that wouldn't help anything. "It's not that bad."

Kit frowned, making the scrunched-up face he always made when he thought one of his friends was doing something stupid. "You have pepperoni in your hair, Ben. O'Reilly's doesn't even serve pizza."

Ben had found worse things in his hair.

When Ben said nothing, Kit groaned and kicked one of Ben's tires. "You've been working at this place for more than twelve years, and I'm pretty sure you hate it."

Ben did hate it, but it wasn't like he had any other options. At least he had a steady paycheck coming in, and he could afford a place to live, even if it was sharing an apartment with their friend Cam. Anything was better than living at home with his parents, where three of his siblings still lived, as well as his sister-in-law and four of his nephews. If he found a new job now, he would probably have to move back home while he worked his way up to a livable wage again.

He knew the way the world worked. Kit should too, being a teacher. It wasn't like he made that much more than Ben.

"It's not that bad," Ben said again, even if it was an utter lie. It was pretty bad. In fact, working at the fun center was awful, and it always had been.

At least he had a trip to the grocery store to look forward to tomorrow, which out of context sounded downright depressing. Still, it was a good idea to offset the misery with a bright spot of happiness and hope, and no one knew better than Ben how important hope could be. At this point, it was one of the few things he had left. Even if seeing a random girl at a grocery store without talking to her was a bit uneventful, it was *something*.

It was the idea that his future had a chance, however slim, of becoming something better.

As tempting as his bed sounded once Kit drove off, as soon as Ben climbed into his car, he knew he would have to wind down before he would ever be able to sleep. Tonight's laser tag fiasco, coupled with Kit's well-meaning but ultimately unhelpful judgment, had left him feeling restless.

Not that that was a new sensation.

Grumbling a little, Ben coaxed his car awake and drove in the opposite direction of home, toward the mountain that loomed on the east side of town.

"You could get a different job," he reminded himself as he gripped the steering wheel tight. It was late enough that there was hardly any traffic on the streets, but the tension in his shoulders kept him stiff. "All you would have to do is pull up a job site and find something new."

He huffed a short laugh. He hadn't had a job interview since he was eighteen, when he got hired on at the cafe in the college library. Eleven years was a long time. What if the whole process had changed and he didn't know it? His friends would be no help, either. The only job Oliver had had was his own company, which he'd sold three years ago after four years of building it from the ground up. Kit had been teaching in the same classroom since graduating college. Cam hadn't even interviewed for his personal training job; the owner of the gym had seen him working out and practically begged him to work for them. Even Madi, Kit's sister and a crucial part of the gang, had been self-employed for the last decade.

If Ben wanted a new job, he would have to find it on his own.

"Your parents didn't raise you to be pathetic," he muttered as he turned onto the road to take him up into the hills. Technically, the area closed after dark, but there was a nice spot several miles up that gave him a great view of the city. Plus, it was an excellent place to scream without being heard.

"Great place for someone to murder you," he tacked on with a shudder. Thankfully, he'd never seen anyone else up this way so late in the night, and he'd come up here enough times in the middle of the night to have a pretty good idea of how well most people followed the rules. They all had real jobs with realistic bedtimes.

His hands tightened around the steering wheel again as he imagined what a real job might look like. Yes, he absolutely wanted a change. No, he wasn't feeling very brave about finding something new. He had limited skills and even fewer talents, and spending half his life working a prize counter hadn't done him any favors. What would he even do?

Having an illustration degree was great until it came to picking a career to go with it.

"What would Grocery Girl think if she knew where you worked?" he asked himself, then rolled his eyes.

Grocery Girl didn't even know he existed, despite the fact that he saw her almost every week because they shopped at the same time. It wasn't like they'd ever spoken. Or ever would. But his negative self made a good point. No woman was ever going to look at him twice if he remained stuck in the same job he'd had since high school. Ben liked to think he was a good person, but what was he supposed to offer someone when the best he could boast about himself was having a top ten high score in laser tag?

As he pulled into a tiny lot and took the short trail out to the lookout point, using his phone's flashlight to guide the way, Ben gritted his teeth. It was time to make a change. He didn't know what that would look like, exactly, but he was tired of being stuck. He was tired of feeling like everyone else in the world was moving on but him.

He was tired.

And it was about time he did something about it.

TWO

SOME THINGS WERE NICE TO wake up to, like the smell of fresh bread or a songbird tweeting a cheery tune outside the window. Some things were less pleasant, like a chilly room or a garbage truck emptying a dumpster right outside. But the worst thing to wake up to? That was undoubtedly Cam Martinez.

"Have you seen my protein shake bottle?" Ben's roommate boomed that question as he came into the room despite it being six in the morning and way too early for stupid questions.

Ben moaned. It was his one and only day off until Sunday, and he had been hoping to spend the bulk of it sleeping and praying he didn't dream about miniature golf and Pacman. "Why in the world would it be in my room?"

Cam shrugged his massive shoulders as he nudged a stack of books with his shoe. Everything about Cam was massive, from his voice to his biceps to the confidence he had in never wearing anything with sleeves. "I was just wondering if you'd seen it. I have to go to work, and I've got some big clients coming in today who might be interested in investing. Gotta keep up my strength."

Ben hadn't been home enough in the last four days to have set foot in the kitchen, which was usually where Cam kept his bottles. But that thought made him wake up a little as he remembered what day it was. Tuesday.

Grocery day.

"Have you checked the dishwasher?" he asked as he slowly sat up. He had gone to the store too late last week, and he didn't want to make that same mistake today. He would have to get up, even if he would rather sleep another six hours.

Cam rolled his eyes. "You don't think I didn't check there first? I'm surprised you even know what a dishwasher is." Bending down, he glanced underneath Ben's bed and scrunched his nose up in disgust. "I don't get you," he muttered, but at least he didn't start cleaning.

He had done it before.

Ben fought to wake up all the way as Cam continued searching the room without actually touching anything. He had to shower and get pizza grease out of his hair from work last night, and already nerves were churning in his stomach and making him sick. It was ridiculous, getting nervous about going to the grocery store, but it happened every week. It would take him at least an hour just to work up the courage to turn on his car and drive to the store, so he needed to get a move on before he made himself too late again.

Cam must have given up on his search, because he moved back to the doorway and folded his arms. "You look like crap, by the way. When did you get home last night?"

Ben ran a hand down his face. "Little after one," he grunted. He had spent a little too long up on the mountain, pacing back and forth as he argued with himself about what to do to fix his sad little life.

Cam grunted back. "You really need to work on your sleep schedule, man. It's not good for you, and if you ever want to get healthier, you can't—"

Ben hated being rude. His parents had always taught him that kindness was one of the most important traits a person could have, and he had taken that lesson to heart. The thing about Cameron Martinez, though, was he didn't respond to a soft hand. His personality was so large that it took large reactions to affect him.

So Ben threw him a glare, knowing it was so out of character for him that it would throw off Cam's equilibrium. "Don't start," he snapped. "Please." He had already gotten enough of a lecture from Kit last night, and he didn't need it from another friend. He had few enough of them, and he didn't want to be annoyed with *all* of them.

Caught off guard, Cam shut his mouth and took a step back. "Sorry," he muttered. "Just trying to help."

And now Ben felt guilty, which didn't exactly combine well with his nerves. He groaned and threw his covers off of him so he could swing his legs over the side and lean his elbows on his knees. "I didn't mean… I'm just tired. Sorry for…you know…"

"You could quit your job."

Ben glanced over. "You know I can't." The two of them were living together out of necessity, not because of the depth of their friendship. Cam was working on opening his own gym and needed every penny he could get, and it wasn't like either of them had ever made much money with their jobs. A fun center assistant manager and a personal trainer at a low-cost gym that skimped on wages weren't exactly rolling in funds, and they both knew it.

Still, Cam scoffed and flexed his massive arms. Was he even aware he was doing that? Probably not. Out of the four of them in their friend group, he had always been the most fit, and he could rival any comic-book hero even on a bad day. Basically the opposite of Ben, who had never been anything but slim and trim, even when Cam tried to help him get a little more muscle.

One of the downfalls of his stick-thin father's genetics, he supposed. That, and a life of stress and late nights that weren't doing him any favors.

"In a couple of months," Cam said, "I'm going to be spending all my time at my gym. I'll be bringing in so many clients that I won't know what to do with them, and I'm probably going to have to move across town to be closer; all the open spaces are over past Bank Street."

Ben frowned. Where was he going with this?

Letting out a sigh, Cam dropped onto Ben's bed, nearly bouncing him off. "What are you going to do then? If I can't split the rent with you…"

Luckily, this had been on Ben's mind ever since Cam got it into his head to start his own gym over the summer. He'd had a few months to look over his options, so this question wasn't completely catching him off guard. He just wished he had better answers than anything he'd come up with.

He could move home and share a room with his nephews, move to a crappy apartment on the other side of town with Cam and have an hour commute to work, or he could genuinely consider the life of a traveling salesman and pretend there was nothing he liked better than talking to strangers.

If only that wasn't his worst nightmare.

"Think Kit would let me take his second bedroom?" he tried.

Cam barked out a laugh. "Kit Morgan? The man who hasn't worn a different kind of shoe since he was fifteen because the thought of trying something different paralyzes him? Yeah, good luck with that. I'm still amazed he got that coffee table last summer."

Ben groaned. Honestly, it was a miracle Kit had decided to buy a townhouse to begin with, and it had taken the man three years after college graduation to work up the courage to even do it. Kit would absolutely do anything to help out his friends, but he would hate someone invading his personal space. Ben would be a little more intrusive than a new coffee table.

"I'll figure something out," Ben said. "Our lease isn't up until the end of the year, so I have a couple months."

For the record, Cam looked genuinely sorry about the situation, but he must not have come up with any solutions either for how quiet he was being about the subject. Hopping up, he clapped a massive hand on Ben's back before he headed for the door. "Look, I gotta head to work, but we'll find you something." He paused and glanced back. "Or, you know, you could find a better job."

Ben shouldn't have been surprised that Cam would loop right back to that. "Maybe," he said, hoping that would be enough to end the conversation.

But Cam wasn't done. "One of these days you're going to have to do something for yourself, Ben. You can't always play the martyr and expect good things to come your way on their own. Sometimes you just have to go for it. Be brave. Your life is only as good as you make it."

Ben watched him go, refusing to move until the front door closed and the key turned in the lock. Then he moaned and fell back onto his bed, throwing his arm over his face. It didn't help that Cam was entirely right, but Ben had never been the brave one. That was always his friends' job, and all three of them had plenty of bravery for Ben to ride in their wake and pretend he wasn't a complete coward.

Even Kit, who struggled with change and was humbler than anyone Ben knew, still had a sense of confidence about him. He knew his worth and knew he was good at his job, and he was the best third-grade teacher Mount Pleasant Elementary had ever had. No one was a better personal trainer than Cam, who had a unique way of being just pushy enough while still having a heart of gold and an innate desire to help anyone who crossed his path. And Oliver…

Try as he might, Ben had always had a hard time being around Oliver, even though they'd hung out all the time during college because Kit and Cam both went to school across the country while Ben and Oliver stayed in state. Oliver was…perfect. He was rich, intelligent, handsome, charismatic. He was the kind of guy who started tech companies from his dorm room and sold them for millions of dollars without breaking a sweat. He'd gone on more dates in high school than the rest of them combined because he was never afraid to talk to the girls, and now he was married to Kit's sister because he was the one person in the world who was good enough for her.

And Ben?

Ben was twenty-nine, still trying to pay off his student loans, working in the same place he'd been working since he was sixteen. He'd been putting off going to the doctor and getting a checkup because that would cost money that he didn't have—O'Reilly's offered horrible benefits. He'd been stalking a girl at the grocery store for months now and hadn't even worked up the courage to say hello.

Slowly sitting up, Ben looked around his mess of a room and had the sudden urge to leave it all behind and start from scratch in some strange small town across the country. Knowing his luck, his car would break down before he even got out of Diamond Springs. Was this going to be his life forever? A crappy job and a crappy car and a crappy apartment that wasn't even technically his because it was Cam's name on the lease? Doomed to be alone forever because he was too shy to strike up a conversation?

"Do something brave," he muttered, testing Cam's suggestion. A new car was out of the question, and he definitely couldn't leave his job until he had something better. But maybe he could say something to the grocery girl. If she shot him down, at least it wouldn't change anything except destroying the possibility of something happening. He had been living on that possibility for months, sure, but it wasn't the real thing. If things blew up in his face, she would just be a hopeful might-have-been.

"Don't overthink this," he told himself as he hurried to take a shower and get the grease out of his hair. "People are always saying how nice and approachable you are, so how bad could it be, really? *Don't overthink.*"

If only his self pep talks ever actually worked.

By the time Ben got to the grocery store, he was definitely running late. His shower had turned into a full-blown conversation with himself, going over the pros and cons of finally making a move after all this time. He didn't know the girl's name or if she was even single, but somehow he had managed to talk himself into finally showing up.

He just hoped he wasn't *too* late.

She usually came in the mornings, before she went into work, he guessed. He didn't even know what she did for work, though he imagined it was in an office somewhere. While not strictly professional, her clothing was usually business casual at the very least with a hint of personal flair. Usually in her shoes.

She had awesome shoes.

"Don't talk about her shoes," Ben told himself.

He had a whole list of things he probably shouldn't mention to her, like how he had noticed once that she was on a baking streak because she kept buying flour and sugar, or the fact that she liked to match her Converse to her outfits and had several pairs of varying colors. And he probably shouldn't tell her about how he had started requesting Tuesdays off back in June so he could shop at the same time she did.

Ben shuddered. It was *October*. At what point did a person cross into stalker status?

He did his usual route across the grocery store anyway, grabbing things at random as he kept an eye out for anyone who looked familiar. Normally, he never let himself get fixated on anything—being the fourth of seven kids had taught him the impermanence of personal things—but something about this girl had caught his attention last spring, and she had been in his head ever since.

Normal people didn't shop at the exact same time every week, so Ben felt like that gave them something in common. She was always on her own, too, which was promising. Plus, she generally bought the kind of food Ben wished he had the energy and time to cook, so he figured they would get along in the food department. It was something. However small.

Had she already come and gone? Ben was halfway across the store when he started to panic. He probably wouldn't be brave again—he wasn't sure he was even brave enough today—so he would be stuck watching her from a distance forever. Or, until she stopped being so predictable or showed up with a partner.

By the time he reached the final aisle, where the ice cream was, Ben leaned over the handle of his cart and let all his breath out at once. She wasn't here. Of course she wasn't. Because why would anything go right in his life? Being the friend of three successful men—big personalities with big lives—had never been easy, but Ben had always been at least a little hopeful that their good luck would rub off on him.

He should have known better.

Glancing at the utter nonsense in his cart—peanut butter cups, a whole pineapple, and a jar of pickles among other things—Ben sighed and pushed forward to work his way back through the store and put everything back except the peanut butter cups.

That was when he saw her.

His breath catching, he tried to figure out how he hadn't seen her earlier. She was at the other end of the aisle, her eyes fixed on the glass case in front of her. He had no idea what color her eyes were—he'd never gotten close enough—but he imagined they were beautiful.

Like the rest of her.

So he hadn't been too late. For once, Ben's plan had actually come together, and all he had to do was walk up to her and start up a conversation. Channel his inner Oliver Hamilton, if such a thing even existed. They'd been friends for eighteen years, so surely Ben knew him well enough to act like him.

"Just walk forward and say hi," he told himself. "Easy."

Then he turned and walked in the other direction, veering off into the next aisle over.

What was he thinking? He couldn't just walk up to her! He could barely have a conversation with his friends, who had known him for years, so what made him think he could talk to someone he had never met? He was being ridiculous, and he should just go home and enjoy his rare day off before he had to get back to his terrible job.

His phone buzzed at the end of the aisle, and Ben paused before he did something stupid, like leave his cart and run for the doors. The staff would probably think he was shoplifting and tackle him in the parking lot, and he would get arrested, and he'd lose his job and have to move back home or join the circus or turn into a hermit in the woods who survived on crickets and leaves.

A shudder ran through him, and he grabbed his phone before his imagination ran away from him. *Too late.*

It was a text from Madi, Kit's sister and Oliver's wife. One of his best friends, she was practically another sister to him.

Madi: Any updates with Grocery Girl?

It was like she *knew*. He glanced around, just to make sure she wasn't somehow watching him, then let out the breath he was holding. She hadn't technically said anything about his cowardice, but Madi knew exactly how long Ben had been avoiding this girl. Maybe she was going to give up on him like the rest of his friends had, and that hurt worse than anything. Disappointing Madi would kill him. Metaphorically. Maybe literally. He'd never put that to the test.

Groaning, Ben took hold of his cart and headed back to the ice cream aisle before he gave himself time to overthink what he was doing. He could do this!

He could also nearly run her over, apparently.

He had mistaken how far down the aisle she was, so as he turned the corner at top speed, his cart collided with hers with a crash.

"Sorry!" he said, eyes wide as she jumped back. "I wasn't looking where..."

Her eyes were blue. Dark, like denim. And they took him in so quickly that he felt exposed. He almost didn't care. He'd never been this close to her, so he'd never known her wavy brown hair was almost auburn in places. It looked softer than he'd expected.

"It's fine," she muttered, turning back to the ice cream in her hands with a frown. A pint in each.

Say something.

Ben cleared his throat. "Rough week?"

When she turned back to him, her expression was wary. Like she was trying to decide if she needed to call the store's ancient security guard over. She swept another look over him that sent his knees shaking. "Pardon?"

What was he doing? He had no idea. He had just said the first thing that came to mind. "You know." He pointed to the pints of ice cream she held. "Girls and ice cream." *Ben, you idiot.* His eyes went wide. "No, sorry, I didn't mean... That was terrible." How had he managed to dig himself a hole so deep so quickly? Most strangers didn't give him a chance to talk this much. "That was really terrible. You don't need me judging your decision to buy ice cream. Not that I was judging. Ice cream is great. Pretend I didn't say anything. Have a nice day." He bowed—*What?*—then tripped over his cart in his attempt to grab it and run away.

He had made it to the end of the aisle by the time she spoke, halting his steps. "I got passed over for a promotion."

Had she just said…? Spinning back around, Ben did his best to act like a normal human. *So much for acting like Oliver.* He would be lucky if she didn't think he was missing a few things from his brain.

"I'm sorry," he said, leaving it at that.

Though she shrugged, her expression conveyed all her disappointment. "The guy who got it is qualified, but he has the voice of a sixty-year-old man."

He had no idea what she was talking about and no clue how to respond, but he did his best. Something told him she needed to talk, and seeing as he was the only person around… "Is…is he a sixty-year-old man?"

She actually smiled, and Ben was pretty sure his internal organs shut down for a second. In all the months he'd gone down aisles a second time to get a glimpse of her, he'd never seen her smile. Grocery shopping wasn't exactly entertaining work.

"Yes," she said. "He is. But that's not the point."

"What is the point?"

"The point is I work for a company that writes children's books."

Now it was starting to make sense, and Ben's heart pattered back to a normal rhythm, even though he knew this conversation was probably a one-time thing. Now that he'd made first contact, the rest of it wasn't so bad. He could do this.

Offering up a little smile that *hopefully* didn't make him look constipated, he folded his arms so his hands didn't shake. "I'm guessing he writes for sixty-year-old men too."

Her smile grew, meaning Ben's shaking did too. He'd thought she was cute the moment he first saw her, but up close… "Exactly. I'm Allie." She shuffled the pints she held to one hand and held out the other.

Red alert! System failure! Danger!

"Ben." He might have said that. He didn't know. All he knew was when his fingers touched her cold ones, something crumbled in his brain and left him a pile of mush. Could he get more pathetic? Probably. He didn't want an actual answer to that question.

Allie wrinkled up her nose a little as she looked him over yet again, and then she turned back to her ice cream. "I've been standing here for ten minutes, and I can't decide which one I want more."

"So get both." *You can't tell her what to do, Ben. She doesn't even know you! You might not have even told her your name.*

But Allie's eyes lit up—holy Toledo, she was absolutely beautiful—and she tossed both pints into her full cart before taking hold of the handle and heading for the checkout. "I like the way you think, Ben." She paused, though, and looked back. "Thanks, by the way. For talking to me. I feel a bit better now. See you around?"

Ben hoped he nodded; there certainly wasn't any sound that came out of his mouth. And as soon as she was out of sight, he collapsed against the ice cream case and pressed his burning forehead against the cold glass. He'd done it. He'd talked to her. After months of psyching himself out, he had finally made a move.

And even crazier?

It had gone well.

THREE

THERE WAS NOTHING BETTER THAN blasting music while cleaning the toilet. At least, that was what Allie kept telling herself as she tried to scrub away the stains that had probably been there for a decade. It didn't matter that she kept telling herself this place had character; some things would be better being gone. Funny, the stains hadn't bothered her when she moved in three months ago.

"What is this song?" she muttered, sitting back against the tub to give her arms a rest. She liked the beat, but she had no idea what the words were, even though it was apparently one of the most popular songs of the year according to the playlist it was on. She'd never even heard it before.

That was because Jeremy thought popular music was a waste of time and only listened to weird, independent jazz trombone. That, and Barbara Streisand. Allie had dated him for over a year, and she had completely forgotten what kind of music she actually liked to listen to. Assuming she ever knew in the first place.

"How sad is that?" she asked the bathroom, which was just as sad as her lack of good music before now. If she was at the point of talking to herself, it was probably time to sit down and write.

Leaving the toilet and its stains behind, Allie slid onto her stool that served as her desk chair. Desk being a loose term, considering it was actually the kitchen counter. Funnily enough—AKA not funny at all—she hadn't looked up what a studio apartment was before she signed the lease, and now she was stuck with a thirty-foot box to call home for the next nine months. Probably longer, considering she didn't exactly make tons of money as a publisher's assistant.

A little voice in the back of her head told her she could probably find a guy with a nicer apartment than hers and solve all her problems.

That voice got her a literal slap in the face.

"You're man-vegan, Allison Ortega," she reminded herself as her cheek stung. "You have sworn off dating for the foreseeable future. Focus." She had sat down to write, which reminded her she still needed to clean the bathroom tiles. She would only jot down the ideas floating in her head before she forgot them. "Then back to cleaning." Ten minutes. Twenty max.

Three hours later, Allie finally sat up straight and stretched her back, mumbling to herself about the woes of getting old.

Why did she always do this? She had work to do—actual work—and she couldn't keep wasting time on projects that wouldn't matter. No one was ever going to read it.

Cursing her uncanny ability to focus so intently on anything unimportant, Allie slid off the stool and went straight for the ice cream in the freezer, telling herself plenty of lies about how she would only have a bite or two and then go back to the bathroom. But she knew that was pointless, even if she told herself that she could have more ice cream after everything was clean. The problem with setting up goals with no one to keep her accountable was her stomach spoke way more loudly than her head, so it always won.

Always.

Two bites in, though, Allie paused and looked down at the paper carton. Not for the first time, she thought back on the guy at the grocery store who was responsible for her having this ice cream in the first place. He had suggested she buy both flavors, and she had complied without hesitation. Yeah, okay, he was cute, but he had a terrible pickup line. One he delivered with the most adorably dimpled smile.

"Dimpled smile that's been watching you for months," she reminded herself. It didn't matter that she'd been spying on *him* for months too. When a guy did that, it was creepy. When a woman did it, it was…well, still creepy. But he probably never thought she might murder him if he ever made eye contact.

Plus, he butted himself into her personal business when he asked her about the ice cream. Who did that? The guy totally stuck his foot in his mouth and made an idiot of himself when he tried to pull it out, and it was completely…

Adorable.

He was *adorable*.

Allie groaned, dropping her head onto her arms as last week's encounter replayed—again—through her mind. He'd actually *listened*. And didn't look at her like she was crazy for thinking she should get a promotion over someone with more experience. And he'd apologized. And convinced her to buy more ice cream than she should without making a comment about how she might get fat. She had let too many boyfriends over the years dictate her body for her along with the rest of her life.

But Ben? *So get both*, he'd said, like it was the most logical thing in the world. It was so different from anything she'd ever experienced, like he found the previously unattainable middle ground in all ways. Especially physical. He was neither slim nor large, and while he wasn't short, he wasn't tall either. Probably an inch shorter than Allie, who was on the tall side. He was just…average. And adorable.

Okay, so his face certainly wasn't average. No, seeing him up close had momentarily made her short-circuit, and those dimples had taken up permanent residence in Allie's brain. He could ask her to do anything he wanted, and as long as he did it with a smile, she would do it. Happily.

"This. Is. Why. You. Are. Single." Allie emphasized each word by tapping her head on her arms. Maybe one of these days the concept would actually stick, even if she did think her apartment was too quiet and she'd been talking to herself a lot lately.

She'd also been able to do a lot of writing, and that was nice. Three months of boyfriend-free time had given her a lot of…useless writing that was never going to see the light of day. But still. She might even finish a project one of these days. That would be a first.

By the time the ice cream was gone—the bathroom still in need of cleaning—Allie's phone rang and interrupted her scrolling of Pinterest. She didn't have to look at the name to know it was her mom calling. The woman operated like clockwork, so Allie answered the call and switched it to speaker so she could keep scrolling. "Hey, Mom."

"You sound funny. Have you been eating ice cream?"

Allie had never been able to figure out if her mom could actually hear a difference in her voice or if she just knew her daughter well enough to know she was often eating ice cream, but it was still creepy. "Of course not," she said, though she made a mental note to go to the gym later. Just to make sure she didn't *actually* gain a bunch of weight she didn't particularly want. Mom would secretly use that as a reason for her not being married yet, though she would never say anything out loud.

"Sweetie, you know that's not a nutritionally sound dinner. You should come over. I made a pot roast, and I know how much you love—"

"Who is he?" Snatching up her phone, Allie figured if she was going to endure this conversation, she might as well clean the bathroom at the same time. It was definitely the preferable activity, and she could kill two birds with one stone. No point in being miserable longer than necessary.

Mom took a while to answer, which meant she was floundering. "Who is who?"

Allie rolled her eyes as she picked up the scrub brush she'd left on the bathroom floor. "The guy you want to set me up with."

"Sweetie, I heard you when you told me you didn't want me setting you up with anyone."

She may have heard, but would she actually listen? The odds were twenty-eighty against. Not a probability Allie was all that comfortable with.

"I just worry about you in that apartment all by yourself," Mom continued. "You must be so lonely, and I know you don't eat well when you have too many things to distract you. Besides, your father and I haven't seen you for weeks!"

Allie held back a groan. The guilt tripping was starting early today, was it? Sitting against the tub again, she did her best to sound cheery instead of weary. She liked to think she was pretty good at it, given how she'd had to tiptoe around José's emotions back when she dated the guy.

"Mom, I'm not lonely." Lie. "And I didn't eat ice cream for dinner." Another lie. "I talk to you and Dad practically every day." True. "I'm just too busy with writing for work to come over as often as I used to." Lie again.

That last one was harder than the others. Allie did miss her parents. They were only twenty minutes away from her apartment, but whenever she went over there on her own, her mom had a habit of looking at the empty fourth chair at the table and letting out little sighs every five minutes.

Helen Ortega was a lot of things, but subtle was not one of them.

"What did you have for dinner tonight, if not ice cream?"

Allie glanced at the cupboards, hoping for an idea to come to her, but she was coming up blank. "I, uh, haven't eaten yet."

"Perfect! Then you can come over, and I can introduce you to Justin."

"Mom!"

"Not like that. He's a new neighbor, and I just wanted him to feel welcome to the area. You of all people should know how difficult it is to be on your own in a new place."

Allie would have gotten angry if her mother wasn't entirely right. She *did* know how hard it was to be on her own. She would never admit it to her mom, but she was pretty miserable. The longer she went without dating someone, the more she started rethinking her decision to stay single for a while. Was it really worth it?

"Yes," she breathed. It was worth it.

"You'll come?" Mom squealed, and Allie dropped her face in her hands.

This was what she got for talking to herself. "Yeah," she sighed, "I'll come. But not because I want to go out with this Justin guy. I'm just coming for the food and to say hi to you and Dad."

"Yes, of course. I understand. Like I said, I heard you when you said you didn't want any more setups. I will do nothing of the sort; I promise. See you soon! And dress nice."

Allie groaned as soon as Mom hung up. She wanted to believe the woman could actually follow through with her promise, but history said otherwise. Mom would never stop trying to find Allie the perfect man, and Allie would never stop saying yes to her. The curse of loving her parents.

By the time she showered and drove to the Ortegas' neighborhood, Allie knew she had probably pushed back dinner by at least an hour. Her parents usually ate early, and she wondered if this Justin guy would actually show up. He probably would, even if he didn't want to. Mom was persuasive like that, and she really didn't take no for an answer. Allie just hoped the evening wouldn't drag on. She had to get up early tomorrow and pretend she loved picking up the coffee for everyone before staff meetings.

An unfamiliar car sat parked in the driveway when Allie pulled up to the house, so she parked on the street and took a deep breath. She could do this. She could be nice to some strange guy who had probably been told all about her already. She could navigate her mother's not-so-subtle attempts to push the two of them together and pretend she had no idea what Mom was thinking.

Mom had done it before, and she would do it again.

"Here we go."

Justin, as it turned out, was in the middle of the house tour when Allie stepped through the front door. Dad was showing him his ships-in-bottles collection and giving him the full history of the largest one.

"It's a perfect replica of the USS Constitution," Dad was saying, his voice full of pride. "Oldest ship still sailing today, in fact."

Allie took one more deep breath before they noticed her, and then she jumped into the fray. The sooner they got this over with, the sooner she could go home to her lonely apartment. "Old Ironsides, they call her. Right, Dad?"

"Allie-cat!" Dad wrapped her up in a tight hug that completely swallowed her, but she didn't mind. It really had been a while since she'd come to see her parents, and she missed these bear hugs of his. "The prodigal daughter returns!"

When Allie finally untangled herself, she caught sight of the confusion on Justin's face only a moment before he put on a smile. "Hi," she said, holding out her hand. "I'm Allie. Dad likes to think I'm his long-lost daughter when I haven't been home in a week."

Justin's handshake was a lot looser than she expected, making her squirm. There were few things she hated more than limp handshakes. Ben's, on the other hand, had been firm and lingering.

"I've heard plenty of stories," Justin said. Ugh, his voice was just as limp as his hand. Like he was in the middle of the world's quietest library and didn't want to disturb the dozen sleeping hungry tigers beside him. "Mr. and Mrs. Ortega are very…uh…fond of you."

Allie bit the insides of her lips to keep from laughing. She could imagine the things her mom had said to try to talk her up to the single young new neighbor. The single part was an assumption, but the rest was accurate. Justin couldn't have been older than twenty-five, putting Allie several years above him. She wondered if Mom had told him how old she was or if she'd avoided that topic.

Not many twenty-five-year-old guys were interested in a thirty-two-year-old who had never paid bills or bought her own car and had signed her first apartment lease three months ago. Generally speaking, she was way behind the curve on the whole adulthood thing. Not that that was her fault. Mostly.

"Allison, is that you?" Before Allie could respond to Justin's comment, Mom came shuffling into the living room looking for all the world like she belonged on the cover of a home and garden magazine from the sixties. She had always looked like that, and Allie had always secretly loved it, even when boyfriends would comment on Mom's somewhat old-fashioned sense of style.

"Hey, Mom." Wrapping her up in a hug, Allie used this moment to remind herself how much she loved her mother. True, she was a little obsessive about getting her daughter married, but it was all with good intentions. Mom and Dad had the happiest marriage Allie had ever seen and wanted her to have the same thing.

Too bad Allie had a terrible track record when it came to dating. Hence the man-fast. She needed some time to figure out her own life before she really tried to share it with someone else, and she couldn't do that if Mom kept thrusting unsuspecting men at her.

"I see you met Justin," Mom said, a twinkle in her eye. "He just moved into the area, so I thought we would show him how we here in Diamond Springs treat our neighbors."

Allie returned her gaze to Justin, trying to figure him out before she did any real conversation attempts. Mom had never really thought through Allie's preferences when it came to dating; as long as he was male and had a pulse, that was good enough for her. Allie, on the other hand, had gotten a taste of just about everything out there, so she was pretty good at making snap judgments.

From what she could tell, Justin was the young business professional type who worked in a good enough job to afford a small house but wasn't cutthroat enough to rise to the ranks too quickly. With the way he comfortably wore his conservative-colored business casual, he definitely worked an office job, likely something in software because he hadn't actually been interested in Dad's ship stories. He *did* keep glancing at the shelf of movies, like he was trying to judge her parents' taste. More on the skinny side and definitely paler than her, he probably spent more time playing video games than he did outside or at the gym.

Allie couldn't spot any red flags from his outward appearance, but she already knew they wouldn't do well together. She'd dated a programmer for six months a few years ago, and she had nearly lost her mind to boredom. Everything was logic and numbers to him. No imagination.

Justin was likely the same way, even if every single one of Allie's assumptions turned out to be wrong.

She hadn't been able to get a good read on Ben, the Grocery Guy. Was he analytical, or did he have a creative streak in him?

Not that it mattered.

Allie wasn't up for dating. At all. *Period.*

Justin was the first to break the awkward silence that came after Mom's comment about him moving in, doing so with a cough and a glance toward the door. *Me too, buddy.* "Thank you for having me, Mr. and Mrs. Ortega."

Mom batted her eyelashes and pretended to blush. "Please, it's the least we could do. And call us Hector and Helen! We're all friends here."

When Justin sent a wide-eyed glance toward Allie, she was pretty sure he was hoping she would help him come up with some excuse to end the night early. He wanted to be here as little as she did. That was refreshing, given the last half a dozen guys Mom had introduced her to had been all too eager to meet her.

That tended to happen when her mom started flashing beauty pageant pictures.

It was only one time, Allie had told people more than once. Her senior year of high school. And she had only done it because it came with a scholarship. The fact that she had won had surprised her more than anyone; she had never considered her curves "swimsuit ready" according to worldly standards. Winning the pageant had come down to great bone structure and cooperative hair, with a semi-decent essay thrown in for good measure.

She had done her best to hide any evidence of the fact that she'd done the pageant, but Mom must have had a secret stash of photos somewhere. Maybe one of these days Allie would try to hunt it down and get rid of anything incriminating.

But first, she had to diffuse the awkwardness in the living room; no one seemed to know what to say.

"So, dinner?" she said.

Mom's eyes went wide. "Yes! Dinner. You must be starving, Justin. I hope you like pot roast!"

"I'm vegan," Justin muttered, but it wasn't loud enough for anyone but Allie to hear. Or maybe her parents did hear him and just ignored it.

They did the same to Allie, and she felt a pang of sympathy for the guy. Maybe he *was* vegan, but he would never be able to be so in this house. The only time Allie ate meat was when she was with her parents and had no other options, which happened quite often. Hopefully Justin wasn't the kind of guy who looked down on others who didn't believe the way he did. Then again, maybe this was just the thing that would keep anything from ever happening between them.

There was still a chance he jumped on the opportunity, and Allie would definitely prefer to shut him down quickly.

Dinner was just as awkward as introductions, and Allie didn't bother trying to fix it. As much as she hated awkward situations, she wanted her mom to understand how weird it was that she invited some random guy over to her house in the hopes of meeting her single—but unavailable—daughter. Mom kept trying to ask Justin personal questions, and he kept responding with single-word answers, and whenever she tried to say something about Allie, Allie kicked her underneath the table.

By the time her mom announced they should play a board game before dessert, Allie was tired of deflecting and ready to be done.

"I can't stay," she said, grabbing up her things before Mom could react. "Thanks for dinner, Mom, and it was nice to meet you, Justin."

He was on his feet in a flash. "I'll walk out with you. Early morning tomorrow."

Allie hoped that wasn't an excuse to get her alone so they could actually talk and get to know each other.

"But dessert!" Mom protested.

Allie grimaced. "Already ate a whole pint of ice cream. I'm good."

"Don't like dessert," Justin muttered.

By some miracle, Allie kept her jaw from dropping. Who in the world didn't like dessert? Crazy people, that's who. Even the ridiculously attractive guy from the grocery store liked dessert!

Before she'd even gotten her jacket on, Allie figured it would be a good idea to get away from Justin and let him carry on with his life away from her. She slipped out the door without a word, ready to leave the whole disaster of an evening behind.

"Hey, Allie?" Justin, on the other hand, was right behind her. "You got a second?"

She didn't like being rude, even if she wished she could be. Allie stopped right next to his car, which was the most basic gray sedan she'd ever seen. Even his car was boring! She'd learned very little about him during dinner—he'd barely spoken a word—but she doubted it would have helped his case even if he'd offered up more than the barest minimum. Allie's life was already boring; she definitely couldn't date someone who wouldn't offer up some excitement to her life.

News flash! You can't date anyone *right now. That's the point.*

Sighing because her inner voice was right, Allie put on a smile just to be nice. "What's up?"

Justin scuffed the toe of his shoe against the driveway, his head down and face red. "I know this was weird, your mom trying to throw us together."

Understatement of the century, but Allie was used to it. Justin probably wasn't.

"Don't read into it," she told him. "My mom does this with anyone even a little bit single."

He nodded without looking at her. "See, the thing is, I don't actually know anyone in Diamond Springs, so I said yes to dinner tonight because I thought it might be nice to have someone who can show me around. You know?"

Grimacing, Allie was glad he was too engrossed by his feet to see her expression. She couldn't fault the guy for wanting a friend, but friendships with the opposite gender always tended to turn into something more. She'd never heard of a friendship where one or both parties weren't hoping for more at some point. Maybe Justin really did just want to be friends, but could she risk that?

She *could not*, under any circumstances, start dating anyone again. Sticking to her guns with this was crucial for her happiness. Unfortunately, her mother would never understand that.

"I'm pretty busy most of the time," Allie said, struggling to find a nice way to shut him down entirely. "But I suppose I could show you around sometime." *What was that?*

Finally looking up, Justin gave her a little smile that might have been cute if it wasn't full of nerves and uncertainty. Surely he had enough going for him that he could have at least a little confidence in himself. There was nothing more attractive than confidence. Wow, when did Allie become such a snob? Justin *was* cute. But that was about the only thing he had going for him in her eyes.

"Thanks," he said. "Your mom, uh, gave me your number, so I'll be in touch. Have a good night, Allie."

Allie watched him drive off, glad that he didn't hug her or anything, but that didn't quell the feeling that Justin would be true to his word and call her up sometime to get together. She would have to work on her excuses to make sure she could get out of it before he fell in love with her.

"Huh," she muttered. "Apparently I'm snobbish *and* conceited. How nice." She would have to work on that, but she blamed it on Jeremy, her last boyfriend. The man had written the definition of conceited, and Allie had spent just a little too much time with him. His cockiness had rubbed off on her.

At least the night was over and she could go back home and write for a bit before she had to go to bed. But first, she had to get away before anyone came outside and tried to convince her to stay.

"Allie?"

She froze with her hand on the door of her car. Why, of all days? Turning slowly, she did everything in her power to smile at the man who had just brought out his garbage cans to the curb next door. "Jake," she breathed. When had he moved back home?

As if reading her thoughts, he glanced at the house behind him. "Dad's gotten pretty bad," he said. "I moved in last month to look after him."

Jake Romney had been Allie's best friend for years while growing up right next door to each other. At least, they'd been friends until they were suddenly more in high school. See? Friendship *never* stays that way. And after they broke up, things got awkward between them, to the point where Allie didn't even know that he'd moved back home.

It was a miracle Mom hadn't told her the minute it happened. Mom *loved* Jake.

"How is your dad?" she asked quietly. Mr. Romney had been suffering from memory problems for years, among other things, and Jake had always talked about how much he hated the idea of putting him in a home. Even with the best care possible, it was nothing compared to keeping him in a familiar environment and surrounding him with people who loved him.

Jake shrugged, his hand still on the garbage bin. "It's up and down. Your dad comes over and plays poker a lot, though."

Of course he did. Her dad was a saint, and for a moment she debated going back inside to spend a little more time with her parents. They were both wonderful, even if sometimes her mom was a little overbearing with the whole dating thing.

"So…" Jake coughed and folded his arms, clearly feeling just as awkward as Allie was. "New guy?"

She glanced in the direction Justin had driven off and snorted. "Uh, no. It's just Mom being her usual matchmaking self."

Did he look relieved? Yes, he did. "So you're not dating—"

"I've sworn off men," Allie said, though she smashed all her words together so it sounded like, "Ifsornoffen."

Jake must have understood, because his eyebrows shot up. "What, like now you're into—"

"Oh! No." As her face burned, Allie wished she hadn't said anything at all. Jake didn't need to know that she was anti-dating. It was none of his business. But she figured she should clarify. "I mean, I'm sort of trying to date myself right now. More than trying. I'm doing it. Soul-searching. You know?"

"Uh, sure."

He clearly thought she was crazy, and Allie didn't feel like correcting that belief. She hadn't been single for more than a few days at a time since she was fifteen. Since the day Jake first held her hand. Maybe they weren't close friends anymore, but Jake definitely knew this about her and didn't seem to believe she would ever be on her own for any significant amount of time.

There was little point in trying to convince him otherwise.

"Well, I should get going," Allie muttered, wishing she hadn't lingered to begin with.

Jake looked like he wanted to say something, but he stopped himself and shut his mouth before anything came out. He simply gave her a nod, stuffed his hands into his sweatshirt pocket, and wandered back up to his house.

Allie let out a sigh. Maybe someday they would be almost friends again, but she stood by her belief; friends never stayed friends. Inevitably, someone always wanted more.

FOUR

ALLIE WOULD *NOT* TALK TO Ben.

She had told herself so five times already, every time she accidentally turned onto the same aisle as him and had to quickly turn around and go back the way she'd come. Apparently this grocery store was a whole lot smaller than she'd realized, though she really couldn't say why she was so determined to keep her distance from the cute guy she'd barely met.

That was a lie. She knew exactly why she was avoiding the cute guy. Emphasis on *cute*. She had enjoyed her tiny little conversation with Ben last week so much that she hadn't stopped thinking about it—or comparing it to her conversation with Justin—which meant further conversations would lead to further thoughts, and further thoughts would lead…

Well, Allie couldn't really resist dark eyes and warm smiles. Puppy dog looks were definitely her weakness.

"You are a strong, independent woman who doesn't need a man to make her happy," she told herself, then smiled at the elderly woman who gave her a strange look as she walked past. "But maybe don't talk to yourself in the grocery store," she whispered as an afterthought.

Problem was, there was something about the cutie, Ben, that really intrigued her. He had noticed her a couple of times this morning, and the only thing he'd done to acknowledge her was give her a nod of his head. Not that she really thought all that highly of herself, but Allie was used to a different reaction when she encountered good-looking men. Generally, if she gave them an ounce of attention, they became a whole lot pushier and made it clear they were interested.

For some reason, the fact that Ben *wasn't* interested only made Allie more determined to get to know him. Exactly what she didn't need to do right now.

As she turned onto the meat aisle, she suddenly found herself face to face with the man, and his eyes locked onto hers. So much for avoiding him.

"Uh, hi," she said, feeling more awkward than she'd felt in a long time as she tucked her hair behind her ear. Had it really been that long since she had to be the one to instigate conversation? Apparently. It was definitely a good idea for her to avoid dating anyone if only because she needed her ego cut down to at least half its size.

At least she was having a good hair day. That somehow made it better.

"Hey," the guy said, and then he turned right back to the package of tofu in his hands.

Wow. She couldn't remember the last time someone had practically ignored her like this. Weirdly, she kind of loved it. "I always have the hardest time with tofu," she said. Did that sound condescending? Johnny had told her many times that she sounded condescending, and sure, she and Johnny hadn't dated for four years now, but she suddenly had his high-pitched voice in her head telling her that she had to be nicer to people.

Funny, coming from a guy who made fun of women on the regular. Somehow, it had taken almost two years of dating the guy for Allie to recognize the misogyny in her boyfriend before she broke up with him and moved on to someone else.

Ben looked over at her out of the corner of his eye, apparently uninterested in having a conversation. Then he looked behind her. And behind him. As if trying to figure out if she was actually talking to him. When he turned pink, Allie had no idea what to do. "Oh," he said. "Yeah. Tofu's, uh, tricky."

He sounded nervous.

To talk to *her*?

Allie had always figured she gave off easy vibes since men were so often coming right up to her and jumping into conversation. Technically she *tried* to make it easy for them, because that made it a whole lot simpler to find a new boyfriend when she needed one. But now that she was determined to stay single, she wasn't sure what vibe she was giving off. Whatever it was, it seemed to make Ben nervous.

It was adorable, and Allie was quickly forgetting her promise not to talk to the guy. "So, are you vegetarian?" A quick glance at his shopping cart—she really shouldn't snoop, but she couldn't help herself—revealed a bunch of vegetables and beans. Exactly the sort of things a newly minted vegetarian would be stocking up on.

Ben cleared his throat. "Yeah. I mean, no, not really. I mean…" He shook his head and seemed to be getting frustrated with himself. He was nothing like the over-confident jerks who usually came up to her while she was shopping, so his flustered nervousness was seriously refreshing. Sure, confidence was attractive, but it turned out humility was even better.

Letting out a sigh, Ben tossed his tofu into the cart and stuffed his hands into his jacket pockets. "I'm trying something new. But I'm a little out of my element."

As she stood there, Allie reminded herself that there was no point in flirting with the man. Sure, he was ridiculously attractive, and not in the "I'm sexy and I know it" kind of way. It didn't matter. He wasn't trying to hit on her, and if she hadn't said anything, they would have gone on their own merry ways and maybe never spoken again. Besides, Allie really was happy trying to learn about herself and figure out who she was without outside influence, so she didn't need to work this conversation into a date.

Then again, people had conversations all the time without flirting. That was all this was. A friendly conversation.

"What are you planning to make?" she asked him. Innocent enough, right? She could talk about food without it turning into flirting.

He grimaced. "I hadn't gotten that far, honestly. I think I was going for a stir-fry kind of vibe? I was hoping Oliver would be able to help me figure it out."

"Oliver?" She had no business asking, but she was curious about the relationship there and couldn't help but ask. Just how available was this guy? Not that she needed to know. It was only to gauge whether he might need help coming up with ideas for vegetarian meals. It was a lot easier to cook for more than oneself.

Ben shrugged. "One of the Wonder…Boys…" He made a face as he turned redder than before. "You didn't need to… Sorry. I'm not usually this…"

Whatever he was trying to say he wasn't, Allie was pretty sure it was a lie, and she smiled. Something told her she was getting full-blown Ben, whether he wanted her to or not. "Who are the Wonder Boys?" she asked. "It sounds like a mix between a superhero team and a sixties band."

"They're my best friends," he said, though it looked like he had no idea why he was still talking. "Madi called us that when we were kids, and the name kind of stuck."

"Who's Madi?" Allie was intrigued by this man and his apparent gang of friends, but at the same time it was making her realize that she didn't actually have friends. She'd never had the time to make them. All of her friends were always friends of her boyfriends, and they inevitably disappeared when her partners did.

No wonder she was lonely.

Ben coughed, glancing toward the door as if he wanted to escape. "Oliver's wife. Kit's sister. You know…"

"I don't know, but she sounds cool." This conversation had been way more entertaining than Allie expected, and all because of some tofu. Suddenly she was wondering why she hadn't talked to this guy before now, considering they'd been shopping at the same time for months. "It was Ben, right?"

"Benjamin. I mean, yes, Ben. I go by Ben."

"Benjamin the Wonder Boy. Nice to meet you."

Now his face was flaming, some genuine embarrassment in his expression, along with a little sheepish smile. "Maybe don't call me… It sounds worse coming from the outside."

Allie bit her lip. "Don't call you a Wonder Boy?"

"Please."

"But it's so cute!"

"I'm happy to be a lot of things, but cute isn't high on my list."

"Why not? A lot of guys are cute."

"A lot of guys don't buy tofu to try to impress a girl they've only talked to once. I mean…" His eyes went wide, and he turned around and headed straight to the checkout line without another word.

Allie was pretty sure that was the strangest interaction she'd ever had with anyone, but as she watched Ben pay for his groceries and start heading for the door, she couldn't help but smile. And when he glanced back her way and offered up his own embarrassed smile, she was pretty sure it would be a good idea to stay away from Benjamin the Wonder Boy. After all, she had sworn off men, and getting to know Ben was the exact opposite of what she should be doing.

FIVE

AFTER A LONG DAY OF work, Ben was stuck behind the prize counter at O'Reilly's, watching an eight-year-old try to figure out how many sticky hands he could buy with his stack of arcade tickets. It had been ten minutes already, and the line behind the kid was growing with no sign of letting up. Technically, Ben didn't even need to be here, with the new guy already done with the training—the job wasn't all that hard—but he wanted to stick around just in case some disaster struck as soon as the kid made a decision.

That tended to happen whenever Ben turned his back on something. It was like the place fell apart whenever he wasn't there.

To keep himself occupied, he'd grabbed an old receipt and was trying to draw the kid's scrunched-up-in-concentration expression. He would never be able to put it into words and describe it to his friends, but he was pretty sure the kid looked exactly the way Oliver did whenever he was trying to solve a problem. Ben's mind may have been melting from boredom, but at least he could laugh about this later with the Wonder Boys.

Any excuse to draw a little was enough to keep him going another day.

"Nakamura!"

Ben snapped up at the sound of his name, his eyes going wide when he caught sight of Mr. O'Reilly himself. What was the owner doing here? He almost never came into the fun center, and when he did, it was usually because he was in a bad mood. Heart pounding, Ben stuffed his drawing into his pocket and hurried over to the mini golf, where Mr. O'Reilly was glaring at him.

"Good to see you, sir," Ben said, holding out his hand. "It's been a while since—"

"No time for chit chat, Nakamura. Step into my office, will you?"

Ben frowned, glancing around. Even the center's manager didn't have an office; he usually just sat in the food court with his laptop. When he realized O'Reilly was gesturing toward the photo booth, Ben fought against a grimace. Surely not...

But O'Reilly pulled back the curtain and slid inside. The seat was hardly big enough for the both of them, but Ben squished inside anyway, his eyes wide in the dim lighting as he closed the curtain.

"This is a confidential conversation," O'Reilly said, his mustache twitching.

Ben could see a pair of pink tennis shoes just outside the booth, probably some girl wanting to take a turn next, but he chose not to say anything.

"I have been noticing some alarming numbers lately," O'Reilly continued, "and it's looking like the common denominator is you."

As he started to sweat—not just because of the heat of the too-small space—Ben silently told himself not to panic. But how could he not? He was getting fired. Had he left the sign on too many times? It couldn't have cost that much. Or maybe there had been too many lost shoes in the ball pit and people had started to complain. Or maybe...

What was he going to do now? This was the only job he'd ever had, unless he counted the few hours he worked in the bookstore coffee shop in college. He was already struggling to figure out where he would live once Cam moved across town!

"What would you say to the idea of opening up your own fun center on the other side of town?"

A buzzing filled Ben's ears, and he was pretty sure he'd heard the man wrong. "Sorry, what did you just say?" He felt dizzy, and he leaned a hand on the console in front of him only to start the camera countdown. Someone must have left a dollar in the machine.

The first flash only made the buzzing worse, but O'Reilly didn't seem to notice the photos being taken. "Every profitable night for the last eight months has been on your watch, Nakamura, and the numbers don't lie. You're good for business, and the perfect location just opened up over on Green Street. We could have it up and running in six months if I get my investors on board, and the place would be yours."

The next photo caught Ben with wide eyes and a gaping mouth. "You want...me...to run the whole place? But I don't—"

"You're perfect, son. You've been working at this place for more than a decade, and I've never seen a more dedicated employee. You love this place more than I do!"

I hate this place, Ben thought, and the camera flashed again. *But what else am I going to do with my life?*

"Think about it," O'Reilly said and literally climbed over Ben to get to the exit, blocking the camera with his rear end for the last picture.

When the little girl outside said something about how he needed to share, Ben finally stumbled out of the booth. He grabbed the stack of photos out of reflex and stared at the shock on his face, sure that he was still wearing the same expression. O'Reilly wanted to start up another fun center? And he wanted *Ben* to run it?

It would be his first promotion in nine years.

He ran into the corner of the counter as he returned to the prize booth, though he barely felt the sharp pain in his hip through his consternation. Why him? Why *now*?

"Hey, that drawing was really good."

Ben glanced over at the new kid, who had somehow gotten through the entire prize line while Ben had been talking to Mr. O'Reilly. "Uh, thanks," he muttered, though he was still reeling too much to really pay attention to what the kid said. What did a little doodle matter when it suddenly felt like his life was imploding?

Imploding in a good way. Was that a thing?

First Allie *talking to him* at the grocery store a couple of days ago—willingly, no less—and now Mr. O'Reilly suddenly realizing that Ben actually worked hard, unlike the general manager of the place who only came into the fun center a few times a week. What was next? Kit announcing he was moving to Europe to become a mime?

Ben shuddered at the thought. It was probably better if the rest of his life just stayed the same. After so many years of constancy, he didn't need everything to happen all at once. For the first time, he was starting to understand Kit's aversion to change. The man had been living his life the exact same way for years and didn't seem to have any intention of switching things up.

Clearly, Ben wasn't all that good with change either.

By the time he closed up the center and got home that night, he was absolutely exhausted and ready to go to bed. Cam was still up, though, which was strange, so Ben sighed and dropped onto the couch next to his roommate. Something told him the night wasn't over yet.

"Looking for a building for your gym?" he asked, squinting at the laptop Cam held on his knees.

Cam grunted. "You'd think there would be more large spaces for lease in a city this big, but no. It's just like I thought, and everything that's going to be big enough is on the other side of town. I can't commute an hour every day, which means…"

"Which means I'm going to have to find myself a new roommate," Ben replied. "I was still holding out a little hope."

"Sorry, man."

"It's not your fault." Ben looked at the refrigerator, trying to decide if it was worth standing up to heat up some leftover tofu stir fry. Thankfully, Cam had had some pretty good ideas for how to cook it up since Ben had high tailed it out of the grocery store before Allie could give him any suggestions.

Nope. The fridge was too far away.

"That face you're making isn't because of me, is it?"

Ben blinked, and it felt like his facial muscles relaxed all at once. He wasn't sure what expression he'd been making, but he had a feeling it wasn't all that pleasant. "O'Reilly wants me to manage his new fun center." Saying it out loud didn't help it make any more sense.

"He has another one?"

"He's planning to build one."

"Is the first one really that successful?"

Ben wouldn't have thought so, but it wasn't like he saw the daily numbers. The general manager had always done that part. "Guess so."

"And he wants you to run it?"

"Apparently."

"That's…cool?"

Ben raised his eyebrow. "You sounded really confident about that statement."

Shutting his laptop, Cam turned his full attention to Ben, which wasn't something he did often. They were roommates, and they'd been friends for fifteen years, but out of all the Wonder Boys, he and Cam were the most different.

Namely in the way that Cam rarely stopped talking. "Can I be honest with you?"

Ben rolled his eyes. "When are you not?"

"Fair point."

Cam was pretty much incapable of lying. Last summer, when Madi was going on fake dates to win the bet, Cam only made it through one date because he was too likely to give everything away. Ben had only made it through one date as well, but that was because by that point she and Oliver were already falling for each other.

Cam looked particularly intimidating when he folded his beefy arms like he was doing just now. "So maybe I'm a terrible liar, but I don't tell you everything, Nakamura. Like how Kit..." He froze, his whole face turning red. "What I mean to say is your job sucks."

The comment hit Ben hard, like it always did when Kit brought it up with him, but it was starting to affect him less and less. At this point, it was beating a dead horse. He was more interested in whatever Cam had almost said about Kit, but Ben wasn't one to pry. If there was something Kit didn't want Ben to know, then Kit probably had his reasons.

"I'm aware my job is awful," Ben said with a sigh.

"So why would you want to get yourself even more stuck than you already are?"

A valid question. "Because I would have control over the whole center. And the pay would be a lot better. Plus, it would be over by your gym, so we could still split rent. Besides, I really know what I'm doing. This is my area of expertise."

Rolling his eyes, Cam grabbed a sketchbook from underneath the couch. Ben had stashed it there the other night, thinking it would be safe, and he stared in horror as Cam opened it up and flipped through it.

"Dude," Cam said, "*this* is your area of expertise. You've gotten so much better since high school, and you have a degree in illustration, for crying out loud! Why won't you use it?"

Ben snatched the notebook back before Cam got to the sketches he'd done of Allie, though if he knew the sketchbook was under there, Cam had probably seen them already.

"What am I supposed to do?" Ben asked. He may have been hugging the book to his chest and looking ridiculous, but that was a lot safer than risking Cam's comments. "It's not like there are tons of illustration jobs out there."

Cam scrunched up his nose. "Have you even looked?"

Ben couldn't argue because he *hadn't* looked. Looking for a job that would use his love of drawing would mean subjecting himself and his art to the opinions and standards of other people, and that was terrifying. It had been hard enough doing that while in school, when everyone else was under the same scrutiny. What if he found out he was no good and no one wanted to hire him? Drawing was an outlet, and he worried that would be taken from him if he risked exposure.

"I'm going to bed," he mumbled, hugging the sketchbook tighter to his chest as he went back to his room.

He collapsed onto his bed in exhaustion, and as he lay there, he opened up to one of his sketches of Allie. He would need to do a new one now that he'd had another conversation with her and knew her personality a little better, but at what point did it turn creepy? He first drew her the day he first saw her. Months ago.

She talked to *him*, though, and he couldn't help but wonder if maybe he had a chance. This was the first time he had ever been really interested in someone, and though he knew he would somehow mess it up, he figured he might as well try.

At least then maybe *something* in his life would be good.

# SIX

OF ALL THE PLACES TO run into Jake, it had to be here. It had to be *now*. Allie crouched behind a display of French bread that smelled heavenly, trying to figure out why in the world her ex-boyfriend suddenly decided to shop on a Tuesday morning clear across town from his house. She'd first seen him in the chip aisle and had nearly crashed into a woman's cart, and she'd run as fast as she could to the other side of the store.

The only reason she hadn't left the store already was the fact that she hadn't seen Ben yet, and she really wanted to talk to him again.

However, that decision to stick around had led her here, hiding behind bread and hoping Jake didn't look up from the boxes of pasta he was examining. She had somehow managed to trap herself in the corner of the store, and she had nowhere to run until Jake left the aisle.

How long did it take for someone to choose between penne and fusilli, anyway?

Allie had had a good week. Nothing from Mom, no word from boring Justin, no major issues at work beyond what she already dealt with on a day-to-day basis. And it was finally Tuesday again, which meant she could get to know the adorable Wonder Boy Ben better. Instead, her mouth watered from the smell of bread while she prayed Jake didn't turn to his right and get a hankering for garlic bread to go with his pasta.

Jake turned.

"Crap!" Allie jumped up too quickly, her shoulder bumping into the bread display and nearly knocking it over. Thankfully, she caught the loaf that slid toward the ground before she was forced to buy it because it was on the floor.

Not that she would complain all that much. Wait, did "you break it, you buy it" apply to food?

"Allie?" Jake glanced around, likely realizing that she couldn't have appeared out of nowhere and was therefore hiding.

"Oh! Hey. Jake. Hi. What are you doing here?"

His eyes dropped to the basket hanging on the crook of his arm. "I'm, uh, grocery shopping."

Well, duh. "I mean what are you doing *here?* Specifically. You don't live anywhere near this place." She probably sounded rude, but she was finally getting to a point where she was comfortable being on her own. Two encounters with Jake within a couple of weeks were messing with her head, reminding her how it felt to always have him around.

There was nothing fundamentally wrong with Jake, and they'd made a good couple. *In high school.* They hadn't dated in more than a decade, and Allie knew for a fact she was a different person from the one Jake had known. That was part of the problem. Allie had changed so much over the years that even *she* wasn't sure who she was.

Rather than reverting to the person she'd been at eighteen, she needed to figure out who the real Allie Ortega was. And she couldn't do that if Jake decided to be all chummy.

Jake's eyes did another sweep of the aisle, almost like he was looking for backup. "I work just a couple of blocks from here," he said. "I thought you knew that."

Allie *did* know that; according to her mother, Jake had been working at the same architecture firm ever since graduating college. So maybe he had an excuse for being in this particular store, but there was no rationalizing his current purchase. Fettuccine at nine in the morning?

"Well, hey," Jake said, and his ears turned bright red at the same time Allie's stomach sank like a rock. Was he really going to do this now? Here? "While I've got you here, do you think maybe the two of us could—"

"I have to go," Allie said in a rush, and she snatched up one of the loaves of French bread before making a beeline for the entrance. Only, she still hadn't seen Ben yet, and for some reason she thought maybe he could help her calm down before she started crying or something stupid. She had no reason to be crying over Jake, but here she was. Like a fool.

Instead of heading straight for checkout, she turned onto the next aisle over. And walked right into something solid and warm. A pair of hands reached out and caught her arms, and Allie scrambled to catch hold of something to keep her balance. That something happened to be a pair of rather nice biceps.

Turned out Ben the Wonder Boy was stronger than he looked.

For a second, Allie stood there with her hands on his arms, trying to figure out how a guy as slim as him could have such definition. And why in the world was he hiding it beneath a shirt that was too big for him?

"My roommate is a personal trainer," he said, which meant he was fully aware that she was absolutely checking him out.

"Oh my gosh, I'm so sorry." Stumbling backward, Allie frantically searched for something to save her dignity. It was a lost cause, considering she'd dropped her basket of groceries and all of her food had gone everywhere, including a jar of jam that had splattered a remarkable distance. Was there a record for how far raspberry preserves could fly? Allie had probably broken it.

She dropped down and started picking things up before her embarrassment sent her running. But then, to her horror, Ben crouched down and started helping, and her face caught fire.

"Oh, you don't have to—I'm really sorry for crashing into you like that."

"What were you running from?"

"No one. I mean, nothing. I just wasn't looking where I was going." And walking at the speed of sound, but that was beside the point.

To try to distract herself, Allie glanced at the basket Ben had set at his feet to help her. He had grabbed more tofu, which made her smile. "Was your friend able to help you cook your tofu the last time?"

Pausing in his attempt to gather up the several bags of candy that Allie instantly wished she hadn't grabbed on impulse, Ben turned a little pink. "Yeah. It was pretty good. And Cam—that's my roommate—he said tofu is a pretty healthy protein option, so I thought… Yeah. Are you… Do you like tofu?"

Allie reached out to grab an apple that had rolled to the edge of the shelf, but Ben beat her to it. Barely. When her hand wrapped around his, he froze. Like, straight up stopped moving. He wasn't even breathing, and he stared at their hands until Allie lifted hers and set him free. Only then did he take a breath, and he handed her the apple without looking at her.

"Sorry," he muttered, even though Allie felt like she should have been the one apologizing. He was clearly uncomfortable around her.

To be honest, that was really refreshing. Most guys that she'd known over the years, including most of her boyfriends, had always been a little *too* comfortable with her. For once, an attractive man wasn't trying to put the moves on her, and she couldn't help but smile.

"Hey, if you want any more tofu ideas, I could—"

"Allie, what are you—" Jake suddenly appeared at the end of the aisle, looking at the two of them crouched down with her basket between them. "Is this guy bothering you?"

Allie had never disliked Jake as much as she did right now. Was he serious? "No, of course not."

Standing up, Ben seemed to be sizing Jake up as he looked him over, but not in a way that made it seem like he was taking in the competition. More like he was trying to read the situation. "We just had a little collision," he said.

Allie hadn't realized it before, but Ben was really gentle when he spoke. Compared to Jake, his words were downright soothing. It was like he didn't have a forceful bone in his body, and outside of the fact that he was apparently jacked beneath those business casual clothes of his, he had always been soft in everything he did.

Like when he offered his hand to help her up.

Before she could even reach up, Jake hoisted her up off the ground. "Maybe be more careful about where you're walking," he said to Ben, completely rude and territorial.

Though Allie was mortified and felt like apologizing for the male population in general, Ben offered up a little smile. "You're right. My apologies." There he went again, apologizing when it wasn't his fault.

"You don't need to say sorry," Allie said. "It was my fault."

When Ben's smile grew, it elicited a flush that ran through Allie like wildfire. Apparently she had never *really* seen him smile before, because she would have remembered a smile like that. The man was breathtakingly handsome. Literally. Had the store's AC just broken? It was definitely hot in there.

Jake stepped forward and put his hand on Allie's shoulder. "Als, are you okay? You look really red. Did he hurt you?" He may have sounded concerned, but every word grated on Allie's ears.

And when he moved his hand on the small of her back, she flinched. Right into Ben again. Based on the way Jake's eyes lit on fire, he didn't like the way Ben put an arm around her to steady her, and a terrible idea popped into her head. One she decided to go for before she thought herself out of it.

She just hoped she wasn't wrong about the kind of guy Ben was.

"Sorry in advance," she whispered to him, and then she took his hand, interlacing their fingers and leaning into him. "I'm fine," she told Jake. "This isn't the first time Ben has made excuses to run into me. It's how we met in the first place" — that was almost true — "and I think it's adorable."

Ben was so tense that his grip on her hand was borderline painful, but Jake was already backing down, his eyes on Allie's hand as she placed her palm against Ben's firm chest.

Ben's heart was pounding like crazy.

"Oh," Jake said, taking a step back. "When did… Never mind."

Allie didn't blame him for being confused. The last time they'd talked, she'd told him she had sworn off men. It had only been a week and a half since then, but he should be used to this. Since the day they broke up, Allie had always been dating *someone*. Why should now be any different?

"Ben," she said, "this is Jake. He lives next door to my parents. Jake, this is my boyfriend, Ben."

Ben made a coughing sound, not quite an actual cough and definitely not a laugh. It was more of a choking sound, and Allie was sure he was going to call her out because this was the last thing he would want a stranger to do. He was already uncomfortable around her, and she had probably just given him a great reason to find a new place to shop.

Maybe file a restraining order.

But then he held out his hand to Jake and offered a smile that *almost* looked real. "Hey, Jake. Thanks for looking out for her, but this was just a case of me getting a little…enthusiastic. I didn't mean to run into her so hard."

Allie could have kissed the man. But she wouldn't. Obviously. Man-vegan and all that.

Nodding, Jake looked even more uncomfortable than Ben had earlier. He opened his mouth as if to say something but changed his mind, looking around as if hoping to find some way to escape. It made sense, given Allie was pretty sure he had been about to ask her out before she ran.

"Nice to meet you, Ben," he said eventually. "I have to get back to work, but… It was good to see you, Als."

He shuffled off, and Allie stood frozen until he turned a corner and headed for the checkout lines. Only when he dropped off his sauce and pasta without buying them did Allie release Ben's hand.

"I'm so sorry," she said when he flexed his fingers. She must have been holding him just as tightly as he'd been holding her. "I really shouldn't have done that, but he was—"

"Ex-boyfriend?"

She blinked. "What?"

Curling his fingers into a fist and flexing again, he looked in the direction Jake had gone instead of at her. "You guys dated, didn't you?"

As much as Allie wanted to deny it, she couldn't. "In high school."

Turning, Ben looked her over and seemed to be trying to figure something out. "So it's been a few years?" It was a nice way of guessing her age without actually guessing.

Allie grinned. He was seriously adorable. Why weren't more men like him? "We broke up just after graduation fourteen years ago." Oh geez, had it really been that long ago? Talk about feeling old.

Ben seemed to do the math in his head, but it didn't seem to bother him when he nodded. How old was he? He had one of those faces that could have put him anywhere from twenty to forty. "And he's still in love with you?"

"He's not—" But she stopped herself. She hadn't ever considered the idea, but... Maybe Ben saw something in Jake's expression; he seemed like a fairly observant guy. Or maybe he was just reading into things.

What if Jake really was still in love with her? *Move on, dude.*

"I shouldn't have roped you into that," she said sheepishly. She must have lost her mind for even thinking up the idea, and Ben probably thought she was at least desperate if not completely crazy. "Apparently I'm not good with confrontation."

"You and me both."

At least she could breathe again, though she hadn't realized just how panicked she'd been until Jake had disappeared through the sliding glass doors. Jake was harmless, but she really didn't need a reminder of the past. She wanted to move forward, not back.

"Can I make it up to you for being a good sport about it?" she asked.

That seemed to catch his attention, bringing back that super-attractive smile again. It was so soft and genuine. If only a smile like that could be bottled; she would be rich from selling it to the lonely hearts of the world. "What did you have in mind?"

A little voice in the back of her head reminded her that she wasn't looking to start dating again, but she told the voice to shut up. This wasn't a date. It was a well-deserved thank you. "I've got a really good tofu lasagna recipe that I could teach you."

His jaw practically dropped, which meant he probably wasn't expecting anything like that. He was probably dating someone. Or married. Or gay. "Are… Are you offering to make me dinner?"

She decided to play it off as far less than she wanted it to be. "I'm offering to teach you. You're not off the hook from cooking with me and sharing the work."

How long did it take to pick yes or no? Ben looked toward one end of the aisle, then the other, and he even examined the contents of the basket at his feet before he turned his dark gaze back to her. Allie was practically shivering with anticipation. "That sounds—"

Her phone chose that moment to start blasting music—the ominous ringtone she'd set for her mom—and her stomach dropped. For her mom to call her this early in the morning instead of sending a cryptic text could mean only one thing.

Jake had spilled the beans as soon as he walked out the door.

"Hey, Mom," she said once she answered. It would be way easier to get this over with than to delay it.

"You're dating someone? Since when?"

It was as bad as she feared, and Allie shut her eyes, wishing this was only a dream and she would wake up on the floor of the grocery store with Ben leaning over her, making sure she was okay after their collision.

Imagining that face being the first thing she saw made her heart rate kick up a notch.

"I don't tell you everything about my love life, Mom," she said into the phone. That was a lie. Her mom had always been all up in her business, which meant Allie was in the habit of telling her everything before she had to ask. It was easier that way.

"You said you weren't interested in dating."

"That was before I met…Ben." She winced the moment she said it and glanced at Ben, who looked absolutely terrified even though he was pretending to read the back of a can of green beans.

"Well, bring him by for dinner on Sunday. Your father and I should meet him."

"Mom, it's not like we're—"

"Jake says it looks serious. We should meet him, Allie."

Mom hung up only a moment later, probably feeling hurt by being kept out of the loop.

Allie groaned and clutched her phone, trying to figure out what to do. She started talking out loud—that was the only way she could properly think this through. "Well, she's not going to let me show up alone. Then she'll think I lied to her. Maybe I could say we broke up? But then she'll think I'm heartbroken and need someone to comfort me, and she'll invite Justin over and it'll be all awkward again. Worse, she'll go next door and get Jake, and he'll probably figure out the truth and try to get back together again."

"Do you not want to date Jake?" Ben's voice was quiet, but he clearly knew exactly what was going on.

Allie sighed. "My dating life is… Complicated. And don't worry. I'm not going to drag you into it. Feel free to go on your merry way and be free of my ridiculous drama."

"I could… I could help." He said it with enough hesitation that Allie knew he didn't actually want to. He was just being nice.

"No, I think that would only make things worse. I…"

Her phone vibrated with a text, and she glanced down. Though it was a number she didn't recognize, the text itself made her squirm:

Unknown number: Hey Allie, this is Justin, your mom's
     neighbor. She said you have some free time this
     week to show me around town since I don't really
     know where anything is yet. No pressure, but I would

love the chance to spend a little more time with you.
We could get coffee? Let me know. Thanks, Justin.

"That little sneak," she hissed. "My mom doesn't even believe we're dating, and now she's going to—"

"I... I have an idea." Though he looked terrified, Ben swallowed and spoke anyway. "My friend Madi, before she married Oliver, she had a friend who kept trying to set her up and get her to go to singles events. So the Wonder Boys stepped in and acted as her fake dates, because she didn't want to date anyone for real. It worked. Or, it did until she and Oliver fell for each other."

A thrill ran through Allie at the thought of going on dates with someone like Ben, but she forced that excitement down. She was supposed to stay strong. "It's a good idea, but I'm not looking to date anyone right now."

"Which is why I could be your fake boyfriend. Get your mom off your back. It doesn't have to involve any actual dating."

"Why would you do that?"

He shrugged his shoulders. "Because I really want to know how to make tofu lasagna."

Goodness, the man was even funny, and Allie shivered when he gave her another radiant smile. It was like he didn't even know how attractive he was. This could be dangerous, but when Allie received another text, this one from Jake asking if he could get to know Ben better, she knew she didn't have much of a choice. Jake was more persistent than anyone she knew and wouldn't give up on this easily.

"Are you sure?" she whispered, waiting for Ben to change his mind. A man as attractive and kind as him probably had better things to do than to pretend to date someone who couldn't get her life together no matter how hard she tried.

"Teach me vegetarian cooking, and you've got yourself a fake boyfriend." He held out his hand.

Allie grabbed hold, noting again his solid handshake, and prayed the two of them could pull this off.

SEVEN

BEN HAD NEVER HAD A lot of time for dating, though Oliver would probably argue to the contrary. When they'd been in college, the two of them spent most weekends together to get through bouts of homesickness. Most weekends, Ben was asked out by the girls on his campus, and he felt bad about saying no.

Almost always, those dates ended up being one-sided conversations that left more than one girl in disappointed tears because Ben clearly had no idea how to act around women.

Things hadn't improved in the seven years since gradu-ation. In fact, they'd gotten worse. With most of his evenings spent at O'Reilly's, he didn't exactly have women lining up to ask him out, unless he counted some of the teen girls who apparently thought he was one of the high schoolers.

So when it came to this whole fake boyfriend thing with Allie, he was entirely out of his depth.

He had changed into his third outfit Sunday afternoon, and he felt like he was back in middle school. Only, this time, he didn't have his two older sisters telling him what to wear. (For the record, both of them had terrible taste and had married the most straight-laced, unadventurous tax guys named Ned. *Both of them.* It was eerie.)

Still, Ben almost wished they were here to give him advice instead of hundreds of miles away in different states. Wearing his O'Reilly's uniform every day had turned him into a polo-wearing weirdo who only owned khaki pants, and he couldn't for the life of him figure out what normal people wore nowadays.

Even his friends were no help when it came to inspiration. Cam always wore workout clothes, and Kit had the style of Mr. Rogers from public television, but in a hip way. Oliver was probably the only one worth imitating since he had been a bit of a flirt up until he realized he was in love with Madi. Problem was Ben didn't own anything that remotely resembled Oliver's sense of style.

Ben opted for business casual after thinking about the fact that he was going to a Sunday dinner, and he felt a little ridiculous for a man who wasn't even the manager of the fun center where he worked. But he could be. If he accepted O'Reilly's offer, he could essentially be running his own business and have something that actually looked semi-decent on his resume.

Maybe then Allie would look at him as more than some guy at the grocery store who bailed her out of a sticky situation.

Ben had seen the fancy watch Jake was wearing, and he knew an expensive haircut when he saw it—Oliver was filthy rich and had always looked the part. Whatever Jake did, he did it well, and something told Ben that if he wanted anything to actually happen with Allie, Jake was going to be his biggest obstacle. That, and Allie's declaration that she didn't want to date anyone.

That one was probably worse.

When Ben came out of his room, Cam was snoozing on the couch, and Ben sneaked by, hoping to avoid notice as usual. He got as far as the door before Cam said, "Why do you look so fancy?"

Tempted to just keep walking, Ben glanced back. "I don't look fancy."

Cam narrowed his eyes as he tucked his hands behind his head. "Put on a tie, and I'd think you were going to church. But you're not wearing a tie. And O'Reilly's is closed on Sundays."

Ben scrambled for something to say, which only interested Cam more, making him sit up and lift his eyebrows high.

"Does Ben Nakamura have a date?"

He considered lying, but he was nervous enough as it was. To say this week had been stressful was a massive understatement, and Ben had nearly gotten stuck in the ball pit because he wasn't paying attention while trying to fish a kid out. The ball pit was the stuff of nightmares. "It's no big deal."

"Is it with Grocery Girl?"

"Her name is Allie."

"So it is with Grocery Girl! Does this mean you actually talked to her? Way to go, champ!"

"Please don't read into this. It's one date." Possibly more, but Ben wouldn't say that. It was bad enough that this date wasn't real to begin with, and he wondered how Oliver had survived his many "fake" dates with Madi before he realized she was as in love with him as he was with her.

That definitely wasn't going to happen with Allie, but a guy could dream.

"Sure, yeah," Cam said, but he had his phone out and was already typing out a text. Ben grabbed his phone with a groan.

> Cam: Guess who has a hot date tonight.
> Oliver: I'm guessing it isn't you.
> Kit: *high five emoji*
> Cam: Rude.
> Oliver: I apologize for my stupid husband.
> Kit: Oliver, do you let Madi read all of our group texts?
> Oliver: *eye roll emoji* Like you guys ever say anything I haven't heard in real life.

Cam: We're getting off topic. Benny Boy has an actual DATE.

Oliver: With the grocery girl?

Kit: It's about time.

Oliver: Yay! You guys should really just add me to the group chat.

Oliver: Stole my phone back. Congrats, man.

Cam: Pretty sure he actually put on cologne for this one.

Kit: Good luck, Watch.

Oliver: He's going to need it. She'll be in love with him in two seconds if he doesn't keep the charm in check.

Cam: He looks like he's about to pass out, so he'll need all the luck he can get but for a different reason.

Ben: I hate you guys.

Oliver: You'd better come borrow my car, unless you want yours to blow up before you get there.

Ben showed up to the address Allie texted him and found himself at an empty field, no houses in sight. He looked down at his phone, trying to see where he went wrong, when another car pulled up behind him and Allie stepped out.

"Hey," she said when she opened the passenger door. "Sorry for the murder vibes, but we'll want to show up to the house together if we want my parents to believe we're actually dating." Her eyes traveled over the car that cost more than Ben made in two years at O'Reilly's. "This is…nice."

Ben had regretted taking Oliver up on his offer to borrow his car from the moment he accidentally accelerated too quickly leaving Oliver's house. The red sports car was ridiculously fancy and the exact opposite of Ben's (in that it actually ran), and he felt like an imposter sitting behind the wheel. This wasn't who he was.

"It's a bit much," he agreed.

Allie smiled as she climbed inside and looked around. "I didn't say that. I was going to offer to drive, but... This'll be way more fun." Only a second passed before her smile shifted into a frown. "You don't have to do this, you know. I can get myself out of this mess, and you can go on with your life as if you'd never met me."

Ben couldn't decide if she felt hopeful that he would change his mind or if she was praying he wouldn't. Based on his experience with women, she probably wanted nothing to do with him now that she'd had more than one conversation with him, but he was her only chance.

"I said I would help," he told her. "Tell me where to go."

It was only a ten-minute drive to Allie's parents' house, but that was plenty of time for Ben to study her out of the corner of his eye. She was nervous, fidgeting in her seat and only speaking when she told him to make a turn. He didn't like how tense she was, and he tried to think of something that would make her feel more comfortable about the situation.

"Maybe we should get our story straight," he said. This was as much for his benefit as he hoped it would be for hers. "When did we start dating?"

Allie didn't even look at him, her eyes on the road. "Two weeks ago. But we've known each other for a few months."

Huh. That was more or less the truth. "How serious are we?"

"I'm not dating anyone else. I've always been monogamous. Jury's still out on you."

Ben wasn't sure if *that* was the truth or not, and his curiosity got the better of him. "Why don't you want to date anyone right now? And I'm not dating anyone else either. In case you're wondering."

She glanced at him that time. "Really?"

"You're surprised?" Surely she'd seen his bumbling excuses of conversation and come to the same conclusion that most people did. Ben was surface level. No one ever felt the need to get deeper.

Shifting in her seat, she turned to face him. "Well, you're such a nice, handsome guy," she said.

Ben tried to hear the sarcasm in her words but couldn't. Maybe she meant it.

"I thought for sure you would say no to this because your gorgeous fiancée wouldn't let you."

He actually laughed at that one. "I'm not engaged. Besides, I'm not the kind of guy who would even consider being unfaithful to a girl I'm dating. Even if it's not real."

Allie didn't seem to believe that, making a face and muttering, "Sure you're not," before telling him to take a left turn.

He couldn't decide if she really thought so little of him or if she thought so little of every man she met. He hoped it wasn't just him, even if that didn't reflect well on his gender.

When they reached her parent's house, Allie cursed under her breath as Ben pulled up behind a car on the curb. "Something wrong?" he asked, his nerves rising.

Allie looked like she might be sick. "She invited Justin."

"Who?"

"Apparently he lives in the neighborhood. She tried to set me up with him a couple of weeks ago."

Ben gripped the steering wheel a little more tightly. He wasn't prepared for competition. "Why would she do that?" he asked, a little breathless.

"My guess? Like I said on Tuesday, she doesn't think you and I are really dating."

"Why not?" Ben wasn't sure he was going to be able to keep up the charade if it was doomed from the start. Then he would lose his chance to try to build something real with Allie. She said she'd sworn off men, but he was still holding out hope.

Allie sighed. "My mom knows I've stopped dating. Though I don't think she ever believed I could do it. I'm… I'm sort of a serial dater."

Ben was so far out of his element that he was suddenly tempted to drive off and give up. Oliver would have done the same, before he fell for Madi, and Kit never would have gotten into something like this in the first place. But if Cam ever found out, he would never let Ben live down the fact that he succumbed to a tiny little challenge.

For Cam, the small challenges were what made a person. Not the big things.

"I'm not," he said eventually. "A serial dater, I mean. I haven't had much time for dating lately. We don't have to do this if you don't want to, but my offer still stands. I'll help however I can. But there's nothing that says you have to pretend to be something you're not."

She set her jaw as she looked up at the house. "You're right," she said, and Ben breathed a sigh of relief. Maybe he wouldn't have to pretend after all. "But if I don't stand my ground, she's just going to steamroll me for the rest of my life. I know this is a lot to ask of you, Ben, but I have never needed a Wonder Boy more than I do right now."

She grabbed his hand, completely unaware of how much that little touch affected him, like his whole arm became electrified. "Will you help me?"

Even if he tried, Ben wouldn't have been able to say no. Not when she gazed at him like he was her last hope. "Of course."

He would have to pull out as much charm as he could muster, though he wasn't sure how much he really had in him. Oliver was convinced Ben made women swoon just by saying hi, and honestly Ben couldn't argue too much against that. He had never fully figured out what it was about him that drew people in, but he wished he knew.

Then he could turn it off.

But for now, he was determined to put on a smile and be the best dinner guest the world had ever known. Allie could use someone like that, and Ben would do just about anything to make her happy.

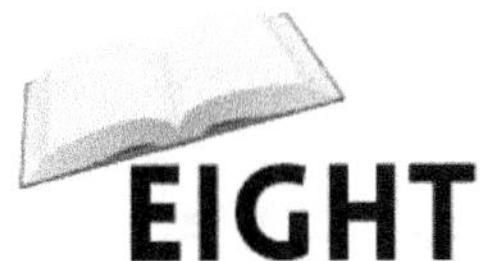

EIGHT

ALLIE HAD NEVER BEEN MORE nervous in her life, and that included pitching her own story idea to the execs at work. (They hadn't even considered her idea, and it had been terrifying.) But bringing someone like Ben to family dinner, someone she was not actually dating? That was the worst thing she'd ever done.

Knowing Justin was going to be inside made her both nervous and angry. She had never lied to her mom before, and it hurt that Mom thought she would be lying now. Even if she was. It also made her so mad that Mom wouldn't listen to her about not dating anyone, but that part didn't really surprise her. Mom wanted grandkids, and that was something Allie couldn't give her on her own.

"Anything I need to know about your parents?" Ben asked as they went up the stairs to the front porch.

Allie wished she would have thought this through and prepared him better. She'd had almost a whole week to fret and stew about this dinner, and she hadn't even thought to give the guy a rundown on what to expect. "They're your typical suburban parents," she said with a shrug. *Hopefully they won't get too crazy.*

He raised one dark eyebrow. "I am the fourth of seven kids," he said, "so my parents barely had time for me because there was always someone who needed them more. And my friend Oliver was raised by strict parents who expected way more of him than he could ever live up to. Kit's parents are probably the closest thing I know to something normal, but they were basically parents to the whole neighborhood and are probably way more selfless than most people. So I don't really know what would be classified as typical."

Allie suddenly felt like she understood Ben so much better. She may not have known much about him, but he gave a lot away when he actually talked. If he were a character in a book, he would be the one who hardly had any lines and was there for moral support to the hero. He probably even wanted to disappear into the background instead of taking the spotlight, but that definitely wouldn't happen at this dinner.

Why had she chosen someone like him to deceive her discerning mother? This was going to fall apart in minutes. "Maybe we should—"

The door opened before she could finish, and Allie felt dizzy when she looked up to see Jake standing there. "Allie!" he said, ignoring Ben completely. "What are you doing standing out here? Dinner's waiting."

Allie barely held back a glare. "What are *you* doing here?"

"Helen invited my dad over for dinner, so I was just dropping him off."

Allie knew what that meant, and she groaned. "She invited you to stay, didn't she?"

"Your mother is an incredibly kind person, Allie. Of course she did."

"But you're going back home." She tried to say that in a way that told him he shouldn't argue.

Jake folded his arms, acting territorial again as he scowled at Ben. "I was just running next door to grab some wine. I would hate to show up for dinner empty-handed."

Ben coughed, and Allie instinctively grabbed his hand as if that might tell him how little she cared that he didn't bring anything. He was already doing her a huge favor to begin with. "Ben offered to host dinner this week, but you know how my parents can be."

Jake glanced at Ben again, narrowing his eyes a little as he looked him over. "Nice to see you again," he muttered and held out his hand with an intimidating glare. "You wanted to go up against Helen's cooking? That's a bold move; where'd you study cooking?"

"I have a chef," Ben said before Allie could get mad at Jake for being rude.

Wait, really? She turned to him in surprise, though she couldn't ask what that meant for fear of blowing things.

Jake glanced behind them, probably at Ben's ridiculous car. "What is it you do, Ben?"

Allie put a hand on Jake's arm. "Jake, you don't need to interrogate—"

"I'm in entertainment," Ben said with surprising confidence. "I work mainly in management, though I've done a little bit of everything."

Allie didn't know that about him, and though she found his answer impressive, she wished he would have been something simpler. His car was obnoxious enough, but if he was going to turn out to be some fancy, self-important exec like her ex Jason, things weren't going to end well. Not that she and Ben were actually dating, but her mom was going to equate the two and guilt Allie into dumping him and dating someone more practical, like Justin.

Mom had never hated someone as much as she hated Jason, though Allie couldn't blame her. Jason had decided he was in a class above Allie and her parents, and he had spent their entire relationship trying to change everything about Allie without ever seeing fault with himself.

She shuddered a little at the memory. That was one reason to like Ben; he wasn't afraid of change. At least when it came to food… She had no idea about the rest of him, but she couldn't picture Ben the Wonder Boy being stubborn.

After Jake gave Ben quite the stare down, Mom eventually found her way to the door and peered over Jake's shoulder, trying to get a good look at Ben. "What are we all doing standing in the doorway? Come in, come in!"

Allie held her breath as they filed into the front room, Mom's eyes locked on her date. Pretend date. Ben was probably going to crumble under her scrutiny, and all of this was going to blow up in her face.

Then Ben did the unexpected: he threw on a smile and held out his hand, his eyes kinder than ever as he said, "Mrs. Ortega, I'm Ben Nakamura. Thank you so much for having me over for dinner. I've been looking forward to this ever since Allie told me all about you and your cooking."

Mom turned into a pile of goo, her eyes alight with what Allie could only describe as pure love. "Oh, what a charming boy. Of course we had to have you over, what with you stealing Allison's heart and all."

"I haven't stolen anything," Ben argued, and he turned that incredible smile to Allie. "I'm just lucky enough to have caught her attention. Your home is lovely, by the way."

Mom turned bright red and sent Allie a look of amazement, as if she couldn't believe anyone could be so perfect.

Honestly, Allie was starting to agree with her, but she was also getting more and more nervous. Ben had seemed a bit anxious in the car, but now he was completely confident, not a trace of nerves on his face. Had she misread him entirely? Maybe he *was* like all the other guys and was just really good at acting.

"Well," Mom said, "let's not stand around! We've got food to eat."

"It smells amazing, Mrs. Ortega," Ben said, right on cue.

"Please, call me Helen!"

Justin and Dad were seated at the table, but they both rose as the group entered the dining room. Allie wished she had been in front so she could try to control introductions, but she'd gotten stuck between Ben and Jake—who had apparently forgotten about grabbing wine—while Mom led the way, so there was nothing she could do when Mom said, "This is my husband, Hector, and this is our delightful new neighbor, Justin. And of course Lewis, Jake's father."

Allie stumbled when Mom suddenly switched places with Ben and held her back, but now she had a great view of the Wonder Boy as he charmed the pants off the entire room.

"Thanks for having me, Mr. Ortega. I'm guessing those were your ships in the front room? They're amazing." Dad beamed. "And Justin, it's good to meet you. You have a nice car—must get excellent gas mileage." Even Justin smiled a little, though he seemed to be trying to figure out just how Ben was connected to Allie as he glanced between the two of them. "Lewis, you have a great son, and I'm sure the apple doesn't fall far from the tree."

Allie dropped her head into her hands. She should have found a way to warn Ben about Jake's dad because now everyone was going to think he was insensitive. The awkwardness in the room was palpable, like they were all stuck in some kind of jelly that kept them in this awful moment.

Well, everyone except Ben. He crouched down next to Lewis's chair and put a hand on his arm, even though Lewis couldn't do much except look at him. "I'll bet you have all sorts of stories about Allie from when she was a kid, don't you? Tell me, was she an angel? No wait, she was probably one of those kids who terrorized the neighborhood, wasn't she? My brothers were like that, and it drove my parents crazy. Drove the neighbors even more crazy." He laughed, even though Lewis hadn't said a word. "You're right; she probably put on that angelic face whenever she was about to get into trouble, and no one could ever stay mad at her. She's used that look on me before, and trust me; it's impossible to resist. I'm jealous of you, you know. You got to see her when she was figuring out who she was."

Did Lewis just smile? Allie hadn't seen him smile in years, and she stared at the two of them in amazement. So did Jake. He stood next to Allie with his arms folded, and he seemed to be trying to find a reason to hate Ben but was coming up empty.

Maybe this dinner wasn't going to be so bad after all.

"Well," Mom said, a little breathless. Was she *crying*? "We should eat before the food gets cold, shouldn't we?"

For the first time in a long time, Allie barely paid attention to the conversation happening around the dinner table, even if Ben was a big part of it. Mom asked him about his family, and Dad told him stories about his ships that Ben listened to with obvious interest, and Justin and Jake were both silent unless they were asked a question directly. Allie didn't really listen to what anyone said, too busy trying to figure out how a guy like Ben could be single.

When she *was* paying attention, she learned a few useful things about the guy. He was twenty-nine and had lived in Diamond Springs his whole life, except when he went to college on the other end of the state. He wasn't very outdoorsy, though he camped a lot with his friends when they were younger. All of his siblings were married except the youngest two, who were both attending the local comminuty college, and he had sixteen nieces and nephews.

Basically, she liked everything about him. Not only was he handsome and sweet, but he seemed to be able to have a conversation with anyone about anything. It was like he could put the whole room at ease with a smile. He didn't talk over anyone, and he let Allie answer questions about herself (which could have been because he didn't know the answers, but she didn't think so), and he was exactly the kind of guy who anyone would want to date.

It was too bad Allie wasn't willing to give up on her plan. Was this really fair to him? Forcing him to pretend and lie to her family? It was a good thing she wasn't really dating him because he deserved a lot better than someone willing to stoop so low.

At some point in the middle of dinner, Ben reached over and took Allie's hand, and she shivered at his touch. He was a complete stranger, but his hand was so comforting. Calming. No one had ever been that for her before, and she had no idea what it meant.

When everyone was finished eating, Mom announced it was time to play games. What was it with her and games? Under no circumstances was Allie going to subject Ben to her family more than necessary, so she got ready to fight her mom like she'd done the last time.

But Ben spoke first. "Actually, Helen, I have an early morning tomorrow, and Allie should probably get to bed at a decent time to combat the stress she's had at work."

Mom's eyes went wide. So did Allie's. What did he know of her work stress? She hadn't said anything about work to him since that first day they talked. Weeks ago.

"Stress?" Mom asked, clear concern in her voice.

Allie waved her off. "It's nothing major. Besides, I've got Ben to keep me from spiraling." She gave his hand a little squeeze before they both got to their feet, though she wasn't sure what she meant by the gesture.

To Allie's horror, Mom was basically in tears as they walked out, like all of her prayers had just been answered. Allie kept a firm grip on Ben's hand, not caring if he wanted her to or not, and she didn't let go until he opened the car door for her.

Once he slid into his seat and closed the door, they both sat there for a second as if going over the whole dinner and trying to figure out what just happened. At least, that's what Allie was doing, and she figured Ben was doing the same.

"She's gonna kill me," Allie whispered. Ben had played his part so well, and things had gone exactly as she planned. So why did Allie feel like crap? She couldn't get her mom's happy expression out of her head.

Ben glanced over. "I'm sorry, I shouldn't have—"

"No, you were perfect." That was the problem. Allie groaned. "If I don't bring you around again, she's going to blame me for messing things up, and she's going to disown me and take you instead."

Ben looked a little sick to his stomach. "I thought you'd be better off if I was the kind of boyfriend Madi deserved."

Allie tried to remember who that was. "Madi? She's—"

"Oliver's wife."

"The one who called you the Wonder Boys."

"Yeah." He gazed out the windshield as he spoke, his eyes distant. "I always thought she deserved a guy who was confident in how he felt about her and not afraid to be a part of her life, you know?"

That sounded amazing, and Allie realized she had never experienced that. Was such a thing even possible? She had had more boyfriends than she could count on her fingers, and none of them had ever been like that. They had always tiptoed around her like they were afraid she might shatter if they pushed too hard. "Is Oliver not like that?"

Ben snorted a little laugh. "No, he totally is. He's perfect for Madi, and they round each other out. Fill in the blanks." He'd gotten quieter, his hands gripping the steering wheel.

She was hesitant to ask, fearing what the answer would be, but she did anyway. "Were you ever in love with Madi?"

He glanced over, a bit of pain in his expression. "No," he said, but it wasn't very believable, which he seemed to realize as he dropped his head onto the steering wheel. "I mean, maybe the *idea* of her. She was such a good friend and exactly the kind of person I could see myself being with for the rest of my life. But she was always meant for Oliver, so I never let myself..." He sat back up and dropped his head against the leather headrest.

Allie sighed. How could anyone choose someone over Ben? She decided to change the subject back before the poor guy got too introspective. "I'm just going to have to tell my mom the truth," she decided. Avoiding Mom's matchmaking wasn't worth the guilt she felt. "I may never be able to convince her I'm not available, but that's better than letting her gush over how adorable you are, because how could she not?"

To her surprise, he turned bright red and kept his eyes locked on his hands, as if too afraid to look at her. "You think I'm adorable?" he whispered, almost too quiet to hear.

Well, now she definitely thought he was adorable, but she was playing a dangerous game with every minute she spent with this guy. She refused to get lost in something that wasn't even real. That defeated the whole purpose, and all of this was pretend anyway.

"Of course," she said as casually as she could. "You played your part so well that even I believed it for a minute there."

"And you don't think I can do it again?"

That question confused her. Again? "I'm sure you could, but—"

"How long before you'll need to bring me around again?"

Was he seriously offering? "Ben, I can't ask you to—"

"Tonight was more fun than I've had in a long time," he said, flashing her that amazing smile before turning away again. "If you don't want to tell the truth to your mom, I can help."

"Why would you do that?" Doubt built in her chest as she thought about doing something like this again. What was he getting out of this? No one did something for nothing. Not even Ben the Wonder Boy.

Ben shrugged, still staring at his steering wheel. "I've been stuck in the same place for the last decade," he muttered. "Something tells me you might be stuck too. Tonight, I felt like I actually accomplished something, and that was a good feeling. So before you go thinking I'm some completely selfless—"

Allie leaned over and kissed his cheek, lingering there because he smelled really good and was super cute and she owed him big time. "Why don't you come to my apartment when you have a free night?" she said, despite the voice in the back of her head telling her that that was a bad idea. "I can teach you my favorite tofu recipe, and we can get to know each other a little bit."

He turned pink again. Allie had never really seen a guy blush this much, and she loved it. It was true humility. "Really?" he asked.

"It's the least I can do. And if you're really going to help me pull this fake boyfriend thing off, you should probably know more about me. And I should get to know you. If nothing else is real, we can at least be friends, right?"

Oh, how she wanted to be Ben's friend. She hadn't had a good friend in so long—she only ever hung out with people connected to her boyfriends—and she badly wanted something to call her own. Maybe then she would stop looking for someone to date every five seconds.

He was quiet for a moment, looking her over and making Allie wonder if he was about to refuse. But then he coughed and started the car. "Yeah," he agreed, and she relaxed. "Friends."

NINE

THOUGH HE PROBABLY SHOULD HAVE been concentrating on the order sheet he was filling out at the end of his shift, Ben wasn't focused in the least. Honestly, what did it matter how many bouncy balls and finger traps he ordered? Kids always went for the candy anyway. Besides, how was he supposed to concentrate on arcade prizes when he was scheduled to go over to Allie's apartment tomorrow to make dinner and have a very-much-not-a-date to get to know one another?

"As friends," he muttered, absently doodling on the edge of the order form.

It wasn't like he didn't want to be Allie's friend, but he hoped for more than that. He'd been working up his courage for months, dreaming of what it would be like to date her, and *of course* he picked the one girl in the world who wasn't interested in dating him. She just wanted to be *friends*.

"You should be grateful she's giving you that," he chided himself. She said she'd sworn off men, and that should have technically meant he had no chance at all. As long as he could be her friend, he could be a part of her life and get to know her better. That was what mattered.

A friendship was better than not knowing her at all.

His phone buzzed in his pocket, and he pulled it out to see that it was Madi calling him. He perked up a little. A chat with Madi always made his day better. "Hey, Madi. What's up?"

"I don't like that sound, Benjamin."

"Sorry?"

"I've known you for more than half our lives, Ben. You're miserable. Why?"

He considered lying, but he had always prided himself on being genuine and didn't like the idea of lying. (His thing with Allie didn't count. That was helping her out.) But his thing with Allie was also the reason Madi thought he sounded miserable, so he sighed. "That's a long conversation," he said.

"Then it's a good thing Oliver is coding and won't notice if I leave the house. Meet me at the usual place?"

Ben smiled, glad that Madi was one of his best friends. She always knew exactly what he needed. "Sure. Give me half an hour."

Ben finished closing up the center, then drove out to Madi's parents' house. Instead of going to the door, he went around to the side gate and straight to the dark backyard.

Madi was already there on the old swing set, her arm linked around the chain of one swing as she slowly moved back and forth with one foot on the ground. Ben took the other swing without a word, sitting sideways with his back resting against the chain. They used to sit here all the time, when the other boys would play basketball or get into arguments, and they would have all sorts of deep conversations.

Ben missed those days.

"So is this about Allie?" Madi asked before he could say anything.

He nodded, scuffing the grass beneath his feet.

"What happened on your date?"

"Nothing."

"She's not interested in you," Madi guessed, and she sounded so sympathetic that it made Ben's stomach twist in his gut. Even Madi, the nicest girl in the world, came to that conclusion without even meeting Allie, so it had to be true.

He still tried to defend his ego a bit. "She's not interested in any guys." When Madi raised her eyebrows, he backtracked. "No, I mean, she's not interested in dating *anyone* right now. She… Our date wasn't real, Madi."

She should understand that; her whole relationship with Oliver had been fake at first.

Madi stared at him, her eyebrows pulled low and her lips pursed in confusion. Ben didn't blame her. He was confused too, but mostly with himself. Why had he agreed to keep fake dating Allie? She'd given him an out, and he could have saved himself the trouble of needing to remind himself that holding her hand at dinner was only for show. He could have told her he was happy to be her friend, even if that was a lie, but that he didn't want to be her fake boyfriend. Heck, he even could have told her he was into her and wanted to date her for real!

Finally it clicked for Madi, and she frowned. "What happened?"

"She ran into…an ex? I think." He definitely knew Jake was an ex, but it was easier to pretend he hadn't been getting jealous glares all throughout dinner. "And I'm pretty sure she panicked when he was going to ask her out again, and I was the closest person to her, so she said we were dating. And he must have told her mom, so things got out of hand pretty quickly."

Ben expected Madi to ask why Allie didn't say she wasn't interested, but Madi just nodded. "Sometimes that's the only thing that helps," she said knowingly. "So that date you went on was to prove she hadn't lied."

Ben was definitely glad he had decided to tell Madi the truth. She had done exactly the same thing before she married Oliver, going on fake dates to get her friend to stop pressuring her into dating. And to win a bet, but that was beside the point.

"We're probably going to keep pretending to date," he said, and he could hear his own misery. "And she's been very clear that we are only ever going to be friends."

"What's wrong with that?"

Ben grew tense at the surprisingly harsh question. "Madi, you've been hearing me talk about this girl for months."

Twisting in her swing, Madi scoffed and let herself spin back to face forward. "Talk *about*, yeah. But not talk *to*. You have to start somewhere, Ben."

Didn't she get how difficult this was going to be? "This isn't like you and Oliver. You've known each other your whole lives." The two of them had a lifetime of history to build off of, so going from fake to genuine had happened over the course of a few weeks. Ben had three conversations and one fake date under his belt, and that definitely wouldn't hold up against any attempt at something more.

Madi rolled her eyes. "So wouldn't it make sense to get started on that whole friendship thing sooner than later? You should marry your best friend, Ben."

Marry? Ben slipped off the swing, landing on the ground with a thump when his leg caught in the swing. "I didn't say anything about marriage," he said in a breath. Even if now he was picturing it. They could do their grocery shopping together and hang out in the evenings watching movies and eating ice cream.

Laughing, Madi hopped off her swing and helped him up. "You are my favorite quiet Wonder Boy, Ben, but you can really be an idiot sometimes."

"What's that supposed to mean?"

"I'll tell you later. I don't think you're ready to hear it yet."

Without letting go of his hand, she started dragging him toward the house even though it was after ten.

"Where are we going?" he asked, baffled.

Madi snickered. "Inside. My dad got it into his head that he wants to take up painting, but he has no idea what he's doing. He needs your help."

This late at night? The Morgans were retired, so they didn't have to be up early, but Ben couldn't picture them staying up late. Duke was the kind of guy who fell asleep in front of the TV just after dinner, and Lydia's favorite thing to joke about was getting her beauty sleep. Back when the Wonder Boys were all in high school, the Morgans had often just told Kit to make sure he locked up after all the guys left because they were going to bed.

Looking back, it was a little crazy to think they trusted a bunch of teenage boys to stay out of trouble.

Wait, Madi wanted Ben to help her dad paint? He stumbled a little when they reached the back door. "I don't paint, Madi."

Sighing, she put both her hands on his shoulders and gave him a piercing stare, one she usually reserved for Cam or her brother. Ben definitely didn't like being on the receiving end of it. "We both know that isn't true," she said. "Maybe it's been a while, but it'll be just like riding a bike."

Ben wasn't sure he believed her, but the thought of holding a paintbrush sparked a little fire in him, from his chest to his fingertips. It had been a long time since he had the desire or motivation to do something beyond a doodle here and there, and it would be a good distraction from his dinner with Allie tomorrow. He had the day off tomorrow, a rare Saturday with no mini golf, so he was even fine with being up late.

"Benjamin!" Duke's greeting came with a poorly covered up curse as he squeezed an open tube of paint too tightly, sending a cascade of cadmium red over his fingertips. "I haven't seen you since the wedding!"

Cringing, Ben glanced around the study-turned-art-studio and hoped he could get away with not addressing the fact that he hadn't come to visit the Morgans in nearly two months. After spending most of his after-school time in this house before he went off to college, he really should have put in more effort with his second family. Duke and Lydia had been as much parents to him as his own.

Anytime he went to visit his actual family, he tended to get lost in the shuffle. Not that he blamed his parents—they had their hands full with seven kids and now with almost a couple dozen grandkids—but Ben was always the kid who avoided causing problems. That meant he was often overlooked.

Middle kid syndrome was no joke.

That had never happened here with the Morgans, though, even with Cam's and Oliver's big personalities.

Forcing down sudden emotion, Ben grabbed a stool and pulled it up beside Duke. "So," he said, making sure he sounded cheery. "What are we painting tonight?"

Duke's eyes were bright with excitement. "A tropical ocean island beach scene. It's a surprise for Lydia."

Taking another look at the red paint covering the man's hands—a color he would barely need—Ben silently thanked Duke. This was going to be a *great* distraction.

TEN

ALLIE FELT ESPECIALLY STRANGE GROCERY shopping on a Saturday afternoon. She had picked mornings as her usual shopping time because it helped her avoid her ex, Joe, who worked early mornings at the local radio station, and then she'd just fallen into the habit. Habit was good; it meant it was something she did for herself and by herself. One of the few things she'd done for herself while dating Jeremy, who hated grocery shopping. Allie didn't, and she enjoyed the consistency of routine.

Just like when it came to watching Ben.

"Okay, well, that makes you sound creepy," she muttered to herself, though there were a lot more people at the store on Saturdays than she was used to. She would probably be better off if she didn't talk to herself.

She'd been too much of a coward to go to the store this past Tuesday. After that nightmare of a dinner, she'd figured it was a good idea to put a little distance between her and Ben.

So, naturally, she was teaching him to cook tonight, because having him in her tiny apartment was totally the same thing as distance.

Stuffing a box of lasagna noodles into her overflowing basket, Allie reminded herself that this dinner was important. If they were going to convince her mother that they really were dating, they would have to know things about each other.

Like, anything beyond last names, which was pretty much the only thing Allie knew about Ben.

That wasn't true. She knew he had a bunch of siblings and a tight-knit group of friends and a fancy car and a really nice job and was so far out of her league that she still wasn't sure why he had even agreed to this whole scam in the first place. Maybe he was just bored.

When she couldn't fit a package of Oreos in her basket because the half gallon of ice cream took up too much space, Allie decided she should probably call it good and check out before she bought half the store.

She had no reason to be nervous. Ben had been nothing but a perfect gentleman, and all they were going to do tonight was cook dinner and go through the list of first date questions she'd printed out that morning. It wasn't actually a date, but the questions were good.

Halfway through checkout, Allie had to dig her phone out of her purse when it started ringing.

Why was work calling?

"Hello?"

"Allison!" Mr. Simmons sounded frantic. "I'm so glad you answered."

The publishing office wasn't even open on weekends. Why would her boss be trying to get a hold of her? Despite her being his assistant, he basically just used her for coffee runs and proofreading when she wasn't answering the phone.

Allie had a bad feeling about this. If this phone call ruined her dinner with Ben, someone would be ruing the day they were born. "Mr. Simmons, is something wrong?"

"Could you come into the office? It's a bit of an emergency."

They were a tiny children's book publisher that had never had a book make it big. Allie highly doubted anything could truly be an emergency, unless the building was on fire, in which case Simmons should probably call the fire department.

Allie handed her debit card to the teenage cashier and held her phone a little tighter. "Uh, what's going on? I'm not sure I can—"

"You're our only hope, Allison. Can you be here within the hour? Great." He hung up without waiting for a response.

What in the world?

Gathering up her grocery bags, Allie weighed the pros and cons of actually listening to the man. It was her day off, and she'd been working extra hours already, helping set up a new imprint that focused on teens. She hadn't actually done any of the important work, but there had been a lot of things to sign and file. She could definitely say no and set that boundary.

Or she could go into the office. It would give her brownie points, and she needed as many as she could get after that failed promotion and the story pitch that had gotten her blank stares and metaphorical crickets when the submission team realized she was trying to pitch her own idea for a book.

She would have to hurry home and drop off her groceries before the ice cream melted, but it would probably be a good idea to stop by the office and see what was going on.

By the time she finally stepped into the Sweet Red Cherry Books offices, Allie had come up with several possible scenarios, each more ridiculous than the last. Maybe Simmons didn't know how to order his own coffee. Maybe someone had broken their leg, and Allie was the only person who could keep them calm. Maybe a criminal had taken the whole place captive, and Allie needed to negotiate for hostages.

But what she found in the conference room was Mr. Simmons and the two editors surrounded by empty donut boxes and coffee cups, all three men staring up at her as if she were their saving grace.

"Uh, what's going on?" she asked, lingering by the door in case she needed to make a run for it.

Simmons jumped up and gestured for her to take a seat. "Thank you for coming, Ortega. We're in a bit of a bind."

Allie had been in this room plenty of times, but she usually sat in the corner and took notes, bored out of her mind. Sitting in one of the big chairs felt like she had done something either very wrong or very right. But she sat anyway, too curious not to.

"What do you need me to do, Mr. Simmons?"

"Well, as you know, we recently acquired a rather wealthy patron to our little publishing house."

That didn't explain why she would have to come in on her day off. "Okay?"

"She has offered to fully fund the new line of teen books," Simmons continued. Though that should have been a good thing, he looked nervous about the fact. "Only… Only she had a bit of a…how would you put it?" He turned to the editors, who both became immensely uncomfortable.

"We're in a unique situation?" one of them offered.

"Essentially, our patron is not fond of Carey," Simmons finished. "And she refuses to let him write the series."

Carey was their strongest writer, the only one able to do more than a line or two a page like most of their books. If he couldn't write the books, they were up a creek without a paddle. Still, Allie wasn't surprised he had gotten on the patron's bad side. Carey was as misogynistic as he was bald. As in entirely.

Her biggest question still hadn't been answered, and Allie figured she would need to be direct if she wanted them to do the same. "Why am I here on a Saturday, John?"

When Simmons sighed, as if he was about to admit defeat, Allie's instincts suddenly kicked in. He clearly didn't want to say what he was about to say, and if there was one thing Simmons hated, it was being wrong.

Was he about to ask her to write the new series?

Sitting up straighter, Allie tried not to jump to conclusions, but she couldn't help it. She had shown Simmons and the editors her writing just a couple of weeks ago, and she knew it was good. She knew because she'd agonized over it for months. She'd been practicing nearly her whole life. She'd had strangers on the internet offer to read bits of it and help her improve until she knew she had the skills to write a half-decent storyline.

This was her moment to shine.

"I need you to find our new writer."

If record scratches were a real-life thing, Allie would have heard the most massive one in the world. The vinyl would have cracked in half with how suddenly her dreams were pulled to a halt.

"Find a new writer," she repeated, in case she had misheard.

Simmons nodded as he grabbed a stack of papers. "We have a whole bunch of applicants, but our patron was really specific. She won't let any of us choose the writer, and since you're the only, uh, woman in the office, well... I've already gone through and picked out the most promising applicants."

Allie took the stack only out of curiosity. Not because she was okay with the situation. After flipping through the first few, all of whom were male, something told her she would not find a female writer among the dozen or so potentials.

Why did she work for this company again? Oh right, because no one else would hire her without experience as an editor or professional writer. This was her only shot at working with a publishing company, and she needed Sweet Red to help launch her into the world as an author. People didn't make a name for themselves on their own. It just wasn't done.

"How soon do we need to find our author?" she asked.

All three men breathed sighs of relief, though Allie was tempted to tell them she hadn't actually said she would do it.

Suddenly she had a lot of power, and she didn't want to give it away too soon.

"By Wednesday, if possible," Simmons said. "And depending on how well this new author works out, we could potentially discuss adding you to the creation team."

Allie dropped the application she'd been skimming. "Wait, what? Really?"

Though he squirmed a little in his seat, Simmons nodded. "If you can prove you know what it takes to write a good book by finding our writer."

So her career depended on someone else? Typical. It would have been way too much to ask that all aspects of her life could be in her own control. At least she had stopped dating and had her own apartment.

Apartment. Dating. Ben! Allie grabbed her phone to check the time. She barely had enough time to clean things up and take a shower before Wonder Boy showed up at her house for their not-a-date cooking lesson.

"I'll find you a new writer," she said quickly, gathering up the applications and trying not to make eye contact with any of them. She didn't want them to know how badly she wanted that writer job; they might take it as a sign of weakness and a way to manipulate her into doing whatever they wanted.

They already did that on a daily basis, and she didn't want it to get worse.

"Ortega?"

Allie paused in the doorway and glanced back at her boss, biting her lip before she said something out of anxiety.

Simmons sighed. "Thanks. Hopefully there's someone up to the task."

Allie hoped so too; she was not about to risk her best chance of being an author by putting her trust in anyone but the best.

ELEVEN

TEN MINUTES BEFORE SIX, BEN pulled up outside Allie's apartment building and tried to figure out why he was more nervous for tonight than he'd been for the dinner date with her family. Then, he'd had a part to play and should have been under a good deal of pressure to not be the one to spill Allie's secret. He still didn't know how he'd managed to act so calm for that, but the evening had been easy.

Now? He had nothing to prove. No one to act for. Somehow that was terrifying, but he would be brave.

He was going to try to be Allie's friend without thinking of her as a romantic interest. He was going to be purely himself, as open as possible, and let her see the man he really was. He had no desire to pressure her into thinking of him more or breaking her ban on dating, but he wasn't sure he would be able to forget how beautiful she was.

Friends could think each other beautiful, right? He thought Madi was beautiful, and they were friends, no problem.

Ben spent the entire ten minutes before six giving himself a pep talk that probably didn't do much good, considering he wasn't very motivating to begin with. He should have had Cam talk him through things… Then again, he hadn't told Cam or the others that he and Allie weren't actually dating, and he could easily imagine his friends' disappointment if he did come clean.

It would probably be better to keep the Wonder Boys in the dark and never let them meet Allie. That way, when they eventually "broke up" once Ben was no longer needed as a fake boyfriend, the gang wouldn't make a big deal about it.

He hoped they wouldn't.

When Allie opened the door, her eyes dropped to the bouquet of flowers Ben held. He'd gone back and forth on bringing them, but one of Madi's florist friends had assured him that these particular roses meant friendship. If he had gone with red instead of yellow, then Allie would have reason to narrow her eyes at him.

"You do remember this isn't a date, right?" she said.

Ben resisted the urge to sigh. "Yes, you made yourself very clear." His jaw nearly dropped. He'd never talked like that to anyone except the Wonder Boys before, and even then, speaking up was a rare thing. "Sorry, I meant it as a gesture of friendship. You can throw them in the trash if you don't like them."

"I never said I didn't like them." Snatching the bouquet from his hands, Allie turned a little pink and offered a shrug. "I'm sorry. This whole thing is new to me."

"You and me both. Can, uh, can I come in?"

"Oh, yeah, of course!" She stepped aside to let Ben in, muttering something to herself as he passed.

Though he didn't hear exactly what she said, he was pretty sure she was getting mad at herself for being impolite, and he had to grin. He didn't talk to himself often, but it was often enough that it was nice to know someone else did it as well.

As Allie busied herself with putting the flowers in a vase—scratch that; in a large bowl with a mug on top of the stems to weigh them down in the water—Ben took a quick look around the apartment. He knew Allie did something that involved writing—something about children's books?—but considering she had been passed up for a promotion, he figured she wasn't super rich. Her apartment confirmed that guess, though she'd done well with the limited space she had. A Japanese screen divided her bed from the rest of the apartment, her many colors of shoes sat stacked up in a massive pile by the couch, and she'd put up a large circular mirror on the far wall that helped the room feel bigger.

The kitchen, Ben noticed, was pretty tiny, and it would be a bit crowded if they were both in there at the same time. He didn't mind that part.

His favorite aspect of the apartment, however, was the decor, which was as eclectic as it was numerous. A print of a Warhol painting sat next to a vinyl sticker of a poodle over the couch, which had no fewer than eight different colors and sizes of pillows, including one of those sequined ones that had different designs depending on which way the sequins were oriented. At the moment, it was half a llama's head and half calligraphic words, of which he could see the words *loco* and *como*. Fake and real plants galore littered the room, as well as trinkets from several different decades.

If he had hoped to learn a little more about who Allie was by coming here tonight, he was likely going to leave with more questions than answers.

"Um, sorry it's such a mess," Allie said, coming to stand at his side. "I would say it's not usually so full of junk, but that would be a lie."

Ben offered a smile. "You have a pretty varied taste. That's fun."

As she squinted at him, she seemed to be trying to figure out if he was making fun of her or not. "Fun isn't necessarily the word I would use. I should probably get rid of most of this stuff, but..."

But what? Ben wasn't about to ask. If she wanted to tell him, she would.

Allie cleared her throat and turned toward the tiny kitchen. "Shall we? This lasagna isn't going to make itself."

Something was off. Ben hadn't noticed at first, but when Allie stepped behind the counter and looked over at him, he realized she hadn't smiled once. She had always been quick to smile before now, and he had a feeling she wasn't fully focused on the task ahead of her.

"You okay?" he asked. He stayed where he was in case his nearness on top of the question would be encroaching too much on her personal space, physically and emotionally.

Allie's eyebrows shot up. "Fine! Totally fine. Um, we should probably get the noodles cooked so we can—"

"Want to talk about it?" Ben didn't like being pushy. He didn't like people who *were* pushy. But if his friends had taught him anything over the years, it was knowing that sometimes people needed to talk, even if they didn't want to. Kit had been the first person to recognize that in Ben, and they'd been friends ever since. If Kit hadn't pushed Ben to admit he was lonely and wanted somewhere to go that wasn't home with his six chaotic siblings, Ben might have been miserable his entire life.

Allie stared at him for a second, as if she couldn't imagine anyone not believing her when she said she was fine, but then her shoulders dropped. "How do you do that?" she asked.

He took one step, waiting to see if she reacted, and then he slowly moved close enough to take a seat on one of the stools at the little counter. "Do what?"

She shook her head. "How do you know when I'm desperate to vent to someone? You did it back when we first met too. You don't happen to read minds, do you? I've been thinking the Wonder Boys sounds like a cool group of superheroes."

Ben laughed, thinking of the many times they had used the name for their team in laser tag. Each of them had their own nickname that matched their personalities. Ben was Watchdog; he generally played laser tag from the corner loft where he could see everything going on below.

"I didn't get a lot of attention as a kid," he said with a shrug. When Allie frowned, his face flooded with heat. "I didn't mean that like it sounded. I just meant I spent—still spend—a lot of time watching other people. Most people tell me a lot without knowing it, mainly in their body language."

Allie leaned across the counter, her hands ending up only an inch from his and her denim-blue eyes locked on him. "What does my body tell you?" she asked, and her voice had gotten lower. Softer.

She was probably baiting him somehow, testing him to see if he would respond to such obvious flirting. And maybe, if Ben hadn't known her decision to avoid dating, he would have fallen for the trap. As much as he liked the idea of pursuing something romantic with this woman, he liked more the idea of actually getting to know her first and respecting her decision.

That didn't keep him from staring at her hands and wanting to hold one again. His hand still tingled from the last time.

Swallowing to clear whatever nonsense had gotten stuck in his throat just now, Ben did his best to answer honestly. He took in her guarded expression, only partially hidden behind her flirty smile, and he would have to be blind to miss the tension in her shoulders. Besides, he had already seen the uncertainty in her eyes, and he doubted this distraction had been enough to make her forget whatever was bothering her.

"I can't say I know your thoughts better than you do," he said warily, "but I'm guessing something happened today that's really bugging you. It must be fresh, or you would have canceled, and you're still trying to process, so you don't really know what to think. And I'm probably getting in the way, so you can kick me out if you want."

He flinched, waiting for her to take offense—perfectly valid offense—to his presumptions.

But Allie stood up straight, her perfect eyebrows rising high. "How did you do that? You're like Sherlock Holmes, only without the arrogance."

Ben wrinkled his nose. "I hate how overused Holmes is in media," he said. Hopefully that admission wouldn't cause some unfixable rift in their friendship. "And I just did the stupid thing."

"Where he blows Watson away with his incredible skills of deduction," Allie finished with a nod. "I hate that too. So cliché."

"Sorry."

"Don't be. You're not wrong." Sighing, she stepped around the counter and sat on the other stool. "I got called into work this afternoon because my boss needs me to help hire a new writer."

Ben quickly replayed their first conversation, trying to remember what she'd said about her job. "Why don't they hire you as the writer?" He was pretty sure getting passed up was the reason for the double ice cream purchase.

"Exactly!" Allie clasped her hand on his knee so suddenly that he jumped, though she didn't seem to notice. "There was a whole thing with one of our funders, and she doesn't want our usual writer taking on the middle grade series she's funding. And she said she wanted a woman to choose the new writer."

"Why?"

She shrugged. "She probably doesn't trust any of the men. So, since I'm the only woman in the office, I have to—"

"Whoa." Ben cut her off. "You don't work with any other women? Why?"

This time Allie seemed to think about that question for a minute, as if she'd never realized her situation before. "Actually, I don't know. I mean, I don't know why they hired me in the first place. It's not like they could have done it by accident since Allison is a pretty standard feminine name."

Though he knew nothing about the company she worked for, Ben suddenly hated Allie's superiors. Weren't they breaching some kind of fair labor law by being so discriminatory when it came to gender? True, Ben mostly worked with guys too, but that was because most girls were smart enough not to apply for a fun center job in the first place. O'Reilly's definitely had a bit of a creepy vibe, something Ben didn't have the power to fix.

But surely there had to be plenty of female writers and editors like Allie out in the world so she wouldn't have to be on her own with so much testosterone, right?

"Why do you work there?" Ben asked. His words came out extra quietly, but he was pretty sure that was because he accidentally asked himself the same thing. Why in the world would he still be at a place if it gave off creepy vibes behind the scenes? He wouldn't be surprised if it had once been a murder scene and Mr. O'Reilly had paid off the news station to keep it quiet.

Allie seemed to realize she was still holding onto his knee, frowning as she lifted her hand up. "It's my only shot at being a writer," she said, just as softly as Ben. "Besides, I need the job since I don't really have any qualifications for anything else. This apartment doesn't pay for itself, so…"

As he gave the studio another glance, Ben couldn't help but frown as well. Yeah, she'd used her space well, but already he was feeling claustrophobic. This place made the apartment he shared with Cam feel like a mansion.

The apartment he was probably going to lose in just a few months.

Letting out a little groan, Ben leaned his elbows onto the counter. "Do you want to order a pizza? I'm not sure I have the energy to cook tonight, and I'm definitely not making you do it yourself."

Allie's smile was one of relief, which made Ben feel a bit better about the suggestion. "That sounds great. I wasn't going to say it, but... Like you probably noticed, I'm still trying to figure out what to do about this whole writer thing. My boss said if I can hire a good option, he'll consider moving me to the writing team as well."

She grabbed her phone, and Ben stared at her while she pulled up the website for the pizza place. She said it so easily that it was as if she had no idea how messed up those conditions were. "Your promotion is dependent on someone else?" he asked.

Allie shrugged. "That's how things go sometimes, right?"

No. It wasn't. At least, it shouldn't be.

Before Ben could go on a righteous—though quiet—rant, Allie asked, "What's your pizza preference?"

"Whatever you want." Ben could hardly think about pizza when he was trying to come up with a way to get Allie some actual support in her career. She knew exactly what she wanted, which should have put her in a much better place than he was, but she seemed to think she had to wait her turn and let some outsider—probably a man—step into her rightful place. There had to be something he could do to help, and she was too smart and beautiful to be kept chasing a carrot on a string.

Though it took him a second, he realized Allie was staring at him, and he flushed hot. He hadn't been thinking out loud, had he? "What?"

She blinked and shook her head a little, as if she'd been in a daze. "Sorry. I just... I don't know what I like on my pizza. Is that weird?"

Definitely weird. "Not at all. My mood always changes."

Still sitting frozen, she seemed to really be contemplating this issue. "Can I be real with you for a second? But you have to promise not to judge me. Of course you won't; you're perfect."

Ben was suddenly dizzy, his words stuck in his dry mouth.

Allie continued on without him. "I've been dating since I was fifteen. Like most people, I guess. But I've been *dating* since then. In relationships. Like, I've never been on my own, without a boyfriend, for more than, like, a week. For seventeen years. And I don't know what kind of pizza I like because I've always liked the kind of pizza my boyfriend liked. I don't know what music I like, or what clothes I like to wear, or if I like to stay up late or wake up early."

She slumped on her stool, looking suddenly exhausted and close to tears. Ben wanted to hug her, but he kept to his seat. Something told him that would be a bad idea. Besides, she wasn't done yet.

"I had a bad breakup a few months ago, and he told me it was because he didn't know who I was. It was like he was dating himself, and why would he want to do that? When I realized he was right, I decided I needed to make a change and figure out who I am, so that's why I'm not dating right now. I'm dating myself so I can figure out if I actually like ironing my jeans or if that's because Johnny told me I should."

Ben waited a second, making sure she was done, and then he cleared his throat. He wanted to say the right thing—she was clearly in the middle of an existential crisis over pizza— but he wasn't sure he was in any way qualified for this. Kit would probably be way better, considering he dealt with emotional eight-year-olds all school year and could talk practically anyone down from an existential ledge.

But Kit wasn't here, so Ben would do his best. What did she need to hear?

He cleared his throat again. "Ironing jeans is weird."

At first, Allie simply stared at him, her eyebrows low and her expression making him second guess himself. But then she slowly softened, and a smile grew on her lips, and then she was laughing so hard that tears spilled from her eyes.

And before he could react, she threw her arms around his neck and pulled herself in for a wild hug that sent his heart racing. *Friends*, he reminded his pounding heart. But that was going to be harder than he thought.

TWELVE

AFTER A RIDICULOUS BOUT OF sobbing/laughing, Allie finally got control over herself and ordered a veggie pizza, thinking it would be a good alternative to their tofu lasagna they were going to make. She hadn't meant to give Ben her whole back-story, but she felt so much better knowing he understood her reasoning for keeping their budding friendship safely on this side of the relationship line. She couldn't afford to lose herself again after making so much progress, and Ben assured her he understood entirely.

The relief that came from him promising to only be her friend had lifted a weight she hadn't realized she was carrying. As long as she made sure *she* kept things platonic, her friendship with Ben could potentially be one of the best relationships she'd ever had.

Maybe, down the road someday, things could change. But only if she managed to figure out who she was first.

While they waited for their pizza, Allie told Ben about growing up and how she always wanted to be a writer. Ben wasn't as forthcoming with childhood dreams, but he talked about his current job which, to her relief, wasn't some big-time entertainment gig that made him ridiculously wealthy. Neither did he have a chef—just a roommate who enjoyed cooking. The more he talked about his job, the more Allie acknowledged he was definitely as stuck and frustrated as she was, just like he'd said, and it was nice to know she wasn't alone in dissatisfaction.

They could be miserable together, which honestly sounded pretty great.

"So you didn't dream of running a crappy little fun center and getting paid barely above minimum wage?" she asked him with a grin. "But who wouldn't want that?"

"Oddly, it's not what I consider a valid career option." He stroked her sequin pillow so the llama disappeared, leaving the phrase *estar loco como una llama*. Allie loved that pillow. It was the only one that hadn't come from a relationship.

They'd moved to the little loveseat Allie had scrounged up from a yard sale, though it was really more of a glorified armchair. Even after tossing the rest of her throw pillows to the ground, the two of them barely fit, which meant they were hip to hip, shoulder to shoulder. If Ben was uncomfortable about the situation, it didn't show, and Allie liked that he seemed to be a pretty chill person. She could work with that. It hopefully meant he didn't have any expectations of her acting a certain way.

For the first time in maybe ever, Allie didn't have to think every little action through. "What did you want to do?" she asked him, eagerly awaiting his answer. Since he hadn't talked about being a kid, she barely knew anything about the guy.

But he only shrugged. "Not everyone has a big dream like you did."

She knew that, she really did, but she had a feeling Ben the Wonder Boy had definitely had dreams before life wore him down. A guy like him didn't go through life just rolling with the punches. Okay, so yeah, she didn't know him that well, but she wanted to believe he was the kind of guy who would throw his own punch now and then. He couldn't possibly be so easygoing and unassuming *all* the time.

"What about now? Any ideas for where you're going now?"

He let out a little laugh. "I got offered to run the new fun center being built across town."

Shuddering, Allie tried not to picture too hard what that kind of life would be like. "I may be making Sherlockian guesses here, but I'm pretty sure you like your job as much as I like mine. Wouldn't running a center make things even worse?"

Another shrug. "Well, I could make it the way I want it, so it wouldn't be that bad."

"Ben, I'm pretty sure those places are designed to suck the life out of the employees. They're boring enough for the people paying to go inside, and I can't imagine it being any better for the ones stuck there day in and day out."

To her surprise, Ben's expression twisted, as if he were actually offended by what she'd said. "You think they're boring?"

Allie was saved having to answer that obvious question by a knock at the door, which meant the pizza had arrived. She jumped up to get it—or, she would have, if she hadn't been wedged so tightly into the couch that she couldn't move. "Um."

Wrapping his arm around her, he attempted to push her out, but she was stuck fast. Which he found hilarious, judging by the laughter that burst out of him when the pizza guy knocked again.

Allie couldn't help but join in, and she gripped the couch's arm and tugged while Ben pushed, even though she was laughing too hard to do much good. With one mighty heave, she finally freed herself, but Ben somehow came with her, and the two of them were suddenly tangled up together on the floor in a pile of limbs and laughter.

"Some Wonder Boy you are," she said through her giggles, meeting his gaze as he bit back more laughing. She should have felt awkward, lying on top of a guy she barely knew, but she'd never felt more comfortable in her life. Was this what friendship was supposed to be like?

Turning a steadily deeper shade of red, Ben cleared his throat and grabbed hold of her arms. "Shouldn't keep the pizza guy waiting."

"Right." Though she accidentally elbowed Ben in the gut trying to free herself, she managed to get to her feet and pull open the door.

The pizza guy in all his teenage glory looked Allie over with wide eyes, and then he held out the box as he turned a matching red to Ben. "Sixteen dollars," he squeaked.

"I've got it." Ben's voice right behind her made her jump, and instinctively she stepped aside, even though she'd been meaning to pay. He already had his wallet out, though, slipping the kid a twenty before leaning in and muttering something to him.

The kid turned an even brighter shade than before and practically stumbled away, leaving Allie completely bewildered.

"What did you tell him?" she asked as soon as the door was closed.

Ben's coloring hadn't changed, though he lifted the pizza box lid as if to hide behind it. "I told him he's allowed to tell you he thinks you're pretty."

That made no sense whatsoever. "What? Why would he want to tell me that?"

"Because it's what I thought the first time I saw you. And probably what every man thinks, if we're being honest."

As much as Allie liked the compliment, it felt like Ben was straying a little too far from the friend zone where he belonged. "Do you really think you should be telling teenagers to hit on women twice their age?"

She expected him to get embarrassed, but Ben just gave her a little smile. "I didn't tell him to hit on you. Just to give you a compliment. I wish someone had told me that when I was his age, because I always thought anything I said was like a declaration of love. It took me a long time to realize I could say nice things without any intent or expectation behind it, and it would probably make someone's day if I did. Besides, you really are beautiful."

This was the strangest man she had ever met.

"I'm starving," Allie said, missing the ease they'd had before the pizza arrived.

Ben held out the box as he took a bite of the piece he grabbed. The pizza looked extremely healthy, but Allie had her misgivings about it actually tasting good. Maybe she should have gone with something else.

"It's better than it looks," he said with a chuckle.

Grimacing, Allie hoped he was right and took a bite. It was…interesting. Definitely not her favorite. But it was edible, and that was something.

Chuckling again, Ben set the box on the counter and gestured to the couch. He took a seat on a stool, probably hoping to avoid another wedging situation. "We'll just have to try something else the next time. And don't think you were saved by the pizza bell. Do you really not enjoy fun centers? Not even laser tag?"

"I've never played laser tag."

Ben dropped his pizza. Literally. It slid from his hand at the same time as his jaw dropped, and he looked so ridiculous that Allie burst into laughter again. After watching him for a couple of months at the grocery store, she never would have expected so much animation from the guy, but he had a whole lot of expression for someone so quiet. Maybe this was a side of himself he only reserved for his friends, and she appreciated knowing she fit into that category so she could witness it.

"You've never played laser tag," he repeated.

Allie shrugged. "None of my boyfriends were fifteen-year-old boys. It was never a date option."

Glancing at his watch, he seemed to be debating something, like his thoughts were whirring too quickly for him to do anything but stare at the time. Allie took this moment to study him a little more deeply than she had so far.

What would he be like as a character in a book? She'd been wrong before. He wasn't the sidelined sidekick offering silent support like she'd thought. There was more to him than that, like his story was only just starting. Maybe he was more of the untrained hero, living his mundane life only moments before he was thrust into some grand adventure he never could have imagined.

"You don't have plans tonight, right?"

Allie frowned at the determined glint in his eyes. "I mean, outside of teaching you to cook? Which we didn't actually do?"

He nodded intensely. Allie hadn't realized that was even something someone could do, but it was the most intense nod she'd ever seen.

"Um, well, no. But—"

"I'm taking you somewhere." Though he moved as if to grab her hand and drag her outside, he stopped just in front of her with his hand outstretched, waiting for her to agree.

She sighed. "You're taking me laser tagging, aren't you?"

And she might have refused, if Ben hadn't gotten a spark of excitement in his dark eyes. Her hero was answering the call to adventure, and he was asking her to go with him. She would be stupid to say no and miss out on something that had the potential to be absolutely epic.

"Fine," she said, slipping her hand into his and doing her best to ignore the spark that ignited inside her at that touch. If she wasn't careful, that was going to be a problem.

THIRTEEN

SHE SAID YES. ALLIE ACTUALLY said yes to going out, and now she was sitting in his nightmare of a car and trying not to laugh every time the radio fizzled to the mariachi station it defaulted to every time he turned on his blinker. Ben might have been mortified if she hadn't found it so amusing, and he was just glad he had no reason to turn on the defroster. Otherwise, she would experience *the smell*.

He really needed to get a new car.

"So..." Allie waited until they'd finished making the turn since the radio only had one volume: loud. "What was that car you brought to Sunday dinner?"

He appreciated that she didn't ask him why he drove this when he had access to something way nicer. It meant he didn't have any kind of expectation to live up to. "That was Oliver's car. He thought I should make a good first impression, and driving this one..." He grimaced when his window slid open on its own, and he could feel Allie trying not to laugh again as he cranked the handle to roll it back up.

"This one has personality," Allie said. "I like it."

"There is nothing about this car resembling personality. I probably should have let you drive..."

"And miss out on all this fun?" Allie snorted when they had to make another turn, bringing back the trumpet-backed

Spanish love song playing at full volume. "You could drive without using your blinker, you know."

Ben gritted his teeth. "I know." But he never would, considering his mother would die of shame and disappointment if she ever found out, and she would warn him that he would surely go to jail if he didn't follow the law to the letter. She may have had her hands full with seven kids, but they'd all had road rules drilled into them before they ever got the keys. Nancy Nakamura was convinced any lawbreaking would lead straight to prison time.

"Oliver must have a crazy nice job. What does he do?"

Had Ben told Allie that Oliver was married? He was pretty sure he had, so he hoped she was simply curious and wanted to know more about him and his friends. However, Oliver wasn't exactly easy to describe. "Oliver Hamilton is too cool to have a job," he muttered. It wasn't that Ben was jealous; he would go crazy without something to do every day. But Oliver was practically a genius and could be out saving the world or building rockets or something. Instead, he taught an after-school coding class at Kit's school two days a week. The rest of his time? Ben had no idea what he did.

"Oliver Hamilton," Allie muttered, and she had her phone in hand as if she wanted to look him up. In fact, it looked like that was exactly what she was doing, and Ben wished he wasn't driving so he could see what she found. "I knew it! We totally went to college together. He was the hot sophomore who flirted with pretty much anyone in the writing center, though I don't know why he spent so much time there when he wasn't even taking any English classes."

Ben suppressed a groan. Though he'd gone to a different school, he'd been less than an hour away and had spent most of his weekends hanging out with Oliver. He'd seen up close how easily Oliver flirted, so it didn't surprise him in the least. *Don't ask, Ben.* "Did he ever flirt with you?"

Allie snorted. "I was dating the quarterback at the time, so… No."

Another question you don't need to ask, Benjamin Nakamura. "How many people have you dated? I mean, you don't have to answer that if you don't want to. I was just…curious."

Thankfully, he pulled into the O'Reilly's parking lot just then, so he busied himself with finding a parking spot instead of watching Allie's reaction to that question. He should have just kept his mouth shut like he usually did, but for some reason it was really easy to let his guard down when he was around Allie. She was way out of his league, and yet he was entirely comfortable around her. At least, as comfortable as he could get around anyone.

He slipped out of the car as quickly as he could, taking the few seconds he had alone to breathe in deeply and remind himself that he had no business knowing about Allie's past loves. Before he had much of a chance to ground himself in smalltalk, though, Allie was at his side and slipping her arm through his.

"How serious are we talking here?" she asked. "Because there were some guys I only dated for a couple of weeks. One guy only lasted three days."

Ben gulped, feeling horribly out of his element despite stepping into the place he spent most of his time. He'd never gotten past a third date with anyone, so he would have been that guy if Allie had actually let him date her. "How about serious relationships only?" he suggested. "The ones that really defined you."

As they passed the arcade, Allie pursed her lips and started counting on her fingers, each finger making Ben more and more nervous until she finally settled on, "Eleven. Ten, if you don't count when I got back together with Jared."

What a great time for Ben to trip on the step that separated the arcade from the prize counter. Thankfully, Allie's arm kept him from falling flat on his face, but she'd turned a little pink and released him as soon as he was steady again.

"I know, it's a lot," she muttered.

"That isn't what I was—"

"This is why I'm not dating." She bit her lip as if waiting for Ben to argue against her choice. "I really need to figure out who I am, Ben. You get that, right?"

How many times would he have to tell her that he understood completely? This wasn't the kind of conversation he wanted to have in front of his employees, however, so he glanced around for any sort of place where they could have a private conversation. He groaned when his eyes landed on the photo booth. It was probably their best option.

"Come here," he muttered, holding out his hand. He started walking as well, in case she didn't want to take his hand, but she slid her fingers into his and let him tug her toward the booth. "Apparently, this is a good place to talk," he said as he climbed inside.

A smile playing on her lips, Allie settled next to him and looked at the screen in front of them. "I've always wanted to do one of these."

"Talk first," Ben said, knowing he would lose his nerve otherwise. "Then we can take pictures. Allie, I am one hundred percent on board with you taking time for yourself. I agreed to be your fake boyfriend so you don't have to stress about your mom setting you up, and I'm going to follow through however I can."

She cocked her head. "So you're totally fine with just being friends?"

Though he knew it would seem counterproductive, he took hold of her hand between both of his. Hopefully he didn't choke on his words and make himself sound unconvincing. "Totally fine. I need a friend right now as much as you do."

"But you have the Wonder Boys."

The Wonder Boys were plenty busy with their own things and never noticed when Ben was gone. Besides, lately they'd only ever talked about how much they hated Ben's job, and he was sick of having that conversation. "The Boys think they already know me, and to some degree they do. But I feel like I can be different with you, Allie. I can be me."

Seriously, how was it so easy to be vulnerable when this girl had the power to break his heart without them even dating? He had built her up so much in his mind over the last few months that if he messed things up, he would definitely feel her absence. That should have made him clam up and melt into the wall, but it didn't.

"You make it easy," he told her.

Allie stared at him for a long time, her eyes jumping between his like she was trying to find something. He'd probably said too much, but he couldn't take any of it back. He just had to wait for her to reply and hope he hadn't just scared her off.

Oh goodness, was she crying?

Ben's panic rose, but Allie laughed and shook her head as she put her other hand on top of his. "Don't worry," she told him. "I do this all the time. I cry about everything, no matter what emotion is behind it. These are happy tears."

He wanted so badly to brush those tears from her cheeks, but his hands were stuck, so he leaned a little closer. In such a small space, there wasn't much room to go, but he would use every inch he could. "Why?"

Sniffling, she lifted her shoulders in a halfhearted shrug. "You basically just said everything I've been thinking all night. I'm really glad to have you as my friend, Ben. And seriously, thank you for that whole fake dating thing. There has to be some way I can repay you."

He could think of a few things, but he would keep those to himself. Tonight wasn't about him, and he wanted to help

Allie do the things she'd never been able to do because her boyfriends weren't up for it. "Take a picture with me," he said with a smile.

She grinned right back. "Absolutely."

They waited until the closing team had cleared out, playing all the stupid arcade games until Allie had enough tickets to buy a squeaking rubber chicken and two sticky hands, one of which she gave to Ben. Ben told the shift lead he would lock up, and then he led her back to the laser tag arena and got her fitted with her vest and gun.

"We'll do the version where you rack up as many points as you can," he said as he set the game up. "Every time you get hit, your gun will deactivate for five seconds. Every time you hit me, you'll get points, and different places on the vest are worth more than others based on how difficult they are to hit."

"Watchdog, huh?"

Ben glanced up at the screen, where his name glowed in orange text next to his high score. He'd been playing long enough that his username didn't have any numbers on the end like most did since they saved all game data from the first day the arena opened. That was the one part of the game Ben really liked, being able to see players return and revisit old games. Oftentimes parents came in with their kids and showed them their old scores before picking a name for the new generation.

"I didn't choose the name," he said, though he'd always liked it. Kit had done the honors for all of them.

Turning to the other screen, Allie started scanning the All-Time Records list with interest. Ben was in the eighth spot, and he would probably be knocked off the board in a year or two. "Who's Captain Morgan?"

Ben smiled, glad to see Kit still at the top of the leaderboard. "Kit. He's kind of the leader of the Wonder Boys. He was the reason we all became friends in the first place."

"FancyPants McGee?" She read the next line down with a raised eyebrow.

"Oliver."

"That makes sense. The guy knows how to dress well."

Ben was suddenly self-conscious of his very boring too-big t-shirt and jeans. He really needed to get a new wardrobe. "El Luchador is Cam," he said to change the subject.

"Another Wonder Boy?"

"Yep. My roommate."

Fourth and fifth place were occupied by a couple of the girls on Team Voldemort, who had been coming in every day after school for the last few years, and in sixth place was Madi.

Allie giggled. "She got her own name, huh?"

"She wouldn't let Kit give her a nickname. She told him she could kick our butts without the help of a pseudonym, and she definitely proved herself every summer."

Ben missed those days. He could get them all in at a discount, and sometimes they would play for hours, sometimes on a team and sometimes against each other. Then they all grew up and split apart to get on with their lives, becoming awesome people with important jobs and talents. And somehow Ben was still here, in the same place he'd spent countless hours in over the last decade and a half.

"What'll my name be, Watchdog?"

Ben dropped his laser gun, glad that it was attached to his vest so it didn't hit the floor. "What? You want me to choose?"

"Why not? I'm as new to this as it gets, so I think someone who knows how it goes should give me a name that will really give me an edge."

That was a lot of pressure to put on someone who was already nervous that she might hate the game entirely, but Ben figured she was right. She had no idea what she was doing, and she probably didn't want to embarrass herself by choosing something weird or silly. Not that having nicknames in the first place didn't make them silly by default. He thought for a moment, and then he typed in *Amaterasu*.

Allie studied it before turning her smile to him. "I like it. Is that Japanese?"

He nodded.

"What does it mean?"

If he told her Amaterasu was the most important deity in Japanese mythology, she might think he was overreaching a bit. To be honest, he really didn't know a whole lot about Japanese folklore. He mostly just knew the name because his grandpa would tell them stories whenever he came over from Japan. But he thought it fit Allie rather well, considering she had been a bright spot in his week for months.

"You can look it up if you want," he said, as if it was no big deal. "But it's, like, the goddess of the sun."

Thank goodness she smiled. "That's really cool. Thanks."

Ben had to try really hard not to breathe a sigh of relief. At least now they were all ready to play, so he led her to the door and opened it up to show her the arena. At the moment, all the lights were still on, so she could get a feel for the layout since he already had the unfair advantage of knowing all the pathways to get around.

"It's easier to shoot from above than from below," he told her. "But fair warning, I know all the good hiding places at the bottom."

Allie lifted one eyebrow, and he could see a determination building in her as she looked around the room. "Something tells me I'm going to lose this game."

"This one, maybe. But the next?"

He hit the button to start the round, and the whole place went dark except for black lights, leaving the arena glowing with neon painted stripes and spots as their vests powered up and told them the game had begun. "You ready?"

Allie's response came as a pull of the trigger, and Ben's vest lit up to tell him he'd been hit square in the chest. "You're going down," she said, and then she disappeared into the darkness.

For a tiny moment, Ben pictured what his life would be like knowing Allie would always be there to catch him off guard. It was the kind of future that involved water balloon fights and nerf wars and surprise kisses. Hidden notes left in a lunch box and breakfast for dinner. Always fighting to be the last to say 'I love you' after a long phone call.

He didn't know if he would ever have that kind of life with Allie or even if this friendship of theirs would last beyond their fake relationship. But he did know one thing:

He wasn't going to waste a minute of the time he did have.

FOURTEEN

NOT THAT ALLIE HAD MUCH to compare to, but she was pretty sure Ben was freakishly good at laser tag. She could only imagine what the other Wonder Boys were like if they were more highly ranked than the man who had managed to get in at least ten times as many shots as she had. She had a hard enough time finding him amidst the neon splatters of light around her, and he seemed to constantly know exactly where she was.

Turned out Watchdog was well-named.

And while she should have been frustrated that she was so outmatched, Allie was actually having *fun*. She didn't generally enjoy physical activity beyond occasional runs, but there was something about huffing through strange and otherworldly terrain with a gun strapped to her back that made her feel powerful.

Even when Ben shouted hints at her before shooting her.

"Don't stay in one place for too long!"

Blam.

"The red lights of your vest are the only red in the arena. Same with my blue. It's easy to spot when you're looking for it."

Blam.

"There's a perfect hiding place on the second level, but I know the secret way to still shoot you if you go up there!"

Blam.

His tips were neither helpful nor appreciated when they always preceded him shooting her, but she liked that he was still kind and considerate even when competitive.

With one minute left in the game, Allie was determined to get in at least one more shot. She would never in a million years beat this man at laser tag, but she could at least get the final attack. She had last seen him running for the ramp on the north end of the arena, so she snuck through the tunnel and hurried to cut him off before he could—

They collided in a crash of plastic and limbs, both of them groaning in pain as Allie fell on top of him and nearly smashed her forehead into his. Snickering, she freed her arm from beneath her chest and was about to tell him she was sorry when his expression stole the breath out of her lungs, leaving her light-headed and motionless.

The look in his gaze spoke volumes, somehow both intense and gentle at the same time, like he was digging into her soul with careful fingers instead of a shovel like most guys.

He was going to kiss her!

He raised his arm, and as Allie scrambled to figure out if she actually wanted him to kiss her, her vest lit up with an explosion sound, telling her she'd just been shot.

"You sneak!" she whispered when Ben grinned, but that look hadn't left his eyes yet. Eyes that slid down to her mouth as the blinding lights flickered on and made his expression so easy to see.

With his face so close to hers, Allie's heart skittered.

So did the bugs.

She screamed when she realized hundreds of little cockroaches were scattering, trying to get away from the light. She probably kicked and punched Ben several times trying to get to her feet, but she didn't care. All she wanted was to get as far from the crawling critters as she could.

Ben, on the other hand, hadn't moved except to turn his head to the side, and he looked alarmingly pale as he stared down one particularly brave—and massive—cockroach that seemed to have pegged him as a threat. It would have been comical if Ben didn't look absolutely terrified.

Apparently, Ben was afraid of bugs.

Though Allie very much disliked creepy crawlies, she was more grossed out than afraid, and she worried Ben would be stuck there until the insect either disappeared with his friends or attacked. And from the looks of things, Señor Cucaracha (who deserved a laser tag name at this point) was gearing up for a full-frontal assault.

Allie acted fast, grabbing the wall for support and jumping forward until she landed on top of Cucaracha with a sickening crunch. As her stomach threatened to launch her veggie pizza back the way it had come, she grabbed hold of Ben's hand and dragged him up to his feet and back to the starting room. She refused to look back and to see if she'd actually killed the cockroach or if he was one of those immortal ones who would live through the world's end and befriend a garbage robot.

Maybe he would lead an army of hexapods and take over the world, enslaving the human race and—

"Whoa!" Allie grabbed Ben's shoulders after he pulled off his vest in the antechamber; he looked about ready to pass out. "You okay?"

He nodded, though the ashen color of his skin said a different story. "I should, uh, probably call the owner. We need to take care of this."

He was right, but Allie had a nervous feeling in her gut. The rest of the center was likely pretty dark right now, and she wondered what would happen if they turned on other lights. Glancing at the scoreboard—Ben had beaten her by a landslide—Allie took hold of his hand and slowly pulled him out into the main room with the arcade. She kept an eye on him in case he wavered again, but his color seemed to be returning by degrees with every breath he took.

She shouldn't have been glad to know the Wonder Boy had a weakness, but she was. Every flaw she found brought him closer to her level and made her feel a little less broken.

"Hey Ben, which one of these switches gets the main lights?"

"Why—oh no." Ben clamped his mouth shut and pointed to the second from the right, clearly afraid to see what would happen.

Allie figured it would be a good idea to know what they were up against, so she held her breath and clicked the switch to illuminate the horror scene.

And Ben collapsed behind her.

Kit Morgan was not how Allie expected him to be. For being the top score in laser tag and the leader of the Wonder Boys, she had pictured him somewhere along the lines of those guys who always played heroes in the big movies. The ones with perfect hair and chiseled jawlines and muscles for days. Besides, he was friends with Oliver Hamilton, the guy who had been voted the hottest commodity three years in a row by the sorority girls Allie had lived with in college. That, plus the fact that he was friends with way-too-attractive Ben, had to mean Kit was totally sexy and confident.

Except… The guy who showed up to O'Reilly's looked like a third-grade teacher who had been woken up because it was way past his bedtime. With his brown hair a mess and thick-rimmed glasses slightly askew on his nose, he had clearly been in bed, if not asleep. Plus, his red flannel pajama bottoms beneath a white t-shirt helped solidify her theory, even though it was barely eleven. He was still attractive, just in a soft and gentle volunteers-to-do-the-dishes-on-Thanksgiving kind of way.

"You Allie?" he asked as he approached the spot where Allie sat next to a still-unconscious Ben, as if there was anyone else who could have called him on Ben's phone.

She nodded, still reconciling her imagined version of Kit with the sixty-year-old-in-a-thirty-year-old's body. He was more of a Clark Kent than a Superman, just without the crazy biceps, though he was by no means small. The opposite of what she'd expected. "Kit, I'm guessing?"

A cockroach scurried close to Kit's slipper, and he jumped back a step with a grimace that turned into a yawn. "Um, I might have been half asleep when you told me what was going on. Something about cockroaches and concussions?" He was being awfully calm for a guy whose best friend was lying motionless on the floor.

Allie had been distracting herself with a story of superheroes saving a city from giant bugs, but now she felt the panic rising again. "It's been, like, twenty minutes since he passed out, and I'm worried he hit his head or something. He hasn't woken up yet."

She'd been *this close* to calling an ambulance before she settled on calling Kit instead. Working at a place like this, she had no idea if Ben had health insurance to cover an ambulance ride.

With another massive yawn as he scratched the five o'clock shadow on his cheek, Kit stepped over to Ben and crouched down. "I think the worst of it is over," he said, though whether he was talking to her or Ben, she wasn't sure. Then he gave Ben a gentle slap in the face, which seemed to do the trick.

Tears of relief filled Allie's eyes as Kit took Ben by the hand and helped him slowly sit up. She'd been so worried!

"That's it, buddy. Take a few deep breaths. He'll be fine," Kit told her as he patted Ben on the back. "He's pretty good about catching himself as he falls to avoid injury."

Just how often did the man pass out for him to be practiced at it?

Ben finally met her eyes and offered a weak smile. "I don't do bugs. When I was eight, my older brother handed me a spider egg sac just as the babies were all hatching." He shuddered. "I haven't been the same since."

As Kit settled next to him, he seemed to finally be awake now as he chuckled. "First time I saw him pass out like that was when he accidentally stood on an anthill the summer after we met. Madi thought he was dead and ran screaming into the house."

"How old were you?" Allie asked.

"Twelve," Ben replied, and only then did he seem to realize who was sitting next to him. "Wait, what are you doing here?"

Kit grinned. "Allie called me."

The smile that Ben gave Allie was small, but it sent her heart pounding all the same. "Thanks."

Allie shrugged, even though she would have loved to see that grateful smile every day of her life. It made her feel needed. "It was sort of a panic move."

"I'm glad you did it," Ben said. "Sorry to worry you." Then he sighed. "I should call O'Reilly. I don't know how long it's been this bad. I don't usually open, and I always keep the lights on until I leave, so… They must have been hiding in the walls or something."

Kit chuckled. "Or maybe they just spawned at apocalypse-level rates."

Ben grinned in a way that made Allie's breath hitch. This was a new side of Ben, and she was here for it. He looked more play-ful. Younger. "I don't think that's how biology works," he said, raising an eyebrow at Kit.

"How would you know? I don't remember you having a science degree."

"I don't remember third graders learning about bugs."

"You did. Firsthand."

Ben shuddered as he rose to his feet. "Why'd you have to say hand?" he moaned, wiping his palms on his jeans as if he could feel the spiders of his childhood.

Grinning, Kit shook his head. "Go make your call, Watch. I'll keep Allie company."

Taking his phone from Allie, Ben seemed to hesitate a moment before he wandered over to the prize counter and was soon deep in conversation.

Allie wouldn't have minded just sitting there and watching him present the problem with that serious little wrinkle between his eyebrows, but Kit had other ideas.

"You have a chicken in your pocket," he said.

"Huh? Oh!" Allie grabbed the rubber chicken out of her back pocket, where it had sat forgotten as soon as laser tag started. She gave it a little squeeze to make it squeak at her, and then she chuckled. It was so useless, and she loved it. Of all the things she could have bought at the prize booth, it had been the one thing calling her name. Just like her sequin llama pillow.

"You called him Watch," she said, still looking at her chicken. The fact that Kit had chosen to sit with her while Ben talked to his boss had her on edge. He didn't need to stick around, but she could feel his gaze locked onto her.

"Watchdog. It's his laser tag name."

"I know. He showed me."

"So…" Kit shifted, stretching his long legs out and leaning back on his hands. "You and Ben, huh?"

Heat spread across Allie's face, and she refused to look at Kit in case he could read minds just like Ben could. They hadn't talked about whether they would pretend to be dating with his friends—just her family. Based on Kit's question, Ben hadn't told them the truth, but maybe the subject hadn't come up. What could she say that would keep things ambiguous enough until she could make a game plan with Ben?

"It's still pretty new," she said. "We're figuring things out, you know?" She chanced a peek at him.

For some reason, Kit frowned as if he *didn't* know, but he didn't respond to her rhetorical question. Instead, he looked over at the prize counter and said, "Ben's a really good guy. One of the best."

"I know." Did she know? They were still barely getting to know each other.

Kit's frown deepened, making Allie's mind-reading fear even stronger. He seemed to read people as easily as Ben did. "I know he's quiet," he said, "but he has a lot to say if you give him the chance."

Allie definitely knew that part, and not just because Ben had told her in the photo booth. After their awkward encounters in the grocery store and the nightmarish dinner with her family, Ben had been so much more confident since the moment he knocked on her door tonight. Even with his somewhat irrational fear of bugs, there was so much to like about him that Allie was already starting to worry what would happen when she no longer needed him as her fake boyfriend. Would he still be her friend?

"Ben has one of the biggest hearts I know," Kit continued, and he put his hand on Allie's shoulder, giving her a look that almost frightened her. The man definitely saw a lot more than he should. "But that also means it's easier to break it if he lets you in."

Allie swallowed. "You think I'm going to break his heart?" She glanced over at Ben and met his gaze, and he gave her that dimpled smile again, the one that pulled her heart up into her throat. "I would never do that." Not intentionally, anyway. She couldn't help but wonder if Kit knew more than he was letting on, but she couldn't understand why he would pretend otherwise if he did. If he knew their relationship wasn't real, it would make more sense for him to let her know that he knew.

This whole pretending thing was giving her a headache.

Giving her shoulder a squeeze, Kit rose to his feet. "That's all I need to hear. As long as he's happy, I'm happy." He tilted his head toward the counter. "You good, Ben?"

Ben gave him a wave, still deep in his phone call, and Kit wandered out to the parking lot.

And Allie sat on the floor, wondering if she had just lied to Kit. With all the fake dating and friendship stuff, inevitably one of them was bound to develop feelings for the other, and it would all lead to heartbreak.

As she watched Ben run a hand through his black hair and wished she could do it too, she feared the first heart to break would be hers.

FIFTEEN

AT FIVE FOOT SEVEN, BEN had never thought himself tall until he tried to sleep on a couch built more like an armchair. In Allie's defense, she had offered him the bed, but what kind of person would he be if he kicked her to the couch just so he could get some better sleep?

What he *should* have done was ask Kit to take Allie home, then crash on Kit's couch, but by the time he'd explained the bug situation to O'Reilly and gotten the place locked down and relatively sealed, Kit had probably been dead asleep again.

So he'd driven Allie back to her apartment, contemplated sleeping in the back of his car, then reluctantly agreed when Allie suggested he get a little sleep at her place instead of trying to drive home while completely exhausted.

He'd managed a few hours of rest, hardly enough to get him functional again, but it was better than nothing. And now he wasn't sure what to do. He would have to go home at some point so he could shower and change, but he didn't want to leave Allie without saying something, especially after she'd been nice enough to let him stay. Neither did he want to wake her up; she'd been up as late as he had and had witnessed his ridiculous fainting act.

He was left in limbo until she was awake, and he didn't know what to do.

Resisting the urge to watch her sleep—that was more than creepy—he wandered over to the kitchen to see if he could make her breakfast. While that was also slightly creepy, he hoped she didn't take it the wrong way and simply saw it as a friendly gesture. She'd been planning to make him dinner before they switched to pizza, so really it was repaying the favor.

At least, that was what he told himself.

Before he reached the fridge, however, a stack of papers caught his eye. Despite telling himself that it was none of his business, he turned his focus to them anyway. It wasn't hard to figure out they were the applications for new potential writers at Allie's company, nor was there any question that every single one of them was male as he looked through them.

"Seriously?" he muttered under his breath.

Each application included a writing sample, and Ben flipped through the first one, skimming the sample until he couldn't bear the pain of it anymore. It was awful, and he couldn't imagine teens finding any interest in a book that used words even Ben hadn't heard before.

The second writer had a juvenile style that made Ben laugh, and not in a good way.

He'd made it through the whole stack by the time Allie finally sat up, bleary-eyed and bedheaded. "You're still here," she mumbled.

Cringing, Ben hoped that didn't mean she was angry about it. "I ordered in some breakfast," he said to soften the sting, just in case. "You...you like breakfast food, right?"

As she slid off the bed, she brought her entire quilt with her, shuffling over like a giant burrito with stunning eyes. "That was a trick question, right?"

With perfect timing, a knock sounded on the door, and Ben hurried over to bring the food in after giving the delivery girl a smile and a tip. Though her answering blush made *him* blush, Ben pretended he wasn't completely hopeless around women and returned to the counter, where Allie had taken a seat on one of the stools.

"Did you look at these?" Allie frowned at the applications she had picked up to make room for the food.

He thought about lying, but that was probably a terrible idea. "Yes."

"They're awful, aren't they?"

Ben hadn't realized he was completely tense until his shoulders relaxed. He could have just blown everything with his snooping, and he would have to be more careful in the future. He had no intention of giving her any reason to dump him like last week's leftovers.

He took a breath, willing his heart to go back to a regular rate. "I mean, they're not terrible…"

"But they're not good either. I'm supposed to stake my whole future on one of these guys, Ben." Sighing, she dropped her chin in her hand. "I just wish Simmons would let me show him what I can do. He barely looked at my writing samples when I tried to take the last writer position. If he won't even give me a chance without involving some strange male author who could end up being terrible, how am I supposed to prove I'm worth it? Oo, are those waffles?"

Ben barely noticed when Allie took the Styrofoam container out of his hands, though he grabbed the next one out of reflex. He'd just had an idea—a terrible idea, probably—and it was crazy enough that it might actually work. At least, it would work if their lives were a movie, which they weren't. Reality was a whole lot different from fiction. But what would Allie have to lose if they tried it?

"Ben, you're putting syrup on that omelet."

"Huh? Oh!" He stopped pouring from the little container in his hands and hoped he hadn't just ruined his breakfast since Allie was already halfway through the waffles with no sign of slowing down. Apparently, she was a fan.

As she chewed, she grinned at him. "I think you got a little lost there for a second. How much sleep did you get anyway? That couch is tiny."

This was a *terrible* idea. He told himself over and over, but he couldn't think about anything else because it was quite possibly the only way to help Allie get what she wanted. "What if I become your writer?" he said, then held his breath.

Allie didn't get it. "You write? Are you any good?"

"No. I mean, no, I don't write. I just meant… If you think your writing is good enough to put it in front of your boss, maybe you just need someone else to be the one to take it to him."

Pausing with a piece of waffle halfway to her mouth, Allie cocked her head to the side and looked absolutely adorable inside her blanket. "I'm not following. I don't want anyone else taking credit for my—"

"I'm a man, Allie."

She leaned back, putting some distance between them.

Ben groaned. This would have been a whole lot easier if he'd actually gotten some sleep. "You already knew that. What I meant was I could pretend to be a writer, and you can tell your boss that you've found the perfect person. And I could show him your writing samples, and when he agrees that I'm the right person for the job, I tell him that it was actually you who wrote it. With only crap as the other options, he'll have no choice but to promote you to the writing team."

She leaned even farther, to the point where Ben was worried she was going to fall off the stool. "That's insane," she said.

"I know." And he counted down the seconds until she finally threw him out of her apartment and told him to never talk to her again.

The longer she sat there, though, the softer her expression and posture became, until she was hunched down with her arms on the counter, cradling the waffle that was right in front of her nose. "You would have to meet Simmons," she said slowly. "Otherwise he would think I was just taking credit for someone else's work."

"I could do that." He had pretended to be her boyfriend in front of her family, so surely he could act like an author for an afternoon. "And once he's ready to put me under contract, I tell him the truth."

Allie grimaced. "It might blow up in our faces."

That was true, but… "Isn't your dream worth the risk?"

Allie sat up straight again, the blanket falling from her head. She was an absolute mess, and Ben thought she was beautiful. "You're right," she said, though fear weakened her words. "I've spent almost ten years working for the company, and I've been too scared to lose it in case I lose my chance to be an author with it. But I'm not an author, and I'm not going to be one if I don't get a good writer, so I'm not losing anything."

Ben smiled. "Exactly."

"Why would you do this for me?" Allie pierced him with a stare that seemed to dig into him. He let her dig, knowing it would help her trust him more.

He took a deep breath, waiting until he was sure she'd seen everything she needed to. "Because that's what friends do, Allie. And I so badly want to be your friend."

SIXTEEN

So FAR, BEN ONLY HAD two flaws: a fear of insects and his propensity to Sherlock things about her. As she drove to the nearest thrift store, Allie added one more to that list, though it wasn't necessarily a flaw, because it was entirely fixable. She planned to rectify the problem today, so it would be crossed off the list as quickly as it was added.

Ben had no idea how to dress well.

She wouldn't have said anything, considering their friendship wasn't there yet, but if she was going to bring Ben to Sweet Red Cherry Books on Monday morning, she couldn't have him looking like an assistant manager at a bug-infested fun center. He had to look like a serious author, with serious writing skills, and she seriously hoped this whole thing wasn't the worst idea in the history of ideas.

"Okay, you're making me nervous," Ben said. To prove it, he was gripping the door handle and staring straight ahead.

Allie rolled her eyes. "I'm a great driver."

"That's not what I'm talking about. I'm rethinking this whole makeover thing."

Apparently, Ben was as afraid of shopping as he was of Señor Cucaracha.

"It's not like I'm going to dress you in drag," Allie told him as she pulled into the parking lot. "I just want to add a little…" She waved her hand around, searching for the word. "Sophistication."

Unless she was mistaken, Ben's hand tightened even more around the door handle despite them coming to a stop in a parking spot. "I wasn't worried about drag until you said that," he said, though he managed an adorably nervous smile before he climbed out of the car.

Allie laughed. "Come on, you big baby." Taking him by the arm, she practically dragged him into the store and to the men's section.

She hadn't been in this thrift store since she dated Jake, and while it felt a little strange to be back, the familiarity of the place brought a strange sense of comfort.

"I love old things," she said as she ran her hand along the rack of mismatched clothing.

"Really?" Ben pulled out a polo that Allie immediately took from him and put back on the rack.

She grabbed a cream-colored t-shirt instead and a brown leather jacket. "There's just something so interesting about having something that used to belong to someone else, you know? Everything has a story, and you wonder why the last person gave it up."

Pulling out a red plaid button-up, Ben held it up for inspection and blushed when Allie gave him a nod. "I've never thought of it that way," he said. "For me, it was always hand-me-downs from my brother. Sometimes even from my sisters. And anything I had was fair game for my siblings to borrow whenever they wanted. I never got to have something that was actually mine."

As Ben turned to the rack behind him to sort through the plethora of jeans hanging there, Allie tried to picture a life with six siblings. It had always been just her and her parents, and she'd never had to share. At least, she hadn't until she started dating, in which case she shared *everything*. Including her own personality. She let her boyfriends borrow her sense of self and make little tweaks and changes until it suited them, and then they would hand it back and tell her she wasn't what they wanted.

"Have you dated much, Ben?" Allie asked, wincing in anticipation of the answer. Of course he had. Just looking at him told her everything she needed to know. He was gorgeous, and kind, and funny, and smart, and she had a feeling there was a whole lot more to him that he didn't let many people see.

But when Ben shot her a glance, he looked sad. "Nah." Though he pulled out a pair of dark jeans that would look awesome on him, he didn't seem to see them as he examined them. "I mean, I went on a lot of dates in college, but it was really because I was too afraid to say no. For some reason, girls really like me."

Anyone else, and that statement would have made him the cockiest guy alive. But with Ben, Allie knew he didn't mean it like it sounded. She fought a snicker as he seemed to slowly realize what he'd said, and then she grabbed his hand before he backtracked.

"I get it," she said. "You're totally hot, and if we'd been at the same school, I definitely would have asked you out too."

He turned so red that he matched the crimson sweater Allie had just picked out. "You think I'm—not that it—I don't…" He cleared his throat and ducked his head, perfectly humble. "Thanks."

"You're welcome. So you never liked any of the girls who asked you out?"

He shrugged and started perusing the shirts again. "I guess some of them were nice. And they were all beautiful. But none of them were…"

Allie almost slapped herself for thinking he was going to finish that sentence with "you." Ben hadn't even known her back then, so he definitely wouldn't have been comparing random classmates to her. Still, a girl could dream.

"None of them were what?" she pressed before her thoughts got away from her again.

"I couldn't be myself with them. Not like I can with you."

There it was, exactly as she'd hoped. And yet Allie suddenly felt slightly sick, remembering what Kit had said to her last night. Ben had a big heart, which meant it was easier to break. So far, Ben hadn't given her any real sign that he was interested in dating her, but Allie still refused to lead him on. Just in case.

Even for a guy as amazing as him, breaking her no dating vow wouldn't do her any good right now. She didn't even know what toppings she liked on her pizza! Jumping into a relationship would only get her lost again, and she'd had to fight and claw her way to get to this point. She felt like she was teetering on the edge of something important. Either way, she was going to fall, but she hoped it was in the right direction.

And that meant keeping her heart safe from Ben in order to protect his. He deserved better than someone who could barely take care of herself.

The friend zone was the only place they could be.

"Well, I feel like this is a good start," Ben said. "I'm going to go try some of this on."

"I'll be here," Allie muttered, glad she would have the fitting room door to hide her budding tears. If she hurt Ben, she wasn't sure she would forgive herself.

As if the universe had decided to laugh at Allie, her phone started to ring. *Mom.* "Hey, Mom."

"Allison, when are you going to bring that delightful Ben around again? I'm making pot pie tonight, and you should bring him!"

Right to the point, huh? Allie sighed and switched her phone to the other hand so she could rub out the building headache that had just appeared. "Mom, I promise we're still dating. But that doesn't mean I have to bring him around every week."

"Nonsense. He could use a good family dinner, I'm sure."

Allie wondered if that was true or if Ben *did* have family dinners now and then. He hadn't talked about them much, outside of telling her about how he often went unnoticed.

She had no idea how that was possible. She'd noticed him from clear across the grocery store whenever they were there at the same time, before she'd even talked to him. Now that she knew him better, she knew it would be impossible to walk into a room and see anything but him.

"Mom, we're busy tonight."

"Oh, are you with him now? Put him on."

Allie groaned, but she knew better than to argue. She pressed her phone to her chest. "Hey, Ben?"

Something crashed into the fitting room door, and then Ben grunted, "Yeah?" followed by a string of muttered curses.

Allie grinned. "You okay in there?"

"Um. Fine."

"Are you sure?"

"Well. I think I might have gained thirty pounds. That, or I've gone blind and couldn't actually read the tag on these pants. I might be, uh…"

Allie snorted a laugh. "Are you stuck, Benjamin?"

"Uh. No?"

Lifting her phone again, Allie shook her head as she wandered just a little ways away so Ben wouldn't be able to hear her. "Mom, Ben's gotten himself into a bit of a pickle, so I should probably go help him out. I'll—"

"Wait! But when do I get to see him again?"

"He's not *your* boyfriend, Mom."

"No, but he's my future son-in-law, and I would like to get to know him better!"

All amusement gone, Allie groaned and wished she could slip her phone into the pocket of the nearest puffy coat and forget it ever existed. She could run away to a cottage in the forest—way less creepy than a cabin in the woods—and spend the rest of her life writing inspiring and thought-provoking women's fiction on a manual typewriter. Or maybe romance. She was a big fan of romance.

"Mom, I've got to go. We'll talk soon, okay?"

By the time Allie made it back to the fitting room, a pair of legs were sticking out from the bottom as if Ben had fallen to the ground only a moment earlier. She crouched down and tapped his foot where it rested hidden in a pair of skinny jeans. "How ya doing, buddy?"

He let out a huge sigh. "One of these days, I would really like to spend some time with you where neither of us ends up on the floor."

"Where would be the fun in that?"

"Any chance you can help me out of these?"

Though she almost asked if he wanted her to go into the fitting room with him, Allie clamped her mouth shut and counted to ten before she said anything. "What do you want me to do?" It sounded like an innocent enough question.

He lifted one leg, letting the bottom hem of the pants flop on the floor. "Pull," he instructed.

Was he serious?

"Allie, I'm pretty sure these are cutting off the circulation in my legs."

Only because he was willing to admit he needed help did Allie shift onto her knees and grab hold of the denim hems. "Just so you know," she said, "I'm using this as extortion in the future."

"Please just save me."

Snickering, Allie gripped a little tighter and gave the pants a tug. They didn't move. She tugged harder, and absolutely nothing happened. "At what point did you realize these weren't going to fit?" she asked. "When your toes turned purple?"

Allie practically heard him roll his eyes. "Ha ha," he said, clearly unamused. "I'll try getting my legs out if you just hold on. Ready?"

She wasn't ready, and when he pulled, he pulled her with him until her head slammed into the door. Though Ben shouted a surprising curse, Allie burst out laughing despite the pain in her forehead. "I'm fine," she assured him and adjusted her stance, standing up most of the way so she could use her body weight in her favor. "Are *you* ready?"

He sighed. "Get me out of these."

Allie pulled with all her strength, sure that the thick fabric would tear before Ben came free. He must have been holding onto something on his end; he didn't move beyond trying to wiggle himself free. This whole thing was so ridiculous that she couldn't stop laughing, but she tried her best to stay focused until suddenly the jeans came free.

And Allie went flying into a winter coat display.

"Allie!"

Though she figured she would probably have a bruise on her head from hitting the door, Allie had never been happier than in that moment, while she lay in a pile of down coats and laughed so hard she cried.

Ben eventually made it to her side, thankfully wearing a pair of jeans that actually fit him. He grabbed hold of her hand and lifted her to her feet, though her laughter didn't make it easy for him because she could barely help. "I'm so sorry," he said, and his utter concern warmed Allie's heart. Not that she'd ever dated straight-up jerks, but not all of them would have taken responsibility for her tumble.

"I should have seen that coming," she said, and then she lifted up the offending jeans to examine them. "Ben, these are size twenty-two. I didn't even know they made a size twenty-two for men." And that was when she saw the bedazzled back pockets, and she burst into laughter again as she turned the jeans around to show him.

Ben couldn't have gone redder if he'd spent three days straight in the sun, and while his embarrassment was adorable, Allie had to stuff down her growing attraction. Had she been wanting to date when she met him, she likely would have passed him over in search of easier prey and never discovered the depth to his character. Never discovered the little flaws that made him real. Without that pressure of romance, however, the more Allie saw these imperfect aspects of him, the more she liked him. Friends weren't meant to be idealized; she could take him as he was, just like he could do with her.

"Hey, Ben?" Tossing the jeans aside, she grabbed both his hands and felt a twinge of regret when he kept his head bowed instead of looking at her. "I hope you know that I have never had as much fun as I have the last couple of days. I'm really glad you're my friend."

When he still didn't meet her eyes, Allie reached up and lifted his chin. "I mean that," she told him. "I really needed this." Then she glanced down to see what had been so interesting down there, and her eyes went wide. "Whoa."

Ben frowned and followed her gaze, as if expecting to see something horrific at his feet. When he found nothing but the floor beneath his socks, he opened his mouth, probably to ask what she was staring at.

Allie put a finger over his lips. Talking would ruin the effect.

Ben looked *good*. Like, crazy good. He'd gone for the t-shirt and leather jacket first, and with the dark jeans he'd put on, the whole look was…breathtaking. Like he'd just stepped into the role of box office hero by changing his clothes. It wasn't that he had suddenly gained more visible muscle or grown a few inches taller; without the polo and khakis that had put him firmly in the dead-end job role, he suddenly looked like he had potential.

"There's the look of an author," she whispered, almost reverently, as if talking too loudly would ruin the effect and turn him back into pre-Godmother Cinderella.

Allie really needed to work on her metaphors.

"How's your head?" Ben whispered back, and he brushed his thumb across her forehead, sending a shiver through her. His gaze held so much intensity, like he was telling her things she would only hear if she listened hard enough.

Desperate to know what he would say, she leaned in closer. Friends could be this close, right? "I'll live."

When Ben's eyes dropped to her lips—only for a second—a jolt of electricity shot through her. He was *definitely* going to kiss her this time.

And she was going to let him.

She closed her eyes, holding her breath, and waited for the moment of collision like his mouth was a defibrillator to bring her back to life.

But Ben's lips touched her forehead, barely a whisper of a kiss, and he stepped away. "I'm really sorry," he said when she looked at him. "Apparently it's...been a while since I last bought clothes, and I didn't think it was possible to get stuck in a pair of, uh, women's jeans."

Resisting the urge to sigh, Allie patted him on the chest. She shouldn't have been disappointed that he stuck to her friends-only rule, but she was. Something was seriously wrong with her. "Happens to the best of us. Now, are you going to try on the rest, or what? This look is great, but you can't wear it 24/7."

As she picked up the coat rack she'd knocked over, Allie reminded herself that being single was good for her. It was important. She was learning so much about herself, and for the first time in her adult life she had someone in her life she didn't have to prove anything to. She'd meant what she said about needing Ben as her friend, and she couldn't risk their budding relationship just because she was attracted to the guy.

Until she knew herself better, she couldn't let herself get lost in something that wouldn't last. When all of her other boyfriends had moved on, why would Ben ever stay?

SEVENTEEN

ONE MORE CHANCE ENCOUNTER PUTTING him within inches of Allie's lips, and Ben was going to lose his mind. With every minute he spent with her, he fell more and more in love with her, and it was starting to mess with his head.

Yeah, he was in love with her. He wouldn't even pretend otherwise at this point. He was pretty sure that made him both crazy and creepy, considering they had been official friends for less than three days, unless he counted their pretend date with her parents. That still only put them at a week. Luckily, Allie had decided they probably shouldn't go to Sunday dinner again after their thrift shopping. Until they were comfortable enough with each other to really pretend they were dating, it was better to avoid potentially dangerous situations.

Apparently, Allie's mom had called him her future son-in-law. Ben was both flattered and terrified by that.

So, once Ben had a week's worth of new outfits, they grabbed a pizza on the way back to Allie's apartment—Ben's least favorite toppings, Hawaiian—and spent the afternoon and evening talking about TV shows and movies so Allie could figure out what she actually liked to watch. As it turned out, Allie didn't like pineapple on her pizza either. She did, on the other hand, decide she loved superhero movies, something Ben particularly appreciated about her.

He finally ended up back home after midnight, thanking Cam's early morning schedule because his roommate was already asleep instead of there to ask prying questions, and he crashed in his bed with a smile on his face.

Now, however, he was as far from smiling as he could get as he sat in his car outside the publishing house where Allie worked.

At what point had he gone crazy enough to think he could pretend to be a kids book writer? Never mind he was in a ridiculous sweater vest that made him feel like an eighty-year-old version of Kit; he had never once thought to himself, "I should write this daydream down because it could make a good story one day." He never really daydreamed to begin with. Sure, he was an artist, and technically that meant he created, but he was better at recreating than coming up with his own ideas.

Okay, so yes, he wasn't even going to have to write anything. Allie had already done that, and she was good.

Ben scoffed as he sat in his car and worked up the courage to walk across the street where Allie was waiting for him inside. She was *way* more than good. Allie's writing was phenomenal, and Ben didn't care if the story was about a ten-year-old who had the power to turn knitted yarn creations to life. One chapter in, and he was fully invested, and he'd almost forgotten to drive over to Sweet Red Cherry Books to meet with the editors and convince them to put him under contract.

He really hoped this plan was going to work. Allie's words deserved to be heard.

Just as he was about to step out into what could be the biggest disaster of his life, his phone pinged with a text. He had to stare at it for a second before he believed what he saw, and for a second he thought maybe his phone was glitching. It was several years old, after all, and the phone company had been hounding him about upgrading.

But when he opened the text, it was definitely from his mom.

> Mom: Hunter and Isaac want you to take them trick-or-treating this week.

Had she texted the wrong person? Ben's nephews generally liked him, but never had they requested to spend time with him. They were always busy taking out their endless aggression in rugby despite being only five and seven. Now that they were living with his parents while his brother and sister-in-law built a house in the next neighborhood over, they got plenty of attention from Ben's younger siblings who still lived at home.

He narrowed his eyes, afraid to text back but doing it anyway. Surely his brother would take his own kids out on Halloween.

> Ben: Why can't Peter and Fiona take them?

Mom's answer came quickly.

> Mom: Peter has a court case that'll be at trial on Thursday, and Fiona has her hands full with the twins.

Something told Ben that Peter had gladly pawned the older kids off on Grandma, and his mom was so overwhelmed by her rapidly growing horde of grandchildren that she didn't have the energy she used to. He couldn't blame his sister-in-law for wanting to stay at home—their newest kids were less than a year old. And his little brother and sister probably had important parties to go to, as all people in their early twenties did.

Well, most people. Ben had always been grateful that the Wonder Boys weren't big partiers, except when Cam had had swim meets in high school and dragged them to the after-parties so he didn't look lame in front of his teammates if he didn't show up.

Ben was already running late to meet Allie, and he groaned at his phone. He couldn't let Mom handle the boys on her own—Dad was on a work trip as always—and he didn't even have the excuse of needing to work since the fun center was going to be closed all week while they fumigated the place. Though he hadn't told his family about the cockroach problem, he figured at least one of his siblings had discovered it and spread the word.

He rarely went noticed by his family, except when they found something to embarrass him.

Honestly, Ben liked spending time with his nephews, but he had hoped to spend more time with Allie this week. The weekend had been a dream, and now that she was back at work until the weekend again, he wanted to claim as many of her evenings as he could.

Ben: I need to check on something, but I'll let you know.

Mom: You could bring those friends of yours along as well. It's been a long time since I saw Kip.

Ben sighed and shoved his phone into his pocket. He would deal with his family problems later, after he'd gotten Allie a writing job.

As he crossed the street, Ben ran a hand through his hair and wished he had thought to get a haircut so it wasn't as much of a mess. Allie had said she liked how long it was, but since he'd never bothered to figure out how to style it when it got too long, he felt like a bit of a slob. Maybe that would play into the whole writer dynamic and help sell the part? That was completely stereotyping, but those overblown traits existed for a reason, so he couldn't be *that* far off the mark from reality.

Once he reached the doors, he forced one hand into his pocket so he wouldn't keep making his hair worse. It was go time, and he would need all his focus to make Allie's dreams come true.

"You sound ridiculous," he muttered, then tugged the door open and stepped into Sweet Red Cherry Books.

To his relief, Allie was waiting for him behind a little desk in the corner of the tiny front room. She gave him a smile, but that—and her eyes jumping to his hair—was the only recognition she gave him. The plan was to pretend they'd never met so Mr. Simmons would think this was a genuine interview.

"Welcome to Sweet Red Cherry," she said brightly. "How can I help you?"

Ben's throat had suddenly closed off, and he coughed to clear it. "Uh, hi. I'm Ben Nakamura. I have a meeting with John Simmons?" That wasn't supposed to be a question. They both knew he had a meeting because Allie had set it up first thing this morning.

Allie's smile twisted a little with amusement, and Ben refused to let himself blush. His face didn't listen to him, though, and he was sure he was bright red as he stuffed his other hand into his pocket as well. He felt completely awkward, and he missed the easy comfort he usually had around Allie.

If someone had told him that the girl he'd had a crush on for months would be the one girl he could talk to without a problem, he'd have laughed in their face—then felt bad for laughing.

"It's nice to meet you, Ben," she said, still with that little grin of hers as she shook his hand. "I'm Allie, and Mr. Simmons should be ready for you in just a minute or two. Can I get you anything?"

Long handshakes were weird and awkward and terrible, but Ben didn't mind when Allie didn't let go of his hand for a second, as if she were hoping to find their connection again just like him. He would take longer handshakes with anyone if it meant he got to hold her hand like this.

Well, he'd rather hold her hand a little differently, but this was better than nothing.

"Mr. Nakamura!" The man who must have been Mr. Simmons appeared from a little hallway, his hand already extended for a handshake even though he was still a good twenty feet away.

Ben reluctantly traded Allie's hand for Simmons's. "Thanks for meeting me," he said. "Hopefully you have good news for me."

Simmons narrowed his eyes but didn't seem to have made any judgment yet. "Let's talk."

Ben hoped he could play his part well enough to help Allie live her dream. If not, he hoped she wouldn't hate him enough to drop him like yesterday's trash.

EIGHTEEN

APPARENTLY, ALLIE HAD NEVER REALLY been in a tense situation before, and it sucked. Her entire body had practically gone numb because of her muscles tensing up while she sat in on Ben's meeting with Simmons and the editors, and she was completely exhausted. If she was making a list of things she liked, being anxious was definitely not one of them.

Ben was *absolutely* on the list of good things, though. She'd been worried about him choking and spilling the beans too soon about who really wrote the samples, but eventually he'd settled into the role and gotten a lot more confident. And it was *sexy*. Of all the people Allie had dated over the years, plenty of them—most of them—had been self-assured and cocky. Full of themselves, forgetting that their pretty little girlfriend had her own thoughts and words because they were too busy praising themselves.

Well, okay, so they weren't *that* bad. Unless she counted Johnny, who was so full of himself that he made Narcissus look like humility itself.

But Ben? Ben's confidence came from somewhere else, and he certainly didn't tout his own accolades the whole meeting like others might have. Anything he had to say was about the writing itself, and each time he mentioned a phrase or passage that really made the samples shine, Allie felt each bit of praise in her soul.

He meant it for her, and Allie loved him for it.

They had almost reached the end of the interview, however, and somehow Allie's nerves were getting worse.

"For general informational purposes," Mr. Simmons said, "the storyline has already been set by our patron, so this is a contracted manuscript with little room for deviation. The manner of the storytelling is up to the writer, as long as he follows the plotline."

"I understand," Ben replied, though he first glanced at Allie to make sure *she* was cool with that stipulation. Honestly, she didn't care what the story was about as long as she would get to write it and prove she was a capable writer. "Is there a contract to guarantee the writer you choose is the one who gets published?"

Simmons didn't seem to like that question, squirming in his seat a little bit. "Yes, once we are sure we have found the right man for the job, he will be given a three-book contract. You can see why we are going to be very thorough in our decision process."

Nodding, Ben seemed to study the three men in front of him as if looking for any sign of deception. "Of course. You will naturally want to choose the best *person* for the project. What does that mean for me?"

"It means you will need to draft the first three chapters of the story by Monday so we can determine if you are up to scratch. Once we have reviewed your submission, we can discuss things from there."

Allie took a deep breath and held it in her lungs for a second, thinking that over. Could she do that? Three chapters in a week was a lot, and she wouldn't have much time to get them done. She knew she could write well because she'd done it, but that included lots of revision time and feedback. Could she write well under the pressure of a looming deadline?

Meeting Ben's gaze, she gave him a tiny nod and hoped she hadn't just lied to him.

Ben offered up a practiced smile as he stood, Simmons and the editors standing with him. "That sounds reasonable," he said, holding out his hand for a handshake. "I should get started right away."

Whether Simmons had intended the interview to be over or not, he had just been backed into a corner. Grasping Ben's hand, he almost said something but shut his mouth, which was probably a good idea; he had a habit of saying the wrong thing when he got flustered, something Allie had had to fix for him more than once when he accidentally insulted an author or client.

"I'll walk you out and answer any questions you might have, Mr. Nakamura," Allie said, hopping up before Simmons could think to stop her. She needed to get out of that room and think over what had just happened.

As she stepped out onto the sidewalk with Ben, Allie couldn't decide which emotion to focus on. She was terrified and excited, nervous and overwhelmed with gratitude. The gratitude was probably the most important one right now, so as soon as they were around the corner from the building, she attacked Ben with a hug and laughed when he fell against the wall with a little *oof*.

"You have no idea how much this means to me," she said into his neck. Holy mama, he smelled good, and she resisted the urge to take a deep breath for a better sample of his body wash. Barely.

As he slowly wrapped his arms around her to return the embrace, Allie melted a little. Even his hug was sweet and gentle, and it was unlike anything she'd ever felt before. She was perfectly capable of living life on her own and taking care of herself, but that didn't mean this protective hold of his would go unwanted.

In fact, she'd be fine to stay there all day.

Ben, however, released her after a moment and slid away from the wall so he could put some distance between them. A reminder that he wanted to be friends and nothing more. This whole relationship of theirs was fake, after all. "I really didn't do that much," he said.

Allie rolled her eyes. "Seriously, Ben. First my mom, and now this. How am I supposed to even the score?"

"Halloween."

The change of subject caught her off guard, and for a second she thought maybe she'd said something else. Had she accidentally asked him his favorite holiday? "What?"

Chuckling, he slid his hands into his pockets and hunched his shoulders a little. "My mom asked if I could take my nephews trick-or-treating, and I thought that might be a good way to show your parents we're still, uh, dating. Reassure your mom that you're fine, you know?"

Allie hadn't been trick-or-treating since she was ten. She and Jake had gone together with his dad, and they'd both dressed up as pirates. She'd been to her fair share of Halloween parties over the years, but she hadn't dressed up often. She only did it when whichever guy she was with wanted her to match his costume, and she never liked wearing the costumes they chose.

"Would we have to dress up?" she asked warily.

Ben shrugged. "Only if you want to. My nephews might force me into it, but you wouldn't have to." He grinned a little, some of his playful side returning. "Not everyone can pull off being a Ninja Turtle, anyway."

"Ninja Turtles?" Allie's jaw dropped, though she was pretty sure she hadn't thought about the mutated teenage super-heroes in years. She'd loved that show as a kid! "Would I get to be Leonardo? I've always wanted to have double swords."

She was pretty sure Ben couldn't have looked more shocked if she'd told him she was a turtle in reality, and she laughed at his expression of utter amazement. Was it really so strange for her to know who the Ninja Turtles were? What *was* strange was how easily she had admitted it. With any of her boyfriends, even Jake, she would have felt stupid for liking such an odd thing.

"Don't be so shocked," she said with a laugh. "You haven't even seen my comic book collection yet."

"Marry me." Ben's eyes went wide before he dropped his face in his hands and mumbled, "I didn't mean that. I only meant… You know what I meant."

She did know what he meant, but that didn't mean a thrill of excitement didn't rush through her when he said it. Honestly, what was wrong with her? People didn't think about marrying their friends, especially when said friends were just making a joke.

Shifting a little closer, Allie grinned at Ben's red face. "So me dressing up as a Ninja Turtle and going trick-or-treating will make up for everything you've done for me?"

He breathed a sigh of relief. "Yeah, that would do it."

"You really need to learn to ask for fair pricing."

"I'm an artist. That's basically impossible."

Well, that was a bombshell, and Allie thought for a second her brain had stopped working. How, in the several days she'd spent with this guy, had she never heard him say anything about art? "You're an artist?"

Clearly, if his hands going into his pockets and his shoulders hunching again meant anything, he hadn't intended to say anything about it. "Uh, yeah, I went to school for illustration."

Oh, she desperately wanted to unpack that, but she couldn't be gone for long if she didn't want Simmons to start asking questions. "I should get back to work," she said, though that was the last thing she wanted. "But don't think this is the end of this conversation. I'll text you about Halloween."

Though she wanted to hug him again, she settled for a handshake and slipped around the corner and back inside, pretending she wasn't burning with heat after that minimal contact.

Simmons was waiting for her, leaning one hip against her desk as she sat. "You seemed friendly with Mr. Nakamura."

Allie shrugged. "He's a nice guy. We were talking about, uh, similar interests."

"I don't tolerate interoffice romances, as they put my employees' safety at risk."

A buzzing filled Allie's ears, and she looked up at Simmons expecting to see anger or frustration. But he looked worried. Did that mean he was worried about *her* safety? Given the age, gender, and marital status of the rest of the office, that concern didn't really apply to anyone else.

She had to respond, but she wasn't sure what to say. "I have no plans to date Mr. Nakamura." Especially now. "But does that mean you're hiring him?"

Grunting, Simmons turned to go back to his office but paused. "Well, most likely. If his chapters are good."

Which meant *Allie* needed to make sure the chapters were good. She had the storyline all set up for her, so all she had to do was write it well, and then she could prove to Simmons that she was worth it. Even if she was a woman.

"You won't be disappointed," she said, and she very much hoped she was right.

NINETEEN

Cam: Are you working Satan's Pit today? I didn't see you
all weekend so I hope not.
Ben: I have the whole week off.
Cam: Wow. Autocorrect really did a number on that one.
Ben: I actually meant it. I'll tell you about it later. What's
up?
Cam: Kit's at school and I need someone to talk to.
Climb?

Ben glanced at his watch, but that hardly made a difference. He didn't have anything to do, and Allie would be at
work until five. For the first time in… He shuddered as he did
the math. For the first time in twelve years, he had seven
straight days to do with what he wanted. No managing teenage employees who hid behind the windmill on the golf course
to be on their phone or makeout with a coworker. No naked
children running through the obstacle course. No frazzled
parents begging him to find a way to make sure none of the
kids knew the birthday clown they'd hired had shown up completely drunk.

Ben had been a stand-in clown more than once, and he'd
gotten surprisingly good at balloon animals.

Ben: That sounds great. I'll just stop at home and grab my
gear.

Cam: Already got it. And a change of clothes. Did you go
shopping or have you been holding out on your
wardrobe all this time?
Ben: You went through my clothes?
Cam: Meet you in twenty?

Ben sighed and typed out an affirmative. Sometimes he still wondered how he and Cam ended up living together. Ben got along with all the Wonder Boys, but Cam had been the last addition, back when they were thirteen. And where Ben was fairly reserved, Cam was…not. With his inability to lie, sometimes he was brutally honest, and he was never afraid to say what was on his mind. Outside of Oliver, Cam was the most confident person Ben knew, and if he felt like he couldn't wait a few hours for Kit to finish teaching to talk to someone, it had to be a big deal.

At least Ben would get to do some climbing because of the impending conversation.

By the time Ben reached the climbing gym, Cam was pacing out front. That made Ben even more nervous about what was going on, but he accepted the duffel Cam shoved into his arms and promised to change quickly. Considering how seldom he got to be helpful to his friends, he was eager to step up to the plate.

"How about some bouldering first," Cam suggested once Ben returned from the locker room. He led the way without waiting for an answer. Thankfully, Ben didn't mind, but he couldn't help but wonder if that was how Allie's life had been. Had she been stuck following the whims of someone more assertive than her?

Since it was the middle of the day on a weekday, the gym was fairly empty, and they had the bouldering wall to themselves. It looked like they'd added some new routes since the last time he'd been here, and Ben eagerly chalked his hands after he slipped on his climbing shoes. He wasn't much of an athlete, but he did enjoy this chance to work his limited muscles and push himself a bit. Plus, it gave him and Cam something in common beyond their shared living space, and they had slowly grown closer over the years because of their love of climbing.

"So, what's going on?" Ben asked as he mapped out the closest route. It looked fairly straightforward, perfect for getting himself back in the groove of things.

Cam leapt up to the second hold on his side, ignoring the first completely. "I found the perfect location for my gym."

Whenever they went climbing together, Ben had to remind himself that Cam's whole job centered around fitness, so naturally his physique would reflect that. But it was hard to look at the massive muscles that popped from Cam's shoulders and not get a little jealous. Maybe, if he'd looked like Cam, Allie might have actually been interested in him.

Clearing his throat, Ben forced himself to focus on the artificial rocks in front of him. "You found a place? That sounds like good news."

One benefit to not being made of pure muscle was not having to pull as much weight; Ben caught up to Cam fairly quickly.

Cam glanced over as they arrived at the same level, shaking out one arm before he continued climbing. "You're using your arms too much," he pointed out, and then he reached up for his next hold. He missed it, though, and slipped from the wall, landing on the mat with a grunt.

Reaching the top of his route, Ben checked to make sure he was clear, then hopped back down to the ground. "Yeah, well, it's been a bit since I hit leg day."

"Why do you have the week off?" Dusting his hands with chalk, Cam moved to the next route, this time waiting for Ben so they could move upward together. "Are you actually taking a vacation?"

Ben laughed, though it broke his focus and made him fall only two holds in. He jumped back to the wall and scurried upward to keep up with his friend. "I'm surprised Kit didn't tell you. The place is covered in cockroaches, so they're fumigating this week."

The memory of all the little beetles hit him hard, and he couldn't help but imagine them coming out of the crack in the wall next to him. He slipped, missed his landing, and ended up flat on his back on the padded mat.

Snickering, Cam finished his route before he jumped down and sat next to him. "Were you the one who discovered them?"

There weren't even any bugs around, and Ben was sweating. *Ridiculous.* Nodding, he sat up and wiped his forehead with his sleeve. "I brought Allie in to play laser tag, and I was on the floor when the lights came on."

"What were you doing on the floor? Wait—Allie? Is that Grocery Girl?" Cam's eyebrows wiggled. "What were you doing on the floor, Benjamin?"

Ben shoved him. "Get your mind out of the gutter, Cam. We knocked into each other at the end of the game."

"Second date, though. That's promising."

Suddenly Ben wished he had thought this through and made a plan with Allie. He didn't want to lie to his friends, but he also didn't want them to tell him he was making a mistake by thinking this whole pretend thing was healthy. Would she be okay with pretending in front of his friends? She'd done it with Kit.

"What's going on with the place you found?" Ben asked. Not the most subtle change in subject, but after spending a weekend with Allie, Ben was realizing how difficult it was to talk to his friends. He'd always been quiet and more on the awkward side of things, but he wondered if it had always been this bad. It was so easy with Allie that the contrast settled heavy on his chest.

Cam sighed, leaning back on his white-dusted hands. For the first time in a long time, he seemed content to just sit there and talk. Usually he filled all his time with something physical, whether lifting weights or doing jumping jacks or deep cleaning the apartment. To see Cam sit still was nothing short of disconcerting, and Ben didn't know what to do. This was Kit's arena, not his.

Ben nudged him. "You said you needed someone to talk to. So talk."

"Someone else has put an offer down." He said it so quickly that Ben could barely understand him. "So I put in a counteroffer. And so did they. And it's been this back-and-forth bidding war for two days, and I'm not sure I can go any higher."

Ben cringed. It was worse than he thought, mostly because he was in no position to offer advice when it came to money. As nice as this week off was going to be, it also meant a week without pay. O'Reilly didn't offer paid time or benefits, seeing as he mostly employed high school students, and Ben barely made enough to cover things as it was.

"Have you talked to Oliver?" he suggested, though he knew Cam wouldn't like that. Oliver, at least, knew what it took to start a business since he'd done exactly that when they were in college. Besides, he was crazy rich after selling said company, and he was basically set for life. If anyone understood good money management, it was him.

The problem, though, was the fact that Cam and Oliver had never gotten along well. If they had, Oliver probably would have joined them on their climbs whenever they did this.

Oliver had known Kit longer than anyone, but Cam and Kit shared a deep bond after getting into a fight when they first met. It was always a constant battle to be first in line for Kit's affection for those two, and the only reason they tolerated each other was for the sake of the rest of the gang. Madi and Kit, in particular.

"He could probably help if you need to put in a higher bid," Ben added.

Cam groaned and fell onto his back. "He's already fronting the down payment because I made the mistake of mentioning to Madi how that would be the hardest part after getting my business loan. No way am I asking Mr. Perfect for more."

Maybe it was because of all the time he'd spent with Allie, but instead of keeping his question to himself like he usually would, Ben asked, "Why don't you like Oliver?"

Cam was quiet for so long that Ben almost thought he hadn't actually said his question out loud. But then he sat up and fixed his gaze on Ben, his eyebrows low. "I like Oliver. You think I don't like him? Wait, does everyone think that? Does *Oliver*—"

"Calm down." Ben punched Cam's arm—that was the only thing that really worked on him. "I only meant you guys aren't super close. I've just never known why." He had his suspicions, though. Kit was a good friend to all of them, but by technicality he could only have one *best* friend. Cam didn't have anyone except the aunt who raised him, and knowing Oliver would always have the top spot in Kit's life couldn't have been easy on him.

Cam let out another sigh, looking pretty stressed for a guy who had both the brains and brawn to live a pretty easy life. Not that Ben blamed him for being on edge. Starting his own business was probably more stressful than anything he'd ever done.

"You're gonna make me say it, aren't you?" Cam muttered.

Ben grinned. He had never been the pushy one in his life, but he was glad Cam thought he *could* be. "You don't have to tell me if you don't want to. But I know how Oliver can be, so I get it."

"He just has it so easy, you know?"

"Are you guys bouldering?" someone asked, interrupting what would have been Ben's agreement.

Both of them glanced up at the woman who scowled down at them. Ben felt immediate guilt for sitting in the way and hopped up. So did Cam, but he grinned at the girl and definitely took his time getting to his feet, flexing everything as he did. He looked ridiculous.

Ben really hoped he'd never accidentally done anything like that with Allie. Doubtful, since he didn't have the muscle to flex in the first place.

"Sorry," Cam said, brushing chalk from his hands. "Sometimes you've got to have a heart-to-heart, if you know what I mean."

The woman rolled her eyes and started braiding her long, dark hair. "Don't even start," she said. "I'm just here to climb."

Cam wasn't deterred. "You need someone to belay, beautiful? I've got you covered. I promise I won't let you fall."

Ben wished he had telepathic powers so he could silently apologize for Cam. As it was, he hoped he had enough skepticism in his expression for the woman to know he didn't condone idiocy just because a pretty girl was around. And she *was* pretty, though not to Allie's level. She just happened to be Polynesian and incredibly fit, the combination of which was Cam's kryptonite; he only ever acted this stupid when he was good and truly attracted to someone.

Plus, Cam hadn't been in a relationship for several months, and he was due for another temporary girlfriend. Ben hadn't realized until now how similar he and Allie were in that regard.

The woman sighed and glanced at the tall wall, as if considering his offer. "I'm good," she said eventually, and then she turned her gaze to Ben. "I think your friend is ready to go."

Based on the ice in her words, Ben knew she wasn't really suggesting, and he grabbed Cam's shoulder. "I think you're right. Sorry we were in the way."

Thankfully, Cam didn't resist when Ben led him over to the taller walls that required ropes and harnesses, though he walked backward and kept his eyes on the boulder wall. Otherwise, Ben would have had to get in between him and the woman who could probably pack a pretty decent punch, based on the size of her shoulders. Though smaller than Cam—most people were—she could still give him a run for his money, and Ben had no desire to get in the middle of that.

It would be like trying to get between two fighting dogs, but one of them was fighting for affection while the other was in it for the kill.

Once they reached a route that was challenging enough for Cam but not so difficult that Ben wouldn't be able to do it, they both started strapping in to the rope. As always, Cam would climb first so he could offer suggestions to Ben, but for the first time in his life, Ben was tempted to suggest they switch it up and he go up blind. The challenge might actually be nice for once, and he was feeling more confident than usual after that meeting with Allie's boss.

But Cam was already tied in, so maybe Ben would do it on the next route.

"I was an idiot, wasn't I?"

The question came out of nowhere, and Ben dropped the rope before he'd managed to slide it into his belay device. He wanted to give an honest answer, but he wasn't sure Cam was ready to hear it.

Cam must have seen something in Ben's face, because he groaned. "Why do I always do that?"

"It's not always," Ben argued. "You talk to plenty of girls without turning into a jerk."

"But not the beautiful ones." His eyes traced the woman as she scaled the boulder wall with ease. "Man, why do girls like that never come into the gym? It's like they were *born* strong."

Ben chuckled. "You do realize there are dozens of gyms in this city, right?"

He wondered if Allie would ever want to get into working out, or if she was content as she was. It wasn't like she needed it, but… Maybe he would suggest a session with Cam, just in case she decided she liked the endorphins. Maybe he could even bring her rock climbing and give himself another excuse to be around her. Or maybe she would laugh at the thought and suggest they binge watch her favorite TV show while eating whole pints of ice cream.

Ben would take whatever he could get and be happy.

Still watching the woman on the other side of the gym, Cam took a breath, then let his shoulders fall with the exhale. "Do you ever think we're missing out on something, and Madi and Oliver are the smart ones?"

Without question. "We just haven't found the right people yet," Ben muttered.

"Maybe you have. You've been after this girl for months, and it sounds like things are going well."

They were going somewhere, that was certain, but Ben wasn't sure he would like the end result as much as he hoped. He reminded himself what Madi had told him about friendships, and it was enough to help him manage a smile. "We'll see," he said, and then he nodded toward the wall. "Are you going to climb, or what?"

TWENTY

ALLIE HAD ALWAYS THOUGHT SHE was an extrovert, always wanting to be around someone else until exhaustion sent her to bed, but after a few days with Ben, she realized she had gotten things wrong. She was outgoing, not extroverted, and all of her boyfriends had always been the reason she ended each day so tired that she fell asleep instantly. As it turned out, Allie was an *introvert*, and that explained why she'd had so much energy over the last few months of being single.

She had credited it to her higher intake of ice cream and the sugars that came with it, but she'd realized the inaccuracy of that assessment when she went the whole weekend without ice cream but still had plenty of energy.

Ben—wonderful Ben—didn't drain her like everyone else did. Being around him simply made her happy, and she'd never been so determined to be around a person before. She didn't find excuses to have a night to herself, which by itself was a strange sensation, and every time he showed up at her apartment after she finished her workday, the day got so much brighter.

The best part, though, was when she told herself she had to sit down and write those chapters for Simmons. Any of her past boyfriends, even the nicer ones, would have guilt-tripped her into giving them the attention they "deserved" and told her she should have done that while she was at work or after they left for the night.

But Ben? Wednesday night, Ben brought over a smorgasbord of snacks so she could figure out what her favorites were, and then he grabbed her laptop and favorite blanket for her and settled next to her on the tiny couch with a book.

"If I'm distracting you at all," he told her, "send me home. I'm sick of staring at my own walls, but I can go to a park or something if you need the space."

And while he had definitely been distracting, Allie had refused to send him away. She liked having him around because he made everything so easy. Maybe they hadn't known each other long, but Ben had definitely become her best friend.

Allie had never had a best friend before—not since Jake, at least—and she absolutely loved it. It was something she could get used to.

When Halloween rolled around on Thursday, Allie was just finishing up the last chapter to send to Simmons when Ben knocked on the door. She hopped up, way more excited to be going trick-or-treating than she'd expected, and had a full-blown grin on her face when she pulled open the door.

"Hey—Jake?"

Jake raised an eyebrow, and his smile as he glanced into the empty apartment behind her made it clear he'd been hoping to find her alone. "Hey," he said, sliding his hands into his pockets as if nervous. Once upon a time, Allie had loved that little gesture, but now she thought it looked far too contrived to be a true indication of shyness. If he was showing up here uninvited, Jake definitely wasn't shy.

Glancing at her watch, Allie hoped Ben would be late for the first time ever. Not that it mattered if he saw Jake here, but she wanted to avoid the inevitable awkwardness that would come if those two met again. "What are you doing here?"

"Can I come in?"

"Now's not a good—"

"That's okay. Mostly, I just wanted to ask if you wanted to come to a Halloween party with me."

Caught off guard, Allie couldn't think of anything to say to that for a second. The only thing that even came to mind was, "But you're not wearing a costume."

As if he'd expected her to say something like that, he pulled two little paper signs out of his pocket that said 'Nudist on Strike' and grinned as if he thought himself the cleverest person in the world. "I know you don't like to dress up anyway, so I figured I would make it easy on you."

It was at that moment, when she felt nothing but disappointment, that Allie realized she really *did* like dressing up for Halloween. She'd been excited all day to see what Ben brought her—she didn't have anything of her own to wear as a costume—and Jake's idea of a costume was entirely lame.

Oh right. Ben. "That's really nice of you, Jake, but I'm doing something with Ben tonight."

"So that's still a thing?"

Seriously? "Why are you so surprised?"

"Because you said you were done with dating, so I figured—"

"So you figured you would ask me out?" Groaning, Allie dropped her head against the door frame and tried to figure out why no one believed a word she said. They didn't believe she didn't want to date, and they didn't think she was actually dating Ben, and they clearly had no idea what she even wanted because they showed up with absolutely awful costumes and thought a party was exactly the thing she would want to go to.

Thank goodness for Ben, who was a better friend to her than anyone ever had been.

"So…" Jake pulled his other hand free and reached out, as if hoping to take her hand, but he put it back into his pocket when Allie just stared at it. "I'm guessing that means you don't want to go to the party with me?"

At what point could Allie declare the man a complete idiot and send him off to the loony bin? Well, that was being a bit harsh. He really was a nice guy, but his persistence seemed to get worse each time they ran into each other. What would it take to get him off her back? Marriage to someone else?

Sighing, she shook her head and hoped she could be as clear as possible. "Jake, I know what I told you a few weeks ago, but that was before I got together with Ben. My *boyfriend*. So no, I'm not going to ditch him just to go to a party with a bunch of people I don't know."

"That's a relief."

The quiet voice behind Jake made him turn, and Allie's first reaction was to scream. Not with fear but with delight.

Ben looked *amazing*. Everything about his costume was homemade, from the tight green shirt and pants that showed off his muscles to the painted disk sled shell on his back. He wore the orange mask of Michelangelo and carried some dollar store nunchucks, and he held a second shell plus a bag that hopefully contained Allie's costume.

Jake, on the other hand, looked like he'd been slapped in the face. Apparently, he still hadn't believed what Allie told him, and seeing Ben standing there had caught him by surprise.

"Jake, right?" Ben tucked his nunchucks under his arm and held out his hand. "Good to see you again."

Jake moved so slowly that Allie wondered if he'd gone into shock. "Hi," he said, and Allie could have sworn he gripped Ben's hand way tighter than he needed to. "Nice, uh, costume. Too bad this one doesn't like to dress up, huh?"

When he jerked his thumb in her direction, anger shot through Allie and propelled her forward. Snatching the bag and sled, she planted a kiss on Ben's cheek and said, "I'll go get changed," before either of them could continue the ridicu-lous conversation. At least, not when she was around. She went straight to the bathroom and changed as quickly as she could, unwilling to leave them alone for too long. She didn't think Ben would do anything stupid, but it had been a long time since she was around Jake for longer than an hour or two. Who knew what stupid idea he might cook up?

Thankfully, everything fit her pretty well, so it only took her a few minutes before she was back at the door, her blue mask in her teeth as she pulled her hair back into a ponytail. Jake gave her a sweeping glance but seemed more confused than anything, and Ben… Heat shot through Allie when she saw his expression, and yet again she reconsidered her stance on dating. Even if he only wanted to be her friend, he still appreciated her costume to the point that his jaw literally dropped, leaving him speechless.

"Oh," Allie said, a little breathless herself, "are you still here, Jake? I thought you were going to a party."

The longer he looked at her, the more confused he became, and eventually Jake shook his head and cleared his throat, as if he'd been as blown away as Ben but wasn't as obvious about it. "Clearly you're going to a party already."

Once she had her mask firmly in place, Allie reached out her hand and breathed a sigh of relief when Ben took it without hesitation. They hadn't had to do any dating-like things for more than a week and a half, and she was glad he was still willing to go along with the plan.

"Actually, we're taking Ben's nephews trick-or-treating tonight."

Jake snorted a laugh but realized pretty quickly she wasn't joking. "*You're* going trick-or-treating?" he asked. His eyes lingered on Allie's hand entwined with Ben's, as if he still couldn't quite believe they were dating.

Thankfully, Ben recognized that as well and slid his arm around her waist to pull her close. "I did try to let her out of it," he said, and Allie was pretty sure that was his way of giving her one more chance to change her mind.

Maybe she might have, if Ben hadn't brushed a kiss against her neck below her ear. She shivered, wondering how he knew the exact spot to make her melt, like she had a button right there that said, "Touch here to make me love you." For a guy who claimed he didn't date much, he was really good at it.

Jake cleared his throat. "Well, I guess I should be on my way then."

Allie fought to focus on anything other than every place Ben touched. "It was good to see you, Jake. Tell your dad hi for me."

Though he lingered a second longer, Jake eventually sighed and wandered off to the stairs, letting Allie breathe again. Of all the boyfriends she'd had over the years, Jake had probably been the best, but she didn't like how little he listened to her now that she was finally making choices for herself. He probably thought he knew her better than she knew herself; that had been the case back in the day. But now?

Now Allie knew she wanted nothing more than to spend the evening as a crime-fighting turtle with Ben and his nephews.

"You okay?" Ben's eyes searched Allie's, and when his arm around her waist pulled her closer against his side, she shivered again. For him, it was probably just a gesture of strength, but Allie was quickly realizing just how much she liked being in this man's arms. "If you'd rather go to the party with Jake, I can—"

"Why would I want to do that?"

Ben winced. "Because you're crying."

Oh goodness, she *was* crying! How embarrassing. At least she'd already told him how easily her emotions leaked out, but she had no idea what had spiked enough to spill from her eyes this time. Overwhelm? Exhaustion? Sheer bliss because of Ben's fingers pressed against her ribcage? Pushing her mask up so she could wipe her eyes, Allie shrugged and dropped her head against Ben's shoulder.

"Sometimes there's just no explanation for the water works," she said, though she doubted that would satisfy him. Watchdog the Wonder Boy probably knew there was a lot more to her tears than she was willing to admit.

Perhaps a change of subject was in order. Tonight was supposed to be a fun night. "By the way, I think I've finished those chapters for you to send to Sweet Red."

Thankfully, Ben's eyes brightened at that announcement, and she silently thanked his enthusiasm. No one else in her life would get this excited over something that technically wouldn't affect them. "You did? Can I read them?"

Sudden fear gripped Allie's heart. She wasn't afraid of critique in general—courtesy of her very blunt classmates giving feedback in college—but Ben's opinion mattered to her way more than it should. "What, now?"

"What if you drive over so I can read them on the way? We're meeting my mom and the boys over in Aspen Heights."

Boy, was she getting emotional whiplash tonight. It seemed everything Ben said or did caught her by surprise. "*Aspen Heights*? Like, that uber-rich neighborhood on the north end of town? Is that where your parents live?"

Chuckling, Ben grabbed Allie's purse and keys from the hook just inside and locked her apartment door for her. "No, that's where *Oliver* lives."

"That doesn't surprise me at all." Already missing Ben's touch, Allie led the way down to the parking lot, telling herself over and over again that everything Ben did was for show and she should be grateful he was even willing to be a little bit physical. Given what she knew of him now, she knew he was incredibly intentional with everything he did and wasn't the type of person who did anything without knowing what it might mean. He wouldn't hold her hand just because, and he wouldn't kiss her neck if he didn't think it would help her case with Jake.

So when Ben put his hand on her shoulder as he followed her to her car, Allie had no idea what to make of that. "My nephews wanted to go where the good candy was," he said, "and they're impossible to say no to. You're lucky they wanted to be Donatello and Rafael, or you would have had to give up your double-sword dream."

He handed her the keys, which Allie took with hesitation. Not because she didn't want to drive but because she knew what the question in his eyes meant.

She sighed. "Yes, you can read the chapters," she said, though reluctantly. "But if you hate them, you *have* to tell me. I can't send in anything bad, or they're never going to promote me to be a writer. Even if they think you wrote it." She almost couldn't picture Ben being that brutally honest, though. He was always so nice, and while he would definitely be the kind of guy who gave good suggestions, he would never tell her if the whole thing was crap.

Pursing his lips, he folded his arms and suddenly looked way stronger than normal thanks to his skin-tight shirt. Maybe he wasn't a bodybuilder, but the man definitely did some kind of physical work. It couldn't be from his job, so Allie wondered where he got that muscle. His personal trainer roommate, probably. But she'd seen pictures of Cam, who was huge, so Ben definitely had a different routine. Allie couldn't see Ben's abs beneath the sewn-on turtle shell fabric on his belly, but something told her they were probably there in ample supply. Maybe she could feel them…

"Do you really think your writing is that bad?" Ben asked.

Allie withdrew her hand only inches from touching him. *Behave yourself, Allison.* "I mean, I thought the chapters were pretty good when I read through them, but—"

"Then I'm sure they're great. You're always going to be your worst critic, and you see everything from a much closer view than everyone else will. So if you think they're decent, then they're probably fantastic." He pulled his head down into his shoulders a little, giving her an adorably sheepish grin. "I still want to read them, though. And I'll have to send them to the editors eventually, so it's just a matter of whether I read them now or later."

Groaning, Allie stuffed her phone into his hands and unlocked the car. "Just... Don't make any comments until you're all the way through, okay? I'm going to focus on the road and pretend you're not there."

Pretending Ben wasn't just a few inches away from her and reading her work required her to blast Justin Bieber at full volume so she could sing along. Not that she liked his songs or was even great at singing, but it was the best way to distract herself until she turned into the first street of the Aspen Heights subdivision and pulled up to the curb of a house that could have fit at least six of her parents' house inside. She'd come to this neighborhood once in high school, when Jake got them invited to a party at the end of their senior year, but she'd been so focused on Jake that she hadn't really paid attention to the neighborhood.

The street looked like the idyllic suburban dream, complete with the most vividly colorful fall leaves she'd ever seen. It was like she pulled into a movie set instead of real life.

As she slipped out of her car, she shook her head at the nature-beautified mansions surrounding them. "How does anyone even use this much space?" she muttered. Sure, she wouldn't mind having money, but she definitely wouldn't spend it on a house with twelve bedrooms.

Home theater? Yes. Indoor basketball court? Definitely not.

As Ben finally stepped out of the car, still reading her pages, Allie pulled close to his side so she didn't feel so small compared to everything.

He chuckled without looking up. "Yeah, I feel the same way every time I come over this way."

"Wait, you said Oliver lives *here*?"

Ben nodded toward a house at the far end of the street, one that was loaded with so many Halloween decorations that she could barely see the house itself. "Fair warning, Oliver *loves* Halloween, and so does Madi. They always chose our costumes every year, even when we weren't dressing up together as a group thing. Just wait until you see their costumes this year."

Allie gulped. She hadn't realized she would be meeting Ben's friends tonight, and she wasn't sure how to feel about that. "Do they know about us?" she asked, grabbing hold of his arm for some support.

Without hesitating, he slid his arm around her again, making their sled-shells bump together. He was still reading, but it looked like he was almost to the end. "Madi knows the truth. Oliver thinks we're actually dating. Well, he knows we've been on *a* date. I haven't told any of them about the others."

Other dates? As far as Allie knew, their dinner date at her parents was their only fake date. What was he talking about? All the times they'd been hanging out? Those definitely weren't dates. Allie had been adamant that they weren't dates. They were just friends hanging out. "What do—"

"Als, this is really good!" His eyes wide, Ben handed her phone back to her and gave her a grin, but he didn't seem to be really looking at her. His gaze was distant, like he was still in the story, and she wondered if he had even realized what he'd said a moment ago about their dates. Maybe he hadn't meant it like it sounded.

In the strangest way, Allie wished he had. If he saw their time together as dates, maybe they could be more than friends. Maybe...

No. She mentally slapped herself, considered *actually* slapping herself, and pulled away from Ben to give them some distance. This was exactly what she was hoping to avoid, and she couldn't fantasize about what it would be like to date Ben when she'd been doing so well. She wasn't ready. Not yet. She needed more time to discover herself so she didn't get lost again.

"Allie, did you hear me?"

She blinked. "What?"

"I said you have a way with creating real characters that stand out on the page. I could practically see them while I was reading, and it was like the story was playing out right in front of me."

Cursing herself for getting so lost in her head, Allie forced a smile and hoped it was believable. "You really think so?"

Ben grinned, back to the present again and looking at her like she was something he'd never seen before. It would have made her blush if she didn't feel so nauseous. "If Simmons and the editors don't hire you on," he said, "they're idiots, and you're better off without them."

She knew she had to stick to her guns on her no dating rule, but the tears in her eyes were a clear sign of just how much she didn't want to. She'd known this man for a few weeks—they'd only been friends for a week and a half at most—but she knew she wanted to keep him in her life for as long as she possibly could. But on the rare chance he decided he didn't want to stay friends, could she really keep stringing him along? For now, things were all good, but what happened when he changed his mind?

And he *would* change his mind. It wasn't conceit; Allie knew she was so far beneath him. But they would never just be friends. That never happened. Allie was proof of that, even if she wouldn't act on her growing feelings. Either he would want more out of their relationship, or he would move on. This wasn't the sort of thing they could drag on forever and be content.

When Ben put his hands on her shoulders, Allie's tears got even worse, and she fell into his arms. He would ask what was wrong, and she would have to tell him *something* because he was way too smart to believe it if she told him she was fine. Crying twice in one night wasn't coincidence.

"No one's ever talked to me like that before," she said into his shoulder. It wasn't a lie, at least. Ben's critique on her writing was so unlike any of her peers or professors, and she hadn't realized how desperately she wanted someone to tell her that she could do something. Her. *Allie*. Without anyone else. Despite being on her own for almost four months now, she'd never actually felt capable until Ben told her she was.

He tightened his hold beneath her shell, blocking out the rest of the world and pressing his cheek against the side of her head. "It probably sounded like I was exaggerating, but I promise I wasn't. You were made to tell that story, Als."

"I like when you call me that." She also liked hearing the rumble of his voice through her ear against his neck, but she wasn't about to tell him that. Especially because his heart was pounding way faster than it would for someone totally unaffected by their closeness right now. Even if it wasn't to the same level that she felt, maybe Ben saw her as more than just a friend too.

She wasn't sure how to feel about that.

Eventually, though Allie wasn't sure how long they'd stood there on the parking strip of grass next to the sidewalk, Ben pulled away and brushed his thumbs against her cheeks to dry her tears. "Are you sure you're up for trick-or-treating? My nephews can be a lot. I'd be fine to take them on my own, and my mom could give me a ride back to—"

Allie grabbed his hand, suppressing a smile when that shut him up immediately. "I've been looking forward to this all week," she told him. "You're not taking this away from me."

His shoulders dropped in relief, bringing out one of his breathtaking smiles and those beautiful dimples. "Good, because—"

"COWABUNGA!"

Something slammed into Allie's hip, pushing her into Ben, and another force knocked them both to the leaf-strewn ground. Ben landed first, Allie on top of him, and a loud crack echoed against the giant house next to them. Ignoring the fact that she'd somehow landed lip to lip with Ben—more painful than it sounded—Allie scrambled off of him just before two matching Ninja Turtles dive bombed the guy.

Groaning, Ben wrapped an arm around each boy and somehow managed to pin them to his sides, even though they put up a pretty good fight to get free. "Hunter, Isaac, the Ninja Turtles don't fight each other. They only fight bad guys."

He looked like he'd just been hit by a train, and Allie couldn't help but laugh. "Need some help there, Michelangelo?" She grabbed hold of the nearest boy, who looked to be about seven, and was glad when he stopped struggling so he could stare at her. "What was that cracking sound?"

Ben grunted again as he sat up with the smaller of the two boys still tucked against his side. He glanced behind him. "That was either my spine or my shell. My money's on the spine."

"It's just your shell, Uncle Ben!" The little one put on an impressive pout as he met Ben's gaze. "Sorry for breaking it. Maybe Gramma has some glue."

"Gramma's already gone," the older said, still fixated on Allie. Had he even blinked yet? "You're really pretty."

Ben chuckled at the same time Allie blushed. "Hunter, that's my friend, Allie. Allie, this is Hunter and Isaac."

"I'm older," Hunter said and puffed out his chest. He and his brother both wore matching turtle costumes, though their shells were a good deal smaller.

Allie had to bite her lips to keep from laughing. "I can tell," she said, as soon as she knew she wouldn't bust up. "It's very nice to meet you, Hunter."

Still a little starstruck, or whatever it was, Hunter blinked a couple of times, then finally got to his feet and grabbed hold of Ben's hand. "We gotta go! All the good candy will be gone!"

Ben definitely moved a little stiffly as he stood, though he put on a smile. Allie had seen his real smile, so she knew when he was masking something deeper.

"Are you really hurt?" she asked, quietly enough that the boys wouldn't hear as they hurried up the steps of the closest house.

Ben rolled his shoulders, testing their movement. "I think I'm in better shape than my shell."

The shell was nearly in two complete pieces, held together by the top ring of plastic but nothing else. Allie was afraid to touch it, even though she wanted to move it to make sure Ben hadn't actually injured himself in the fall.

She opted for a different route, one that didn't involve touching him. "Sorry for falling on you. And, uh…" She resisted the urge to touch her mouth. It hadn't exactly been a kiss, but her mouth had definitely been on his.

And his lips were *soft*. She wanted to explore them more, see if they really were that soft or if they had just felt that way because her chin hitting his had been especially solid and hard. Either way, her little sample had made her want to order the full entree and devour that mouth of his.

Stop thinking about his lips!

Ben adjusted his mask, pulling it a little lower over his red cheekbones. "Don't worry about it," he said.

As the boys rang the doorbell and shouted, "Trick-or-treat!" when the door opened, Allie silently repeated her vow to remain single. Again. And again. She would probably have to keep repeating it the rest of the night, and she hoped she would make it through. A little time and distance would be good for her, even if she didn't want it. Good for both of them since Ben hadn't exactly told her he was interested in that way. But before she could get some distance, she had to make it through tonight.

When the boys came crashing back into them with full-size candy bars in tow, Ben sent her a subtle smile that made her chest burn, and Allie knew making it through the night was going to be a lot harder than she hoped.

TWENTY-ONE

DON'T THINK ABOUT KISSING HER. Do not *think about kissing her. You're definitely thinking about kissing her, and you have to stop. Stop it. Stop!*

It wasn't working. No matter how many times Ben told himself to think about something—anything—else, all he could think about was Allie's mouth landing on his when they fell. He couldn't call what had happened a kiss, but that didn't change the fact that now he almost knew how she tasted, and all he wanted to do was find out for sure.

He was glad his nephews had both taken a shine to Allie and decided she was their new favorite person; it meant they got her full attention as they made their way through the neighborhood. It meant Ben could follow behind them and repeat his silent mantra without having to check his expression except when Allie glanced back to make sure he was still there.

He wouldn't be anywhere else.

That was the problem.

He'd thought he was in love with Allie at the thrift store on Sunday, but that had been nothing compared to this. It was only four days later, but those four days had felt like a lifetime. Spending every evening with Allie this week had reminded him of his junior high days, when he would go over to Kit's house after school every day and hang out with Madi. When

Kit and Oliver were busy playing their video games or basketball outside, Ben had helped Madi with her homework or worked on his while she read a book. They'd often done their own thing, but being around another person had made it more comfortable for both of them.

They just…vibed.

It was the same with Allie. Only, Ben had never wanted to kiss Madi.

"I seriously can't get over how cute your nephews are," Allie said, bringing Ben's head snapping up from where he'd been staring at his feet. She grinned at him, clearly loving everything about the evening, and he wished he could do the same.

"You should see them when they're not getting pounds of candy," he said, forcing a smile. "They're nightmares."

Allie frowned. "How's your back doing?"

He was so glad he had the excuse of pain keeping his smile from being real. Honestly, the sled-turned-shell had taken the brunt of their fall, so he was only a little bruised. He couldn't tell her why he was really miserable, so it was nice to have something to fall back on. Literally.

"I'll live," he said. "Makes me wonder if the Turtles stopped fighting after they got old, though. There's a reason you don't see the Middle-Aged Mutant Ninja Turtles."

Allie giggled. "Well, at that point Shredder would be geriatric, so it makes sense! No one wants to see that fight."

Ben almost groaned, barely managing to hold it back. How was it he had found the perfect woman, and she was the only woman who didn't want to date him? "That would be the most boring fight in the history of comics," he said.

"Oliver's house!" Hunter took off running toward the faux cemetery up ahead, Isaac right behind him.

Ben gritted his teeth. He was eager for Madi to meet Allie, but not so much for Oliver. He still hadn't decided if he wanted to tell his friend the truth, and he was going to have to pick in the next two minutes. On the one hand, if he told Oliver that their relationship was all fake, Oliver would joke about how he knew where that would lead. He would be wrong. On the other hand, if Ben pretended Allie was his girlfriend, Oliver would make a big deal out of him actually committing to someone rather than letting Allie down easy after their first date.

No matter what he did, Oliver would turn it into a joke, and Ben wished his friend could take things seriously for once. For the genius that he was, Oliver could be pretty clueless about other people and what mattered to them.

"Are you ready to meet Wonder Woman herself?" Ben asked as they approached the door. The boys had gotten into an argument over who got to pull the old-fashioned electrical switch that had replaced the doorbell for the night, so the door hadn't opened yet.

Though she bit her lip and looked a bit nervous, Allie nodded. "Madi sounds awesome, and it'll be fun to see how Oliver has changed. I wonder if he'll recognize me."

"I don't know," Ben muttered, though what he really wanted to say was, "You'd be impossible to forget if he saw you the way I do." That would be coming on too strong and the opposite of sticking to friendship. Besides, he was a bit distracted by the way she kept biting her lip; he wanted to take over and do it for her.

Hands to yourself, Nakamura.

The boys decided to pull the switch together, and a ridiculous clanging sounded from inside the house. It was bad enough that the yard looked like a movie set from a horror film, but did they really have to go and change their entire doorbell? They'd only bought the house a month ago. At least it jarred Ben out of his imagination, which had been pulling him down a path he probably shouldn't go, and he braced himself for utter ridiculousness on the other side.

The door opened in a puff of smoke—they literally had a smoke machine in the front room—and from it emerged Superman himself. From the artificially dark hair to the suit to the cape, everything looked silver screen worthy. Oliver even had the winning smile to go with it. And while he probably had a practiced response to the chime of "trick-or-treat," the instant he caught sight of Ben standing behind the boys, Oliver's smile dropped at the same time as the bowl of candy in his hands.

"*Ben?* What are you—" His eyes landed on Allie as the boys wasted no time in scooping all of the fallen candy into their bags, and a ridiculous grin spread across his face the longer he stared at her. "What do we have here?"

Ben pressed his palm into his face, wishing he had told Oliver the truth days ago. He wasn't sure if that was the best option now, though. He took a deep breath, though he knew that wouldn't help him sound any less mumbly. "Oliver, I'd like you to meet Allie. My…girlfriend."

Allie glanced at him, but luckily she held her hand out to grasp Oliver's. "Hey. Ben's told me a lot about you."

"I know you from somewhere," Oliver replied. "Where'd you go to school?"

Her eyebrows lifting, Allie flashed him a smile that made Ben jealous even though it shouldn't have. It wasn't like she was flirting with Oliver, but that didn't mean he wanted her smiling at anyone but him.

Get a grip, Ben. Even if you were a real couple, she could smile at whomever she wanted.

"Jefferson State. Is that why you look familiar?"

"You dated Hammond, didn't you? The quarterback?"

"For a little bit."

Oliver looked more than amused, his grin comically big as he folded his arms and looked her over. "What are the odds?" he muttered. "Hey Mads! You'd better come see who's at the door."

Madi materialized out of the smoke in her own superhero costume, and Allie's gasp was a pretty good assessment of her stunning outfit. "Ben! It's so good to see you! And you must be Allie." She pulled Allie into a tight hug that squeezed the air out of her lungs—Ben heard it as much as he saw it—then helped steady her as she stepped back. "You guys look amazing! Come on in. Hunter, Isaac, I've got some hot chocolate in the kitchen if you want some."

Ben had hoped to simply say hi and continue on, but deep down he knew his friends would never let that happen. So instead of staying out in the crisp October air and keeping his head clear, he took hold of Allie's hand and stepped into the indoor fog, hoping the night wouldn't end in disaster.

As they followed Oliver back to the kitchen, Allie leaned close. "You weren't kidding about Wonder Woman. I thought that was a reference to the Wonder Boy thing."

Ben chuckled a little. "Madi has loved Wonder Woman since she was a kid, and she dresses up as her at least every other year. The costume gets better every time, though."

"She looks like she walked out of a movie. No wonder Oliver fell for her."

The boys had already settled on stools at the kitchen counter, their legs swinging as they waited for Madi to give them their favorite liquid form of sugar. Oliver took up a seat at the table with a good view of his wife, and Allie joined Madi in the kitchen, though Ben didn't know if that was by choice or because Madi decreed it.

"She's cute," Oliver said as Ben settled in a chair opposite him. "That's Grocery Girl, right?"

Ben nodded. "Things are still pretty new." *Or nonexistent.* "But we get along pretty well."

Madi laughed at something Allie said, and Ben resisted the urge to sigh with contentment at the sight of both women getting along so well. For Allie's sake. Madi, though she was never great at making friends when she was younger, could get along with anyone and make them feel special. She was very much like Kit in the way she approached people, and it had served her well in her photography business that somehow kept growing, from what Ben heard. Madi did look a bit tired, and Ben wondered if she was working a little *too* hard.

"Do you think things are getting pretty serious with you two?" Oliver asked. Thankfully, he was smart enough to keep his voice down so he wouldn't be overheard by the ladies, and it helped that Hunter and Isaac were getting louder and louder the more impatient they got.

Ben shrugged. It was the perfect chance to tell the truth, but he held back. For once, he was having a conversation with one of his friends that didn't involve convincing him to quit his job, and he didn't want to offer up any reasons to change the subject. "It's only been a couple of weeks," he said, "but I definitely like her. We have a lot of similar interests."

It was more than that, but he didn't know how to put it into words. Allie made it so easy to be himself, without living through a dozen different filters that had been in his way his whole life. A year ago, he definitely wouldn't have put on a ridiculous costume like this, and he probably wouldn't have agreed to take his nephews in the first place. He was also drawing more than ever, even if no one was holding him accountable for stretching his creative talent.

He felt alive again.

"I hope it works out for you," Oliver said, his words still soft. "I really do. You deserve someone awesome, and the fact that Madi likes Allie makes her even better, in my opinion. So maybe don't screw this up."

"I don't plan to," Ben replied. Even if he didn't know how to keep this little relationship of theirs going. He would just have to push to keep the friendship alive since that was likely where things would stay. He would be the best friend Allie ever had, and maybe then he would get to keep her.

Not a lot of people kept their childhood friends into adulthood, and Ben counted himself lucky that the five of them had stuck together like they had. Things were different, though, and they were all moving on to bigger and better things. Ben had spent a lot of time lately wondering what would happen when they all got too distant to keep things up. Madi and Oliver dating had brought the Wonder Boys back together after a bit of a rough patch, but now they were married. Eventually, they would have kids, and they wouldn't have as much time for club meetings. Cam was opening his gym, and that would keep him way busier than he'd ever been. Plus, he was moving across town, leaving Ben practically homeless until he figured out somewhere he could afford.

Life was shifting, and more than ever Ben was understanding why Kit had such a hard time with change. He was moving into unfamiliar territory, and that frightened him more than it should. Becoming friends with Allie had given him something new to hold on to, but how long would it last?

Allie laughed at something as Madi handed her a mug of hot chocolate, and Ben felt himself pulled in her direction, though he kept himself firmly planted in his seat. He needed to give her space as much as possible so she could choose him rather than let him decide her life for her, like everyone else seemed to.

He wanted so badly for her to choose him that his chest hurt, and he forced himself to focus on Madi before his heart preemptively broke. There was something different about Madi, though he couldn't quite place what it was. Beyond the superhero costume and the underlying exhaustion beneath her eyes, there was something…warm…about her.

Oliver was watching her with a dopey grin on his face, which wouldn't have been weird if it had been a smile Ben had seen before. He had known Oliver for eighteen years, and never once had he looked at someone like…

Ben's arm slid off the table as the realization hit him. "Wait, is Madi…?"

Oliver's eyes went wide. "You can't tell anyone. Did she tell you? How did you—"

"Madi's *pregnant*?"

Oliver practically jumped across the table to slap a hand over Ben's mouth, and he looked completely terrified. "No one is supposed to know," he hissed. "Not yet at least."

That didn't make any sense to Ben. Well, it didn't until he remembered who Madi's brother was. It was hard enough on Kit to watch his sister get married and move on from the way things had always been, and throwing a kid into the mix? Considering they had only been married since the end of August, that would challenge him for sure, and Ben wasn't sure Kit was ready for that.

Pulling himself free of Oliver's hold, Ben nodded. "I won't tell him."

Oliver sighed with obvious relief. "Or Cam. He wouldn't be able to keep a secret that big."

Cam couldn't keep *any* secret.

"How far along is she?" Ben asked as Oliver returned to his seat. Now that he knew, he could see Madi's little smile as she helped the boys put mini marshmallows in their hot chocolates. Like she was imagining her own kids down the road doing the same thing.

"Couple months," Oliver said, his goofy smile returning.

A honeymoon baby.

Ben had never pictured Oliver as a dad, so it surprised him how easily the image came now. Oliver would be the dad who encouraged his kids to do whatever made them happy. He would take them to soccer games and piano recitals. Teach them coding at the same time he taught them to read. He would throw the most epic birthday parties and make their lunches and be the most present dad in the world who was always there, no matter what time of day.

Those kids were never going to feel like they were lost or ignored.

"I thought I couldn't love her any more than I already did," Oliver said, his voice going reverent. "But then she told me the news a few days ago, and… Man, there's just nothing that compares to that feeling. I really hope you find that, Ben. I hope you all do." With that declaration, he stood and crossed into the kitchen with determination. He was kissing Madi even before he'd pinned her against the pantry door, and Madi definitely wasn't complaining.

As the boys made sounds of disgust, Allie giggled and covered their eyes before meeting Ben's gaze. She looked so…happy. Relaxed. Though he had no way of knowing how she felt about him unless he asked her—and that would take courage he didn't have tonight—at least he made her happy.

If they were only meant to be friends, shouldn't that be enough? Ben could love her without being in a romantic relationship with her. There were all different types of love, and the love he felt now could easily change and adapt if he willed it to. As long as he could keep her in his life in some form, that could be enough. She was good for him, and he liked to think he could be good for her.

Maybe down the road she would finally feel comfortable about who she was and would change her mind about not dating. Maybe she wouldn't. Maybe they would only ever be friends.

Ben had to be okay with that.

When the doorbell clanged and Madi and Oliver barely even paused for breath, Allie grabbed the half-full bag of candy on the counter and practically bounced toward the door. "I've always wanted to do this!" she told Ben and grabbed his hand to bring him with her.

"Trick-or-treat!" Three kids at the door held out pillowcases weighed down with candy, all of them dressed as characters from the latest teenage fantasy book craze. Ben hadn't read it, but from the look of delight on Allie's face, she had.

"Holy cow," she gasped. "You all look amazing! Are you dressed as Hawkstone? And you're the Fairy Prince! That is the best Gullbar costume I have ever seen, and don't let anyone tell you differently. I love the *Fairy Prince* books too." She dumped half the candy into their bags and squealed as they skipped away in triumph, and Ben had the sudden urge to drop to one knee.

He would work on changing his love tomorrow. Tonight, he just wanted to imagine Allie dressing up her own kids as their favorite book characters. She would be a phenomenal mom if she wanted kids, and all of her children would love reading as much as she did. He could picture her sitting in a window seat, surrounded by several little imps with books, all of them lost to the worlds inside the pages.

Ben's phone buzzed, and he reluctantly pulled his eyes away from Allie to glance at the text he'd gotten.

> Mom: I'm here to pick up the boys.
> Mom: Is that Maddy in the doorway with you? She looks different.

Ben glanced out onto the street and waved at the head-lights, even if he couldn't see the car behind them. "My mom's here to pick up the turtles," he told Allie, debating if he wanted to have the two of them meet. It would be risky, introducing someone as his girlfriend when it wasn't true, but Mom might forget after a day or two with Hunter and Isaac hopped up on sugar and tearing the house apart.

No, better to be safe.

> Ben: Yeah. I'll send the boys out.

"I'll go grab them," Allie said, though she squinted at the headlights as if hoping to catch a glimpse of his mom. Did she want to meet her? Maybe it would happen eventually, once their friendship was more established, but it would be safer to keep things compartmentalized until Ben figured out what he was doing with this relationship of theirs.

The boys must have hit their post-sugar crash as they trudged from the kitchen looking half asleep. Ben handed them their surprisingly heavy bags of candy and watched until they were safely tucked away in the car. Mom double-honked her usual goodbye and drove off, and the house was quiet.

Well, mostly quiet. Allie snickered when she realized what the muffled sounds in the kitchen were, and then she grabbed Ben's hand. "I don't want to go home yet. Want to go on a walk with me?"

Ben would have said yes no matter what she asked him. He debated calling a goodbye to the married pair, decided against it, then tugged Allie out into the cemetery yard with a smile. Tomorrow they would be friends, he reminded himself. Tonight he could pretend to be something he wasn't, and he was going to make the most of it.

TWENTY-TWO

ALLIE LOVED BEN'S FRIENDS. OLIVER was charming and funny and laid-back, the kind of guy she could picture having a barbecue at which he grilled up a mean veggie burger without judgment. And Madi was exactly the kind of girl Allie had always wanted to be friends with. Maybe she would have, if she hadn't always been friends with the guys her boyfriends hung out with. Madi was sweet and confident and ambitious, and she wasn't afraid to be herself. Even just the few minutes they'd interacted had been enough for Allie to know she wanted to keep Madi in her life.

She hadn't interacted with Kit much, but based on what Ben had said about his best friend over the last week, Allie imagined he was the steadiest person in the world who always took care of his friends. The kind of guy she could call to help with a flat tire or give her a ride to the airport. She suspected there was more to him than that, but Ben was reluctant to bring her around his friends too much.

He hadn't said that in so many words, but she'd seen his hesitation when Madi invited them into their house. He was worried about what the Wonder Boys would think about their relationship, and he probably couldn't decide if he wanted them to know the truth or not.

Honestly, Allie just loved that she could even deduce that much from him. She'd never known anyone she could actually read, and his transparency was so refreshing.

Unfortunately, it was for that reason that Allie was nervous as they walked Oliver's neighborhood. Ben had been acting different ever since leaving Madi's house, and Allie was still trying to figure out why. It could have had something to do with the couple making out in the kitchen, but she didn't think so. He was quiet as they roamed the streets, like he was deep in thought about something that had to do with Allie. She had discerned that much, but it wasn't enough, and she was desperate to know what he was thinking about.

Desperate? Yes. Brave? No.

"Have you heard anything about O'Reilly's?" she asked.

Ben glanced over at her, his eyebrows sinking lower. So he thought it was a strange question too? "Should be bug-free by Monday."

"Is it going to be hard to go back to work?"

He shrugged. "It'll be hard to have my evenings taken up again."

Allie hadn't thought of that, and she frowned. "I'm sure it's hard to do anything with people when you have opposite schedules." *And by people I mean me.*

As he tucked his hands under his folded arms, Ben seemed to be wishing he had pockets to stuff his hands into. Allie knew the feeling. A wind had picked up, and the dark skies were threatening rain. If it got cold enough, it could even snow, and Allie definitely wasn't dressed for that. She cupped her hands together and blew into them, a not-so-subtle hint that her fingers were cold.

Ben gave her a little smile, pausing in the middle of the sidewalk. "Here," he said, holding out his hand until she slid her fingers into his. He picked up her other hand as well and held them both against his warm chest in a protective cocoon of fingers. "Thanks for coming with me tonight."

He spoke so quietly that Allie had to lean in, though she might have done that anyway in an effort to find some warmth. She was desperate to get back to the car, but that didn't mean she had any intention of leaving this spot.

"I owed you," she said. "Though I'm pretty sure tonight doesn't begin to cover things, especially after Jake showed up like that."

Ben's eyes crinkled with his smile. "Can't say that I blame him."

At what point had Allie gotten so close that her entire leg was pressed up against his? Their faces were only a few inches apart. "What do you mean?"

Ben swallowed, his eyes shifting downward for half a second. "Allie."

She wanted this. She wanted to be held like this, to be desired, to know there would always be someone in her corner. And she was tired of resisting his pull when it was so strong. What was even the point? The longer she spent with Ben, the more attracted she was, and it was silly to think she would ever be strong enough on her own when someone like Ben could fill in the gaps.

You're better than that, Allie.

She froze only a breath away from his lips, only then realizing that Ben had never moved closer. She'd been the only one to cut the distance between them, and Ben had shut his eyes tight, practically grimacing as he stood there. He clearly didn't want what she wanted and was there to be her friend. Nothing more.

A drop of ice-cold rain landed on her cheek, telling her that she'd made the right choice in holding back, even if she didn't agree. "We should probably head back to the car before we freeze." Her voice sounded hollow with disappointment.

Ben, on the other hand, seemed to breathe a sigh of relief as he looked at her. "Wouldn't want you getting sick," he said with a nod. "Come on." He released one of her hands and tugged her toward the car.

Allie would have liked to keep walking the neighborhood so she could work up the courage to ask him if she had imagined their connection, but she was already starting to freeze. Plus, a few more drops had fallen, and her rather thin costume wasn't going to protect her from the thickening storm. Besides, she was pretty exhausted from everything that had happened to-night, so maybe it would be a good idea to keep her questions to herself until she was more awake.

To keep her attraction tamped down, locked in a vault where it belonged.

When the rain started to fall heavier, they both picked up their pace, and Allie slid the shell off her shoulders to hold it over their heads. To her confusion, Ben let go of her hand so he could slide his arm around her waist, and he took hold of one half of the sled as they half-walked, half-ran back to the car. Talk about mixed signals.

"How far away is it?" Allie gasped when the rain started to pelt them from the side, rendering their little shelter useless.

"Just up ahead," Ben replied. "Are you okay if I drive?"

Allie's teeth had started chattering, so she nodded, even though he probably couldn't see it. He took her silence as an affirmative and took the keys she held out to him. Was it raining or snowing? Allie had closed her eyes, so she couldn't tell, and she was relying entirely on Ben at this point as the slush from above soaked her to the bone with ice water.

When they finally reached the car and she climbed into the dry passenger seat, Allie had never been so glad to see her little Jetta, and she kissed the dash while Ben slipped into the driver's side. He fumbled with the keys, his hands probably as frozen as hers, but quickly got the car to turn on. Allie cranked the heat, and they both sat there shivering as they waited for the air to warm up.

Allie was the first to laugh. Though frozen to her core, she pictured what the two of them had looked like, dressed as second-hand Ninja Turtles as they ran for their lives through the darkness. Ben soon joined in, and the pair of them laughed until the heater had thawed them out enough that he could drive them back to her apartment, his hand securely around hers to keep it warm. Maybe they were stuck as friends, but that was okay. Better than okay. It felt so good to laugh with Ben that she would take him however she could get him.

Allie wasn't laughing the next morning, though.

She woke with a deep ache all over her body and a nose so congested that for a split second she thought she was suffocating. The headache that went with it was the clincher, and she moaned as she fumbled for her phone, which she had left in her purse all night despite several texts that had come in while they were trick-or-treating. It had probably been her mother demanding updates, so Allie had ignored them.

Now she wished she'd had the foresight to put her phone on her dresser so she didn't have to crawl across the floor to get it.

What had Ben said when he dropped her off? The rain had made it hard to hear, but he had mentioned taking a hot shower to keep warming up before she went to bed. She'd been so cold and tired, though, so she had thrown on some pajamas and slid beneath her covers without even brushing her teeth.

Worst mistake of her life.

By the time she finally found her purse buried beneath her wet turtle costume by the door, Allie was tempted to curl up in a ball right there on the floor and fall asleep. She would definitely regret that in a few minutes, though, so she forced herself up onto the couch, which was closer than her bed.

Once she was buried beneath several pillows—her blankets were just out of reach—Allie sent off two texts. The first went to Simmons, telling him she couldn't come into work because she was dying—well, the professional version of that—and the second went to Ben, who responded almost immediately.

> Allie: Please tell me you're not sick too.
> Ben: Oh no, are you sick? I was worried that would happen.
> Allie: So you're fine?
> Ben: The Wonder Boys always say I have the best immune system in the world. I almost never get sick. I'm crediting the ball pit that I have to clean every week.
> Allie: Gross.
> Ben: What do you need? I can be there in ten minutes.
> Ben: Make that an hour. Cam just said he's making you his famous chicken noodle soup. Sans chicken.

Allie smiled at her phone, even though that simple movement of her lips was exhausting. Cam didn't even know her, but he was willing to make her soup, which meant he was just as amazing as the other Wonder Boys.

> Allie: He doesn't have to do that, and it's probably best if you don't come over. I don't want to get you sick.
> Ben: If you really don't want me to come, I won't, but if that's you trying to be noble and self-sacrificing, I'll be there in an hour.

This time, Allie hugged her phone to her chest, feeling warm all over. Though, maybe that was the fever…

> Allie: We could pretend that I'm selfless, but I'm not. Soup sounds amazing.
> Ben: I can't promise it will be good. He's never made it for me.
> Ben: One of the downsides of never getting sick.

> Ben: Do you need anything else? Cold medicine? Aspirin?
> Allie: How about a hammer and chisel to clear out my head?
> Ben: I can arrange that.
> Ben: Cam says that's a terrible idea.

Another text popped up from a number Allie didn't recognize, but she had a feeling she knew exactly who it was and couldn't help but tear up as she read it.

> Unknown number: If you put a warm wet towel over your face, that will help with the congestion. Or take a really hot shower to let the steam fill the bathroom. You'll want to drink a lot of fluids, too. I'll send some good electrolyte drinks with Ben that aren't full of sugar like the ones you can get at the store.
> Unknown number: This is Cam, by the way.
> Allie: Hi, Cam. Thanks. For making me soup. And sending me electrolytes.
> Unknown number: Thanks for making Ben happy. I've never seen him like this.

Allie's heart sank a little. Though now she was extra glad she hadn't kissed Ben last night, knowing she had made the right choice didn't exactly make her feel better. She'd thought maybe he felt... But if Ben was happy with the way things were, who was she to mess with that and try to change their dynamic? After everything he had done for her—was still doing—she owed it to him to stay strong in her determination to be single.

She owed it to him to be his friend.

When Allie woke, she was in her bed. She'd fallen asleep soon after getting Cam's last text, but she didn't remember getting up and moving to her bed. Nor did she remember her apartment smelling like eucalyptus and something else soothing. Poking her head out from underneath her blankets, she searched the apartment until she found Ben in the kitchen. Either he'd let himself in—she didn't remember locking the door last night—or she had been in such a fever haze when she let him in that she couldn't remember opening the door.

"You're here," she said, though she sounded like she'd swallowed several rocks and had to talk around them.

The counter was completely covered in several bags, mugs, and bottles, and from the smell of things, Ben had turned her apartment into a full-service coffee shop. At the sound of her comment, he paused whatever he was doing and smiled at her. For a guy who had been caught in the same storm as her, he looked amazing and perfectly healthy. Apparently that whole magic immune system thing was spot on.

"How are you feeling?" he asked.

He was too far away. Allie's head pounded so badly that she could barely hear him, and she wanted nothing more than to curl up into a ball and break into tears. She had never been all that great when she got sick, unlike her mom who just powered through it even if she had full-blown pneumonia. (True story.) But Allie? She had lost boyfriends during colds because she turned into a nightmare.

She would have to work really hard not to scare Ben off. Especially after last night.

"Not great," she said with her gravelly voice. "You don't have to be here, Ben."

Leaving his project behind, he settled on the side of her bed and pushed some hair from her forehead. She knew her hair was sweaty and stringy and gross, but he didn't seem to care. "I want to be here," he assured her. "Besides, your mom called earlier, and I told her I was looking after you. I'd hate to break my promise to her."

Her mom knew she was sick, and she hadn't shown up with the entire medicine cabinet? That was a first.

Allie glanced at the loaded countertop again, feeling awkward but not sure why. Maybe it was all of this attention that she wasn't used to from anyone but her mom. "What did you bring me?"

Ben smiled gently. "Hot drinks. I figured it would help your throat."

"What kind?"

"All of them. I wasn't sure if you knew what you liked, so I figured I could help you figure it out. We'll start with hot chocolate. Something tells me that might be a winner."

Tears pricked at Allie's eyes. This man was so amazing, and she didn't deserve him. As he stood back up and returned to the counter, she tried to understand why anyone would do what he'd done when she had given him basically nothing in return.

She wanted to understand. "You're not my boyfriend."

Ben paused again, though a drop of milk landed in the cup he had been about to pour into. "I know," he said, a hint of anger in his words. He clearly didn't like the idea of being her boyfriend any more than he'd liked the idea of kissing her, which stung a bit. But it also helped solidify Allie's confusion.

"So why are you doing all of these things for me?"

His eyebrows slid down his forehead, not with anger this time but with sadness. "Because that's what friends do, Allie. They help each other."

"I've never had a friend like that."

"Then you've had the wrong friends."

"Can I steal yours?"

Thankfully, he smiled at the joke and returned to his milk pouring. "I'm pretty sure they like you better than they like me, so they're already yours."

"What if we share them? Joint custody. You can have weekends as long as I get holidays."

Finished with the hot chocolate, Ben slowly brought the cup over and set it on the nightstand. He sat on the bed, so close that Allie was tempted to grab his arm and snuggle up to him. "You can have my friends whenever you'd like, as long as I can be there too."

Tears filled Allie's eyes at the thought. "Does that mean you want to be my friend?"

"Have I ever given you a reason to believe otherwise?" The sadness had returned to his expression, and Allie couldn't help but reach up and smooth the skin on his forehead. He took hold of her hand and kissed her palm before tucking her arm back underneath the blanket. "I would love to be your friend, Allie. For as long as you'll let me."

"Forever?" How presumptuous of her! But she wanted to know, so she'd asked the question. Would she get to keep him as a friend, if nothing else? "Will you stay in my life forever, Ben the Wonder Boy?"

He chuckled, and this time his kiss brushed her forehead. "Sure. Try some hot chocolate, then see if you can get some rest." He rose and started picking up all the pillows Allie had dumped onto the floor earlier.

She definitely didn't deserve this man.

Hot chocolate sounded amazing on her throat, though. Pulling her eyes away from the best guy she'd ever known, she lifted herself up onto her elbow so she could take a sip of the cocoa. But when she saw the contents of the cup, she gasped.

Ben furrowed his brow again as he looked over. "What's wrong? What do you need?"

Allie needed her phone so she could take a picture of the masterpiece in the foam. It was a Ninja Turtle. Clear as day. How was that possible? "I didn't know you could do latte art."

He chuckled, resuming his tidying. "I worked at the coffee shop in the school bookstore my last few semesters of college, and sometimes I got really bored in between customers. Had a lot of time to practice."

"I never did ask you about your art degree." Allie took a sip of the hot chocolate, reluctantly destroying the image in the foam, then moaned with delight. "Oh, this is amazing. I was expecting the powdered stuff you get from the supermarket."

"Never. Hot chocolate is meant to be enjoyed, not tolerated."

She had to work really hard to keep from guzzling the stuff, knowing her empty stomach wouldn't appreciate that much sugar all at once. Besides, she needed to savor it. "I'm going to force you to make this for me every day, even if it puts me in a sugar coma," she said as she sank back onto her pillow.

Though Ben didn't say anything, his little smile was enough to make Allie's heart pound a little harder. He didn't tell her no, and imagining this view every morning made the future a much brighter prospect. She was pretty sure friends didn't see each other every morning unless they lived together, but if Allie lived with Ben, the line between friends and more would most definitely get blurred. She wasn't sure she would be able to resist pushing the boundary.

Once the living room was clean, Ben grabbed a bowl and filled it with something from the stove. He sat on the bed again and held onto the spoon he'd put inside, as if he was about to spoon feed her, and Allie almost decided to let him. Instead, she slowly sat up and propped herself up against the wall, wishing she looked a lot cuter than she knew she did.

At least her sickly state would help keep them in the friend zone, which was exactly what she needed. She wouldn't try to kiss him when she knew she looked terrible.

"Cam swears by this soup," he said as he handed her the bowl. "But, like I said, I've never had it, so I can't testify to its healing properties."

Allie only ate one spoonful before she was convinced Cam was a culinary wizard. "This is amazing," she said, though maybe part of that was because she was starving. She'd been too excited about Halloween and finishing her chapters last night to eat much dinner, and a few sips of hot chocolate this morning definitely didn't count as food. Still, Cam knew what he was doing, and she finished off the bowl in just a couple of minutes.

And Ben watched her the whole time, smiling at her as if he'd never seen anything better. It should have made her feel self-conscious, but it didn't, and she couldn't resist grabbing his arm as she curled back up beneath the covers and cuddling it like a teddy bear.

Ben held back a laugh, his face rather close to her because she'd pulled him down. "Do you plan to hold me hostage all day?"

She wanted to, but that wouldn't be fair. "Just until I fall asleep." With how easily her eyelids closed, she figured it wouldn't take that long. His arm was warm and comfortable, and she felt entirely safe. The perfect conditions for falling asleep. "Then you can go home."

"I've got nothing to do at home," he replied. "Would you mind if I stayed here?"

She smiled. "Of course not."

"I could email those chapters to your office, if you think they're ready."

That made her smile fall, and she looked up at him again. "I don't know. Do *you* think they're ready?"

As he grinned and brushed a bit of hair from her forehead, Allie knew she would believe whatever he told her. "I think they're perfect. But I won't send them unless you want me to."

How was he so amazing?

"They're on my laptop," she said and pointed with her nose to the foot of the bed. "You can send them. Just do it when I'm asleep so I can't stop you."

His quiet laughter rumbled through her like a strange lullaby, and her eyes drooped again. "I'll wait until you're asleep," he promised and brushed his hand over her hair again.

She was out only a few seconds later.

TWENTY-THREE

BEN EMAILED THE PAGES OVER to Simmons first thing after Allie fell asleep. He was no writer, so he couldn't say if they really were the best they could be, but he'd meant it when he told her he thought they were phenomenal. If the editors at Sweet Red Cherry Books didn't like the chapters, then they were all idiots, and he would help Allie find somewhere else to work. Somewhere that deserved her.

He figured he should clean up his coffee mess while Allie was still sleeping so she wouldn't worry about it when she woke up, but with the kitchen so close to her bed, he worried about waking her up if he accidentally made some noise. It would probably be better to stick to the couch so he could keep an eye on her without being creepy.

He counted himself lucky she was letting him stay in the first place. He had almost kissed her last night, and it had taken all of his willpower to keep himself in one spot. Hopefully she hadn't noticed how close he'd come to breaking his promise to only be her friend. He'd been too scared to open his eyes and see her expression.

Just as he was about to close her laptop and grab a book to read, something on her desktop caught his eye. He knew he shouldn't snoop, but his curiosity overcame him again, and he clicked the document open before he could stop himself.

It was a novel. Or at least the bones of one. More of an outline, really, but the longer Ben read through it, the more he smiled because he knew exactly what this was and what had inspired it.

Allie had written a story about the Wonder Boys.

It was a superhero story, and all of them had names so similar to their laser tag names that Ben knew Allie had written them down after their misadventure with the cockroaches. She'd been thinking about this for almost a week now, from the plotline to personality traits to character descriptions.

Ben's favorite by far was The Sentinel, who wasn't the leader of the team but was considered the most important because he kept an eye on the others through a telepathic bond he created with each of them. A silent defender who saved the lives of his team every day. He was also the only one with a love interest in this story, apparently, and Ben glanced over at Allie when he got to that part. She was sound asleep, and he couldn't help but wonder if there was any truth to her plotline.

Did Ben have a love interest?

What really intrigued him about that facet of the story, though, was the fact that the love interest was the villain, a shapeshifter who had lost her memories before turning down the path of evil. Was that really how Allie saw herself?

Grabbing his sketchbook from the backpack he'd brought with him—he'd figured Allie would spend a good chunk of the day sleeping—he flipped to the first blank page and started drawing based on the descriptions Allie had written down. The Sentinel didn't look much like Ben, it sounded like, but he knew he was the inspiration. Just as Cam had inspired Matador and the tech genius billionaire had been patterned after Oliver, though he was the only one not described as attractive, which made Ben chuckle. Kit and Madi had been turned into twin elemental wielders who could build off each other's strength and both led the team to victory, and each villain who populated the page had their own backstories and motivations. Something told him they had come from past boyfriends.

There was so much to draw, and Ben lost himself in the work, feeling more on fire than he had in years.

Ben wasn't sure what woke him, though the first thing he noticed was the ache in his back from falling asleep on Allie's mini couch again. Grunting, he struggled upright and rubbed the sleep from his eyes until he realized Allie was sitting on the floor right in front of him.

"Whoa!" He jumped to his feet and almost toppled into the wall behind the couch, barely catching himself as Allie grinned.

There was something else in her grin, though, something beyond amusement, and it made him nervous.

"Sorry for scaring you," she said gently.

Ben glanced at his watch. He'd been asleep for almost two hours, which was a whole lot longer than he'd planned. Not that he'd planned to fall asleep in the first place, but drawing for three hours straight had completely drained him. "Don't worry about it," he said and settled back onto the couch. "Do you want to come sit up here?"

Her grin twisted, and that was when he saw the sketchbook in her hands.

He gulped. "Oh. Um. I shouldn't have looked around on your computer. Sorry."

But she shook her head, her eyes bright after her long nap. She still looked sick, but she seemed a lot less miserable than when he'd gotten here. "When you said you had a degree in illustration, I thought maybe you were really good at stick figures."

What was he supposed to say to that? "Thanks?"

"Ben, these are the most amazing drawings I've ever seen."

Well that definitely wasn't true, and he scoffed as he stretched the pinch in his back. "You can tell me they're horrible," he said with a little smile. "I can take the criticism."

"I would have said that if I thought they were horrible." Suddenly, she was right next to him, wedging herself in the couch until she could lean her head against his shoulder as she flipped through his dozen or so sketches.

He hadn't really been paying attention to what he was drawing—he had wanted to get a rough representation of the images in his head—but looking at them now had him wondering if he'd been possessed by the ghost of Steve Ditko for the last few hours. He'd never drawn comic-style before, but apparently he was decent at it.

"I'm serious, Ben. I just cried for, like, ten minutes because these are so incredible. They're…you drew my characters."

"I shouldn't have—"

"Have you ever thought of doing a graphic novel? Because I have, but I don't know how to draw. You do."

Ben froze when those words hit him, and he was pretty sure he'd heard wrong. It had sounded like she wanted to create a graphic novel with him. "No," he said, knowing he should probably elaborate on that answer but unsure what else he could say. Maybe… "I've never been good at storytelling."

"Well, that's not true. Remember that story you told me about the time Oliver and Kit got pulled over for having Cam hogtied in the back of the car?"

Ben snorted a laugh. He had, thankfully, been absent for that one because he'd had to work, but his friends had told him the story often enough that he'd felt like he was there. For some reason, they had decided it was absolutely necessary to transport Cam from the homecoming game while roped up like a pig. Something about him getting into a fight with some-one… Somehow, they hadn't gotten in trouble, and Cam had never felt the need to explain why he'd gotten into the fight in the first place.

"That's different," Ben said, shrugging. "It's not like I could create a story like you can."

Allie grabbed hold of his hand, and she looked more excited about this than Ben had ever seen her. Like she had never wanted anything more in her life. "Ben, I know I've asked so much of you already, and I will owe you so many favors for the rest of forever. But if you try this with me, I really think we could make something amazing, and you will be the best friend I've ever had."

Ben swallowed, almost wishing she wasn't so close so he could actually think straight. Outside of taking up some of his time, he really didn't have a reason not to agree to her suggestion. He had lied when he said he hadn't thought about it, though it had been years since he'd toyed with the idea of making a comic book. But the fear of failure loomed over him like a thick cloud of suffocating darkness. A familiar darkness. The kind that had followed him his entire life and kept him from moving on from the job he hated and finding something worth doing.

What if he couldn't do it? It wouldn't just be his failure but Allie's as well, and that was a lot of pressure. It would ruin everything. He had just gotten used to the idea of only ever being Allie's friend, and if he lost that?

She flipped through the sketches again, her fingers lingering on the character based off of her. "I couldn't figure out what she looked like when she wasn't shapeshifting," she said, cocking her head to the side. "She's beautiful."

"She's you." Ben didn't actually say that. He wanted to, but the words stuck in his throat. He had to say *something*, but he was afraid of what was going to come out when the important things wouldn't.

"I…" He had to swallow again. *C'mon, Ben. You've got this.* "I don't want to disappoint you."

Allie deflated. "Oh."

"No! I mean, I want to do it, I just don't know if I…" Why was it so hard to admit out loud? "What if I'm terrible at it and ruin it? You've clearly got a good story here, and…" He reached over and turned the pages of his sketches, as if showing her his terrible art would convince her to pick someone else. He turned a few pages too far, however, and landed on one sketch of Allie. Not her character. *Allie.* Perusing the produce at the grocery store.

Ben flinched, waiting for her to freak out and call him a stalker. To throw him out of her apartment and tell him to never come back again.

But Allie let out a little sigh and leaned into him, her head falling onto his shoulder again. "When you can draw like this, how could you possibly think you would ruin it? Whaddya say, Benny?"

She sounded like she was falling asleep again, which meant Ben was stuck. Both in his seat on the couch and with his decision about the graphic novel. How could he say no when she trusted him so completely?

He shifted, sliding his arm behind her and pulling her close so she could more comfortably rest against his chest. "I'll try," he said quietly. It was the best he could do, and he hoped it would be enough.

TWENTY-FOUR

ALLIE ARRIVED AT WORK ON Monday with a pit in her stomach the size of Texas. Ben had emailed Simmons the chapters she wrote, and today she was going to find out if her boss would even accept the writing, let alone her. Ben had also agreed to come in for a meeting to discuss the chapters, and thankfully he had convinced the editors to meet him earlier in the morning, rather than after lunch like they had suggested.

Otherwise, Allie wasn't sure she would have survived the day.

Allie owed Ben big time. Not only had her Wonder Boy spent the entire weekend taking care of her while she recovered from that nightmare of a cold, but he had also spent that time convincing her that she had nothing to worry about when it came to the teen series. He had a plan, he said, and he would do everything in his power to make sure she didn't lose her job when the truth came out.

Then there was the graphic novel.

If she was being honest with herself, Allie hadn't exactly dreamed of writing a graphic novel. She preferred regular novels full of words rather than pictures since she *knew* how to paint a scene with words. She didn't even read many graphic novels anymore, though she had a few favorites on her shelves that she went back to whenever she needed something to re-read. As a kid, she'd loved comics, and she had a few she'd kept, but most of them had gotten lost over the years when she realized her boyfriends either thought comics were lame or called her a wannabe nerd because she didn't like the right ones.

But when she'd woken up to find Ben asleep on the couch, his sketchbook open on his lap, she'd fallen in love with the characters he'd drawn, and the graphic novel idea, which up to this point had been nothing but a few bulleted lists for a potential plotline, had basically written itself. Besides, it was the perfect excuse to spend as much time with him as she could, and she wanted that more than anything. Even if she had no right to ask him for more, she hadn't been able to help herself.

She was glad she'd pushed him.

Within two days, they'd created something amazing. Sure, it was only a few pages of concept art and a couple panels of storyline, but once they went over to Ben's apartment so he could get onto his computer to create a colorized version of his sketches, everything had started falling into place. She'd never been more excited to make something in her life, and something told her Ben felt the same way. He'd come alive once they put her words with his art, in a way Allie had never seen before.

Ben was born to create.

Allie settled at her desk at Sweet Red Cherry, wishing she could still use the excuse that she was sick but knowing she wouldn't be brave enough to postpone learning her fate. She had less than ten minutes before Ben was supposed to arrive, and the fact that the only breakfast she'd had was leftover hot chocolate meant she was shaking like a chihuahua in January.

When her phone buzzed with a text, she practically shouted a thank you to the heavens for the distraction, no matter how small.

> Mom: You didn't come over for Sunday dinner again. Is
> everything okay?

Allie smiled, glad her mom hadn't mentioned anything about setting her up. Sending a picture of her and Ben in matching Halloween costumes must have helped.

> Allie: I got a little sick on Halloween, so Ben and I thought it would be a good idea to stay in. His roommate cooked for us, though.

In fact, Cam had been thrilled to whip up some lettuce wraps while he offered suggestions for their character designs. Ben told her afterwards that he had never seen his friend so invested in someone else's interest before and it was nice to know he could be a little selfless sometimes. Allie had yet to see it, but Ben was convinced Cam had more ego than anyone he knew.

From Allie's perspective, Cam had so much goodness in his heart that he didn't know what to do with it most of the time. Once he got his gym up and running, he would be a spectacular trainer and boss.

> Mom: Roommate? What did Ben say he did for work?
> Allie: Entertainment.
> Mom: What does that mean?
> Allie: A lot of things. He might get a new job soon, though.

Allie didn't actually know that part, but she hoped it was true. Ben had been so much happier this week, being away from the fun center, and she knew he was dreading going back to work that night. And not just because of the potential bugs.

O'Reilly's Fun Center sucked the life and joy right out of him, and she desperately hoped working on this book together would keep him alive long enough for him to find something new.

> Mom: Does Ben have family nearby?

Well, that was an odd question, and Allie hesitated with her fingers hovering over the keys. What was she getting at?

Allie: His parents live in town, plus a few of his siblings.
Mom: So he has a big family?
Allie: Pretty big.
Mom: Maybe he wants a break this year.

What did *that* mean?

Mom: Think he would come over for Thanksgiving?

The front door opened, and Allie slammed her phone onto the desk as Ben stepped into the lobby. "Ben! Hi!"

He lifted one dark eyebrow, approaching her desk with a bit of hesitation. "Everything good? He hasn't said anything about the chapters yet, has he?"

Mom wanted Ben to come to *Thanksgiving*? Allie hadn't brought *anyone* to the big holidays. Not even the guys she dated for years. She always found some excuse, or went to their families, because she refused to let her mom think she might get a son-in-law unless it was a for sure thing. Allie had never had a for sure thing.

Mom had only met the guy once, but she seemed to think Ben was The One, and Allie wasn't ready to break her heart when their fake dating ended.

They had never discussed an end date to this charade. The last week had been a dream, and while that wasn't a long time for some people, it was for Allie. It had been a week of being herself, with no one telling her she should be something else. She'd discovered some of her favorite things and admitted to her love of comics. She'd been so relaxed that she let Ben spend the entire day in her apartment while she lay sick and dying in her bed, something she never would have done with any of her boyfriends.

She'd actually been happy.

"Allie, are you okay? Are you still feeling sick? You look..."

He didn't even have a word for how she looked, and Allie bit her lip before she burst into laughter. She had no idea why this whole Thanksgiving thing was suddenly so funny, but she had to spin around and face the wall before she cracked.

"Allison, why didn't you let me know Mr. Nakamura had arrived?"

As heat flooded her face, Allie spun back to find Mr. Simmons shaking Ben's hand. "Sorry, sir, I was just about to—"

"Never mind, I know he's here. Let's sit down and discuss those chapters you sent over."

Ben took one step to follow but paused and looked back at her, a clear question in his eyes.

Allie smiled. "I'm great," she lied. "I'll follow you in."

Mom hadn't said anything else, but Allie knew she wouldn't drop the subject. She would keep asking about Thanksgiving until Allie gave her a firm answer. Probably until Allie said Ben would come. They would likely have to "break up" before then, which gave Allie less than four weeks left with a solid reason to be around Ben.

That graphic novel was the only thing that gave her hope for this friendship of hers.

Grabbing her phone, Allie slipped into the conference room just as Mr. Simmons cleared his throat to begin. At least her mom had sufficiently distracted her, but now was the moment of truth. Now was the moment she would learn if she could be a real writer.

"Thank you for coming in, Mr. Nakamura," Simmons said, the two editors nodding along with him. That was a good sign. "We've reviewed your submission, and we have come to a decision about working with you."

He paused there, and Allie sat forward. Why did he feel the need to drag this out?

Ben coughed. "I've been eager to know what you thought."

Simmons grunted, rubbing his beard and looking at the two editors as if hoping they would step in just like they had the last time. Bad news. He only had bad news, and Allie held her breath as if that might make the sting hurt less.

"Well, I'll just come right out and say it. We want you to be our new writer."

"What?" Allie clapped a hand over her mouth as four pairs of eyes turned in her direction. "Sorry, I just... That's great news! Isn't that great news, Mr. Nakamura?"

Ben smiled, his twinkling eyes belying his outward calm. He was probably just as excited as she was. "Very good news," he agreed. "So what now?"

Simmons slid a thick stack of papers over to Ben. "Now you sign the paperwork to hire you on as a contract writer. We still have to approve the final product, and it will go to the patron before any money exchanges hands, as she has final say over whether it gets published, but from here on out you will be a contract employee of Sweet Red Cherry Books."

Though he had nodded while Simmons was talking, Ben held up a finger before he even looked down at the paperwork in front of him. "I have one condition," he said, sounding rather intense as he did so.

Simmons frowned, as did the editors. "What condition is that?"

"I write under a pen name."

Of course! Allie bit back a grin as the three men considered this, glancing amongst themselves. It wasn't strange for someone to want to use a pen name, but Allie was pretty sure she knew which name Ben would choose. It was genius, assuming he could actually pull it off.

"What name would you like to use?" Simmons asked.

Ben shrugged. "I'll know once the book has been written."

"I'm sorry?"

"The name of the author is an important part of any work," Ben explained. "Until I know the story, it is impossible to know who wrote it."

"You wrote it." Poor Simmons had only dealt with children's book authors up until this point, and he had probably never dealt with a diva before. He must have found Ben ridiculous, but the pull of the writing seemed to be the winning force as he looked around the room one last time. It gave Allie a strange sense of pride. "Very well, Mr. Nakamura. Assuming the name you choose to print under is appropriate, we will allow a delay on that information, until the first book has been written. Anything else you require?"

Ben seemed to ponder that question, though Allie had no idea what he could possibly ask for. "You said the patron is a woman?"

Simmons nearly groaned. "Is that a problem?"

"Of course not. Why would it be?"

"Oh, I thought perhaps—"

Narrowing his eyes a little, Ben leaned forward until he practically commanded Mr. Simmons's attention. "A woman is just as capable as any man would be, if not more so," he said. "Sometimes even I'm a woman."

"Mr. Simmons," Allie said, before her boss said anything stupid. "Mr. Nakamura told me he has another appointment to get to."

Ben sent her the flash of a smile. "Yes, thank you for reminding me, Allison. I will have my assistant look this paperwork over and send it back as soon as it is finished, if that works for you."

Simmons shook his head, apparently a little dazed. "Of course."

"Great. Allison, if you could accompany me outside, I have a few questions I hoped you could answer."

With the eyes of her coworkers fixed on her, Allie slipped out of her chair and followed Ben out to the sidewalk, checking to make sure none of them randomly decided to follow them. Then she threw her arms around his shoulders in the tightest hug she could manage.

"You are amazing," she said into his neck.

He chuckled, and the sound rumbled through her. "I'm pretty sure I was ridiculous. I didn't know what I was saying."

"I think it might have worked, though. At the very least, you scared them silly with that little feminist speech."

Ben pulled away, his eyes dancing as he gazed at her. "I meant it, you know. Except the part about me being a woman. I'm not that cool. But you are, and you're going to prove that to them when you fill out this paperwork for yourself." He handed her the stack, which she took with some measure of hesitation.

"I can't do that," she said, even though she badly wanted to. "They're going to notice and tear it to pieces."

He shook his head. "Who is it who files all the paperwork, Allie?"

"I do."

"So who's even going to see it until it's too late? I'd bet you can get them to sign it without even looking at the name on the signature line, and then they'll have no choice but to let you write the story. Especially when I tell them to put your name on it."

In a perfect world, it would work just like he said, but Allie had been disappointed too many times by too many things to believe it would all work out. Mr. Simmons would see her name before he signed, or he would find a way out of the contract, or he would simply refuse to let her take the credit for the story because he would be convinced she had stolen it from Ben.

"It's not going to work," she mourned. "Ben, they're just going to reject my story and tell me they won't publish it."

Putting his hands on her shoulders, he gave her a little squeeze. "Allie." Apparently, his nearness wasn't enough for him, and he moved closer, shifting his hands to her neck. "You are a phenomenal writer, and if Simmons doesn't take your work, then you can publish it yourself."

"The story belongs to the patron."

"You can't copyright an idea. Even if you could, you would just have to change up a few things and make the story your own. You've already proven you're capable of coming up with original content."

How was he so good at making speeches and making her feel like she could do absolutely anything she put her mind to? She seriously owed this man big time, and she had no idea how to pay him back.

"What was so funny earlier?"

Payback definitely wouldn't come from answering that question. As she turned what was probably the color of a tomato, Allie shrugged. "Um. Nothing."

"Yes, I totally believe that."

"It was just my mom."

"Is she still trying to set you up?"

"In a manner of speaking." Allie really didn't want to have this conversation outside of her workplace, but she knew she wouldn't survive if she didn't tell him sooner than later. He would be at work all night, and she couldn't wait until tomorrow. "Um, my mom wants you to come to Thanksgiving at our house."

Based on the expression that filled his face, Allie imagined an error message popping up in Ben's brain. He got halfway to forming a word but stopped there, staring at her as if she'd just spoken gibberish. He clearly hadn't expected that response, and he clearly didn't know what to do with it, and the two of them stood there on the sidewalk in awkward silence, wasting what precious alone time they had.

"You don't have to come," she added, though she was pretty sure the damage was already done. He probably didn't want to go to Thanksgiving because that was a big step in their fake relationship. He probably didn't want to keep the fake relationship going in the first place. He had probably been finding the right time to tell her that he wanted out of the relationship and maybe the friendship too because she kept asking too much of him.

That was the problem with being in a solid relationship—even if it was a friendship—with a decent guy. She'd never felt like she could ask things of people, so this was a new experience for her. She had definitely abused it, and now she was paying the price.

"Sorry I mentioned it," she muttered, then turned to go back inside.

Ben grabbed her arm. "Hey, Allie?"

She refused to turn and look at him in case she started crying. "Yeah?"

"I'm going to do that stupid Sherlock Holmes thing and pretend I know what's going through your head just by looking at you, okay?"

She shrugged, unsure what she could say to that.

"I would love to go to Thanksgiving with your family. You caught me by surprise. No, I'm not backing out of this thing just because this is a big step in a normal relationship. No, I'm not going to abandon you to your mother's misguided attempts at making you happy. And no, I don't want to stop being your friend. I *really* don't want to stop being your friend. So don't push me away, okay? If you're ever asking too much of me, I will let you know. I promise."

Well, she definitely wasn't going to be able to hold back her tears now. Pulling Ben out of the sightline of the office doors, Allie fell into his embrace again and wished she could stay there forever. "How do you do that?" she whispered, tucking her face in his neck.

"I mean, you're a pretty expressive person, and I've spent my life watching people, so—"

"No. How do you keep making me realize how terrible all of my past relationships have been? I mean, outside of a few of them, I've always thought they were pretty good guys, but you… You're perfect, Ben. How do you exist?"

His heart pounded in his chest at a pace that surprised Allie since he seemed reluctant to return her embrace. "I'm really not that great," he said.

"You really are," she argued, pulling away. "But… I should probably get back to work. Are you going to survive tonight?"

"Without you?"

That made her blush, though his grin told her he was trying to repay the favor of her unasked-for compliment.

He chuckled. "I'll be fine. I've made it through more than a decade of O'Reilly's, so I doubt a single night will kill me. I'll probably just hide in the mini golf windmill and work on our book, anyway."

Our book. That was the best thing Allie had ever heard. "So I didn't make up this weekend in a fever-induced utopian dream? That's good to know."

"You're ridiculous, Allie." He nodded to the pages in her hands and offered a breathtaking smile. "Make sure you don't bring that paperwork in until tomorrow, so it's like I actually had my assistant fill it out."

She hugged the pages a little tighter to her chest; they were her best shot at becoming an author. "Technically, with what you said, that makes me your assistant. I'm not sure how I feel about that."

"You're definitely the boss. I could fill it out for *you*, if you'd like."

Allie dodged his hand as he swiped for the paperwork, laughing and wishing she didn't have to go back to reality.

Was it always going to be this way with Ben? She missed him already, and he was literally standing right in front of her. Last week had definitely spoiled her.

Sighing, she glanced back toward the doors. "Are you sure we have to be adults again? I just want to be a teenage turtle fighting fake crime and taking candy from strangers forever. None of this job nonsense."

As he offered a matching sigh, Ben pulled his keys from his pocket and stared at them as if hoping to find some sort of solution to their problem on his keyring. "I know how you feel. I'm pretty sure my boss is going to bring up the new center the next time he comes in, and I don't know what to tell him."

Allie knew what he should tell him. Ben should absolutely tell the guy *no* because Ben was way better than a stupid fun center that would probably get infested with bugs just like the last one. But no matter how much she wanted to tell him that, she knew he would have to make the decision himself. At least, it was the kind of decision *she* would want to make for herself.

In fact, she *did* have to make it. She held a stack of papers that would tie her to Sweet Red Cherry for the next who knew how long, and she almost didn't want to fill it out. Sure, she could write whatever she wanted after she told the patron's story, but was it worth waiting to get there?

"Let's get through the next month," Ben told her, giving her shoulder another squeeze. "Simmons won't ask for any more pages until the first of the year, and O'Reilly hasn't even found a venue for his center yet. We've both got time. How about we just focus on our graphic novel before we make any big life decisions, okay?"

Allie would have taken a deep breath if a weight hadn't settled on her shoulders and made that impossible. "You think our book will make it easier to face the future?" she whispered.

Ben snorted a laugh, shoving his hands into his pockets. "Definitely not. It'll only delay it. But I'm hoping it makes the present a little more bearable. It'll give me something to look forward to. Along with grocery shopping, of course."

He gave her one last smile and wandered off toward his nightmare of a car. And Allie couldn't move. Not because he looked so dang attractive in his cuffed jeans and maroon sweater—which he did—but because her heart was threatening to pound out of her chest. Ben hadn't said anything strange or suggestive, but each word had hit Allie hard. Right in the gut and straight to her soul.

She was falling for him. Falling hard. And she was pretty sure she'd never felt this way about anyone before.

That absolutely terrified her.

TWENTY-FIVE

IT TOOK A FULL WEEK before Ben stopped jumping at work every time he saw something move out of the corner of his eye. He kept expecting a cockroach to leap out at him, and he absolutely refused to go into the laser arena. (He had a feeling he would never be able to look at the game the same way again, which was a shame.) O'Reilly never came into the center, and Ben avoided mentioning anything about a second location to anyone, and time continued to tick by at the pace of a slug.

Only when he was with Allie did time pick up its pace, and he hated it. His time to leave her side and go home always came way too quickly.

Depending on how their schedules synced up over the next few weeks, they split their time between Allie's apartment and the fun center. Though Ben generally worked the evenings after Allie was off work, she could at least sit in the broken racing game in the arcade and write down dialogue and narration for their graphic novel, while Ben checked and cleaned the machines around her, offering up feedback when he could.

It was better than going to his own apartment; he and Cam only had until early December before their lease was up and Cam moved closer to the area he was hoping to set up his gym.

Ben still had no idea where he was going to live, but he started packing anyway during the mornings he was off and

Allie was at work. He would have to tell her eventually, but he worried his stress would put a strain on their friendship, causing her to back away so he could get his crap together without distraction. He wanted the distraction—needed it—so he pretended nothing was wrong and everything was normal.

Besides, Cam was a little too excited about their relationship, but eventually he would figure out that they were nothing but friends. Ben hoped to postpone that discovery as long as possible. So he went about life as normal, answering Cam's questions as vaguely as he could.

Tuesday grocery mornings were brainstorming days. Ben and Allie spent way too long wandering the aisles talking plotlines and villains, and Ben always bought Allie a pint of her favorite ice cream, which changed each week based on her mood. He loved how much she had discovered about herself since the day he officially met her, and he loved that she still tried new things as she continued to figure out who she really was. Really, Ben just loved *her*. Every little facet that made up Allison Ortega.

Sundays were gifts from above: the one day they both were off work.

On the Sunday before Thanksgiving, Ben showed up earlier than he would have normally and let himself into her apartment, knowing she was likely still asleep. He hadn't been able to wait any longer; being around stacks of moving boxes was far more depressing than he'd like. He had been up extra late the night before after a long night at the fun center, but his nervous energy had fueled something he couldn't wait to show her.

Sure enough, she was fast asleep in her little corner of the room, her dark hair a wild mess around her head as she hugged a bundled-up blanket. Ben grinned at the duvet tangled around her, then set about making some hot chocolate. Allie was not a morning person, just like Ben, and he had quickly discovered chocolate helped soften the blow of being woken up before she wanted to be.

Any other day, he would have let her sleep. He probably would have joined her, curling up on the tiny couch until she finally joined the living because no sane human woke up before seven. But today he couldn't wait.

Twenty minutes later, he seated himself on the side of her bed with a steaming mug in his hands and brushed her hair out of her face. "Good morning, beautiful," he said gently. Though he had settled comfortably into the role of Allie's friend and nothing more, it didn't stop him from finding her the most enchanting woman he'd ever known. For the last couple of weeks, he had gotten in the habit of telling her she was beautiful and talented and kind, simply because she deserved to know.

She stirred after a moment, her nose in the air before she'd even opened her eyes. "I love you," she murmured before her hands reached out and found the mug he held and pulled it to her lips.

Ben's heart twisted a little. He knew that was anatomically impossible, but it was how it felt. She hadn't said those words out loud before, but he knew she didn't mean them how he wished she did. She loved hot chocolate. She loved the way he treated her. She loved knowing he would always be around if she wanted him to be.

But she didn't love *him*. And that was okay.

That lie was getting harder to believe.

"You're going to spill, you glutton," he said, and he cradled her hands with his before she dumped the chocolate all over herself and her bed.

She finally opened her eyes to grin up at him, making his heart do that little twist again. "You've got me spoiled, by the way. I'm going to expect this kind of treatment for the rest of forever."

He would do this every day for the rest of his life if she let him. No one had ever really *needed* Ben before. Sure, he was a good sounding board for his friends, like when Cam spent three hours complaining about how he had finally been outbid and had to find a different location for his gym. But the Wonder Boys could talk to each other or Madi as easily as they could talk to Ben, so he was replaceable in that sense. Technically, Allie was strong enough that she didn't need Ben either, and she would eventually find herself and be able to go live her life without someone like him to help her avoid getting lost again. But for now, she had decided she needed him around, and he loved that.

"I'm still waiting for my own breakfast in bed," he said and gave her a smirk. "How about we start repaying the favor? And you still haven't taught me how to make tofu lasagna."

She had, however, figured out that classic cheese was her favorite pizza, especially with a bit of garlic sauce drizzled on it. She had tried mini golfing and gotten bored halfway through, so instead they played it like hockey and tried to be the first to get the ball into the hole, stealing it from each other as they moved through the course. She had attempted rock climbing and had gotten scared ten feet up, forcing Ben to rescue her because she refused to let go. She had memorized the words to Ben's favorite album and belted each song in the car even though she was a poor singer and an even worse dancer. She had thrown out a lot of her random decor and most of the throw pillows, except for the sequined llama one they both loved.

She and Ben had created something amazing with their book, and he couldn't wait to show her.

Letting Ben hold her hot chocolate so she could sit up, Allie scooted over to let Ben lift his legs onto the bed and sit directly next to her. It was far more comfortable than the couch, something they'd figured out after one particularly bad wedge moment on the little loveseat, and she almost always put her head on his shoulder when they sat like this.

Maybe it was a bit masochistic of him, but Ben loved when she did that. It was easier to imagine a different kind of future.

"I'll teach you that lasagna someday," Allie said with a sigh. "I just wish you didn't work so many nights."

Another twist to his heart. "It's not as bad in the summer when we open earlier, but with all the kids in school right now…"

"Yeah, yeah. I don't need your logic solidifying the fact that I barely get to see you except on weekends." She took hold of her hot chocolate again and guzzled half of it down, and then she grabbed his hand.

With her mug-warmed skin against his, Ben could almost picture them sitting like this every winter, cozying up in front of a fire and watching their favorite movies. Then he considered the fact that they clearly didn't need to be dating to sit like this, and he chided himself for yet again wishing he had more than he did.

Allie had become his best friend, and he wouldn't trade that for the world.

"I brought you something," he said, reaching into his pocket with his free hand.

Her eyes traced his movement, her expression guarded as she waited to see what he grabbed. For one brief moment he wondered if she thought he was pulling out a ring, but that would have been ridiculous for so many reasons. They weren't even dating, for one, despite everyone they knew thinking they were, but beyond that they had only known each other for a month and a half tops. Ben wasn't Oliver, who went head-first into everything he did and proposed to Madi the day after they'd started dating.

Okay, in their defense, Oliver and Madi had known each other for more than twenty years before that point. But Ben was far more cautious, and he would never catch someone by surprise with a proposal. He'd want her to know it was coming.

When Ben pulled a flash drive from his pocket, Allie relaxed beside him and reached for her laptop. "New pictures?" she asked as the computer booted up.

"Something like that."

Ben grabbed the half-full mug of cocoa just in time. Allie gasped and sat up straight as soon as she opened up the file on the computer, and Ben took a long sip of chocolate to keep himself from freaking out as she scrolled. He hadn't told Allie how close he was to finishing the artwork for their novel, and he'd spent most of the night putting the finishing touches on the cover he'd designed. While he wasn't a cover designer by any stretch of the imagination, he had looked up the most popular graphic novels out in the world and created something that hopefully looked like it belonged alongside them.

Menace Unknown, the story of the Wonder Boys, was complete.

"Ben," Allie whispered, and she let go of his hand so she could more easily scroll through the finished pages. "This is amazing. When did you do all this?"

He smiled, though he still had a hard time relaxing. Allie's approval didn't mean the product was any good. "While you were busy writing the next great middle grade book series," he said. "Or, you know, after you've gone to bed each night. I'm more of a night owl than a morning person, and your story was easy to draw."

Next thing he knew, she had her hands on his jaw and was pressing a kiss to his cheek, though she lingered there just long enough that he was so tempted to turn and match his lips up to hers.

"So you like it?" he asked, his voice shaking. *Get a hold of yourself, Ben.*

Allie apparently liked it so much that she kissed him again, her lips warm against his jaw. Her breath smelled of chocolate, so tantalizing that he nearly gave in and just went for it. Consequences be damned. "This is the most incredible thing I have ever laid my eyes on, Ben. *You* are incredible."

Something shifted.

Ben didn't know what it was, but when his eyes met hers, he could feel it in the air, as if the room had suddenly become charged with an electric current. The earth had moved beneath him and left him a fraction of an inch off from where he'd been.

He just didn't know which direction he'd gone.

"So what now?" he asked. He meant it about their book, but he also wondered what finishing the project meant for the two of them now that it wouldn't give them a reason to spend all their free time together. Thanksgiving was four days away, and with all the schools closed for the week, he was working extra hours at O'Reilly's. Today was his only chance to spend any real time with Allie before he showed up at her parents' house again, this time with the implication that things between them were getting more serious. Casual boyfriends didn't show up to big family holidays, at least not without it meaning something more.

At what point would the charade end?

Grabbing Ben's arm and lifting it over her head so she could snuggle into his chest as she scrolled, Allie took a long time before she said anything. As much as Ben wanted to know what she was thinking—did she have the same question running through her head?—he was also terrified.

She was quickly coming to that point where she didn't need him anymore. Their graphic novel was finished, and they could easily "break up" after Thanksgiving so Allie could use the excuse of needing some grieving time before she dated again, buying herself another few months of peace. Once Ben convinced Sweet Red Cherry Books to sign Allie on as a writer instead of him—they hadn't discovered the contract with her name on it yet—she could continue on her merry way and leave him behind if she wanted.

That had always been the plan, and he knew it, so why was it so hard to consider a life without Allie?

That was a stupid question. Ben loved her, and he probably would for the rest of his life. He could survive without her, but life would be so much brighter with her in it.

"I guess…" Allie pulled herself a little tighter against him, as if she might be unwilling to let him go just yet. "We need to find a publisher who will print it, though there aren't a lot of people who take on new authors, especially without an agent."

Ben hadn't realized how complicated the publishing world was until he met Allie, and he was glad he had her to walk him through things. Not that he ever would have made something like a graphic novel in the first place… Knowing what she knew, she wouldn't give him a false hope that their little book could actually end up going anywhere, but she had enough optimism to believe they had a chance.

He was the same way with their relationship. They had a chance, but he wouldn't let himself *expect* a future with Allie. He just had to hope.

"You're really quiet right now, Ben. Is something wrong?"

Ben let out a little laugh, shaking his head. She probably didn't feel any of the weirdness that had grown between them, and he envied her for it. From the very beginning, she had only ever seen him as a friend, and that probably wasn't going to change. "I'm just blown away by the fact that you convinced me to do something like this," he said. "Imagining it actually printed and existing outside of that flash drive is a weird sensation."

Allie paused on a page that featured their first antagonist, the shapeshifter Ben had designed with Allie in mind. By the end of the book, she turned to the good side, but for the bulk of the story the shapeshifter was fighting to be seen by any means, no matter who got hurt along the way.

She sighed. "Everything about this book has just felt so right, you know? I've never had a project like that before, and I'm pretty sure it means it was meant to exist. We were meant to make this, Ben."

"Do you really believe that?"

"More than anything."

At least one of them was confident. Ben would do what he could to hide his fears and insecurities, but when a good chunk of the problem was Allie herself, it wouldn't be easy to mirror her undying optimism.

It might be a good time to change the subject. "Madi wants us to come over for lunch today," he said, even though he probably should have come up with some sort of transition. "But I'm happy to stay in, if you'd rather do that."

Allie glanced up at him. "Has she told anyone she's pregnant yet?"

"Nope." In fact, Ben honestly wasn't sure how *Allie* knew about the baby. He hadn't said a word about it to anyone, and they hadn't seen Oliver and Madi since Halloween almost a month earlier. Kit was still blissfully in the dark, and Cam wouldn't know until everyone else had been told since he wouldn't be able to keep the secret to save his life.

Madi must have told Allie on Halloween, but Ben was too afraid to ask if that was the case. Afraid of what, he didn't know, but he feared the question nonetheless. Allie knowing Madi's secret made everything feel a little too…real. Especially because Madi was the only one who knew this relationship was fake.

"Lunch sounds fun," Allie said eventually. "As long as we don't stay a long time."

Ben did his best not to look disappointed. "That's fine. I can drop you off after—"

She clapped her hand over his mouth, shutting him up completely. "I was hoping to try out some new TV shows with you today," she said. "We've been so busy with *Menace Unknown* that we haven't had any downtime, you know?"

She wanted to stay in and watch TV? "Oh."

She deflated, muttering, "We don't have to do that," and Ben cursed himself for letting things get awkward just because he had no idea how to handle being surprised. He kept doing that, and it was the only time things were not easy with Allie.

"That actually sounds nice," he said, grabbing her hand and hoping that would emphasize his point. "You're right about not having a lot of downtime. We could start this morning, and if anything catches your eye, we can keep watching it tonight."

If smiles could save lives, the one Allie gave him just then would heal millions. "Really?"

"I would never lie about time I get to spend with you."

Snuggling up next to him—somehow she always managed to get closer, even when Ben thought she was as close as she could get—Allie let out a sigh. "You probably think I'm so ridiculous. I'm sorry for always jumping to conclusions."

A weight settled in Ben's stomach, just as it did every time she reverted back to her insecure self. They'd been hanging out for more than a month now, and she still fell into that uncertain Allie that he'd first met. The problem was it didn't matter how many times he told her she was amazing, or how many things she chose for herself; Allie had spent her whole life under the direction of someone else, and it was going to take her a long time to break herself out of the habit of requiring someone else's approval.

He wanted so badly to help her, but he didn't know what else he could do on top of what he'd already done. That wouldn't stop him from trying, but he worried about what would happen if their relationship changed from how it was now. In either direction. Unless he knew exactly what she wanted, he would have to do whatever he could to keep things the way they were.

As for right now, he had to say something—anything—to bring her spirits back up.

"I have spent my life around ridiculous people," he said slowly, not sure where he was going with this. "I mean, you've met Oliver and Cam. And Kit is the king of jumping to conclusions. I'm not saying you're either of those things, but even if you were, you'd fit right in."

He knew she had started crying because she sniffled into his shirt, but he figured it would be best not to point it out.

Ben took a breath, hoping he didn't make a wrong choice. "You know what?" he said. "What if we do a rain check on lunch with the Hamiltons? I think we could both use a day off before we have to face this week."

Allie pulled herself even tighter against him and simply nodded, reaching out to pull up a streaming website so they could pick a show to start with.

It wasn't much progress, but it was something, and Ben hoped he could do more in the future. Allie deserved to be completely confident in who she was.

One of them should be.

TWENTY-SIX

When it came to holidays, Allie had never liked many of them. Most of them were reserved for family, which meant long, forlorn gazes from her mother every time Allie showed up alone. While she definitely could have been worse, Allie's mom had perfected the subtle sadness and casual mention of future grandkids, to the point that Allie had, on occasion, considered never getting married or having kids, just to spite her.

But then she'd think about how lonely of a life that would be and all of the dreams she would miss out on, and she would remind herself that her own desires were way more important than what her mom wanted. Eventually, their dreams might coincide, but Allie didn't have a whole lot of control over that.

So she'd taken to avoiding holidays whenever possible.

Though she'd explained all of this to Ben, he didn't seem to fully comprehend her reasoning and had been asking questions all morning while they made a green bean casserole to bring over for Thanksgiving dinner. After her little meltdown on Sunday, she was glad he wasn't treating her like she was delicate. Things felt normal again, even if she loved him more than ever.

Seeing their finished novel had done something to her, and she'd spent all week trying not to think about what might happen after dinner tonight. For some reason, today felt like the end of something, and she was terrified that he was going to move on and let her go at it alone.

Him asking questions about holidays and pretending their conversation wasn't strange was helping her avoid a full-blown panic attack.

"What about Christmas?" he asked as they made their way out to Oliver's car, which he'd borrowed again to keep up appearances.

Allie groaned as she hugged the casserole. "Mom has started giving me fewer presents, telling me that she's saving them for my kids."

"Ouch."

"I don't care about the presents, but the sentiment hurts."

Ben opened the door for her and took her hand to help her down into the ridiculous car. "One year, I didn't even get any presents because my parents just forgot."

She gaped at him. "You're not serious."

He smirked. "They forgot my birthday once, too."

"No!"

"Yep."

"Wait, when is your birthday?"

Chuckling, he waited until he'd climbed into his own seat before he answered. "March. And you'd better not turn it into a big deal. I don't actually like big birthday celebrations."

March. That was four months away, and Allie clung to the hope that he thought they would still be friends by then. If he wasn't planning to leave, she didn't have to worry. At least, not *too* much.

"Mine's in July."

"Isn't that when you broke up with Jeremy?"

Allie groaned. Jeremy had flat-out dumped her, something she hadn't really experienced before. She was usually the one to initiate the leaving. "Birthday breakup. Good time."

Maybe she imagined it, but she was pretty sure Ben was gripping the steering wheel way tighter than he needed to, considering he hadn't even turned the car on. "You okay?"

He nodded stiffly and hit the ignition, and he pulled out just a little too quickly. "Sorry. Um. If I ever meet this Jeremy guy, can I punch him in the nose?"

Laughing, Allie pried his right hand from the steering wheel so she could kiss his knuckles. Thankfully that made him relax so he didn't accidentally turn their short drive into a race to see how quickly they could get there. "Jeremy's a weakling, so you would definitely kick his trash. I'd like to see that."

By the time they arrived at her parents' house, they were back to discussing the various holidays, which Allie appreciated. Though, learning that Ben's dad was rarely around for the holidays made her ache for him. At least he had Kit and his family to look after him when his own family forgot about him. Apparently, when his dad was home for the holidays, he focused mostly on his wife. Ben spoke as if he didn't care about how often his dad was gone, but Allie could see the longing in his eyes, clear as day.

"My dad's big into barbecuing," Allie said to lighten the mood after Ben's casual revelation, "and the fact that he can't make his jokes with someone else at the grill with him is definitely a sore spot. So that kills the vibe at Memorial Day, Fourth of July, and Labor Day."

Ben grimaced. "Too bad I'm not much of a barbecuer. Cam is big on alternative protein sources, and living with him the last half a decade has mostly broken me out of my meat habit."

Allie raised an eyebrow. "Says the new vegetarian who doesn't know how to cook tofu."

This time Ben laughed. "I didn't say I'm good at eating well. I'm pretty sure Cam thinks I'll keel over dead any day now based on my low-nutrient diet."

"Well…" Allie sighed as she looked up at her childhood home. "I'm afraid my mom doesn't understand vegetarianism, and she *will* expect you to eat your weight in turkey. Sorry."

"For you, I'll eat anything."

He missed Allie's blush because he stepped out of the car just then, and though she usually preferred to open her own door, this time she decided to wait. Just to give herself a chance to calm down. Watching him walk past the hood of the car, she could so easily imagine this sight for the rest of her life. Was that completely ridiculous? Probably. But when he opened her door and held out his hand, the thought struck her so suddenly that she couldn't move. She wanted that. So badly. She wanted Ben to be in her life.

All of it.

"You good?" Ben crouched down to be at her level, his shoes probably getting wet in the dead grass. Jeremy would have hated that, but Ben didn't seem to care. His focus was entirely fixed on her. "I'll admit I can't read your thoughts this time, so no Sherlocking for me today. What's going on?"

Could she really tell him how she felt? It would change everything. But would it change for the better or worse? She had no idea; Ben was just as hard to read as he seemed to think she was. She hadn't spent enough time around his other friends to know if the way he acted with her was different from how he acted with them, so she couldn't know if he thought their relationship could be more than a friendship. Being honest with him could either be the best or worst decision of her life, and she didn't know if that risk was worth it.

Could she afford to lose him?

"Allie?"

She blinked, taking him in as much as she could before her tears blurred her vision. "I'm nervous," she admitted.

He cocked his head. "Why? I don't think today's dinner will be all that different from the last one."

"You don't know that." Allie shuddered. He *really* didn't know that. Mom thought this relationship was real, and lasting, and the only one Allie would have from here on out. Maybe that was true.

Maybe it wasn't. She still didn't know if Ben would ever want to be more than her friend.

Her heart picked up speed, and she felt like she was running the hundred-meter dash while sitting in this ridiculous car.

"Ben," she whispered, her tears escaping down her cheeks.

Ben reacted quickly, grabbing the casserole off her lap and setting it on top of the car. Then he took hold of her hands and pulled her from the car as well. Once she was in his arms, she felt monumentally better, and she burrowed into his hold like she always did whenever he held her like this. It happened often, and she had never been able to tell him how much it meant to her that he was willing to embrace her whenever she needed it.

No one had ever been so accommodating before. No one had ever been so…loving.

Her heart constricted. What if Ben loved her as much as she loved him?

Allie pulled away as determination set in. She had to tell him. Before her mom's over-sentimental spiel scared him away. At least this way, if she told him she loved him as more than a friend, he could decide if he even wanted to stick around for dinner or if he would be better off cutting ties as soon as possible.

Allie swallowed as she met his eyes and saw the concern in them. She could be brave. She could. "I have to tell you something," she whispered.

Ben leaned a little closer. Was that fear pulling his eyebrows together? "What's wrong?"

"Um."

"Allie, you can tell me anything. You know that, right?"

She did know that, and the longer she looked into the man's beautiful and caring face, the more confident she became. She had just spent four months learning who she was and figuring out what she liked. Ben had helped her learn to be independent and go for what she wanted.

Go for what you want, Allison.

"Ben, I'm—"

Movement caught her eye, and she glanced over just as Jake and his dad stepped out of their house and headed their way. Allie's stomach dropped when she met Jake's eyes and he gave her a look that clearly said he hadn't given up on her yet. He still didn't believe she was with Ben. He was still determined to be in her life, and he was coming over for Thanksgiving because he thought he had a chance.

Allie cursed under her breath and did the first thing that came to mind.

She grabbed hold of Ben's jacket collar and tugged him forward until their lips met, and then everything but him vanished.

Oh boy. Allie had kissed a lot of people. *A lot.* And she knew she was good at it. Multiple guys had told her so, and she took pride in that. But kissing Ben was unlike anything she'd ever experienced, and she credited that entirely to him. He kissed her with a slow fervor, at the same time with a restrained intensity that made her wonder what he was holding back. It was an exploration, a searching for something deep inside her as he pulled her tight against him and cradled her head to protect her from anything that might come their way. Allie wrapped her arms around his neck and let him search, as if he might learn everything about her if they stood there long enough.

She lost track of time out there on the parkway, and when Ben finally released her, they both fought to catch their breath.

Allie had no idea what to say, and Ben seemed just as tongue-tied. She could think of one way to help fix that, but she figured now was not the time to dive back in. Especially when the front door opened and Mom poked her head out.

"What are you two doing out here? It's freezing!"

Jake was nowhere in sight, which meant he must have already gone inside. As much as Allie wished she could stay right where she was, Mom would never let them continue what they were doing. Even if Allie desperately wanted to have a conversation with Ben, a conversation she was sure he wanted to have as well based on the question in his dark eyes.

She hadn't meant to jump him like that, but he definitely hadn't seemed to mind.

"I guess we should go inside," she said, biting her lip.

Ben's expression smoldered. Allie had never seen a smolder, but that was the absolute best word to describe the look on his face. "If we have to," he said, his voice low and his eyes fixed on her mouth.

Allie shivered and couldn't help but slide her hand to the back of his neck. She was so tempted to ignore her mom and pull him in for another kiss that her lips were on his before Mom shouted her name again.

Snorting a laugh, Ben touched his forehead to hers and pulled away, though he threaded their hands together before grabbing the casserole with his free hand. "I guess we have to go," he muttered, his reluctance clear.

So she definitely wasn't alone in this. Whatever she felt for Ben, he felt some measure of it too, and they had to figure out what that meant for the future.

But first, they had to get through Thanksgiving dinner, and with the way Ben was looking at her like she would taste so much better than any meal, that was not going to be easy.

TWENTY-SEVEN

BEN WAS FREAKING OUT. HE hoped he had an outward calm, but he was so caught up in his head about what had happened outside that they were halfway through dinner already and he had no idea what he had said whenever anyone talked to him.

Even Allie had pulled him into conversation, and he'd probably responded because no one had given him any strange looks. But all of it was a blur.

All of it except the way Allie had kissed him.

He knew she'd done it because Jake had come outside. Deep down, he *knew* that. It was proving a point and protecting herself. But if that was how Allie kissed to prove a point, he couldn't imagine what a real kiss would be like.

Now he understood what Madi and Oliver had gone through when Kit suspected there was more to their relationship than faking it. Kit, as always, had been right. He'd asked Ben and Cam to keep Oliver and his sister from being alone, and Ben had absolutely felt the tension between them. In fact, he had almost left them alone just to see what would happen, but he had promised Kit that he would stick around until Kit got off work.

Madi had told him later that Oliver had kissed her a couple of nights before that day, and they hadn't had a chance to talk about it by that point. If it was anything like what Ben was going through right now, Oliver must have come within inches of losing his mind.

No wonder they locked lips every chance they got.

"Ben?"

Ben jumped and pulled his eyes away from Allie to look at her mom. "Sorry, did you say something?"

Helen gave him a knowing smile, not at all subtle about telling him he had been staring at her daughter. And probably grinning like an idiot. "I only wondered if your family is missing you today."

"I doubt it." He cringed, even if it was true. His dad was home for Thanksgiving for the first time in years, which meant all attention would be on him. "I mean, I often spend Thanksgiving with my friends. My parents don't have a lot of space." That wasn't any better. "I'll be there for Christmas, so it's fine."

"And what about you, Allie?"

Allie jumped too, and her hand suddenly rested on Ben's thigh, making him tense up. "Sorry, what?"

Helen and Hector both snickered, completely unaware of the way Jake was glaring at his mashed potatoes.

"What are your Christmas plans?" her mom asked. "Are you coming here? Or going with Ben to his family?"

Ben could only imagine the chaos that his family was going to be, particularly compared to this gathering. As much as he would love for Allie to meet his family, they were more likely to scare her away than anything, and he would need to be sure she might stick around before he subjected her to the Naka-mura madness.

Allie's hand tightened in the spot just above his knee that had always been extra ticklish, and he squirmed. Her eyes went wide, and she mouthed a "sorry" and let him go. "We haven't talked about that yet," she said as her face turned red.

If he wasn't being stared down by the rest of them, Ben would have invited her in a heartbeat. But they still had a month before Christmas, and they had to talk about their relationship before they started going into holidays, particularly ones Allie didn't like.

Ben didn't like losing the contact they'd had a moment ago, so he grabbed Allie's hand and gave it a squeeze. She squeezed back, and suddenly they were in a sort of Morse code conversation even though neither of them actually knew Morse code.

This was maddening!

"Hey Ben," Jake said suddenly, the first thing he'd said directly to him since they arrived. "You got a second?"

A buzzing sound filled his head, and with the way Allie was biting her lip again, this time because of clear nerves, Ben was tempted to say they had to be somewhere so he could drag her outside and kiss her again. But he still had a part to play, so he reluctantly let go of Allie's hand and stood.

"Sure," he said, though it came out strained.

Once he checked to make sure his dad was doing okay, Jake led the way into the kitchen, far enough that they could talk without being heard but near enough to the dining room that they were within sight of Allie's family. That meant this would be a decently short conversation and would remain civil, but that didn't mean Ben was looking forward to it.

Leaning against the sink, Jake folded his arms in a way that was probably supposed to be intimidating. But Ben had known Cam most of his life, so displays of machismo didn't go very far with him.

Jake narrowed his eyes. "So, you and Allie are getting pretty serious, huh?"

Ben had no idea how to answer that without potentially being wrong. "That's not something I can define on my own. I'm only half the equation."

"How chivalrous of you."

Ben really didn't like the sarcasm in Jake's tone. "Are you trying to insinuate Allie shouldn't get a say in her own life?"

Jake scoffed. "I'm not insinuating anything. I just know her better than you do, so I know that whatever it is you think you have with her, you're wrong."

Ben was never prone to anger. He'd learned to roll with the punches and always see both sides, and that way of thinking had served him well. But when it came to Allie and the way she'd been hurt so many times over the years, Ben could feel his frustration and empathy churning inside him, threatening to explode. Anger would absolutely not help this situation when Jake had already decided he knew what was best, so Ben took a slow breath and forced himself to stay calm.

"What Allie does and who she decides to be with is entirely up to her," he said, silently applauding his control over his voice. He wanted to shout, but he kept his words calm. "If she chooses me, then I'll be the happiest man in the world. And if she doesn't, then that's her decision."

As he stood up straight to look down at Ben, Jake clearly didn't like that response. "She won't choose you," he spat. "Allie has proven time and time again that she needs someone who's willing to fight for her, and that's clearly not you. Maybe things have been good so far, but as soon as you hit a hiccup, she'll be gone, and you'll be forgotten. Just like the rest of them. You do know how many people she's dated and dumped, don't you?"

Ben had heard about each and every one of them, probably in more detail than Jake ever had. Most of them had become villains to go up against Allie's Wonder Boys, and Ben had honestly appreciated knowing more about them. It helped him understand Allie and who she was beneath all of the masks they had made her wear.

"This isn't a conversation we should be having," Ben said, though he did wish he had a little more of Cam's intimidation. "Who Allie dates is none of your concern, and who she's dated in the past is none of mine. That includes you. If you'll excuse me."

Jake grabbed his arm before he could take a step, though he let go as soon as he looked over and saw Allie and her parents unashamedly watching the pair of them. "However good things seem on the outside," he said quietly, "she's still going to leave you the second you do something wrong. I should know."

That last bit came out strained, and Ben stared at the man as Jake returned to the dining room and said something about the football game being on. The one ex Allie hadn't told him much about was Jake, so Ben didn't know how things ended between them. Something told him it hadn't been easy on either of them.

"What did he say to you?" Allie asked the instant she arrived in the kitchen.

Her mom had started cleaning up while the men moved into the TV room, and Ben was itching to go grab all the dirty dishes but worried he would lose his cool as soon as anyone pushed him over the edge. He was especially worried that Allie would be the one to make that push, and he refused to lash out at her just because a guy she used to know had staked his claim on something that couldn't be owned.

Ben tried to take a deep breath but failed. "Ask me later," he said, practically begging. "I promise I'll tell you, but right now…" He met her gaze and softened at the sight of the fear in her eyes. "Right now I need a distraction. Anything."

He did not expect her to grab his hand and pull him so hard that his wrist popped, but he followed her down the hall and out the front door without hesitation. She stopped on the porch and turned around, and the hungry look in her eyes was so easy to read that he didn't question his interpretation of it.

It was an invitation.

Ben took his opportunity, pulling her into a fierce kiss that stole his breath when they collided. Their first kiss had pulsed with electricity, but Ben had been caught off guard by that one, unsure if any of it was real. He'd been cautious. But this? This was fire, the kind of kiss that made history. He had wanted to do this for so long, and as she guided him up against the side of the house to lean into him and return the favor, he knew he hadn't imagined the spark between them earlier.

She wanted this as much as he did.

"I love you," he said the first chance he got. It surprised him as much as it surprised her—she froze with her eyes closed—but the words came out easily. For the first time in his life, the important thing had been easy to say, even if Ben was regretting saying it with each passing second.

Tears slipped from Allie's eyes as she looked at him. "What?" she whispered.

Ben swallowed. As much as he wanted to take hold of her waist so she couldn't run away, he forced himself to keep his hands at his sides. "I'm sorry," he said. "I know you're off dating right now, and I know this messes up our friendship. But I'm in love with you, Allie Ortega. Deeply. Madly. Completely."

"You love me?" she repeated, as if she couldn't believe it. Or maybe she was simply angry, and Ben wouldn't blame her.

Saying more wouldn't help things, but his mouth had apparently grown a mind of its own. Or maybe talking was the only way to keep from kissing her again. "You're my best friend, Als, and I don't want to lose this friendship. But I want it to be more. I want you to let me help you find yourself, and I want to make dinner with you and order cheese pizza when we're too tired to cook, and I want to take turns going to family holidays, and laugh together when your dad realizes I have no idea how to use a grill."

She hadn't moved, still standing right in front of him with her hands clasped around his arms and an expression on her face he'd never seen before as she stared at his chest.

He had no idea what to do with that except to repeat what he'd already said more times in the last two minutes than he had his entire life. "I love you, Allie. Always have, always will."

She finally looked up at him, her cheeks wet with tears, and he braced himself for her inevitable rejection. "I love you too," she whispered.

The floor seemed to disappear beneath him, leaving him weightless. "What?"

This time she smiled, biting her lip as she did so. "I love you, Ben. I've never said that to anyone before and meant it, but it's true. I love you."

Reaching up, he brushed the tears from her cheeks with his thumbs and willed himself to believe he'd heard her right. "I don't... Really?" Why in the world would he question her right now?

Allie laughed and kissed him with a gentleness that made him groan. "Really. I think it's been a long time coming."

"But you don't want to date anyone." *Stop talking, Ben.*

With a little shrug, she ran her hand through his hair and made him shiver as she said, "I don't want to date anyone but you."

Somehow their next kiss was better than the others before. Spinning them around so Allie's back was to the wall, Ben wrapped his hands around her waist and took control of the kiss, putting his whole heart into it in a way he'd never done before. In a way that made him feel important and wanted.

He was half convinced he'd died and gone to heaven because there was no way he could be this happy. All of this was probably a dream, and he would wake up in his crappy apartment on a random Thursday, stuck driving his crappy car on his way to his crappy job. He wouldn't have a graphic novel or an amazing woman in his arms who made it so easy to be himself like he'd never been before.

Eventually, Allie broke free of their embrace and laughed at what was probably a ridiculous expression on Ben's face. "Where did you come from, Wonder Boy?" she breathed as she cupped his face with her soft hands.

"The grocery store," he replied, leaning into her touch. "Don't you remember?"

Rolling her eyes, Allie kissed him one last time, then took hold of his hand. "We should probably go back inside."

Ben didn't move. "Not yet," he begged. "I just want a little longer with you to myself. Please."

That got him a smile and another kiss, both of which he accepted with utter contentment. He had to work a double shift tomorrow since a good number of people had taken the day off for the holiday, so he wouldn't get to see her again until Saturday afternoon after he worked the morning shift. For now, he just wanted to soak in the moment and never let go.

TWENTY-EIGHT

ALLIE HAD NEVER SLEPT SO well in her life, and she gave Ben all the credit for that. True, she would have liked the night better if Ben hadn't insisted he go back to his own apartment, but his goodnight kiss had made everything worth it. For a guy who hadn't dated much, he sure knew how to kiss, and she suspected it was because he put his whole heart into everything he did, no matter what.

His whole heart. Ben *loved* her. Not just as a friend but as something more. So much more. Allie squealed as she lay in her bed and hugged her blankets tight with utter joy rendering her pretty much useless. Of all the things she thought might happen at Thanksgiving, his admission had definitely not been one of them. How could she have gotten so lucky, especially after all her insistence that they were nothing but friends?

Unable to help herself, Allie booted up her laptop so she could pull up their graphic novel again. *Menace Unknown* looked just as good as it had on Sunday when Ben showed it to her, and she couldn't wait to see it in print form. No one would buy it, most likely, but having something in her hands that she had helped make was going to be the best feeling in the world.

Well, second to hearing Ben list the reasons he loved her. That would always be top of the list of amazing things, and he had done it the entire drive from her parents' to her apartment.

Allie had started making her own mental list, and she couldn't wait to share it with him. Hers was considerably longer.

Not that it was a competition, but if it were, she would win.

Allie stared at her pretty little novel until she finally had to get up and get ready for work, cursing the fact that Sweet Red refused to take off any holidays other than the major ones. If she had had today off, she could have gone to O'Reilly's and spent the day with Ben, even if he happened to be working.

Before she hopped in the shower, she sent off a text to Ben because waiting to talk to him sounded like the perfect way to ruin her day. She wanted him to know how much yesterday had meant to her and how willing she was—desperate—to turn their relationship to something more.

> Allie: If I could pick my top favorite days of my life, nothing would come close to ranking as high as yesterday.

By the time she was showered and dressed, Allie was definitely running late now, and she cursed her imagination for running wild in the shower and replaying yesterday's kisses. All of them. She would really have to hustle now, so when someone knocked on the door, Allie almost ignored it.

Thinking it might be Ben here to surprise her, she rushed to the door and pulled it open with her heart racing. Her mood plummeted. "Jake."

He stuffed his hands into his pockets and glanced behind her. "Can we talk?"

"I'm late for work."

"This shouldn't take long." He pushed his way inside without invitation, and Allie cursed herself for being too nice to force him to leave.

At least she didn't feel the need to give him her full attention. She started gathering her things as he sat on the bed and watched her.

"I take it things are going well with Ben?" he said.

Allie really didn't want to have this conversation now. She didn't respond, too busy chugging a protein shake so she wouldn't starve until lunch.

"He seems to like you," Jake continued. This time, he sounded a little distracted, and Allie realized he was staring at the graphic novel still pulled up on her screen. "Did you guys do this?"

Allie rolled her eyes. "Don't act so surprised," she said on her way to the bathroom to brush her teeth. "Jake, why are you really here?"

The sound of her toothbrush covered up anything he might have said, but she didn't really care to hear it anyway. For the first time since she was a teen, maybe in her life, she was genuinely happy, and nothing Jake could do or say would change that.

When she returned to the main room of her apartment, Jake had moved to the door, his hands in his pockets and his eyes on the floor. "I just want to make sure you're okay, Allie," he said. "I care about you. You know that, right? I just want you to be happy."

Ben hadn't texted her back yet, but he was probably at work so it didn't matter. He would reply as soon as he got the chance, and Allie knew he wasn't the sort of guy who would kiss her and immediately ghost her. He was better than that.

She must have been frowning at her phone, because Jake leaned in closer, probably not realizing he was blocking her way out and making her later than she already was. "Something wrong?"

Allie's head snapped up. "No, nothing's wrong. I have to get to work, Jake. And you have to stop coming here and acting like we stayed friends all these years." That was probably too harsh, something she realized when Jake's shoulders slumped.

Sighing, she put her hand on his arm. "If you want to be friends, then great. We can be friends. But that means you have to be friends with Ben too. He's not going anywhere anytime soon."

Jake had grown up a lot appearance-wise since they dated, but as Allie looked him over, she realized he still had the same half smile that didn't quite reach his eyes when he wasn't actually happy. He hunched his shoulders the same way, and he could never decide which eye to look at when he met her gaze. He really hadn't changed all that much, and that made her sad. She had changed so much that she was a completely different person, and she was beginning to like that about herself. She had discovered the real Allie Ortega.

Was this the real Jake, or did he still have some self-discovery to do?

"I hope you're right about him," Jake said quietly, and he leaned forward to kiss Allie's cheek. "See you around?"

"Sure."

Allie waited until he'd disappeared down the stairs, and then she hurried to her car and sped to work before she was so late that she would get into trouble.

While she didn't often pray for a crisis at work, Allie was more than grateful when one popped up today. It was already going to be the longest day of her life, so at least she had a good distraction. Apparently, all of their proofreaders had gone on sudden vacations for the holiday, and they had three different manuscripts that were supposed to go to press on Monday.

Mr. Simmons didn't hesitate when he asked Allie if she could step in and comb through the books with the editors and writers, even offering to bring in lunch. He had never once bought Allie lunch, though he did it all the time for the creation team, so she felt like she was actually a part of the company for once. Though it was a strange feeling, she absolutely loved it and dove right in.

Ben didn't respond to any of the texts she sent throughout the day, which meant he must have been as busy as she was, but when she still hadn't heard from him by the time she finally got home after eleven that night, she started to get a little worried. This silence wasn't like him, and she couldn't help but wonder if something had happened to him at work. Or maybe…

As she crawled into her bed, exhausted, Allie hugged a pillow tight and did everything she could not to think the worst. She couldn't help it, though. After one of her boyfriends broke up with her by disappearing into the wind rather than talking to her, her mind tended to stray in that direction.

What if he'd changed his mind? What if that goodnight kiss had actually been a good*bye* kiss, and Allie had been too lost in a fantasy to realize it? What if Ben had never loved her and had kissed her because… Because why? Any man in his right mind would have pushed things farther before he vanished, getting what he wanted first. He wouldn't have gone home instead of staying the night.

"Ben's not like that," she whispered. She *knew* that. But she also knew he was so nice that if he wanted to break up with her, he probably wouldn't know how to do it without hurting her. He'd picked the easiest option and decided to simply ghost her. No words exchanged and no feelings in sight.

Tears pooled in her eyes as she tried to stop her thoughts from spiraling. She always did this, and this was exactly why she had been so determined to stay away from men for as long as she could. She wasn't strong enough on her own, and the moment she attached herself to someone, she lost all sense of confidence.

Was she even ready to love someone? What if she was falling back into the same trap as always?

"He'll text you back," she told herself and prayed she was right.

She woke late the next morning to her phone buzzing, and she snatched it up before she'd really woken up yet. She had to squint at the screen and blink several times before she could even make out the words in the text, but cold disappointment washed over her pretty quickly as she realized it had come from Mr. Simmons.

> Simmons: Why is Mr. Nakamura self-publishing when he's under contract with us? This is a clear violation, and I need you to contact him and set up a meeting with our legal team.

What was he talking about? He'd included a link, which Allie clicked with growing dread. The page seemed to take forever to load, but when it did, she suddenly couldn't breathe.

It was *Menace Unknown*. Their graphic novel. Ben had sent it to a popular comic site where people could download it for free. But worse than that?

He'd taken her name off of it.

Menace Unknown by Benjamin Nakamura.

Clicking the download button, Allie scrolled through a few pages but knew she wouldn't find any changes. The words were still the same. *Her words.* He'd taken them and claimed them as his own, and there was nothing in the book that even mentioned her.

The worst part was the fact that the book was trending. Like, a lot. A quick search showed links all over the internet, and people had been downloading and sharing the thing since late yesterday morning. It was all anyone was talking about in forums and social media sites, and Allie's world was crashing down around her as she realized what this could have meant for her if Ben hadn't been like every other man in her life and cut her out of his to suit his needs.

People clearly loved her writing, and she could have made it.

She could have been something.

Without having to deal with Simmons and Sweet Red.

Though she didn't realize she was doing it until the phone was ringing, Allie pulled up Ben's name in her contacts and hit the call button. She had to ask him why. She had to know what she'd done wrong to convince him to destroy her like this so she could avoid doing it again in the future.

Of course, he didn't answer. He'd probably been screening her texts and calls since yesterday morning so he could make sure she didn't discover their book until it was too late. She sent him a text anyway, asking him how he could have done this to her, but she knew he would never answer that question.

He could get any job he wanted now. So many people were talking about his artwork that he would be getting hundreds of emails from all over. He would finally be able to leave that stupid fun center, but Allie would be stuck living her awful life because he hadn't had the decency to pull her up with him. No, he decided to take full credit for all of the hard work she'd put in over the last month.

The fun center. He was probably still going to be at work today; he would have to keep getting money from somewhere until he actually accepted one of his million job offers that would be coming down the line. If nothing else, Allie could look into his eyes when she told him she never wanted to see him again. There was nothing she could say that would actually hurt him like he'd hurt her, but she would do her best.

O'Reilly's had opened only an hour or so before, but the place was chaos. Kids were everywhere, running around like they were living off of several days' worth of pumpkin pie sugar-high and their parents had dropped them off for a moment of peace. Every employee Allie passed seemed on the verge of a breakdown, but she only felt marginally bad about that because she thought of all of them as an extension of Ben. He was their supervisor, after all, and he deserved to have his life flipped upside down in the course of a few hours, just like she had.

She found him in the middle of the mini golf course, stuffed halfway into the windmill as several people watched on. From the sound of things, a kid had gotten herself stuck inside, and Ben was trying to get her out.

If Allie hadn't been completely heartbroken and torn to shreds, the moment might have been funny.

"I'll let you choose any prize you want from the arcade," Ben was saying as Allie approached the edge of the crowd. His voice sounded muffled and dull, exactly how Allie felt.

A high-pitched whine was the response from inside the windmill.

"How did you even get in here? Let's get you—ouch! Alright, kid, maybe no one has told you this before, but it's not nice to bite people."

Knowing she would lose her nerve if she didn't ride the anger wave that had brought her here, Allie crept forward and touched Ben's knee. "Ben?"

He jumped, and the thud that came with it meant he had probably hit his head on something. But he scrambled out of the windmill quickly enough, his face bright red as he met her gaze. "Allie! Hi. Sorry. You've probably been texting me, but I dropped my phone in the ball pit yesterday while I was cleaning up a puke fest and…" He swallowed when he realized the two of them were not alone and his audience was fully captivated. "Um. How are you?"

Curse her tears! Allie wanted to stand there in confidence and righteous fury, not break into sobs as the one good thing in her life fell apart.

Ben was on his feet in an instant. "What's wrong?"

She slapped his hands away before he could touch her, which made him jump back. *Good.* "How could you?" she whispered.

His eyebrows dipping low, Ben glanced at the crowd around them. "Do you want to go somewhere and talk? I have a break in a minute."

"No, I don't want to *talk*. Why would I want to talk to you ever again?"

"Allie, I don't… I don't understand. Is this because I didn't text you? I told you, my phone—"

"Like I'm going to believe that bull." Folding her arms tight, Allie searched deep inside herself for every bit of strength she had. She was going to need it. "You know," she said, "I thought you were different. I've spent my life being used up and walked over, and I thought for once I'd found someone who could let me have my own life. And here you are, just like everyone else."

Ben shifted his weight on his feet, clearly uncomfortable, though his focus never wavered from her. She had come to like that about him, how he wasn't afraid to really see her. But right now, she wished he could show at least a little shame. Some proof that he wasn't the monster she thought he was.

"Allie," he said slowly, "I don't know what I did, but I want to fix it. Please, tell me what's going on."

How long would he play dumb? "You ruined my chances of being a writer," she spat.

The color drained from his face. *Finally* an acknowledgement. "Allie, I swear I haven't done anything. I'm going to make sure Simmons puts your name on the books, and—"

"This has nothing to do with that!" Her strength was fading fast, and the fact that he wouldn't even admit to what he'd done made all of this so much worse. "You think I care about those stupid books? No one's going to read them anyway! This is about you stealing the one thing I was proud of."

The kid in the windmill made a whimpering sound, and Ben glanced back, clearly torn between arguing his case and finding an excuse to walk away. "Allie, I want to talk about this, okay? Whatever it is. But..."

But she would never come first. She should have been used to that at this point, and she berated herself for ever thinking things in her life would go her way. "What's the point?" she said, all of her anger making way for misery and disappointment. "You got what you wanted, and I'm done. With all of it. Thanks for ruining my life, Ben."

"Allie, wait!"

But Allie didn't look back as she made her way back through the fun center. She'd meant what she said, and for once she was going to follow through. This was one time she wouldn't falter.

She couldn't.

TWENTY-NINE

BEN STOOD FROZEN TO THE spot, watching as Allie disappeared into the sea of kids that had been his nightmare for the last twenty-eight hours. He wanted to run after her and make her explain what in the world she was talking about, but the parents watching him and the cell phones still trained in his direction kept him rooted to the spot. That, and the kid who had started crying behind him, finally realizing that sitting inside a tiny windmill wasn't as fun as it had looked.

He would fix this. As soon as he could.

"You ready to come out?" he asked the stuck child.

She mumbled something through her sobs, and Ben took that as an affirmative, climbing back inside the little opening so he could grab her foot and direct her way out.

With that problem solved and the girl safely in the arms of her parents, Ben took a deep breath and prepared himself to move onto the next item in the never-ending stream of catastrophes he'd been fixing since yesterday morning. It had started with a kid getting sick at one of the tables in the food court, which had launched a chain reaction of vomit throughout the attendees of a birthday party. Things had only gone downhill from there, and Ben hadn't gotten home until two in the morning, only to return at six to deal with everything he and his team hadn't managed to solve last night. All while occasionally jumping into the ball pit to try to locate his missing phone.

"Ben, I found it!"

Ben hadn't moved from the windmill when one of the teen employees rushed over with his dead phone in hand. He knew he would have to face reality eventually. But the look on Allie's face and the hurt in her eyes told him something bad had gone down, and he hadn't been there to help.

She had needed him, and he'd failed her, and that hurt so much worse than the way she'd looked at him like she hated him. Which had sucked.

"Ben!" Another employee ran up to him, her eyes wide and desperate. "We've got an emergency situation in the bathrooms!"

Before he could even respond, maybe tell her she would have to handle it because he had more important things to take care of—away from this awful place—another employee approached with a phone in his hand.

"Someone found this in the garbage," he said and handed it to Ben.

Allie's phone. She'd thrown it away? Though he could think of so many better ways she could have dealt with her anger, like blocking his number, this was a very Allie move to make. Head first, no hesitation. He would have been proud of her for knowing what she wanted if what she wanted didn't involve him. The message was clear: she wanted nothing to do with him.

Ben had no idea what had happened over the last day and a half, but he was going to find out. And he was going to fix it if he could, because that was the only way he would convince Allie to give him a chance.

THIRTY

Unwilling to go home, with her apartment full of memories with Ben, Allie went straight to her parents' house in search of something comfortable and familiar. She had no idea what she was going to do next, but maybe her mom would have some magical solution to fix heartbreak. Moms were great for that.

When she arrived, however, the house was empty, and she sank onto the couch as sobs finally broke free. She'd been holding it together pretty well, but here in the safe space of her childhood home, she let loose.

Until the doorbell rang.

It was probably Ben, and though he was the last person in the world Allie wanted to see, she still crept over to the door with some lingering hope that he would know how to make it all better. Ben had always had a solution for things. A way to look at the bright side. She wouldn't take excuses, but apologies on his knees she could handle.

But it was Jake at the door, his eyebrows pulled low as he took in her blotchy face and red eyes. "Allie."

Allie closed the door.

Jake stuffed his foot in the way before she could close it all the way. "Allie, I saw you pull up and run inside. What's wrong?"

This was none of his business, but Allie didn't have the strength to tell him so. Instead, she fell into his arms and let him hold her. It wasn't the embrace she truly wanted, but it wasn't like she could go to Ben for that. She would take what she could get.

"I've made a huge mistake, Jake," she said into his chest once she'd stopped bawling her eyes out.

He rubbed slow circles on her back, which from anyone else might have felt soothing. But his touch did nothing but emphasize how wrong he was for her. She'd outgrown him, and they didn't fit anymore. "Allie, I'm sure that's not true. What happened?"

She stuttered through her basic explanation, though he didn't seem all that surprised. Maybe he had been right about Ben the whole time, and Allie had simply been blinded by his charms. At least she felt justified in her feelings on the subject when someone else validated her reaction without hesitation.

Something about it all didn't sit well in Allie's stomach, but she was too miserable to think about it right now.

"I don't know if I can ever trust anyone again," she admitted. Saying it out loud made it far truer than it had been in her head, and she shuddered. Surely her life wouldn't end up so completely awful, would it? She would find someone real, and true, and so entirely good that he would make Ben look like the worst boyfriend in the world.

There were two problems with that statement: No one could be better than Ben, and he had never been her boyfriend. Not really.

Jake shifted Allie in his arms, keeping her close enough that he could brush the tears from her cheeks. "You're going to get through this, Als," he said. "I'll be here to help you through this."

Then he went in for a kiss.

Allie slapped him. She'd slapped a good number of guys over the years, but never someone she actually *knew*. Still, despite her own surprise at her actions, she stared at Jake and tried to understand how he could have read the situation so completely wrong.

"What was that?" she demanded.

Jake massaged his cheek. She must have hit him hard. "I thought…"

Allie had never been so insulted in her life, and that included what Ben had done to her. "Have you ever heard a word that I've said to you?"

"Of course I—"

She stepped out of his reach when he went to touch her again. "This is why I'm going to be alone forever," she said with a huff. "Ben is the only person who has ever actually listened to me."

"He's also the only one who sent your book to Hayday Comics," Jake grumbled.

"Okay, yeah, he…" Allie's words stuck in her throat as everything fell into place. "I didn't tell you anything about Hayday," she said, taking a step back.

Jake turned red. "Sure you did. You said…" He couldn't even come up with a lie, and he dropped his chin to his chest. "Allie."

Suddenly dizzy, Allie fell back against the door. "*You* sent my book. *You* took my name off of it."

And if she was being honest with herself, she wasn't even surprised.

"Allie—"

She shut the door with a finality that didn't feel final enough, her heart pounding in her chest like it wanted to escape. *Jake* had sent the book. Probably trying to get her to break up with Ben so he could make his move. Of all the stupid, asinine, *manipulative* things… But the worst part? It *worked*.

Allie sank to the floor, hugging her knees tight as she started to cry again. She hadn't even questioned it. One little doubt, and she'd blown up on poor, sweet Ben who probably still had no idea what she'd been talking about. She'd thrown away the best thing to ever happen to her, and Ben deserved so much better than her.

He deserved someone who had it all put together and could actually be a support to him instead of a burden. And that wasn't Allie.

"Not yet," she murmured, wiping the tears from her eyes and sitting up straight. She'd spent the last few months learning who she was, but she hadn't done anything to learn how to stand on her own two feet. She still needed someone else to hold her up.

Maybe Allie wasn't the woman Ben deserved, but she *could* be.

She *would* be.

THIRTY-ONE

IT WAS NEARLY IMPOSSIBLE TO go without talking to Ben when he wouldn't leave her mind no matter what she did. Not that she really wanted to stop thinking about Ben, but it wasn't exactly easy to focus on improving herself when all she could think about was his dimpled smile. Or the quiet way he laughed. Or how perfectly he kissed when he wasn't holding back…

Every single day she thought about finding Ben and explaining everything. Every single day she lost her courage. He probably didn't even want to see her. With the way she blew up at him, he likely hated her, and she wouldn't blame him if he never wanted to talk to her again. It was better if she gave him a chance to move on, no matter how much she wanted him to take her back when she was more worthy of him.

That was going to take a lot of work to get to that point, but Allie wanted to do it. For Ben, yes, but mostly for herself. She had spent too long believing she was only worth the value someone else assigned to her, and that needed to change.

The Monday following Thanksgiving, she quit Sweet Red Cherry Books. Simmons practically begged her to reconsider, but she'd had the whole weekend to think about it. With the way *Menace Unknown* had exploded, she knew she could definitely make it on her own as a writer. So many people had been talking about the storyline, and while Ben's art had helped get attention, the story was all her.

She was done holding herself back, so she left Sweet Red and didn't look back.

That was Step One.

Allie had it all lined up in five steps that she called "Operation Worthy of Ben." (It was a terrible name, but it did the trick.)

> *Step one: stop letting men dictate your life*
> *Step two: come clean about everything with Mom*
> *Step three: prove you can write without validation*
> *Step four: fix yourself for real*
> *Step five: apologize to Ben — groveling if necessary*

She put the apology part last because she knew herself too well now. If she saw Ben too early, she would fold like a card table and ignore all the other important steps in her important plan. She'd thrown her phone in the O'Reilly's garbage — an overly dramatic move she'd regretted almost immediately — so she couldn't text him either, and getting close enough to his apartment to leave him a note would inevitably result in her lurking until she caught a glimpse of him. Too dangerous.

Nope, any contact with Ben would have to come last if she wanted this self-love thing to work.

With no income, she sold her apartment lease and moved back home. Though her mom was worried about her, and understandably so, for once she kept her distance and let Allie mope in peace for a full two days. After that, though, she wouldn't leave Allie alone until she talked about what had happened.

Allie told her everything. Admitting to the truth — that the relationship hadn't been real at first — hadn't been easy, but the weight of the guilt she'd been carrying disappeared after her mom spent an hour crying with her. She would have to build back up to a place of trust, but at least her mom didn't hate her.

Step Two complete.

In fact, Mom had forgiven her quickly and even offered to read some of Allie's work and help her write something good enough to self-publish.

For Step Three, she sequestered herself in her room except for bathroom breaks and meals with her parents and managed to get the first draft of a novel written out. It was the story of a girl discovering who she was, and Allie had never been prouder of something. It would be a while yet before she tried to publish it, but at least it existed.

She wanted so badly to show it to Ben, but she knew that would only throw her right back into her old ways. She didn't need his validation or his love to be proud of herself. She clearly hadn't been as strong as she'd thought—thinking Ben had refused to give her credit had broken her—and she spent the days after Thanksgiving deep diving into herself. She even talked to a therapist a couple of times, learning ways to help her rely on her own mind and heart instead of putting her fate into anyone else's hands.

Step Four had been more successful than she could have hoped. For the first time in her life, she could let herself just...be. To do whatever she wanted to do and not think about what anyone else might think. It was good for her, even if it was a bit lonely.

Okay, really lonely. But she discovered she *could* survive on her own, as much as she didn't want to, and that was more important than anything. If she could get through life without relying on someone else, maybe she would be able to give back for once. To be an equal half of a whole.

Step Five was going to be telling that to Ben, something Allie promised herself she would do soon. Facing him now was more terrifying than she expected it would be. She didn't know how he would react, and the chance that he would turn her away kept her overthinking the whole exchange. She told herself she would be brave enough tomorrow. Then again the next day. All the while, a hole in her heart seemed to grow bigger with each passing day.

When Allie woke late one morning and found her mom decorating a Christmas tree in the TV room, something inside her brain snapped. They always decorated the tree on Christmas Eve. Dashing back to the kitchen, she stared at the calendar and tried to understand how it had been a month since Thanksgiving. A *month*!

Time had flown by, but it also felt like she hadn't seen Ben in years. With how deep the ache had settled in her chest, that might have been true, and she could only imagine what he was thinking on his side. A month! How was that even possible? She almost thought he would have tried to reach out by now, but she didn't blame him for keeping his distance. After how she'd treated him, he had every right to still be angry and hurt.

"Mom, I'll be back in a little bit!" She didn't even wait for her mom's response as she slipped on her shoes.

Would Ben even listen to her? She didn't know, but as she headed out the door with her heart beating wildly with fear and anticipation, she knew it was time to find out.

She found Jake instead, who had just gotten the mail and was halfway up her driveway.

He stopped upon seeing her, his eyes downcast. He'd tried a few times to apologize over the last few weeks, but he'd finally figured out after she threw a half-eaten donut in his face—what a waste—that he would do better to keep his distance. Thankfully, he'd been good at that.

Until now.

"Sorry," he said. "I was already at the box, so I figured I could grab yours too. I was just going to leave it on the porch."

Allie took the stack of letters and shuffled through half of them, hoping to avoid eye contact as much as possible. *Really mature, Allie.* She could be the bigger person here, even though she refused to give him longer than a few minutes. She had more important things to do than let him soothe his guilty conscience. She took a deep breath. "Thanks. How've you been?"

Jake's eyebrows shot up, as if he hadn't expected her to say anything. "Oh. Uh, fine, I guess. Dad's doing okay, and work is keeping me busy."

"Designing anything fun?"

He shrugged as he stuffed his hands into his pockets. "Just a new bank downtown. Nothing fancy."

"That sounds—"

"Allie, I'm sorry." He took a deep breath, letting it out in a huff. "I was way out of line. With the book, with Ben, with everything."

As much as she appreciated the apology, she wasn't sure what to say to that. It didn't change what happened. "We're different people now," she said slowly. "You know that, right?"

"I do now. I guess I hoped, after the way things went down in high school, we might still have a chance. I thought it was only a matter of time before you were ready to come back."

"Jake. Things between us ended years ago."

"Why?"

Allie took a step back. She hadn't expected that question, and she wasn't sure why he had even asked it. Did he really not know the answer? "Because you asked me to marry you," she whispered. "And we were *eighteen.* Barely out of high school. Neither of us was ready for something like that."

He swallowed. "I was."

Maybe that was true. Maybe Jake had been perfectly ready to slap a ring on her finger and start a fancy little life. But Allie had only now figured out who she was, and her decision to leave Jake and go to a different school had been the first thing in her life that she'd done for herself. She hadn't known why they needed to break up at the time, but she had always been glad she listened to that gut feeling that had told her to walk away.

"I wasn't," she said. "I'm sorry for the way things ended, Jake, but I've moved on. You should too." Looking down at the stack of mail in her hands and trying to come up with a good way to end the conversation, Allie continued shuffling through the bills and letters until something made her pause.

It was a black-and-white photo of Ben, taken with some definite skill. Allie's heart skittered at the sight of him, as if it hadn't been weeks since she saw him, and she cursed herself for being so easily affected after so much time. Maybe it was the expression on Ben's face, which was like nothing she'd seen before.

He looked exactly how Allie had felt for the last month.

Allie recognized Oliver and Madi's front room, and it looked like Kit was in the background talking to someone— maybe Oliver. But the photo's focus was on Ben and his utterly miserable expression.

"Who would leave—"

Allie turned and walked back to the house without letting Jake finish what was probably a question full of righteous anger and spite. She was far too focused on the picture and how easily it worked its way into her heart and made her ache for the man she'd fallen in love with. Had she made the wrong choice in staying away from him?

No. She'd had to stay away. But she'd thought Ben would be okay. He had every right to hate her for the way she'd re-acted, and he'd made no attempt to tell her he wasn't angry. But Allie's heart throbbed as she swallowed that thought. Her phone in the garbage had been a pretty clear message to stay away. And Ben was perfect. He would have taken that sign and understood exactly what she was saying.

What had she done?

Instinct told her to flip the picture over, and she found a few lines written there. Lines that brought tears to her eyes and stole all of her strength until she sank to the floor in a heap.

> *I've known Ben since I was nine years old, and he has always been the kindest, sweetest, most honorable person I have ever known. I had to do some investigating into what happened because he wouldn't tell me, but I can promise you that he didn't do what you think he did, and he has tried everything he can to fix it. Something tells me he thinks he can never be happy again until he makes this better, but he's out of options. So I need you to step up, Allie.*
>
> *I need you to fix Ben.*
>
> *He has loved you from the moment he first set eyes on you. Maybe that's weird for you, but anyone who knows Ben knows that he has never put his faith into something like he put his faith in you.*
>
> *Don't ruin this, Allie. You both deserve to be happy.*
>
> *Please bring my happy Ben back before he dies of heartbreak.*
>
> *- Madi*

"What do you mean, they moved?" Allie knew she was being ridiculous, but she still tried to peer over the shoulder of the woman who stood in Cam and Ben's doorway, blocking her view of the apartment. From what little she could see, namely the Christmas decor and abundance of glitter and pink, she was pretty sure the woman was completely right.

The woman rolled her eyes. "I've been in this apartment for three weeks, honey." Then she slammed the door.

It didn't make any sense, though. Ben hadn't said anything about them moving. Ever. And if they had moved out more than three weeks ago, they had probably been planning and packing long before Thanksgiving. Before the breakup.

Had Ben been planning to leave her anyway?

Allie didn't think so. Not that she could claim she knew everything about Ben Nakamura, but she trusted Madi and her opinion of the guy. That, plus the things Allie *did* know, meant this little secret wasn't as much of a surprise as it could have been. Ben probably hadn't told her because he didn't want to add his stress to hers while she was writing the Sweet Red book along with their graphic novel. While he probably could have used the support, he was thinking only of her.

It was just another reason to make Allie glad she had fixed herself, though she still had a long way to go before she reached his level of love. Ben was, without a doubt, the best human she had ever known.

"What am I supposed to do now?" she asked the empty hallway. No one answered her, of course, and she knew she couldn't stand there forever. At some point, she was going to have to figure out how to find Ben and explain why she had stayed away as long as she had.

She just hoped he would listen.

As she headed back to her car, Allie pulled the photograph from her coat pocket and gazed at it like she'd been doing since she found it. It killed her that he looked so sad, and Madi was right. Allie needed to fix this. She just wasn't sure how. O'Reilly's was closed today, so she had to figure out how to find someone who might know where Ben would be. He hadn't tried texting or calling her, so she didn't have his number anymore, and no one…

Madi. Cursing herself for being so stupid, Allie started the car and headed for Madi and Oliver's house before she reconsidered. Allie should have told Madi about what Jake had done from the beginning. She couldn't have gone to Ben—seeing him would have broken her resolve to keep fixing herself—but she could have at least let Madi and Oliver fill him in.

One of these days, Allie would figure out how to make a relationship work. She hoped it happened sooner than later, for Ben's sake.

Maybe Ben wouldn't even like this new, stronger Allie. Maybe he would spend five minutes with her and realize he preferred the moldable version of her.

"Don't be stupid!" she shouted to the quiet car as she sped through the heavy Christmas Eve traffic. "Ben would never make you change, and you know it." He was too good to ever do something like that.

By the time she reached the giant Aspen Heights house (though she barely recognized it beneath the insane Christmas decorations that had replaced Halloween's), Allie was shaking with anticipation. She didn't see Ben's car parked anywhere, but she thought she recognized the little BMW in the driveway as the one that Cam drove. Maybe she wouldn't even have to go anywhere else, and she would finally get a chance to have the conversation she wished she'd been strong enough to have a month ago.

When she rang the doorbell, the first couple lines of "Jingle Bells" rang through the house, and Allie bit her lip to keep from laughing. Apparently Madi and Oliver liked Christmas as much as they did Halloween. "What do they do for St. Patrick's Day?" she wondered out loud. "Put a real leprechaun under the actual rainbow leading to their house?"

Allie hadn't quite prepared herself for when the door opened, but it turned out she didn't need to. Cam took one look at her before he shut the door again, turning the lock with a deafening click.

"I deserve that," she muttered before ringing the doorbell again, this time filling the house with the first line of "Deck the Halls." At least they had some variety.

Though she had to ring the bell several more times, playing several more songs, the door eventually opened again. This time it was Kit who stood there, still looking like a PBS television host in his sweater, and with a glare to rival Cam's. "What are you doing here, Allie?"

Allie took a deep breath. She *definitely* hadn't prepared to deal with the best friend. Where was Madi when she needed her most? "I need to find Ben," she said. "Is he here?"

Kit looked her over, his brown eyes narrowed behind his glasses. "I wouldn't tell you even if he were," he said after a moment.

"So he's not here." Allie tried not to be too disappointed, but Diamond Springs was way too large for her to try to find him on her own. She needed help, and the only people who could give her any sense of direction were the ones inside this house.

"I didn't say that," Kit argued, but he seemed smart enough to know that he'd slipped up. Sighing, he folded his arms and filled the open space of the doorway with his obnoxiously festive Christmas sweater. "I warned you," he said. "I told you not to break his heart, and you went ahead and did it anyway."

If Kit thought Ben was heartbroken just like his sister did, then it was probably true, and Allie felt completely awful for assuming all wrong. She hadn't handled things well—she knew that—but didn't she deserve a chance to make up for it?

"I can explain everything," she said.

"This I gotta hear," someone said behind Kit. Cam was back, his massive arms folded over his own terrible sweater as he approached. Allie had dated a firefighter and several foot-ball players, but none of them compared to Cam when it came to brute strength. He had the intimidation stare dialed in.

Allie swallowed, and it didn't help when Oliver joined in with the others in the doorway, the three of them like a body-guard set who had just been thrown into a second-rate Christmas sweater factory. Individually, none of them were necessarily all that scary. But put the Wonder Boys together like this?

Ben had a powerful team behind him, and Allie knew she would have to fight for her chance to make things up to him.

"We're waiting," Cam said.

Allie took a deep breath. "I've dated a lot of people," she began. When Kit grabbed hold of the door and went to close it, Allie shoved her shoulder into it before he could. "You didn't let me finish!"

Sighing, Kit glanced at the other two and seemed to have a silent conversation with them before gesturing for her to continue.

"I've dated a lot of people," she said again, "so I realized I needed to have some time on my own, to figure out who I am."

"That's why you stomped on Ben's heart?" Oliver asked with narrowed eyes.

"That's why when I met Ben, I told him I wasn't interested in dating him," Allie replied. This wasn't going to be easy, but she needed them to understand everything if they were going to trust her with their friend. "Everything about our relation-ship was fake." She held her breath.

Hopefully at least Oliver would understand that, but it was Kit who spoke first. "Explain."

Allie would do her best. "My mom wants so badly for me to settle down and start a family, so she constantly sets me up with people. She didn't understand when I told her I wanted some time on my own, and when an ex-boyfriend tried to ask me out, Ben offered to be my fake boyfriend to get everyone off my case."

After a long stretch of silence, during which Allie was tempted to run and hide from the piercing stares directed at her, all three men seemed to catch on at the same time, their expressions varying from sympathy to anger to amusement.

"You've got to be kidding me," Oliver said with a crooked grin. "This is the funniest thing I've ever heard."

Kit elbowed him in the side. "There's clearly more to this story, or Ben wouldn't be so miserable," he said, still focused on Allie. He was the angry one out of the three. "Keep talking, Heartbreaker."

Actually, that was a pretty good laser tag name, though Allie wasn't about to say so. Maybe down the road, if Ben managed to forgive her…

This was the moment of truth, and Allie willed herself to be brave. "I fell in love with him," she said. "I mean, how could I not? He's amazing. But he was so kind about helping me discover myself, and he never pushed the boundary beyond friendship even though I'm pretty sure he wanted to. He was the best thing that's ever happened to me, so when Thanksgiving rolled around, I decided to tell him that I wanted to be more than his friend, and—"

"That's why he was completely mute when he got home that night," Cam interrupted, and then he raised an eyebrow when the other two looked at him. "I mean, he's been happier in general, but Thanksgiving had me wondering if something happened."

For some reason, that comment prompted a whack on the head from Kit, and Cam cringed.

"So what went wrong?" Oliver asked, ignoring the other two's glares at each other. "All we know is something went down that weekend, but he won't talk to us. He won't even tell Madi."

"Playing the martyr, as always," Cam grumbled.

Remembering how she'd felt when she discovered the novel still hurt, but she'd had a lot of time to process Jake's actions. If Madi was right and Ben really had tried everything he could to fix it, maybe there was still a chance for the two of them. Maybe he hadn't given up on her. She couldn't know until she talked to him about it, and she couldn't talk to him about it unless she made it past the gatekeepers.

"We made a graphic novel together," Allie said. "Cam, you already knew that. But we were going to publish it together, and it was going to be awesome. Then my idiot neighbor slash ex-boyfriend stole the flash drive and put it up on the internet after taking my name off of it, so it looked like Ben had taken all the credit."

Kit frowned. "Did you seriously think Ben Nakamura could do something like that? Maybe you don't know him as well as you thought."

"You're probably right," she agreed. "But I've never wanted to know someone as much as I want to know Ben. I could spend my whole life learning about him. I haven't had the best luck with dating, and I have a hard time trusting people. So the way I felt about Ben was terrifying. I got scared. I think, the whole time, I was secretly looking for a reason to end things just like I did with all my other relationships because that was easier than admitting I'd fallen for him."

Unconvinced, Kit turned to his friends for another silent conversation. They'd known each other so long that they were probably saying all sorts of things she couldn't see in their expressions. Finally, Kit turned back to her and looked her over again. Not in a creepy way but in a searching way. "Why now?" he asked. "Why wait all this time to try to fix things?"

Allie quickly searched for an answer that might finally convince them to listen to her. She couldn't very well tell them she'd lost track of time, even if that was partially the truth. She needed to explain why her apology had been Step Five instead of Step One. "Because I had to be sure I didn't need Ben."

"Excuse me?"

Allie straightened up. She didn't need these men questioning everything she said, and she hoped she could make them understand. "I have spent my entire life relying on other people. Men, mostly. And even though I thought I was doing well, I completely fell apart when I broke up with Ben. I had nothing to stand on without him. And if I needed so much from him, how was I supposed to give anything back?"

Tears pooled in her eyes, but she willed them to go back inside her tear ducts. Not that they listened. "I've spent the last month learning to be strong," she said. "I've been trying to be someone who deserves a man like Ben, though I'm pretty sure he'll always be out of my league no matter what I do."

"Dang straight," Cam said.

"Shut up," Kit and Oliver said together. They shared a look, and then Kit took one step back, a gesture that Allie hoped meant he was close to forgiving her. At the very least, he was letting her into the warm house that smelled of cinnamon and something sweet.

It smelled like Christmas.

"We're not ready to tell you where Ben is yet," Oliver said slowly, "but we're willing to consider it."

Cam lifted an eyebrow. "We are? That's a bad idea. You guys didn't have to live with Ben in the aftermath before he moved in with—"

Oliver elbowed Cam in the gut, cutting him off, and Kit folded his arms yet again as he stepped in front of his friends. He wasn't as frightening this time around, maybe because he must have pushed on a certain spot on his sweater and started up a little battery-powered version of "Up on the Housetop."

Oliver and Cam both snickered as Kit fought a smile, changing the whole vibe of the front entryway in an instant.

"There you guys are!" a voice said behind them, and Allie nearly started crying when Madi appeared. She had started to show, her pregnant belly protruding just enough beneath her own ugly sweater that Allie was sure the guys all knew by now, but she looked happy and healthy. "I was wondering where—Allie!"

Allie hadn't expected the hug that came once Madi had elbowed her way through the guys. She'd only met Madi the one time, even though they'd texted several times before Thanksgiving, but Allie had hoped they would one day become friends.

Madi was the one person in the world who knew how Allie felt about Ben before Ben did. She had guessed it on Halloween, even though Allie had vehemently denied it.

"Why are you fraternizing with the enemy?" Oliver asked in clear horror.

Keeping one arm around Allie's waist, Madi scoffed at her husband. "Grow up, Ollie. She is not the enemy."

Oliver made a face. "Of course she is."

"You saw what she did to Ben!" Cam complained.

"Should you be standing right now?" Kit asked. "Maybe you should sit down."

That comment sparked a flurry of activity as all three Wonder Boys scrambled to make the most comfortable seat on the couch, complete with several pillows for back support. Apparently, Kit was handling the baby news decently well, considering how much Ben had said he hated change.

Madi rolled her eyes, giving Allie a little side hug as she watched the guys make her a nesting spot. "They're all ridiculous," she muttered. "I'm not sure I can stand another five months of this, but it's nice to know they care. I'm glad you got my note, Allie. Ben needs you."

Kit's head snapped up. "Do *not* tell her where he is, Madi. You know he won't want that."

"Ben hasn't missed Breakfast Eve in fifteen years," Madi argued. "He should really be here. I don't care if he hates asking for help; he clearly needs it."

Kit leveled his sister with a pretty impressive stare, the kind that must have given his students mini heart attacks whenever he had to use it. "You don't think I tried to force him to come?"

Madi matched his glare. "You didn't force anything, and you know it. You've always had a soft spot for Ben and let him do whatever he was the most comfortable with."

"Yeah," Oliver agreed, "which is pretty unfair, if you think about it. You forced me to do all sorts of—" He cut himself off the instant Madi's glare shifted to him. "We're not talking about me. I know."

"I still think we should have just brought the food to his parents' house instead of letting him skip out," Cam grumbled.

Oliver and Kit both groaned and whacked Cam in the back of the head in unison. "You idiot," Oliver breathed.

Allie turned to Madi, grabbing her hands in desperation because she was finally getting somewhere. "Where do they live?"

Frowning, Madi looked at each of the Boys in turn, then sighed. "Technically, Cam spilled the secret, so I don't have to feel guilty about this." She grabbed a piece of paper from a nearby end table and scribbled out an address, holding it out to Allie with a little hesitation. "You're going to fix him, right?"

Allie nodded, but Madi moved the paper out of her reach before she could grab hold.

"I'm not asking if you'll get back together with him," Madi said. "If Ben doesn't want you back in his life, then you have to be willing to stay out of it. Do you understand?"

As much as Allie hated the idea of never seeing Ben again after today, she had to give Madi some credit. She really did know Ben, and she knew that if Allie asked him to take her back, he would probably do it. Even if he didn't want to. Madi was right, and Allie needed to tell Ben everything about what Jake had done and admit to the fact that she hadn't been strong enough to love him yet. Losing him and not knowing if she would see him again had been what she needed to finally figure out what she was capable of and what she wanted in life.

Allie took a slow breath, holding it in her lungs as she looked at each of the Wonder Boys in turn. She wanted them all to believe her, not just Madi. "I will do everything I possibly can to give Ben some closure and make him happy again," she told them. "Even if that means I have to let him walk away. At least he'll have you guys to get him through this."

She took the address that Madi handed her as if it were an ancient artifact that could fall to pieces at the slightest disturbance. It wasn't all that far from her own parents' house, which meant she'd been within a couple miles of Ben all this time. Now that she knew how to find him, though, her fear was back in full force.

"Do you think he'll listen to me?" she asked Madi as she brushed her tears from her cheeks with her sleeve. She hadn't bothered to dress up nice or even put on makeup this morning, and she worried what would happen when Ben saw her. Would he have the same reaction as his friends and shut the door in her face?

Taking Allie's hand, Madi gave her a sympathetic smile. "Honestly? I have no idea. I've never seen Ben like this, and he's never been in love before, let alone heartbroken. This is new territory for everyone."

"I hope he listens to you," Kit said softly.

Allie turned in surprise, staring at the man who wouldn't make eye contact with her anymore. A moment ago he'd still been wary, and she couldn't help but wonder if he really meant what he said.

When Allie said nothing, Kit glanced up and met her eyes. "Ben is one of my best friends," he said. "And I miss him. As much as I hate to admit it, he was happier when he had you as a friend. Nothing I've tried has brought him back, so maybe it's your turn to give it a shot."

As her tears started up again, Allie threw her arms around Kit even though he tensed and clearly didn't like the affection. "I'll do my best," she said, then hurried off to her car.

THIRTY-TWO

ALLIE ABOUT HAD A HEART attack when Ben opened the door just as she was raising her fist to knock. The only thing that saved her was the fact that it *wasn't* Ben, just a slightly older carbon copy with shorter hair. He looked her over with a raised eyebrow, apparently unconcerned by the raucous screams echoing through the house behind him.

Allie swallowed. "You must be Peter." *Ben's older brother.*

He narrowed his eyes. "Do I know you?"

"Um, I'm Allie. I'm looking for Ben. Is he around?"

"You do know it's Christmas Eve, right?"

"Yes, of course."

"So maybe you should come back later."

Allie wondered if Peter knew what had gone down and was being protective, or if this was his natural state. Maybe he just couldn't handle any more people entering his parents' house; it definitely seemed full to the brim. The narrow hallway leading from the door didn't offer Allie much of a look inside, but she watched six different people ranging in size and age pass from one room to the next in a matter of seconds.

How many people had Ben said were in his family? Seven kids. More than a dozen grandkids. If everyone had come back for Christmas, that meant there were nearly thirty people running around.

"I was really hoping to talk to him," Allie said. "So maybe I could—"

"ALLIE!"

Two little bodies careened down the hall at lightning speed. Allie flinched, but somehow Peter caught an arm of each and held the boys back before they could crash into her like they had on Halloween. The fact that Hunter and Isaac seemed to know her must have changed something in Peter; he looked at her a little more closely.

"You know Ben?" he asked, though that should have had an obvious answer.

Allie smiled. "He and I took the boys trick-or-treating."

"She was Leonardo," Hunter added with a huge grin. "Ben was Michelangelo, and Isaac was—"

"I really need to talk to him," Allie said quietly, even if she was interrupting Hunter's explanation of the evening.

Peter nodded, lifting Isaac into his arms and nudging Hunter back into the house. "He's around here somewhere."

The hallway led to a living room with every seat occupied by so many beautiful faces that Allie knew she wouldn't be able to tell them apart. Like Ben, everyone in the family was ridiculously attractive, and even the kids would probably grow up to have people falling at their feet. She had thought Ben's handsome face was a one-in-a-million sort of deal, but it looked like all of his siblings had been equally blessed.

Especially his sisters, who looked over at Allie and instantly made her feel shabby and unimportant. She probably should have reconsidered her choice to go without makeup, if only to not feel so intimidated.

"Anyone seen Ben?" Peter asked, setting Isaac on his feet and reaching out a hand to a cute redhead who sat sandwiched on the couch between nearly identical Nakamura sisters.

"I think I saw him playing games with the kids," one of the sisters said with a shrug.

"No, that's Mark," the other sister argued. "Ben was talking to Mom in the kitchen."

"I'm not in the kitchen," a blonde woman said from the other couch, though she was mostly hidden behind four kids who had turned her into a jungle gym.

Her comment was answered by a series of progressively louder shrieks coming from up the nearby stairs.

As much as Allie was desperate to meet Ben's mom, as well as his other siblings, she first needed to talk to Ben. No way would she butt herself into his life if he didn't want her there. But seeing the chaos that was his family made her understand him so much more. No wonder he was so used to being unseen or forgotten.

More than ever, she needed him to know how much he meant to her.

"Is Ben even here?" Peter's redheaded wife asked.

No one responded, all of them jumping back into their own conversations and leaving Allie forgotten. Just like their brother. For a moment, Allie thought she would never find him unless she started wandering the house (which she wasn't keen on doing), but then she caught the eye of little Isaac, who was smiling at her from his mother's lap.

Allie crouched down. "Do you know where Ben is hiding?" she asked quietly.

Isaac nodded.

Her heart racing, she swallowed her nerves and asked if he would show her.

Without anyone noticing, Isaac hopped to the floor and grabbed her hand, and she nearly burst into tears as the boy led her past the bustling and crowded kitchen and out the back door.

The snow had been packed down across the little yard, and a misshapen snowman stood in the middle of it, smiling with a pretty remarkably carved face. Something told Allie her

Wonder Boy had had something to do with that, and she grinned at it as they passed. Ben had probably been giving his little nieces and nephews some good attention because he knew how it felt to be overlooked.

Isaac, who wore only a t-shirt and had to be freezing, stopped at a large tree at the back of the yard and pointed upward before running back inside.

An impressive treehouse sat within the branches of the tree, and as Allie stared up at the open trap door at the top of the ladder, she really hoped Ben wasn't actually up there. It was freezing out, and if his family hadn't seen him in a while, there was no telling how long he'd been out here.

Taking a deep breath, Allie grabbed hold of the first board that had been nailed into the trunk. It wouldn't be easy to climb up, but she would do it if it meant finding Ben. Her shoes were just a little too big, though, and her fingers couldn't get a good grip; she only made it halfway before she slipped back down.

She would just have to be brave and see if he would come down. After several more deep breaths, she lifted her head toward the treehouse. "Ben?" *Too quiet.* "Ben, are you up there?"

Though the only sound that came back to her was an icy breeze whistling through the bare branches, something told her she wasn't alone out here. She'd never been much for spiritual thinking, but she couldn't ignore the way her heart pounded in her chest as if it knew how close she was to the man.

"Ben, I know you're there. I want to talk."

The tree creaked as something moved inside the house, and Allie nearly panicked and ran away when his head appeared in the doorway above, his eyes fixed on hers and full of confusion.

He looked just like he had in the picture: miserable. "What are you doing here?"

Allie shivered as the wind picked up around her. Ben was probably frozen! "Can you come down? Please? We really need to talk."

He shook his head.

Gritting her teeth, Allie grabbed hold of the boards again and heaved herself up. "Then I'm coming up."

This time, when she slipped, a hand wrapped around her wrist and held her in place. Not willing to waste this literal handhold he had given her, she scrambled up as best she could and let Ben lift her the rest of the way. Those rock climbing muscles of his were really doing him a lot of favors, and he did most of the work to get her up.

She collapsed onto the treehouse floor with a gasp and had to catch her breath, trying to ignore the way Ben was doing the same thing but in a far corner of the house, as if he wanted to put as much distance between them as he could. Seeing him in the dim afternoon light, especially without his smile, was doing bad things to her equilibrium, and she was desperate to help him get back to the way he was before.

Even if she had to leave for that to happen.

Leaning against the wall, Ben hugged his knees and watched her as she sat up. "What are you doing here, Allie?"

His voice had lost its life, and Allie started crying immediately. She'd really broken him.

"I'm here to tell you I'm sorry," she whispered. "I overreacted, and I didn't give you a chance to defend yourself, and I wasn't ready to love you. I'm sorry."

Ben frowned, his eyes moving to the floor instead of her. "I don't know what happened with the book. I tried to contact all the sites and get them to fix it, but I wasn't the one who sent it in so they didn't believe I was really the artist. Every comment I made about you being the author got down-voted or flagged as spam. I thought if maybe I fixed things you would... But I couldn't. So you didn't."

He'd thought the only way she would come back was if he fixed everything? Ben was too good for her, putting that much responsibility on himself. She wanted to grab his hand and tell him so, but something told her he wouldn't want that. They weren't there yet. "It was Jake," she said, waiting until Ben looked at her again. "He stole it from my computer the day after Thanksgiving and was trying to turn me against you."

"It worked."

"For a little bit, yeah." Mirroring his position and hugging her legs, Allie so badly wished she had been able to find herself *before* she met Ben. All of this would have been so much easier. "I found out it was Jake after I left O'Reilly's," she said. This was the part she was most worried about, but she had to be honest with him.

Ben swallowed. "That was a month ago."

"I know."

As he processed that, Allie could see the pain building behind his eyes. She should have been making this apology weeks ago, but she hadn't. With no job to help her keep track of the days, she'd been so focused on herself that everything else had disappeared. Everything but the ache she felt without Ben.

Sitting up straighter, Ben lost all expression in his face as he stared at the boards beneath his feet. "You gutted me," he croaked. "Jake warned me you would leave if something went wrong, but I trusted you, and then you…"

Why would Ben listen to *Jake*? But that didn't matter. What mattered was Allie explaining what happened. "I know."

"You *don't* know." Now there was an edge to his voice, a sharpness she'd never heard before. Not anger, but an acute pain that Allie knew well. "You have no idea what it's been like to be me. To be forgotten, overlooked, nothing but surface level to everyone who knows you. You don't know how it feels to finally be seen and think things will be different, and then get dumped on the side of the road when something goes wrong." When he looked up, his eyes flashed with something deeper. "I'm not The Sentinel, Allie. I'm not some superhero who can read your mind and fix everything with a snap of my fingers because I know exactly what you're thinking. You didn't give me a chance. After everything I—"

He cut himself off, clenching his jaw as he rose to his feet. His voice softened, closer to his usual gentleness. "You broke me, Allie. And I'm not sure that can be fixed. I don't know if we can go forward from here."

Even though she'd expected a response like that, it still hurt. It felt like he'd plunged a knife in her chest and twisted it, but in the nicest way possible. Of all people, she thought he would be good enough to recognize she was trying to fix her mistake. But even Benjamin the Wonder Boy couldn't be perfect. Something like this could never come easy.

"Ben, I told you. I wasn't ready to love you. Even if I *do* love you."

"And telling me that is supposed to make everything better?"

Brushing her tears with her sleeve, she shook her head. "Love isn't enough to fix something broken. It takes more than that."

He finally looked down at her, curiosity peeking through the pain.

She slowly rose, making sure she kept her distance so he didn't feel threatened or anything. Not that she felt all that intimidating. Really, she was barely holding it together, but she would be strong. "Ben, I didn't mean for it to take so long, but it took me a month at rock bottom to learn how to pick myself up again and rely on my own strength instead of someone else's."

"I never tried to—"

"I know you didn't. You helped me learn who I was, and I love that about you. But…" She sighed. "But I wasn't ready to stand on my own. I was still hanging on to you for dear life, and I had to learn how to survive without you."

He didn't like that, his eyes filling with tears. "And you had to break me to do it? You could have *told* me. I would have given you space."

Allie was saying everything wrong—she'd *done* everything wrong—but she didn't know how to fix it without going back in time and including him in the process like she should have from the start. If only he *could* read her mind and know how much it had killed her to stay away from him. But if she had known he would be there waiting for her, she never could have built a good enough foundation. "I *know* you would have given me space. But *I* wouldn't have. I know I overreacted, but I—"

"You should go, Allie."

Was that it? Had she lost her chance? "Is there nothing I can say that will convince you to give me one more chance? I know I don't deserve it, and I know I've burned all my bridges with you. But give me a rope and I'll swing. Anything. Anything to be your friend again."

He took a slow breath. "Friend."

"Maybe this will help." She grabbed her phone, which her parents had graciously paid for after they couldn't find her old one at O'Reilly's, and pulled up an email she'd gotten almost two weeks ago. "I've been trying to pretend this email doesn't exist, and I honestly don't know why he sent it to me after everything… But I think you should read it."

Thankfully, Ben took her phone and skimmed over the message. It was from Mr. Simmons, telling her about how he'd found the contract with Allie's name on it and was glad she'd quit because it meant he didn't have to fire her for taking the credit of a man's hard work. But also attached was an offer to publish Ben's next graphic novel. Since he hadn't heard back from Ben, he hoped Allie would be able to get a hold of him.

Ben's eyebrows steadily drew lower as he read, until they shot up high at the end. "He wants to publish the next Wonder Boys?"

Allie shrugged. "He's seen the success as well as anyone and wants to capitalize on his connection to you."

"He still has no idea you wrote it." That wasn't a question; the email had made it clear that Simmons had no reason to think Allie was capable of writing something decent. "I'm glad you quit."

Allie managed a little smile. "Me too."

Ben returned his attention to the new contract Simmons had sent, his eyes lingering on what Allie guessed was the substantial royalty advance Sweet Red was offering. "I was kind of convinced I would never do another one," he said, and the tiny smile he sent her way was enough to make Allie start crying again. It was small, but it was something. "Hard to make a book with no story and no one to write it."

"Sweet Red could easily find you an author to partner with."

Ben looked up, a question in his eyes. "Is that what you want? Someone else to write it?"

Allie hoped she could say what she needed to say without falling apart. They were getting to the end of this conversation, the part where Ben would decide if she could be in his life or not. She would be okay with whatever he chose.

She had to be.

"It doesn't matter what I want," she said, her eyes on the floor. "This is all you, and you deserve to have something that's yours. I would love to make another book with you—I would love to spend the rest of my life with you—but the only thing that matters is your happiness. You helped me figure out what I want, and I want to do the same thing for you. You're my best friend, Ben, and I love you with all of my heart, but if you want me to walk away, then—"

The thud of her phone hitting the floor made her jump, but then Ben lifted her chin and his lips met hers in a desperate kiss. Though his hands were freezing at her neck and made her shiver, she didn't even care, pulling him closer and kissing him until she was warm again. Then kissing him again. And again. Somehow, this kiss was different from all the others, like each brush of his lips was saying something new. Asking a question and seeking an answer and making a promise. So many promises.

After a while—she lost track of time—Allie pulled away to catch her breath and bit her lip when she caught the disappointment in Ben's eyes, which were focused entirely on her mouth.

"You have to stop doing that," he growled and stole her lip back with another kiss. This time, he guided her to the wall, keeping one hand in her hair while the other pressed against her waist.

She laughed when his finger barely grazed a spot of bare skin beneath the hem of her sweatshirt and sent a shiver through her. Though she was glad she'd built up their friendship first, she really had no idea how she had resisted this man for as long as she had. "Has anyone ever told you that you're really good at that?" she asked him, brushing her thumb over his mouth and then his dimple when it appeared with his smile.

"No one ever kept me around long enough for that." His eyes traced her face for a moment, as if he wanted to memorize every part of it. Hopefully he didn't think she would let him get very far after this; he would never have the chance to forget any part of her.

He pressed his forehead to hers, clasping their hands between them. "I'm sorry. I'm sorry I gave up on you. I'm sorry I wasn't stronger."

There he went, apologizing for things that weren't his fault. "Hey, Ben?"

"Yeah?"

Allie smiled when he met her gaze again. "You *are* strong. You're one of the strongest people I've ever known. And I love you. I love your kindness, and the way you take care of people, and the passion you don't let anyone see. I love you so much that if you ever decide I'm too much work for you, you can send me away. I won't fall apart this time, so you don't have to worry about—"

Ben cut her off with a kiss. "I am never letting you go again unless it's what you really want," he said. "Say the word, and you're free."

"Never."

At some point, they would have to go inside, and Allie couldn't completely abandon her parents on Christmas Eve. She hoped Ben would go with her, but she wouldn't push him either way. They were both capable of making choices, and they had plenty of time to be together.

But for now, she really just wanted to kiss him. She had a whole month to make up for, and Ben seemed happy to help her rectify the situation.

"I told you they'd make up."

"Pretty sure you mean make *out*."

Ben and Allie broke apart, looking out the window to find the Wonder Gang standing near the snowman and watching the goings on in the treehouse. Though Kit looked a little sick and Cam angry, Madi and Oliver both smiled as they stood in each other's arms.

Bright red, Ben looked around as if searching for an escape. "What... What are you guys...?"

Allie didn't know why Ben was so quiet around his friends when he had quickly grown out of it with her, but she was glad he could at least be himself with her. Maybe she could help him work on opening up to the Wonder Boys.

"What *are* you doing here?" Allie added when no one said anything. If they were planning on coming, why couldn't they have just brought Allie with them?

"We wanted to make sure Ben was okay, whichever direction he decided to go," Madi said brightly.

"Only, it took us a while to figure out where you were," Cam said with narrowed eyes. Allie would have to work harder to get back on his good side.

"I forgot this treehouse was here," Oliver said, and he moved his hands to his wife's belly as he held her from behind. "Madi, we are building a treehouse as soon as spring hits. Our kid is gonna love it."

After giving Allie's hand a squeeze, Ben hopped down to the ground and held his arms up to help Allie follow, though she wasn't nearly as graceful. As soon as she was steady on her feet, he threaded his fingers through hers and pulled her close.

"Kit?" he said.

Kit swallowed, still looking a little nauseous. "There are exactly three people in that house who knew where you guys were, and none of them are older than six." His eyes jumped back and forth between the two of them before settling on Ben. "You missed Breakfast Eve, Watch. That's against club rules."

Though Oliver rolled his eyes, the rest had taken on perfectly serious expressions. Ben included.

"Sorry," Ben said, dipping his head. "I didn't want to bring the mood down. I know our traditions are important, and—"

"*You're* important, Ben," Kit interrupted, and he'd gotten softer. "I was worried about you."

Allie felt like she shouldn't be standing right next to them as the two men gazed at each other, but with how tightly Ben was holding on to her hand, she had a feeling he wouldn't let her give him some privacy.

Ben leaned closer to Kit, and when he spoke, it was so quietly that the others probably couldn't hear. "You can't protect us forever, you know."

Kit ducked his head. "I know. Won't stop me from trying." Was that a tear he brushed away? It was there and gone so quickly that Allie knew she wasn't meant to see it.

Ben reached out and put his hand on Kit's shoulder. "Thanks for looking out for me, as always," he said, louder this time. "But maybe we should go inside. It's freezing."

Allie tucked herself against Ben's side, halfway into his leather jacket that definitely wasn't warm enough for him to have stayed out here this long. When he thanked her by kissing the top of her head, she bit her lip before she squealed with happiness and was glad Ben couldn't see her; they probably would have gotten lost in a kiss for a while if he had.

Not that that was a bad thing.

Everyone hurried back toward the house to go in and get warm, but Ben lingered a moment, keeping Allie up against him. "Do you want to meet my family?" he asked softly. "I know that's a big step, so we can wait until—"

"I would love to." Allie stepped back so she could look into his eyes when she said this part. "I'm in this long term, Benjamin the Wonder Boy. I want to know every part of your life, if you'll let me."

His smile was so incredible that her knees almost gave out beneath her. How had she managed to snag the most hand-some man she'd ever seen? "I love you," he said, thankfully leaving a kiss on her cheek instead of tempting her with an actual kiss. "We should go inside, though. It's very cold."

Though she knew she probably shouldn't, given the dozen or so faces surreptitiously peering out the windows, Allie still ran a finger down Ben's chest and grinned when he seemed to melt at her touch. To her delight, he really did have some impressive abs down there. "I can think of something to warm you up," she said, then bit her lip.

For a moment, Ben just stood there dumbstruck, but he recovered quickly, grabbing her and pulling her against him as he locked her in a kiss that was somehow better than all the others, like he would never be able to get enough of her.

Three things happened simultaneously. Four, if you counted Allie turning to mush in Ben's arms. A thunderous cheer came from inside the house, someone whistled loudly, and Allie's phone buzzed in her pocket. The whistle had apparently come from Cam, who had wedged himself in the doorway to prevent any of Ben's family from coming outside. The text was from Jake.

While Ben laughed and turned bright red, Allie stared at the text and tried to comprehend what it said.

> Jake the Snake: I really am sorry for what I did. I shouldn't have tried to control your life, and you deserve better than that. I registered the book in your name when I took it, by the way, so it's all copyrighted. In case that matters. Probably should have told you that a month ago.

"What is it?" Ben asked, but Allie was already shoving the phone into his hand because she needed someone else to understand for her. He read quickly, his eyes going wide, and then he grabbed her hand and pulled her inside. He didn't stop until he found Peter in a wrestling match with his boys down in the TV room. "Tell me what this means," he said before stuffing the phone into his brother's hand.

Peter glanced at Allie first, then quickly read through the text while the two boys climbed all over him. "Book?" he asked, raising an eyebrow.

Ben grabbed his own phone and pulled up the original site, which was still advertising free downloads of *Menace Unknown*. "Allie and I made this," he explained. "Her neighbor is the one who sent it to the site and took her name off of it, but if he got it copyrighted in her name before he sent it, what does that mean?"

How did Peter manage to ignore the boys bouncing against his head? Lots of practice, probably. He seemed to think for a moment, his eyes darting between Ben and Allie, and then he shrugged. "It means she could sue you for a whole lot of money," he said with some hesitation.

"Let's say I don't want to sue Ben but the websites who are giving it away when we were planning to sell it?" Allie asked.

His eyebrows rose, as if in appreciation. "Then the two of you could probably win yourselves a pretty good settlement. From what I can tell..." He scrolled for a moment, his eyebrows rising ever higher. "This book has a lot of popularity. There's a lot of potential royalties you could have gained. It would take a solid case beyond just the copyright, but..."

Ben's grip on Allie's hand tightened. "We have sketches. Story notes. Voice memos. The whole process is on my computer."

Allie felt the people gathering behind them more than she heard or saw them, and she was too afraid of what Peter was about to say to turn around. This was a very big deal, and Ben's entire family (plus the Wonder gang) were about to learn their book's fate as Ben and Allie did.

Peter, on the other hand, could see them all, and he didn't seem to like the attention. He was the second oldest in the family, so it had probably been a while since he got this much notice. "There's no guarantee," he said slowly, "but you probably have a case. I could help. If you wanted."

Ben turned to Allie. "Do we want that?"

Allie could definitely use some money, jobless as she was, but it sounded like a lot of work. "If we did," she said, thinking out loud, "that could potentially hurt the sales of future books."

"Or it gets us good publicity," Ben countered. "You, in particular. I've already got my name all over the internet."

"Sympathy can be a big motivator for fans," someone in the crowd added. One of Ben's sisters, probably, though Allie didn't turn around to look.

"What do you think?" Allie asked. "I care more about you than I care about the book."

"And I care that you can do what you love and be happy," Ben said. "If we try to make another Wonder Boy book without giving you the proper credit for the first, people might think you're a copycat."

"Or they'll think you just brought on help for the next," Allie countered.

"You deserve credit for your work, Als."

"And you deserve your time in the spotlight."

"Will you two just make a decision already?"

This time Allie did turn around, but only because it was Kit who spoke, and he looked completely frustrated as he stood at the back of the family gathering.

Ben chuckled. "If the choice were up to me, I'd say we have Peter help us. Even if we don't try to get any money, at least we can get your name on the book."

Allie had been hoping he would say that, though she wouldn't tell him so. Smiling, she kissed his cheek. "A little money would be nice too, but I'll settle for attribution if I need to."

"Finally!" Oliver pushed his way past several kids and a few unamused sisters/sisters-in-law until he reached Ben and Allie. "First of all, your family is way too close-knit and I feel like I'm suffocating. Only child, and all that." He sent Allie a wink, which made her laugh. "But that's not important. I have a Christmas present for you, Ben."

Ben raised an eyebrow. "We don't do Christmas presents."

"This year we do." Stuffing his hand into his pocket, he pulled out a silver key and held it out on his palm. "Technically it's just from me and Mads, but the other two want to take credit, so pretend it's from them too."

Ben stared at the key. "Please tell me you didn't buy me a house." At least Allie wasn't the only one thinking it.

Oliver, however, made a face. "Okay, I'm rich, but I'm not that rich. No. This is a key to our guest house, which I'm fully planning to charge you rent for, so don't go getting any crazy ideas about charity. We just figured you might want to, uh…" He glanced behind him at the multitude of Nakamuras. "You know. Have your own space."

At first, Allie thought Ben was going to refuse. It was probably hard enough for him to have friends who knew how difficult it was for him to pay the bills working at the fun center, and this extra act of sympathy could easily be too much. But he needed this, and Allie knew it, so she silently cheered when he reached out and grabbed the key.

"It'll be farther from Allie," Madi said from the crowd. "But closer to the new fun center, so that'll be nice."

"Oh, I'm not running the new center." Ben kept his eyes on the key, but he turned red enough for Allie—and probably everyone else—to know there was more to that statement.

Cam pushed his way through the gathering next, though he accidentally knocked a couple of kids over. "But you told me that's why you were working mornings instead of nights. You were helping get the new place ready."

A little smile played at Ben's lips, though he still didn't look up. "Yeah, that was a lie. I don't even know if O'Reilly is still planning on starting the new one. He, uh, sort of fired me a month ago."

"What?!" Half the room spoke at the same time, Allie included.

Ben chuckled and pulled Allie a little closer. "Well, some lady came into the center last month accusing me of ruining her life, and when several people posted videos of the incident online, O'Reilly thought that might be bad for business."

Allie's heart sank, and though she tried to pull away, Ben only held onto her tighter. "Ben, I didn't mean to—"

"I was going to leave anyway. I've been working at a coffee shop down on Hackberry Road," Ben said with a shrug. "It actually pays the same as O'Reilly's, and the hours are way better. Well, technically I make even more now, if you count tips." He flushed red again. "There's sort of a hashtag for me? I do latte art, and it's starting to gain a following, so I bring in a lot of business."

Along with several of Ben's siblings, Oliver had his phone out and was typing furiously. Only a few seconds later, his jaw dropped, and Madi snatched his phone out of his hand to see.

"Whoa!" she said before passing the phone to Cam, at the same time Ben's younger brother—another clone—got wide eyes and told his sister what the hashtag was. "Ben," Madi said, "these are amazing! I didn't know you could do that with a latte."

"For clarification," Oliver said, "she means 'you' in the general sense, not you specifically."

Madi winced. "Yeah. Thanks, Ollie."

"I didn't know you could draw," Ben's youngest sister said as everyone burst into a buzz of conversation. Or maybe it was a niece. At this point, Allie would be lucky if she could remember names let alone put them to faces.

But she would get there eventually, and she would make sure Ben never went unnoticed again.

When Cam loudly cleared his throat, everyone went silent and looked at him, but he didn't seem to notice. Or maybe he did but didn't care about being the center of attention. "Um, why did you tell me you were taking over the new fun center?" he asked.

Ben grinned. "Because I knew you would tell everyone else, and it was the best way to keep things on the down low while I was figuring things out."

Cam didn't like that answer, scrunching up his face in disgust. "Why didn't you want us to know you'd switched jobs when this is clearly better than Satan's Pit?"

"Why didn't you want *me* to know?" Kit added quietly, his eyes on his feet.

Ben frowned, clearly hurting right alongside his friend. "I didn't want you to worry."

"We were all worried." But it wasn't Kit who said that.

At first, Allie had no idea who had spoken, and the whole family looked around in search of the man who had commented. Based on the way Ben grew tense, though, she had a pretty good guess that was confirmed when the family stepped aside to let the aged-up version of Ben through. He was the only person Allie hadn't seen yet, and everyone seemed surprised to see him.

"Dad," Ben said, standing up straighter. "I thought you were going to be in Japan for Christmas."

Mr. Nakamura gave his wife a kiss on the forehead as he passed her, and then he put his hand on Ben's shoulder. "I finished up my work early so I could check on you. Your mom was so worried when you moved back home, and no one knew how to help you. Even Kit called me, but I was already on my way to the airport by that point."

Ben took a step back. "You came back early...for me? But..."

Mr. Nakamura chuckled, and he sounded just like Ben. "I've always thought you were the most like me," he said, so quietly that everyone had to lean closer to try to hear. "More of a watcher than a doer. Always on the outskirts so you can be there when someone needs you. I've always admired that about you, but your mom and I worried you would forget to look after yourself. It's easy to get lost if you're not looking where you're going."

Though he seemed reluctant to let go of Allie's hand, gazing at their entwined fingers for a moment, Ben released her and fell into his dad's embrace as if he'd never needed anything more. He shut his eyes tight, tears leaking from his eyelashes, and the family swarmed in for a group hug right behind him.

Allie ended up stuck between Madi and Peter, but she didn't mind. She was just glad they would include her when they definitely didn't have a reason to pay her any attention. When someone broke into a Christmas carol and everyone else joined in, she felt even more out of place because they all had angelic singing voices.

"Of course," she muttered under her breath.

Next thing she knew, someone grabbed her hand and pulled her off balance, and she was sure she would crash into the ground. Only, she landed in a pair of familiar strong arms, wrapped in his delicious scent as Ben stole a kiss before setting her on her feet.

"Come on," he muttered with a gentle smile and led her away from the family choir. The other Wonder Boys had already extricated themselves and were waiting in the hallway. "They'll be at this for hours, and I guarantee they won't notice if we disappear for a bit."

When Allie glanced back, she caught the gazes of both of Ben's parents. Though they hadn't officially been introduced, both of them waved and mouthed, "Thank you," before turning their attention back to the rest of the family.

Maybe Ben had been more noticed growing up than he'd thought.

"It may be long past breakfast," Kit said once they all got outside, "but I will not let you miss Breakfast Eve, Ben."

Allie wrapped her arm around Ben's waist, thrilled when he put his arm around her shoulders, and she had to take a moment to appreciate how well they fit together. It was like they had literally been made for each other. "What exactly is Breakfast Eve?" she asked.

"It's only the best morning of the year," Madi said, her smile wide as she snuggled against her husband. "It started when we were kids, when Oliver's parents wouldn't let him come over on Christmas."

"Christmas morning at the Hamilton house was quieter than a funeral home after hours," Oliver explained. "I knew I was missing out on something magical."

Kit grinned, far more animated than Allie had ever seen him. "So I convinced my parents to do Christmas a day early so we could invite Oliver over."

"By the time I joined," Ben told her, "it was a regular thing."

"The Morgans let us do our own thing every year after I joined the club," Cam added, though he still seemed a little grumpy about Ben using him to distribute false information. Or maybe there was more to it than that.

"How's the gym coming, Cam?" Allie asked, even though the question was completely out of the blue. She'd missed a month of Wonder Boy life, and she was eager to catch up.

Cam, however, wasn't eager to answer that question, stuffing his hands into his hoodie pocket and clenching his jaw.

Kit caught on quickly, his stance and expression shifting into what Allie could only describe as 'protection mode.' "What happened?" he demanded.

Cam grimaced. "This isn't something in the spirit of Christmas, so I don't want—"

"Spill it, Martinez," Oliver said.

Groaning, Cam ran a hand through his dark hair. "Turns out that other bidder for my perfect space was another gym owner. He's opening the same week as me. And I'm only one block away."

Yikes. If Allie had any idea how to help with a bombshell like that, she would do it in a heartbeat, but she didn't even have a job, let alone her own business. The rest of the gang seemed to be at a loss as well, but Kit had the sense to hide his anxiety after letting it slip out for a second in his expression.

"Boys," he said in a commanding tone, "do you know what this means?"

"Not another pros and cons list," Oliver groaned at the same time Kit said, "A pros and cons list!"

Madi laughed. "Sounds like breakfast is turning into a war meeting. Allie, you're going to want to stick around for this. I probably have an extra sweater for you, too!"

"We'll meet you there," Ben said as the four of them squished into Cam's car.

As they drove off, Allie moved to unlock her own car, but Ben grabbed her hand and tugged her close.

"You don't have to come, you know," he said, though his eyes said otherwise as they traced her face, this time like he was drawing her in his mind. "I know you've got your own family to get back to. I would hate to leave Helen without her favorite daughter on Christmas Eve."

Allie laughed, and now that she and Ben were alone again, she could focus on the way her heart beat so steadily that she knew she had no more fear when it came to Ben.

Whether their relationship lasted, she didn't know, but she knew she would survive either way. Now that he knew his family cared about him more than he'd thought, Ben would probably make it through too.

"I love you," she said. "And my mom will be fine without me tonight if you promise to come over for Christmas dinner tomorrow. Besides, I brought you a pizza." She nodded toward the box sitting on her passenger seat.

Ben's eyebrows rose. "A pizza?"

"It's barbecue chicken. Your favorite."

This time his eyebrows slid downward, and his grip on her hand tightened. "I never told you my favorite," he said, his voice coming out strained.

"You didn't have to," Allie replied with a grin. "I like to think I pay attention now and then, and I know you better than I've ever known anyone."

Tears welling in his eyes, he swallowed hard. "You see me," he whispered. It wasn't a question.

"I see you, Ben."

And when he wrapped her in a tight embrace, she felt like nothing in the world could touch her, like all of her problems melted away with every passing moment in his arms. She never wanted to leave that spot, and she imagined spending the rest of her life enjoying these stolen moments alone. But then she pictured holidays with the Wonder Boys, several little kids running around while their parents wore matching sweaters and played laser tag and built a giant patchwork family.

She imagined growing old with Ben and constantly learning new things about themselves and each other.

No book could compare to that life.

"How did your mom handle our, uh, breakup?" Ben asked after a long while. He pulled away, but only far enough to meet her gaze before moving back in to kiss her cheek. Her jaw.

Allie's answer came out a little stilted when Ben kissed the magic spot below her ear. "Better than I expected. I..." She closed her eyes for a moment so she could appreciate the way his lips caressed her skin as he moved back along her jaw. "I told her the truth. All of it."

Ben paused, his gaze wary. "Is she going to hate me now?"

"Not if you keep being your adorable self." Though, he really needed to stop looking so kissable if they wanted to get anywhere. "We should probably get to Oliver's house before they send out a search party."

"They can wait," Ben replied. "I already did a month of that, and I don't want to waste any more time."

So Allie grabbed him and pulled him in until their lips met in a kiss that would be just one of many to come.

This was never going to get old.

The End

Special sneak peek of Book 3 in the Wonder Boy Series,

Love on Display

EXCERPT FROM *LOVE ON DISPLAY*

> Cam: I know you and I are both busy, but I'm not giving up on you yet. How about a twenty-minute coffee date next Thursday sometime between 10 and 11:30?

Not even a text from Cam could improve Kailani's mood this morning. Not when Mr. Martinez had just played his next move in a way she would never be able to match. Free nutrition guidance with every personal training contract? If Kailani wanted to do something like that, she would have to hire a nutritionist, and it wasn't like those grew on trees. That would cost money. Money she didn't have. Money she couldn't use even if she had it. How could Riptide afford something like that?

Letting out a sigh, Kailani looked out her office window at her little gym and wished she knew what she could do to make it thrive. If she could get some actual income instead of bleeding out money every day, she could do something to help her parents and siblings. At least the protein shake thing had brought in more people, and the place was pretty full today. Enough so that Kailani wanted to be out there, actually working with her clients instead of watching from behind the glass like some zoo animal.

That was the whole point of this. She *loved* working with people. But she also had a business to run, and that side of things had been taking up all of her time since the moment she opened her doors. She had had to force herself to go out onto the floor a few times a day and interact with people so they at least recognized the face behind Horizon Gym, all the while knowing she had work to do because the gym around the corner existed where it shouldn't.

Was this going to be her life? Sitting behind a desk and wishing she'd never chased her dream in the first place? This was awful.

Her phone buzzed with a call where it sat on the desk, making her jump. Guessing it was her mom, she answered without looking at the screen. "Hi."

"Oh good, so I didn't imagine you?"

Her stomach did a strange somersault at the sound of Cam's deep voice. She definitely hadn't expected *him* on the other end of the line, and heat pulsed through her as his crooked smile filled her mind's eye. "Cam! Hi. How—how are you?"

"Better now that I know you're real." He chuckled, and she imagined it rumbling through his chest. Though she'd tried not to dwell on it, she'd been revisiting his pectorals for weeks. Her up close and personal view as he'd cradled her at the race had lodged itself in her brain, though she couldn't be too angry about it. As someone who prided herself on her own personal fitness, she'd appreciated feeling small and protected in his hold. Yes, she was strong enough to take care of herself. No, she didn't dislike the idea of someone being stronger if she needed it.

"You thought I wasn't real?" she asked, cursing the way she'd gone breathless. She hadn't seen the guy in weeks; how did he still affect her so much? She didn't even know him!

"Yeah, well, when all I've got is faceless texts, I was starting to think maybe someone was catfishing me. Why else would you cancel all of our plans?"

Because she was drowning, but she wasn't about to tell him that. Cam was the one good thing she had in her life despite only talking to him for an hour and a half at the race. Taking a deep breath, she told herself that she couldn't mess things up with him before they even started. No matter how much she was struggling, she had to make this effort. "You canceled too," she reminded him. "But Thursday sounds great."

"I changed my mind."

Her heart sank. "What?"

Though he laughed, it wasn't enough to quell the fear that she'd already lost her chance. His next words, however… "Thursday is too far away. I've been wanting to see you again since the moment I walked away. Got anything going on today?"

Too much. But surely she could spare an hour, right? Her two trainers had been handling everything anyway, and Kailani could definitely use the caffeine boost if she was going to find a way to compete against Martinez's nutrition strategy. Brainstorming was easier with a little shot of energy. Maybe Cam would be able to offer up some ideas, seeing as he was a trainer as well.

Hoping she wasn't going to shoot herself in the foot by sharing her many problems, Kailani took another deep breath and took the plunge. "I've got some time. What part of the city are you in?"

"East side. What about you?" Cam's happiness was clear in his voice.

"Same. That makes this easier!"

"There's a smoothie shop on Hunter Ave."

"I know it." In fact, it was one of Kailani's favorite places to go when she wasn't being extra frugal. Their acai bowls were incredible, and their coffee even better. "Meet you there in half an hour?"

"Can you make it fifteen minutes? I'm feeling impatient."

Kailani laughed. How had she put this off for so long when Cam was such a breath of fresh, honest air? "Sure. Let me just make sure my team is good, and I'll see you there."

"Your team, huh? You never did say what you do for work."

Hadn't she? They'd talked about so many things at the race and while texting over the last few weeks, but Kailani had intentionally strayed from anything too personal. Cam didn't know where she lived or what she did, and she definitely hadn't said anything about her family. But why? She'd told herself it was for her own safety, until she knew Cam wouldn't serial killer murder her in her sleep, but she really doubted he had a dangerous bone in his body, despite his size.

She'd been protecting her heart, plain and simple.

Maybe that should change. "I'll tell you all about it at Blended Perfection."

"Hearing you say those words is perfection." He cursed, and then he hung up.

Grinning, Kailani sat at her desk for a minute as she processed what had just happened. With one phone call, Cam had managed to convince her to get her away from her stress and do something for herself for once. Not that smoothies were all that indulgent, but every penny counted. Hopefully it would be worth it.

That was when she realized she only had fifteen minutes to make sure she looked cute and alert and not at all stressed. No big deal.

Twenty-three minutes later, she sprinted down the sidewalk and hoped Cam was like her and not super great about punctuality. She hadn't meant to take so long, but one of her clients had been squatting with terrible form, and the other trainers had been busy, so she'd spent ten minutes walking the woman through the exercise. Then she'd seen herself in the wall of mirrors and realized her hair was an absolute mess, and it took three different braids before it finally cooperated.

She also may have hunted down a Horizon Gym t-shirt to wear so she could impress Cam. He already seemed to like her, but a little power play couldn't hurt.

Finally reaching the smoothie shop, Blended Perfection, Kailani tugged the door and rushed inside.

Directly into a pair of strong, warm arms.

"I wasn't expecting this kind of greeting," Cam said with a rumbling laugh, "but I'll take it."

"Sorry!" She probably should have pulled away as soon as she recovered from the collision, but her feet refused to move. Probably because his hold seemed to chase away all of the lingering doubt she'd been harboring about this guy for the last few weeks. She shifted a little deeper into his arms, pressing herself up against his hard chest and wishing she wasn't so starved for attention that she could so easily ignore the strangeness of hugging someone she'd only known in person for a couple of hours.

"Bad day?" he asked, and his warm breath tickled the loose little hairs by her ear.

He hadn't smelled this good at the race. Not that he'd smelled bad—apparently Cam was one of those rare breeds of men who still smelled pretty great when all sweaty. Those genes should have been illegal. But today, Cam didn't just smell okay. He smelled *amazing*. Whatever cologne or aftershave he used, it filled her nose like a wave curling over her toes on a sandy beach. That metaphor didn't even make sense, but it was how it made her feel, and she breathed him in without shame.

"Are you smelling me?" he asked.

Okay, maybe a little shame. Her face flaming, Kailani slowly pulled out of his hold and stepped back so she could give him a sheepish smile. "You smell good. Sorry for running into you. Literally."

His eyes sparkled, despite there being no twinkling lights anywhere nearby to make that happen. Eyes didn't just sparkle on their own, but apparently Cam's did. She hadn't paid much attention at the race, but his eyes were such a unique color of brown. Like cinnamon. She'd never seen eyes that color, and she loved them.

"I'm guessing you were excited to see me?" he said, one corner of his lips lifting to create that adorable half smile.

Kailani grinned right back. He said everything with such ease that it made it easy to be open and honest with him. Usually when she dated, she felt like she had to hide pieces of herself and be strategic about when she pulled them out for display. A first date was almost like a job interview. But Cam had yet to give her any reason to think she couldn't be entirely herself, and it was utterly refreshing.

"Well, when you kept rescheduling," she said.

He narrowed those fascinating eyes as his hand found hers. "Excuse me, but *you* were the one who canceled more times than me. Now, I believe you owe me a smoothie."

Kailani loved that he gave her a gentle tug to pull her into the line with him. "You're really going to let me pay?" she asked, giving his hand a little squeeze.

He shifted an inch closer to her. "Only because this means I can pay for dinner the next time we get together."

He was impossible to look away from. She didn't know how he did it, but Cam was like a magnet, drawing her in with his open expression and big hand wrapped around hers and that delicious smell of his making her wonder if he would taste as good as he smelled. She was never one to kiss on the first date, but he seemed worth the exception. She'd almost kissed him at the race, after all, and all those text conversations over the last few weeks had definitely made this feel less like a first date and more like a reunion after a long time apart.

"What can I get you guys?"

Kailani jumped when she realized they'd reached the front of the line. Just how long had she been staring at the man?

Grinning as if he knew exactly how she felt, Cam gestured for Kailani to order first. "Just so I know how much you're willing to spoil me," he said with a wink.

He joked, but Kailani truly appreciated his thoughtfulness. By letting her order first, he could gauge her budget, something he proved when he ordered something slightly less expensive than the green smoothie she chose for herself.

Smoothies in hand and fingers laced together, they headed for the outdoor seating without saying a word. It was like they'd been on this date a million times already and knew the routine, and Kailani's heart kept beating faster with every minute that passed. Both with excitement and with fear. All of this felt so much like they were meant to be together, but there was no way Cam was *this* perfect. She could live in the fantasy of this moment for a little longer, but at some point the other shoe was going to drop and leave her dreams shattered on the sidewalk.

As soon as they'd sat on some high stools at a round table outside, hands still clasped together, Cam shook his head as if clearing away a fog. "Can I say something?"

"Please." Kailani sipped at her smoothie, intentionally drinking the smallest amount that she could to draw out this date as long as possible.

His expression held some measure of reverence beneath his easy smile as he took her in inch by inch. "I'm gonna sound crazy, but it feels like you and I…"

Like they what? Kailani might have asked if he hadn't lost his smile at the same time he lost his words. Following his eyes, she glanced down at her t-shirt with her gym's logo splashed across the front. "I'm actually a trainer too," she said warily. Maybe she had made a mistake in choosing to impress him. He had already admitted he was intimidated by her, so she probably should have eased him into the idea of her being in the same sphere as him.

"You work at Horizon Gym?" he asked. His voice had dropped almost to a whisper, his face turning slightly green.

Kailani wasn't sure if she wanted to answer that question with the way he was looking at her like she'd run over his dog. "I, um, own it."

"No, you don't."

What kind of response was that? "Yeah, I do?"

"No."

"You don't believe I can own a gym?"

He slid off the stool and started pacing, though he didn't have a whole lot of space to do it. Not only were the tables all packed closely together, but he was so big that he used up every square inch as he rubbed his palms along his thighs. "No," he said, making her heart sink. But then he kept talking. "No, I don't want you to own *that* gym."

What did he have against her gym? "Why not?"

He glanced at her and stopped pacing, nothing but pain in his expression as he stuffed his hands into his dark hair. "Because if you own Horizon, we can't be friends."

As she gripped her smoothie cup, she wished she wasn't so entirely confused so she could make sense of this conversation. "What does that…" That was when she saw it. His jacket had covered it before, but with his arms up, she could see the wave logo printed on his shirt over his heart.

Riptide.

Kailani's heart dropped, and she was pretty sure it had left her body entirely instead of falling into her stomach. It wouldn't be enough for him to be an employee there. He wouldn't freak out this much. "Cam, what's your last name?"

She already knew the answer to that question, but she wanted to hear him say it.

He winced. "Martinez. And you're Adams." It wasn't a question.

Of all the gyms in Diamond Springs, why did Cam have to own *that* one? The only one that Kailani hated.

"We can't Romeo and Juliet our way out of this one," Cam muttered and clenched his jaw, moving his hands from his hair to under his arms, making his shoulders look even bigger.

"Romeo and Juliet die in the end," Kailani replied. Her smoothie suddenly tasted sour, and she regretted making the purchase. The fifteen dollars she'd dropped ten minutes ago could have been so much more useful somewhere else.

Cam looked miserable. "Exactly." And then his expression shifted, his eyebrows pulling together as his thoughts worked through his head. When his eyes snapped back to hers, something had changed. His entire body had gone stiff, muscles tensing as he gazed at her. "What's your next move?" he asked.

Kailani's eyes widened. *Seriously?* "As if I would tell you."

"You've got to be planning something after my nutrition play."

"Yeah, and if I tell you what it is, then you'll just do the same thing and be one step ahead of me again."

"No, I won't." He turned slightly green and pressed a hand to his mouth as he swallowed. "Fine. You don't have to tell me."

She narrowed her eyes as she stood. "Don't act like you get to tell me what to do. I just bought you a smoothie."

When he stepped closer, he seemed to grow in size. Instead of protective and safe, he looked almost terrifying. "I'll pay you back if going on a date with me is so repulsive to you."

Kailani rose up on her toes, trying to match his height as she closed the distance between them. "I wouldn't have gone out with you if I'd known—"

"Is that why you kept canceling on me?"

"What?"

"You flirt with me to throw me off my game and knock me off balance?"

"Are you insane? I didn't flirt with you!"

Eyes flashing, he leaned closer as if hoping to add power to his words. "You were totally into me."

She scoffed. "Ego, much?"

He let out a bark of a laugh that had no trace of humor. "You almost kissed me at the race. Admit it!"

"I wouldn't be caught *dead* kissing you." But as if they weren't paying any attention to the conversation, her eyes slipped down to his mouth. She'd been dreaming about that mouth for weeks. *Rein it in, Lani.* "You could be the last man on earth, Cam Martinez. You could smell amazing, and you could have abs of steel, and you could have the most tempting lips I have ever seen, but I still wouldn't—"

For being so big, the guy moved fast. He grabbed her waist and pulled her against him, his mouth only an inch from hers, and he went so still that it was like he was made of stone.

"You sure about that?" he breathed.

Nope. She definitely wasn't sure. And despite her brain screaming at her to get out of there, her body decided it was a great idea to take the reins.

ALSO BY DANA LECHEMINANT

The Wonder Boys
Love on Camera

Simple Love Stories (Sweet Love Stories)
Simplicity
Growing Young
Bittersweet Brews
In Front of Me
As Long as You Love Me
Dear Dalia
Let Go

Terms of Inheritance (Sweet Romance)
Forever You and Me
Holding On to Everything
A World without You
Love, Strictly Speaking

Historical Romances
The Thief and the Noble
A Twist of Christmas (part of The Holly and the Ivy Christ-
mas anthology)

ABOUT THE AUTHOR

Dana LeCheminant has been telling stories since she was old enough to know what stories were. After spending most of her childhood reading everything she could get her hands on, she eventually realized she could write her own books too, and since then she always has plots brewing and characters clamoring to be next to have their stories told. A lover of all things outdoors, she finds inspiration while hiking the remote Utah backcountry and cruising down rivers. Until her endless imagination runs dry, she will always have another story to tell.